Daisy May
THE SEQUEL

Trevor L Evans

First published 2025

A self published title designed and produced by Adala Publishing
www.adalapublishing.com.au

 A catalogue record for this book is available from the National Library of Australia

ISBN 978-0-6453485-7-6 (Print)
ISBN 978-0-6453485-8-3 (eBook)

CHAPTER 1

I woke up from a deep sleep. I could hear the jet engines of an aircraft and rushing wind. Though the seat was comfortable, my back was a little stiff. I rolled my head slightly to my left and reached up with my right arm to push the little curtain to one side so that I could see out of the window. The view took my breath away. I sat up straight, pushed my hair out of my face, and sat there enjoying the view. I could see a range of snow-capped mountains, so beautiful and majestic with the early morning sun touching them. The colours were pinks, blues, yellows and greys, all the colours of the rainbow. They changed as the sun rose. I sat there mesmerised. This was God's creation, and I was seeing it. I looked at my watch, 7.30 am, but was this the right time?

The flight attendant spoke. 'I wonder if you could close the curtain madam, other people are still sleeping.'

She startled me. I know I snapped when I replied, 'And miss this?' She leaned over and looked out of the window.

'Yes, madam, I understand, yes.' She walked off. I sat there, still mesmerised, watching the beauty of it all. I could see where the mountains rose up from the green valleys, sandy yellows where rivers and creeks gouged their way through the ground. I wondered who lived there and what their lifestyles were. There was so much we did not know. I could hear my husband, Ted, snoring in the next seat. I sat back in my seat and watched him with his mouth wide open, his little moustache quivering as he snored. His grey hair was untidy, which was not like him at all. He liked his hair perfectly groomed. I felt very lucky to have found the perfect partner, and we've been married for ten years now. I loved his support and understanding. He was always able to look at both sides of the fence when we had our discussions. He was a senior officer in the Australian police force and was very, very methodical. I suppose we got on well because I am a lawyer, and we had so much in common. I loved being his wife – Mrs Peggy Jones. My given name was Margaret, but people always called me Peggy. I found it amusing. My maiden name was Johnson. We had recently received a telegram from a solicitor in London, England, telling us of the passing of my sister Lesley. She had left all her estates to me, and he suggested that we come to England. Ted had taken his long-service leave, and we were on our way. I gently rolled over, my elbow accidentally leaning on his bladder. I kissed him on the end of his nose, and he opened one of his eyes.

'What does ye want of me, young maiden?'

'Oh dear, sir, what I want, you cannot give me here!'

He gave me that wicked smile of his. 'I would very much appreciate it, dear, if you would ease the pressure off of your elbow. I think there's something I need to do!'

'Before you do dear, look out of the window.'

Ted leaned over, placing his elbow where I had placed mine, but he didn't ease the pressure off. He stared out of the window and, in a low voice, replied, 'You could not put a price on this, could you dear? It is so beautiful, but I must go somewhere.'

We both got up and headed down the aisle. I don't know which one of us was in the most need. We returned to our seats. They were very comfortable with a small table in front of us. This was a Comet aircraft, and in this year of 1959, it was a new beginning in technology, and we were flying in it.

CHAPTER 2

We eventually landed in London. It was such a smooth landing, and we had certainly enjoyed our flight.

We picked up our luggage from the carousel and went through to customs. The officer looked at our passports, then he seriously studied Ted and handed back his passport, also giving me mine back. Then, in a low, hushed voice, he said, 'Good to see you, Ted.'

Ted stared at him, then started to chuckle. 'Well, I never! Are there many of us left?'

'Yes, Ted, there are. We meet at the same place, same time, each day.'

Ted put his thumb in the air and nodded.

'What was that all about, Ted?'

'We were all together in the police force many years ago.'

Ted had worked his way up to the top in the police force in England and was subsequently transferred to a special assignment in Australia. He liked Australia so much, he decided to stay.'

Ted had booked a room at the Ritz for one night. I told him I definitely wouldn't be able to sleep as I was wide awake, but as soon as my head touched the pillow, I was asleep.

I woke in the morning and looked at my watch, 6 am. It's too early; wait another hour, at least. Just then, Ted walked in with two cups of coffee and put them on the side table. He sat down on my side of the bed and slowly sipped his coffee. He reached out with his left hand, laying it gently on my side. His eyes looked into mine; could he see something in them I didn't know?

Ted sighed. It seemed to come from a long way away. 'Peggy, seeing that old codger of mine brought a lot of memories back. It all seems like a lifetime ago, and I thought I'd left it all behind, but it's back. I have a feeling I've got to sharpen up the game here in England. It is different from Australia. Here, everything has to be politically correct; politics play a big part, and it interferes with justice. Australians seem to know the difference, so you can do your job without obstructions.'

We quietly drank our coffee. I put my cup back on the table.' I'm going to have a shower now, and then we can have a lovely continental breakfast.'

Ted shook his head. 'No. Kippers and jellied eels, and good old English bacon and eggs with fried bread in dripping for me, Peggy. I'm a Cockney, and nobody will change me. Bread and dripping, my knife and fork, like chalk and cheese. These things will never change.' Ted lent forward and kissed me on the tip of my nose.

'Not going to argue that one with you, Ted, but before I have a shower, I will phone the solicitor, Mr Fredericks, to make an appointment.' I made the call and placed the receiver back down, and called out in a loud voice, 'Ted, the solicitor will see us at 10.30 am this morning.'

Ted's voice boomed back, 'Will I have enough time for my breakfast?'

'It's a 15-minute walk from here, dear,' I replied. We went down to the restaurant, and I sat there watching Ted shovel food into his mouth. His little moustache quivering away. When he started to eat those jellied eels, it was just too much for me to watch, so I excused myself and went to the ladies room to freshen up. When I returned to the table, Ted was waiting for me, his Mackintosh over his arm. He winked at me and said, 'I thought you were beautiful, but those jellied eels were beautiful, Peggy.' I turned around and walked towards the door. Ted followed me.

CHAPTER 3

We arrived at Mr Fredericks' office on time. The office was very impressive. It was situated on a curved road, with a beautifully kept park right opposite. The buildings were all three storeys, with stairs going up to the front door, which was on the first floor. The ground floor windows were below the path, and this is where the kitchens usually were. Alongside the front door was a big brass plaque with the name *Mr Fredericks, Barrister, Solicitor, and Business Advice* engraved on it. Ted looked at it, then turned to me, raising his eyebrows, 'This will be fun Peg, watching you two together.' Ted rang the doorbell, and a young man, extremely well-dressed, opened the door.

'May I help you sir, madam?'

'My name is Margaret Jones. We have an appointment.'

The young man nodded slightly and very politely ushered us into a waiting room.

'If you would excuse me, Mrs Jones, I will inform Mr Fredericks you are here.'

With that, he went through a big panelled door. He returned after just a couple of minutes. 'Mr Fredericks will see you now.' He ushered us through the door into Mr Fredericks' office. The room was quite large. It had panelled walls with large paintings. There was a beautiful, large fireplace and mantelpiece. Mr Fredericks was standing in front of the fireplace, waiting for us. He had a big smile on his face and put both his arms out, which took me a bit by surprise. He didn't actually embrace me; he just put his hands on the sides of my arms.

'I've been waiting so much to meet you; please sit down.' I sat with my back to the door. Mr Fredericks shook Ted's hand with a very strong grip. 'You are a very impressive man, Mr Jones. My colleagues have told me a lot about you.'

I noticed the handshake. So, he was a Freemason as well.

Ted and Mr Fredericks nodded to each other in acknowledgement. I watched Ted's eyes scan the room. They stopped at the certificates on the wall. I read them: one was a certificate that said 'Master' and the picture of a Freemasons chapel. One was that of Rosicrucian's, the same thing: people standing in a chapel around him. The next one said Rose Croix, same type of picture, but the fourth one startled me a little: Knights Templar. I know they called them the Keepers of the Holy Grail, and that they were Crusaders, all tied up with Jerusalem. Ted sat on a chair where he could see the door, the desk, and me.

Mr Fredericks asked to be excused for a moment. He picked up the phone, 'Yes dear, they're here.' He smiled at me with so much warmth and joy. 'My wife has been waiting so long to meet you.'

I heard the other door open behind me and was startled to see Ted's eyes light up. He sat straight up in the chair, then stood up. I turned around to face the door. There was a beautiful woman standing there. She had olive skin and was dressed in a sari, beautiful reds, greens, gold, and silver. It reminded me of the mountainside and the views from the airplane window.

'Margaret, I would like you to meet my wife, Marcia. Marcia, this is Margaret, Lesley's sister.' I watched the light shine in her eyes, then a deep sadness. I stood up, and Marcia put her arms around me and embraced me.

'She was my best friend, my very best friend,' she said in a low voice. Then the tears started to flow. I could feel the sobbing in her body and I cuddled her a bit tighter. Tears were coming into my eyes. I could sense her grief was as bad as mine.

Marcia looked at me and said, 'Lesley was my very best friend, she was the only one who really understood that society in England can be a bit cruel sometimes when your skin is a different colour. We would sit and talk for hours in the garden. She loved the warm sun, the flowers, and the trees, everything that surrounded you, which was nature. I miss her so terribly. My husband and I don't understand the circumstances of her death. That wasn't her; she was too strong in character, and she fought so hard to get where she was in the British Navy.'

Mr Fredericks' voice broke in. 'There is a lot we don't understand. Lesley disappeared just before September, at the beginning of the war. She then turned up some weeks later, bright and alive; her skin, her hair, she looked so beautiful. You would have thought that she had been on a world cruise.'

'I know that she was in love,' Marcia said as she chuckled to herself. 'I tactfully asked her, but she told me that she was under the *Secrecy Act* and smiled at me.'

Mr Frederick's voice broke in again. 'During the war, she would disappear for a while, but each time she returned, she was more tired, more weary. She stayed with us each time, and towards the end of the war, she asked me if I would look after all her affairs. She had a postbox number and gave me the key and all her personal documents.'

'Lesley returned here and stayed with us for two weeks,' Marcia went on. 'She was in a very bad way. Her hair had thinned and was very untidy. All she wanted to do was sleep. She also had trouble with her lungs, but told us nothing. We last saw her at the end of the war. She said that she was going away for a while and would notify us later.'

Mr Fredericks spoke again. 'I received a letter saying that she had taken her own life.'

Marcia started to cry again. I put my arms around her and held her tight. Mr Fredericks went and picked up a letter from his desk. He pushed his spectacles, which sat on the end of his nose, closer to his eyes and read the letter

It is with deep regret that I must inform you that Lesley Johnson has died. Her body was found on the path. It is believed that she jumped from the eighth floor to her death.

Mr Fredericks shook his head, and in an angry voice said, 'Nothing makes sense. Lesley was not the type of person to take her own life. I received a death certificate, which also doesn't make sense. It is a civilian death certificate. Lesley was a high-ranking officer in the British Navy; her death certificate should have been a naval certificate. I had one of my colleagues check it out. All he found out was it came under MI5 and MI6. We came to a dead end and couldn't get any further information.' Mr Fredericks handed me Lesley's death certificate. It stated that the deceased died in her flat. Usually, it will give an address. Then, in the second column, it had Name – *Lesley Johnson*, third column Sex – *female*, and in the Age column, no age given. In the fifth column, nothing was noted as to her occupation. Column 6 was the cause of death; it just had *impact*. In the last column, where it should have stated who had registered the death, there was nothing listed. There was a signature, but it was illegible.'

I handed the certificate back to Mr Fredericks, who put one hand in the air in frustration. 'This death certificate is a load of crap and would not stand up in any court!'

By now, Ted had taken a small notebook out of his inside pocket and was jotting things down.

'Could you give me the number of the death certificate, please?'

Mr Fredericks replied, 'PAS5006.6/F/ but the year isn't here. DEX204231.'

Ted nodded to him to say thank you. They just stared at each other. Ted nodded at him again; no words were spoken, but they were understood! Mr Fredericks took the spectacles off his nose and handed me Lesley's birth certificate. I took it, then looked at Mr Fredericks. 'Could you please call me Peggy from now on? Everybody calls me Peggy.' Mr Fredericks nodded.

Marcia smiled and said, 'Lesley always called you Peggy.' Then she said, 'Oh, excuse me, you are stopping for lunch aren't you? We are having honey chicken and vegetables, followed by apple pie and cream.'

Ted's voice boomed out, 'Certainly, we are stopping for lunch; honey chicken and apple pie sounds really good.' I shook my head and thought to myself, *where is he going to put that after his big breakfast?* Ted grinned at me. Marcia nodded politely and went into the kitchen.

I opened the birth certificate and read it, and read it again, and again. Then I read the last part, Mother's Name, then the word at the end of that: *Indigenous*. I felt the tears start to well up in my eyes. I looked at Ted. He looked at me, puzzled.

'What's wrong, Peg?' I broke down in tears, but at the same time, I felt happy.

'Nothing is wrong; everything is alright. My aunt never told me who my mother was, and now I'm so happy I know she was mine, my beautiful mum. I have always wanted her to be my mother; she was the most kind, beautiful person I've ever known. She used to hold me and cuddle me and tell me stories of the Dreamtime. Stories that I have never forgotten.' I handed the birth certificate to Ted.

Mr Fredericks had a beautiful smile on his face and said, 'Lesley has left everything to you, her apartment, and all her shares, which amount to a fair bit of money, if you wish me to still look after them, I will.'

'I would be grateful to you if you would,' I replied.

'Now there's a lot of paperwork here for you to sign.' Mr Fredericks picked up his phone and spoke with the young man we had met at the door. 'Could you please come into my office? I want you to be a witness for some paperwork.'

The young man knocked on the door and entered. Soon, all the legal work was done. Ted sat there listening to the two lawyers chattering away. It all sounded mumbo jumbo to Ted. He did want to know more about the shares, but knew better than to ask questions at this point in time. He was content to wait for the honey chicken and apple pie and cream.

I watched Ted as he was licking the cream off his spoon with a very contented look on his face. Where did he put it all? Mr Fredericks offered him more wine, which he politely accepted. We chatted well into the evening. Ted had booked the hotel room for another night. We said our goodbyes, and we left the Fredericks feeling quite content.

Mr Fredericks asked Ted if he would keep him informed. Ted nodded. But instead of going to my left, which was kerbside—he always did this to protect me from any traffic—he turned around, facing the road and the park, and was on my inside. I dismissed this in my mind as we walked back to the hotel. I was pleased it was only a 15-minute walk.

We arrived back at our hotel, went up to our room, and being jet-lagged and having had a few drinks, fell into bed. It was 7 am when I awoke the next morning. I rolled over to put my arm around Ted, but he wasn't there. He was sitting in one of the armchairs, smoking his pipe. He only smoked his pipe when he was deep in thought. I stared at him, thinking *I'm half Aborigine. I wonder what he thinks about that?* I pushed those thoughts to the back of my mind.

Ted looked up and smiled, 'I don't think you've slept so soundly for such a long time dear.' He put his pipe down and walked over to the bed, sat down, and put his arms around me. 'I told you when we arrived in England that I knew I had to sharpen up.' He sighed. 'I'm back,' he chuckled to himself. 'Breakfast, dear?'

I looked at his face and put my arms around his neck. 'Not before you give me some attention, my dear'. Ted came back to bed. An hour later, we showered, dressed, and went down to breakfast, again, as yesterday.

CHAPTER 4

Ted had a really good English breakfast. He wiped his mouth with his napkin and said, 'What first? The apartment?'

I replied, 'Yes, Ted.' We collected our bags from our room and checked out of the hotel. We were able to get a cab quickly, and soon we were standing in front of Lesley's apartment. The traffic on the road was quite busy, and there was a park opposite. Ted looked up at the apartments. He looked at the verandahs. They were staggered; the bottom ones were bigger than the top ones.

He turned around, looked at me, grinning. 'Will you be alright carrying the suitcases up the stairs, dear?' I didn't look at him but grabbed the two small ones and took off into the foyer, where, to my relief, I found a lift. Lesley's apartment was on the eighth floor. When we got to her front door, I stood for a moment wondering what we would find inside.

Ted's voice broke through my thoughts. 'The key, dear.' He opened the door slowly, not picking up the suitcases; he just stood in the doorway, looking into the apartment. I was nearly going to say something, but he put his hand up to stop me. He put his finger to his lips, which startled me, he shook his head at me. I saw him looking at the couch, one end of which was slightly away from the wall. There was a beautiful picture of the Victory at Sea hanging on the wall, but this, too, was lop-sided. On the sideboard, one of the drawers hadn't been closed properly. Ted walked into the bedroom. One of the drawers in the dressing table had a piece of material hanging out of it, and the dressing table looked as if it had been moved away from the wall. His eyes flashed quickly around the room. He stared at the bed for a few moments before coming back into the lounge and looked at the picture on the wall again. He squeezed himself between a small table and the couch, placing his head against the wall so that he could see behind the picture. He put his hand up behind the picture and took out a small, round object and put it in his pocket. He walked over to the telephone and unscrewed the mouth plate, looked at it, and appeared angry and annoyed. He took another small, round object out of the mouthpiece and put that in his pocket as well. He turned to me with a very serious look on his face and put his hand up to say, *just stay there and wait*. He walked back into the bedroom and looked at a picture on the wall above the bed. He slowly lent on the bed and looked behind the picture, but found nothing. He stood back for a few minutes, then looked behind the bedhead, slowly shook his head, then reached behind the bedhead and took out another small, round object. I watched him scanning the apartment again. He seemed satis-fied and walked into the bathroom. I was going to say something, but stopped. I was biting the inside of my lip. Ted came out of the bathroom and wrapped the three round objects in a towel, placing them in the top drawer of the dressing table. I looked at Ted and raised my eyebrows.

'Peggy, somebody has bugged this apartment. If you notice the draw-ers, the dust on top of them has been disturbed by somebody's hands; they have been looking for something. They've looked under the couch and behind it. Look at the marks on the carpet. They have looked under the bed and everywhere else they could think of. But what were they looking for?'

'We're being followed. I first noticed someone outside the hotel and I noticed the same man when we walked down to Mr Fredericks. When we came out of Mr Fredericks', he was in the park.'

I thought that made sense. I watched Ted walk outside the door and bring in the suitcases. Then he stood, staring at the French doors. He slowly took his pipe out of his pocket, walked over to the French doors, but had trouble opening them. They obviously hadn't been opened for a long time. He stood there for a moment, looking out at the verandah, then walked outside, slowly filling his pipe. He struck a match and let the smoke pour out of his mouth slowly while he looked at the surroundings and the park across the road. He went over to the verandah and looked at the other verandahs in the building. He turned his head slightly, looking towards the park, and turned his body slightly so that he could see the park, but anybody below could not see he was watching them. There was a man wearing a trilby hat and a Mackintosh. Ted looked back towards the park. I heard him mutter to himself, *the man is good; he knows how to conceal himself.* He kept looking at the park whilst enjoying his pipe. His mind started to go to work.

He said, 'So Lesley's death certificate is false, why are we being followed? Why has Lesley's apartment been searched and bugged? Nobody has lived here for quite a long time.' Ted tapped his pipe out, emptying out the ash, whilst at the same time scanning the park again to see if the man was still there. He turned, put the pipe back into his pocket, and walked back into the apartment, closing the verandah doors. I studied him with a serious look. He stared at me for a moment before shaking his head.

'Peggy, Lesley did not jump off the verandah. If she had, then she would have landed on the verandah of the apartment below us.' Ted shook his head. 'There is no way she could have landed on the footpath. Peggy, I don't believe she's dead! Somehow, I've got to prove this. We have to find out where she is. I know we are being followed, but why

16

Peggy? I have a strong feeling this is all political. Tonight I'm going out to have a drink with the lads; they may be able to double check some information for me. But first of all, I have a little thing to do and let them know the game begins!'

CHAPTER 5

Ted put on his Mackintosh and his trilby hat. He went into the bedroom to get the three bugs and put them in his right coat pocket. Then,
he picked up my roll of peppermint Polos, unwrapped the roll, took
out all of them bar two, leaving the loose Polos on the table. He put
the wrapper with the other two into his left-hand pocket. I was totally
confused.

'I'm going to have a bit of fun, Peggy.' With that, he walked out of
the front door, down the lift to the foyer, then went to the back of the
foyer and out through the back door to the alleyway. This was London,
and most of the buildings had a back alley. Ted walked down the alleyway, turned left, and he was facing the park. He checked to see if the man
was still there. Yes, he grinned to himself. He crossed the road and went
into the park, turned slowly, and walked up beside the man who was also
wearing a Mackintosh coat and a trilby hat. The man spun around. Ted
asked him, 'Any movement?' The man looked back up at the verandah.

'No. A man came onto the verandah and smoked his pipe. Other
than that, no. I've been here all night, and it was bloody cold and wet.'

'Well, I'm here to relieve you,' Ted replied. He walked up alongside the man and took a Polo out of his left pocket, and offered the man the other one. He took it. Ted put the Polo in his mouth, slightly brushing the man on his left side with his right side. He reached across the man to throw the empty packet into the wastepaper basket with his left hand. The man just accepted what Ted had done. Ted said to the man in an annoying voice, 'Not much to report for the night is there?'

In a frustrated voice, the man replied, 'No, she won't be happy with that.'

Ted thought to himself, *who is she?* Pushing a little more, he put his right hand on the man's shoulder in a comforting gesture.

'You can't give what you don't have, especially on a cold, wet night.'

The man replied in a sharp voice, 'Jackie Evans is a very hard woman to please; like an English Bulldog, she never lets go!'

Ted realised then that he knew this man. He was in his squad a long time ago. Ted replied, 'She was taught by the best: Winston Churchill.' He turned and looked towards the verandah, 'I hope I have a better day.'

The man replied, 'All I want is a good, hot bath and sleep.' He turned and started to walk away.

In a low, soft voice, Ted said, 'See you later, Michael.'

The man stopped walking for a second and thought I'm too tired and wet to play games anymore and walked off towards the underground station. Ted watched him go down the steps to the station, waited a few moments to make sure he had gone, then looked at his watch. 10.15 am. He went back to the alleyway, into the foyer, and back up to the apartment. Peggy heard the front door open, turned around to see Ted.

'Coffee, dear?'

'That would be nice, thank you.'

CHAPTER 6

The next morning, the man, Michael, stood in front of a big, impressive desk in front of a large government office window, looking out towards the Houses of Parliament. A plaque on the desk said, Jackie Evans. Jackie looked at the man with a look of annoyance on her face. 'It would have taken you a long time to write that report, wouldn't it?'

Michael replied, 'That was all that happened ma'am.'

Jackie slapped her hand on the table. 'Could you please explain to me why you left your post at 10.15 am?'

Michael replied sharply, 'Because I was relieved at 10.15 am!'

Jackie suddenly stood up. 'The man who was sent to relieve you said you were not there. He made that phone call to me at 10.30 am, the time you were meant to be relieved! Please explain.'

'A man relieved me at 10.15 am'

Jackie kept staring at him. 'This man doesn't lie, he is one of the best. What was the name of the man who relieved you?'

Michael blinked, 'I don't know.'

Jackie looked at Michael, thought to herself, *there is something wrong here,* and in a low voice asked, 'What did he look like Michael?'

'Well, he was dressed in a Mackintosh and hat, just like mine. He had a small, grey moustache, his nose was a little bit large and slightly hooked on the end. I know I've seen it before.'

There was a knock on her door. It opened slowly, and a man walked in. He seemed a bit timid.

Jackie asked him, 'Well, what is it?' The man hesitated for a moment, then replied, 'The three bugs we placed in the apartment.'

'Well, what about them?' Jackie asked sharply.

'We can hear your voice on them, the noise of the underground, and muffled train noises.'

Jackie looked puzzled. She looked back at Michael, 'You say that the man who relieved you was about your height, with a grey moustache and slightly crooked nose?'

'Yes, ma'am.'

'What exactly happened when you were with him?' Jackie asked.

'He asked if anything had happened, and I told him. He handed me a Polo with his left hand, then had a Polo himself and threw the empty packet into the wastepaper basket with his left hand.'

'Stop!' She shook her head backwards and forwards. 'Then he brushed past you with his right side, didn't he Michael?'

'Yes, ma'am, he did.'

Jackie shook her head slowly. 'Michael, could you reach into the right-hand pocket of your Mackintosh?'

Michael did so and took out the three bugs. He stood, staring at them.

Jackie said, 'You should have known better Michael.' She stood staring at him for a moment before asking him, 'How many hours was your shift Michael?'

Michael replied, '12 hours ma'am.'

Jackie picked up the phone, 'Could you please put me through to customs.'

There was a reply, 'Yes.'

'Jackie Evans here. Has a Ted Jones from Australia entered the country?'

The voice came back, 'Yes ma'am, he flew in on the comet with his wife Margaret.'

Jackie looked annoyed and asked the customs officer, 'Why didn't you inform me?'

The customs officer replied, 'We had nothing in the way of a report to say we should. After all, he is a British citizen, and his wife is an Australian citizen.'

Jackie thought for a moment, then said to the man on the phone, 'Yes, he was one of yours, not mine!' With that, she hung up the receiver.

'Michael, you spent a lot of time with Ted Jones, and you didn't recognise him? Didn't he teach you that little trick about bugging people?'

Michael gritted his teeth and said, 'Yes ma'am.'

Jackie shook her head, then said to Michael, '12 hours in the rain, no shelter, freezing cold, your senses would have been dulled. Wait here, Michael.'

Jackie went through the door, down the corridor to another door, she went through. The lady sitting at the desk stood up and, in a very distinctive voice, said, 'Yes ma'am?'

Jackie replied in her commanding voice, 'Is he in?'

The lady replied, 'Sir John is ma'am.'

Jackie walked up to the big, panelled door, knocked, and entered. Sir John looked up and said, 'You must have a problem Jackie!'

Jackie looked him straight in the eyes with a sharp look. 'No, Sir John, you have the problem! Ted Jones is back. He is married to Margaret Johnson.'

Sir John raised his eyebrows. Jackie continued, 'Customs has confirmed it and my people have also confirmed it.'

Sir John stared at Jackie for a few moments, got up out of his chair, and lit a cigarette, drawing in deeply. 'I thought I'd gotten rid of him, Jackie.'

Jackie replied with a mocking grin on her face, 'Yes, he was too good for you wasn't he?'

Sir John replied loudly, 'He was a bloody good placement, but he couldn't play politics; he was too dangerous, he had to go!'

Jackie was annoyed. 'You made a bumble of Lesley's death; he will see straight through it. He has a whole network of colleagues who highly respect him, and he trained most of them. He is still registered as a high-ranking police officer. You bugged her apartment, and Ted found them. He slipped them into the pocket of one of my surveillance officers, letting him know the game now begins.'

Sir John shouted, 'Who is he, the incompetent?'

Jackie flew back at him in an equally loud voice, 'You cut my budget, so my officers need to work 12 hours in the pouring rain, cold and wet, all through the night. Would you be so sharp and on your toes if you were to do those hours? After that, with the short conversation he had with my man, he did manage to get my name. He still has that sense of humour letting you know he's ten steps ahead of you.'

Sir John sat down in his chair, looking at Jackie with frustration in his eyes. 'I remember, a long time ago, we were at a dinner party. He was sitting at one end of the table, and I was sitting at the other. I had a bottle of Scotch alongside me; he also had a bottle of Scotch. He caught my attention, winked at me, and poured himself a glass of Scotch and drank it in one gulp. I thought, *you bastard, you will not beat me!* And I did the same. He winked again and poured himself another glass and downed it in one. I did likewise. Then, one of the guests did a small talk, and Ted filled up his glass again and downed it like before. I wasn't going to let him beat me, so I did the same. Now, I'm not a drinker, and I soon got the first signs of too much alcohol, but he downed another glass, so I had another. I knew my wife was scowling at me. Then a waiter came up to me and said in a very soft voice, *'He is drinking tea!'*

Jackie chuckled, 'I've heard that story before somewhere.'

Sir John replied, 'He is just ten steps ahead of you, with a sense of humour, but the tables might turn yet. He may find what we are looking for; then we will have him and also find what we're looking for.'

Jackie's eyebrows lifted, and she sighed, 'Who is a better chess player, you or Ted?'

With that, she turned and left the office.

CHAPTER 7

I made Ted his coffee and watched him take out his pipe and put it back in his pocket, while he slowly sipped his coffee.

With a serious look on his face, he said, 'Peg, I'm going to lie down for a while; jet lag has gotten the better of me. We'll go out later and meet the boys and have a bite to eat.' He got up and went into the bedroom, kicked his shoes off and lay down. The minute his head touched the pillow, he was asleep.

I sat there watching him, going through everything in my mind that had happened since our arrival. I could quite understand why Lesley and Marcia got on so well together, both being part Indigenous and part white, although Marcia was from India and Lesley was from Australia. Someone had been searching Lesley's apartment, looking for something. Would Lesley have hidden anything in the apartment for me, like she did when we lived with our aunt? You couldn't keep anything from her. When we were at school and university, she would go through all our things. She'd hide things behind the top of the curtain, pinned in the fold, so you wouldn't see them. I picked up a chair and walked over to the curtains, thinking, *if I put the chair here, I could be seen through the window,* so I moved a small table and placed the chair where I couldn't be seen. I slowly moved the curtain so that nobody would see it moving and looked behind it, but there was nothing there. I ran my hands over the pleats. One of the pleats seemed to have been stitched together very carefully. I went back into the kitchen and got a pair of scissors and very slowly undid the stitches. There it is! So, this is what they've been looking for. Slowly, I reached up with both hands and undid the safety pin on the envelope. The scissors slipped out of my hands and clattered to the floor. They bounced off the wall, making more noise. I got down from the chair and picked up the scissors, put the envelope in the same hand, and with the other, picked up the chair and took it back to the table. I turned around to see Ted who had been woken up by the sound of the scissors hitting the floor.

He stood there, studying me with a small grin. 'What are you up to?'

'I think I've found what they were looking for!'

Ted nodded. 'Never get between two sisters; they will outsmart you every time!'

I put the scissors down on the table and looked at the envelope, turned it over, and read the words written on the back. *I knew you wouldn't forget, little sister*. I handed the envelope to Ted. 'Lesley always called me Little Sister.'

Ted picked up the scissors and glanced at me, asking permission.

'Yes, Ted, go ahead and open it'.

Ted frowned at me, slightly closing one eye. 'How would Lesley want you to open this?

I looked at Ted, puzzled.

'Peg, your sister worked for MI5. She may have fixed this envelope just in case the wrong person got it. The game is too serious.'

Ted saw me frown; my mind went back. 'Lesley always used to cut the corner of the envelope and look inside to see whether it had been tampered with. She always had a suspicious mind and didn't trust my aunt. Ted, turn the envelope towards you as if you were reading the address, and cut off the corner on the bottom left, but hold it away from you while you're doing it!'

Ted did as instructed. When he cut the corner off, brown powder came out. I burst out laughing. Ted dropped the scissors and quickly stepped back. The envelope fell onto the floor. I continued to laugh, which confused Ted.

He put both his hands on his hips and shouted, 'What is so bloody funny?'

'It is pepper Ted, had you opened it from the top, the pepper would have gone into your face,' I replied.

I watched Ted bend down to pick up the scissors and envelope. 'Very, very funny, dear, very funny! I'm the one normally playing the jokes!' With that, he went over to the sink and emptied out the rest of the pepper.

He didn't turn on the tap but examined the pepper very carefully to make sure it was indeed pepper. He then opened the envelope with the scissors and shook it. We were very surprised when a key fell out of the envelope and into the sink. Ted picked up the key and examined it, then handed it to me.

I frowned and looked at Ted. 'This is a safety deposit key from a bank.'

I watched the grin on Ted's face. 'She plays a mean game, doesn't she, Peg. I've got to make sure she's dead. I've got to have the proof, so tonight I'll get somebody I know to get the information from Somerset House.'

I saw that grin come over Ted's face again; his moustache was quivering. 'But, Peg, we're going to the theatre tomorrow. I will ring up and book the tickets. The game is afoot, my dear friend, Mr Watson.' Ted gave me that cheeky, seductive grin. 'I think we should lie down and rest for a while, with that, he gave a courtly bow and gestured me to go before him.

I shook my head at him, saying, 'Does that mean I submit?' I walked into the bedroom with the key in my hand and put it on the bedside table.

CHAPTER 8

Later that afternoon, I woke up and put my arm out to touch Ted, but he wasn't there! The last thing I remembered I was in his arms. I rolled over and sat up. Ted was standing at the bottom of the bed, stark naked, wearing nothing but a cheeky grin. 'Coffee, dear?' He was holding two cups of coffee in his hands.

'Yes, please.' Ted walked around to my side of the bed and sat down. He handed me my coffee.

'Peg, I suggest you put the key around your waist, under your clothing, so no light-fingered person can get it.'

I shook my head. 'Ted, I thought you were going to be romantic.'

He grinned at me. 'Now that's a good suggestion. We still have time to play!'

'No, Ted, I need a shower, and so do you!'

Ted looked at me with those puppy eyes. 'I think all men are the same and don't like the word *No.*'

We both finished our coffees and had our showers. Ted ordered a taxi, and we went downstairs and waited for it to arrive.

The taxi arrived, and we got in. Ted gave the driver the name of a pub, I thought it sounded like The Bell. The taxi driver nodded, and we were on our way. I thought I knew London well, but I didn't really know where we were going. The taxi driver turned down a side street, turned down another little street where there was a pub on the corner. He stopped the taxi and Ted went to pay him, but the driver shook his head, 'No Mr Jones, I won't accept any money from you, because you looked after me in the old days when I was in trouble with the Police. You knew the barristers were setting me up politically.' He chuckled, 'You fixed them good and proper and I don't think you were very popular after that.'

Ted frowned at him, 'Yes, I remember. In future, just call me Ted, not Mr Jones. I consider myself Australian now.'

The taxi driver replied. 'Well, Ted, if there is anything I can do for you, just let me know.' He handed Ted his business card.

'How's the family?' Ted asked the driver.

'Ted, the kids are all grown up now. My wife's got bigger, but she's my missus and looks after me well. She'll laugh when I tell her I've met you.'

Ted turned and looked at me. 'Please excuse me, let me introduce you to my wife, Peggy.' Ted looked at the frown on my face. 'I will explain it all to you later, Peggy.'

We got out of the cab and walked into the pub. The barman glanced at us coming in the door, stopped what he was doing, and shouted, 'Look what the cat's dragged in!'

Ted stopped, put both his hands on his hips, and said to the barman. 'Well, I never. I thought they'd buried you a long time ago. What went wrong?'

'As you know, Ted, I'm too slippery for them, something you taught me. To weave, duck, and dive, and land your punch in the right place. Do you still drink the same thing, Ted?'

'Yes, please, I do, and the lady is my wife, Peggy. Peg, this is Slippery. This slippery sod can't use any stronger words in front of you Peg, he's number one; you can rely on him. But if he starts to complain, just ignore him and tell him what you want. A brandy and dry ginger, for the lady.'

Slippery looked at him seriously and said, 'Yes, back room.' Ted led me into a back room. There was another bar, tables and chairs, women were sitting there. The men all stood up and clapped when we entered. I thought I saw tears in Ted's eyes as he looked at each one of them. They meant so much to him. They were his team before he left England.

He looked at one of the men and said, 'Michael, I didn't think you'd fall for that trick!'

Michael shook his head. 'I didn't know you were back, but I do know you've got Jackie worried.' Our drinks arrived, and one of the women stood up and put her hand out to shake mine.

'I'm Janet, please come and sit with the other women. Leave the men to play, boys.'

The women talked about the old days when Ted was their boss. I looked around the room surprised, 'You all worked under Ted?'

'Yes, we did. You could write a book,' Janet said. 'Ted was the best, but strict. He used to tell them that they were not working for politicians; they were working for the people, and that's why they all respected him so much.'

Janet asked me if I had met Slippery at the bar. 'Yes, I did.'

'The hierarchy set him up, but Ted stopped them. That's why he was sent to Australia, but we all think it may have backfired.'

Ted was talking to three others in the corner. Slippery turned up with the drinks and sat down with them.

Ted looked serious. 'I've got a problem.' He explained it all to them. 'So, I would like it if you could check out Lesley Johnson's death certificate at Somerset House, see if you can find out anything different about it. The numbers on the death certificate don't make any sense. Peg, my wife, is her sister. Lesley has left everything to Peg in her will, but is she really dead or not? And who is the Lesley Johnson on the certificate and is there a file on her in the police archives?'

Slippery looked at him and said, 'It will be done!'

I saw one of the women look at her watch. She said, 'If we don't stop them talking, they will be there all night, and they have work in the morning.'

With that, the woman got up and walked over to her husband, tapped him on the shoulder, and with words of command said, 'Home, you've got work in the morning!'

They all broke up. They had been given a command from a lot higher authority. As we walked out of the pub, I felt the cold chill of England's winter.

Ted and I got back to the flat about 12.30 am. As we crawled into bed, Ted said he had booked a matinee show at the theatre for that day.

'Just wake me in the morning with a cup of coffee, please.'

'Yes, my lady, certainly.'

Before I could blink, I was asleep.

I heard a terrible voice calling me, 'Wakey, wakey sleepy head, it's time to leave your bed.'

I rolled over and there was Ted, grinning at me with two cups of coffee in his hands. 'As you ordered, my lady.'

'Well, Ted, what's today going to bring?'

He winked at me. 'All sorts of fun and games.'

I replied, 'You love being a detective, don't you?

He moved his head slightly to one side. 'I suppose you could say that, yes.'

'And you love meeting your old colleagues.'

'Yes, I did.'

I touched him lightly on his shoulder.

'You do miss them, don't you?'

'Yes, I do.'

I watched Ted. He appeared to be thinking very deeply. He shook himself. 'Come on, old girl, we've got work to do.'

With that, he disappeared into the bathroom. I sat there thinking of my sister, Lesley. The tears started to come. I was devastated when I was told she had died. She was the only person who understood me. I could no longer talk to her or write to her. What is happening now? I can't understand or get used to it. I want to reach out and touch you, to be safe with you, like the old days. I still wanted to lean up against my big sister, to feel the warmth and compassion she always gave me, just like our mum used to do. The one thing I have learned is that my mum was the person I wanted her to be.

Just then, the bathroom door opened. 'Come on, lazybones, out of bed!' Ted was hurrying into the kitchen.

I got up and went into the bathroom. When I came out, Ted had bacon and eggs on the table with fresh toast. The smell of breakfast made me very hungry. I reached over and took Ted's breakfast as well. Ted's protest made me laugh.

'But Ted, I'm hungry!'

Ted put both his hands flat on the table. 'That is my breakfast.'

I replied, 'But Ted, yours is bigger than mine'

He gave me a serious look, but had a twinkle in his eyes. He deepened his voice and said it was his, and took it back. We ate our breakfast and had two cups of coffee.

CHAPTER 9

We went downstairs. Ted hailed a taxi, and we went on our way to the theatre.

I loved the theatre. The marble stairs, mirrors on the walls, and pictures of all the old actors. Ted bought a brochure and appeared to be reading it, but I noticed he was really looking in one of the mirrors. He looked up and said, 'Would you like a Walls ice cream?'

'Ooh, yes please, I would; they are so creamy, and I haven't had one since the last time I was in England as a student.'

Ted walked up and joined a small queue waiting to buy their ice cream. He took a small purse from his pocket. It was a horseshoe shape, made of very soft leather. He appeared to fumble with it, like he was trying to sort out some change. A woman started to walk past him with an ice cream in her hand. Ted dropped his change, and just as she was passing, he bent down to pick it up. They accidentally nudged each other, the women looked down at Ted; you would have thought she had seen a ghost, she hurried off. Ted bought the ice cream and handed me mine. I thought of the woman; there was something wrong, but I couldn't put my finger on it. We went up the stairs into the theatre, sat down, and ate our ice cream. The lights dimmed, and Ted said, 'Come on, let's go!'

I wanted to argue with him, but thought better of it. We didn't go back through the foyer but through an internal side door. We turned left down a corridor, right through another door, down some steps, and out through the fire door into an alley. Ted was walking quickly whilst holding my hand. I could see traffic on the main road at the end of the alleyway. There were some rubbish bins in front of a door. Ted took me through the door; I was totally and utterly confused!

We were in a kitchen. A man with a black beard looked up and raised his eyebrows. Ted put his finger to his lips; the bearded man nodded. We went through another door into a small restaurant that was divided into small cubicles, giving the diners privacy. The decor was beautiful, old English style. Ted chose a cubicle where he could see out of the window, but if you were outside, you wouldn't be able to see in. Outside, I could see a statue of a man on a horse. There was a very beautiful building behind it, with tall columns like you would see in Rome. I knew it was the Exchange building. I could also see the Bank of England.

Ted grinned at me and said with a chuckle, 'That is Threadneedle Street and the building is nicknamed *the old lady*.'

I frowned at him. He chuckled, stood up, and took off his Mac and hat. He folded his Mac and put it neatly on a seat where it couldn't be seen. I was even more confused.

I looked at him and shook my head. 'What's going on, Ted? You need to explain it to me.' I watched the wicked smile in his eyes, the same smile a little boy has when he is up to no good.

'Peg, see the lady standing at the traffic lights? Have you seen her before?'

'Yes, Ted, I have. She was buying an ice cream when you dropped your change. I remember because it didn't look right.'

'Peg, there is something wrong. She was one of mine and one of the best, then she was transferred to MI5.'

Ted took a small card out of his pocket and showed it to me. *Jennifer Howard*. It was her warrant card.

I shook my head. 'You're like a little boy, always playing games. You took that when you dropped your change, didn't you?'

Ted hunched his shoulders and grinned. He glanced back at the road. 'She's coming in here, dear.'

He turned to face me and took both my hands as though he was going to talk to me very seriously, so anyone coming in the door could only see his back and part of me.

Jennifer came through the door. She glanced around the restaurant and walked up to two cubicles, which were at the back of the restaurant. She looked in each one as if she were looking for something or someone, excusing herself to the people sitting there, then she went into the kitchen.

Ted sat there with a cheeky grin all over his face. After a while, he said, 'Peg, she's gone out through the back door and down the alleyway because she is now back at the traffic lights. She would have gone to the back two cubicles because we used to sit in them many years ago.'

'What do you mean, you used to sit in the cubicles at the back?'

'Well, Peg, we had a bit of a thing going on for a while, and then it got too dangerous.'

Just then, we saw a car pull up at the traffic lights, and Jennifer got in the back seat.

Unbeknown to us, Jackie Evans was also in the back seat. Jennifer said to Jackie, 'I lost them! I think they may still be in the theatre.'

Jackie shook her head. 'That would be Ted! Always playing damn games.'

The black-bearded man walked up to our cubicle, carrying a tray with three cups and saucers, milk, sugar, and a small teapot. He placed them down on the table and sat down next to me. He stared at Ted, and Ted stared back at him. Ted looked at me and, in a soft voice, said, 'Peggy, this is my older brother, Peter.'

Ted winked at his brother. 'Sniffy, this is my wife Peggy, we met in Australia.'

Peter gave a loud, throaty laugh. 'So, twinkle toes, you're not so good on your feet anymore; a woman finally got you!' Peter had a strong Cockney accent, and I didn't understand why Ted called him Sniffy. Just then, Sniffy gave a small sniff!

I now understood! Ted looked at me for a minute, then said, 'Peggy, our mum and dad owned this restaurant. They left it to Sniffy.'

Just then, a man walked in the front door. He looked straight at Peter, then walked up to our table and put some money down in front of him, nodded, and walked back out into the street. Peter took a notebook out of his pocket and wrote something in it. He then put the money in his top pocket. Peter looked at me and saw the puzzled expression on my face. He glanced back at Ted, who gave a little chuckle and said to me, 'Peggy, we Cockneys stick together love, if you are a little short of money, you come and see Sniffy. Before Sniffy, you used to come and see our mum. You borrow the money and pay it back as you can. No set amount, no set time, whatever you can afford, just so long as you pay back your debt. If you are having problems paying, talk to Sniffy, and he will work it out. As I said, we are Cockneys, we stick together, we are the original Londoners. The little book Sniff has is called the Slate.'

With that, Peter's voice broke in. 'Tea, sugar, and white.'

I gave a small sigh, raised my eyebrows, and said, 'Yes please.'

Then I smelled something in the men's teacups and knew they were drinking something a little stronger. Ted and Peter talked about their families for a few moments, then customers started to come in, and Peter had to go back to work.

'I don't think I'll ever call him Sniffy; I'll stick to Peter,' I said to Ted.

Ted picked up his Mac and said, 'I think it's safe to go now Peggy.' He turned and looked at his brother. Their eyes met, a thousand words were spoken between them. They just nodded to each other.

Ted turned and took my arm. We left the restaurant and headed towards the bank. It had a beautiful marble foyer. Ted nudged me and asked, 'Have you got the key dear?'

'No, Ted, I don't. You didn't tell me we were coming to the bank.'

Ted looked at me with a worried look. I couldn't help but laugh. If Ted can have his sense of humour, so can I.

'Yes, Ted, I do have the key.'

'Peggy, you have the key, but we also need a password. Lesley left you the key in the envelope, but she also left you the password, and I believe it is *little sister.*'

I looked at Ted. 'Yes, I believe you're right. You are one great detective.'

We walked up to the counter and told the man what we needed. We were ushered through a door into another room. The man asked to see the key. After he handed it back to me, he asked for the password, which I gave him. He nodded, then left. We were ushered into another room. The man left and closed the door behind him.

There was a safe deposit box on the table. Ted and I stared at each other for a few moments. What was in the box? It was like looking at the Holy Grail. I walked towards the table, the key in my hand. I hesitated before putting the key in the lock.

Ted stood back. As he did, I turned the lock and the lid sprung open. The safe deposit box was full; there were lots of photos. I picked up one of those, which was on top. I started to cry. It was Lesley. She looked so beautiful. I stood staring at the photo for a minute, then handed it to Ted.

I picked up the second one. It had a well-built man wearing a Navy uniform. He had strong cheeks, although his face appeared serious, it was also warm and friendly. On the bottom of the photo, it read, *Captain William Farquhar.* I handed it to Ted.

The minute I saw the eyes in the next photo, I knew who it was. Jacko, my greatest friend when I was on the Diamantina River.

His hair was white, and so was his beard, but I still knew him. His eyes still had that wicked look in them. He was called *The Peacemaker* and would sort out any problems among our people. He was the law, the wisest of them all.

I handed the photo to Ted and picked up another one. It showed a tall, thin man with a worried, stern look on his face. He was also dressed in a naval uniform. At the bottom of the photo, the words read, *Captain Ted Coe*. I handed it to Ted. There was one more photo of a man with black hair that had a beautiful wave on top. He was dressed in white and was wearing an apron. He had a beautiful smile and dancing, twinkling eyes. He appeared to be standing on a sailing vessel. The name at the bottom of this photo was *Leslie Evans*. I handed this to Ted, then picked up a logbook. Written on the front was *Daisy May, Captain William Farquhar*. I opened the logbook. It stated that the *Daisy May* had departed Melbourne on September 20th, 1939. I read the crew list. Ted Coe—Bosun, Michael Theodore—Sailmaker, Les—Cook. No surname listed. When I got to the end of the page, it had Lesley Johnson—reporter for a magazine.

Further on, I read about the cargo—wool bales—destination—England. I turned the pages, which were full of various courses and longitude and latitudes, winds and tides, but very little actual information. I handed the journal to Ted and picked up the next book, which was a journal.

I started to read. It said that Lesley was assigned to a project in Australia in September 1939, at the beginning of the war. Lesley and three British naval commandos were signed on to a barque sailing clipper named *Daisy May*. She was a writer; the other three were signed on as crew. Lesley wrote that they were assigned to protect the cargo at all costs. I kept scanning through; everything was in detail, nothing appeared to be left out. From the beginning of the voyage in Melbourne, to sailing around Madagascar, Lesley had written something here and underlined every line.

I realised I knew who William Farquhar was, and Jacko. I have kept it from them that I know who they are. They were from the Diamantina River. Jacko is the Peacemaker, and William Farquhar is the cook's son.

I kept on reading. She talked about submarines and a spy who came on board, about Jack Fox and them all arriving at Dartmouth. Everything was in detail, every single thing she had written down: her assignments during the war, names of people, their ranks and positions in the forces or the government. Lesley worked closely with Winston Churchill, she highly respected him, and talked about being caught between Churchill and the upper class in England who were sitting on the fence, backing Germany in case they won and also their own country England, in the hope that they would win. They were using their positions in society for their own protection for the future.

I realised how dangerous these journals were for the British government or those in higher levels of society. There are those who would want these journals to disappear, and others who would use them to control some people. My lawyer mind was now clicking in. Political blackmail was definitely not in the British interest. Should Lesley's journals be destroyed? No, they are history. Keep them hidden for fifty years or longer? But what have they done with Lesley? If she is dead, where does that leave Ted and me? What lengths would they go to get her journals?

I turned and looked at Ted, who had been sitting patiently waiting, browsing through the ship's log.

'Ted, we've got big trouble!' I explained to him what I had read and what I thought the circumstances would be. He listened, but didn't say a word.

'Ted, if Lesley is dead or alive, where does that leave us? How far would they go to get the journals?'

Ted looked at me; he appeared to be deep in thought.

'Peggy, first of all, we've got to find out where Lesley is. I've got to protect both you and Lesley. Everything will be safe while it's in the deposit box. What else is in it? Look inside.'

I turned around and took the rest of the items out of the box. There was a folded bundle of five-pound notes. I took out another envelope. Inside was a piece of white paper; the sides were neatly folded into the centre. Straightaway, we knew what this was. It's how they wrapped diamonds! I opened the package. There were four large diamonds the size of a thumbnail.

'Ted, these are worth a fortune!'

Ted lifted his eyebrows and shook his head, 'Peggy, Lesley is a very wealthy woman.'

I wrapped the diamonds up and put them back into the safe deposit box. Next item was a leather pouch. I slowly opened it and saw a beautiful pocket watch with a note. I opened the note and started to read out loud, '*To my son Jacko*'. I put the watch back in the case, then picked up a beautifully made pair of canvas gloves. Written with intricate stitching were the words, *Daisy May*. I couldn't resist trying them on. I put the left one on. Judging by the size, they had definitely been made for a woman. I put the right-hand one on; there was a piece of paper inside. I took it out, unfolded it, and read the words

Little Sister, I knew you couldn't resist putting on the gloves. You have found what they've been looking for. Keep them safe for me. Love you. Lesley.

I folded the piece of paper back up and put it back into the glove. I could feel a tightness in my chest and started to cry. My sister had spoken to me for the first time since we arrived in England.

Ted reached out and touched my hand. 'Are you all right, Peggy?'

'Yes, Ted. Everything has just caught up with me. I just want to know that Lesley is alright.'

'Peggy, the Captain's logbook tells us of a voyage from Australia to England. To me, he has deliberately kept it very brief. I don't think it's a problem for anyone, but as you say, Lesley's journals are a powder keg; they can be used in many ways. Politically, I envy your ability to speed-read, but you are a lawyer.'

I looked at Ted very seriously. 'Ted, I would like to read more details, but so far, it frightens the hell out of me! Where has she been? What has she done? My sister certainly isn't an ordinary person.'

I shook my head and picked up the journals and put them back into the safe deposit box, closed the lid, and locked it. I stood up and cuddled into Ted's arms for support.

By the time we left the bank, it was dark; time had vanished.

'Peggy, I want to go to the Bell and see if the boys have any information for me. I will give Slippery a phone call.'

We found a phone box, and Ted stepped in. He rang the bell. A voice at the other end of the receiver, in an unfriendly tone, said, 'What do you want?'

'Ted here, Slippery.' There was a chuckle at the other end of the phone.

'You'd better get your backside down here, me old cock sparrow. The boys are awaiting. I'll have your drinks waiting.' With that, the receiver went click!

We hailed a taxi and asked the driver to take us to the Bell Pub at the Pen. The taxi driver laughed, 'Haven't heard that for a few years!' It didn't seem to take too long, and we arrived at the pub. Ted paid the driver, who said to Ted that it was good to meet a true Cockney. Ted nodded, and the taxi took off. I asked Ted what he meant by the Pen.

'See that building over there? That's where they made pens.'

'Ted, there is another language here I have never known before, and I was educated in England!'

We walked through the door of the pub, and Slippery came around the corner of the bar, over to a door. He looked at it, nodded his head, and we followed him to the back bar. Men were sitting at a table; they nodded their heads to Ted. They all stood up when I came in and ushered me to a chair. I sat down, then they all sat down. I smiled to myself; I wasn't used to this respect paid to ladies.

Slippery spoke first. 'We've heard a whisper that they are stepping up surveillance on you.'

Another man spoke. 'I've been in touch with Somerset House.' He laid some papers on the table. 'This is Lesley Johnson's death certificate. According to the numbers you gave me, she died of pneumonia and heart failure, so I did some more research on her. Her husband died overseas during the war. Her four children died in the Blitz. She had no fixed address and lived a very rough life on the streets, getting a quid wherever she could. She was just another victim of the war. So, this death certificate is not your Lesley Johnson's!'

He handed me the paperwork.

Another man spoke. 'I did some enquiries with the Navy Department. Lesley Johnson, nationality: Australian. She is still a high-ranking officer in the Navy; where she is posted is classified information.

'So, she is still alive!' My voice boomed out. 'You're saying she is not dead, but that she's alive!'

'Yes, madam.'

I looked at Ted with tears in my eyes. He gently nodded to me.

The first man spoke again. 'So, we have a problem. A crime has been committed; somebody has forged a death certificate. If Peggy accepts the death certificate, she can be charged as well. She doesn't rightfully own the assets. I also researched you, Ted. You are still a high-ranking British Officer, you out rank us all, so we are researching a crime for you.

Lesley Johnson is a high-ranking British Naval Officer. Anything she has belongs to the British Navy, not MI5.' He thumped his fist on the table in annoyance. 'So we are tied up in bloody politics again. The war is over! The British Navy hasn't faked her death, so it can only be MI5. Is there something we should know about Ted?'

Ted's eyes looked straight into mine. He wanted a legal way out. I replied, 'Yes Ted. It is my problem, gentlemen. Ted and I are very grateful for the information you have given us. I now know my sister is still alive. Where she is, that's another question. We don't want to tie you up in something extremely political, which could be very harmful to your careers. I can say that during the war, Lesley was involved in a lot of high-ranking… I don't have an actual word… as to say, *funny business*. It did involve the War Ministry, MI5, MI6, and many high-ranking aristocrats, so it was political. Lesley kept journals. She wrote every detail in them. These journals, as you realise, can do a lot of damage to a lot of people if they get into the wrong hands. I'll use the words Political Blackmail. As a lawyer, the point is, if we go back into history, Queen Victoria had a Scottish Gillie, his name was Mr Brown. He kept diaries, and when he died, the diaries disappeared. Nobody knows where they are or who they belong to. His family or the Queen. If they got into the wrong hands… I'll leave that question open, but to protect you all and Ted, Lesley's journals will remain hidden. Yes, I have read them briefly, and they frighten the hell out of me, but I do believe she had a great part in protecting England. Winston Churchill had picked the right person to play the politics.'

At this time, Ted spoke up. 'So, I will have to take this to somebody a lot higher up to protect you all, but at the moment I don't know who. If MI5 is responsible for the forgery, they will say it is in the interest of national security. Please give me time to work on this a little more.'

Sniffy's voice boomed out. 'Yes, boss. More drinks are coming.' He put our drinks on the table and said, "I'm just popping upstairs to have a look outside, just to make sure we are not being watched.'

I laughed. 'You all have Mackintosh coats and that same hat. Do you have a spare one for me, please?'

Sniffy grinned. 'Yes. I do like the way you think, Peggy. It must be rubbing off from someone else.'

As he started to walk out of the room, he nudged Ted on the shoulder. When he returned, he said that there were two of them together in the doorway of the Pen, trying to keep dry.

'Peggy, Ted, I will get you a taxi, but I will order three taxis, and they will all leave together, but go in different directions. It should be confusing, especially when you are all dressed identically. Peggy, you are wearing high heel shoes; those two will be sharp out there, so be careful.'

As Ted and I got into the cab, he pushed himself in front of me so that you couldn't see what I had on my feet.

'Good morning,' the taxi driver said. We looked at him and saw it was the same taxi driver we had met before. I briefly glanced at my watch; it was morning. 'Sniffy said we could have company, so sit back and enjoy the ride.'

All three taxis took off together and went their separate ways, but we met them all at the next intersection. Anybody watching would have been totally confused. Which one was going where? They all looked the same.

I nudged Ted on the elbow. 'Life isn't boring, is it?'

Ted grinned and pulled his trilby hat down over his face as if he were going to have a sleep. I thought, what a good idea, and did the same. Very soon we arrived back at the flat and fell into bed, exhausted.

CHAPTER 10

Next morning, I woke up, rolled over to see Ted lying on his back, snoring away, his little mustache quivering every time he breathed out. I wondered whether I should wake him. I grinned and thought if I held his nose with my fingers, if I touched him somewhere, I knew that would get complicated. I decided to leave him in peace. I quietly slipped out of bed and went into the kitchen and made myself a cup of coffee. I sat down to drink it, but felt very sad. There were so many unanswered questions. I was asking myself, *where are you, Lesley? Are you safe? Are you well?* I sat up straight, shocked, spilling my coffee in the process. I heard her voice. No, I didn't hear it, but the feeling was that of a cool breeze on a hot day. *Little sister, I am well and I am safe!* I jumped again as I felt a hand touch my shoulder, but there was nobody there. Then, in my mind, I saw Jacko's eyes; I instantly knew it was Jacko. I sat there, mesmerized, not believing what had just happened. I felt that I was back in the desert with Mum and Dad and sensed the voice again. *Use your inner senses; go back to the desert.*

I heard Ted's voice. 'Are you alright, Peggy?'

I looked up at his face. 'I think so. I was asking questions in my mind, and I got the answers.'

'Peggy, I've been married to you for ten years. I know that you have special senses I do not have. There is something very special about you. Sometimes, when we are talking, you give me answers that surprise me, and I ask myself where do they come from. When we were with Marcia, you read Lesley's birth certificate and told me you are part Aboriginal and came from the Diamantina River. Your natural senses are far sharper than mine; I perfectly understand what you're saying.'

Ted walked over to the sink and picked up a cloth to wipe the coffee off the table. He folded the cloth and held it over the top of my coffee cup. 'We can't afford to waste coffee, darling!' He pretended he was going to wring out the cloth. I sharply pulled the cup out of the way.

'Ted, you always take the seriousness away with humour.'

'Peggy, after breakfast we are going to see Mr Fredericks and Marcia, and explain things to them.'

I nodded. 'Ted, I should have squashed your nose!' He looked at me, totally confused. With that, I went off to have my shower.

Ted phoned Mr Fredericks and made an appointment for 10.30 am. We had plenty of time and decided to walk to the office. As we were walking, Ted stopped, took two paces backwards and whispered to a man leaning on a fence, reading a newspaper. 'We are going down this road here, then we will be turning right, then left, so please don't get lost, Michael!' They smiled at each other.

Michael replied, 'I told Jackie Evans it wouldn't be any good trying to follow you discreetly.'

Ted put his hand on Michael's shoulder, 'Walk with us Michael, but hold up the newspaper; it will look good.'

Michael chuckled, 'You are still a bastard Ted!' They walked together talking and laughing about the old days and some of the cases they had worked on.

We soon arrived at Mr Fredericks' office.

'Will you wait here for us, Michael? We will be here for quite a while, why don't you go on and have a nice cup of coffee? If anybody should criticize you, tell them Ted Jones told you to have coffee because he outranks them.' Ted turned and started to walk up the steps.

Michael raised his hat and said, 'Good morning, Mrs Jones.'

I nodded to him and followed Ted. Ted looked at the big brass plaque. 'Do you think you would like to have one like that, Peggy?'

I nudged him. 'Yes, if you would keep polishing it!'

Ted started to push the bell, but the door opened before he could do so. Marcia was standing there, ready to greet us. Before I could get through the door, Marcia's arms were around me, embracing me with so much affection. Then she looked at Ted and said, 'Pork in batter with honey drizzled over, served with vegetables, then rhubarb and apple crumble served with custard and cream.' She raised her eyebrows.

Ted gave her that schoolboy look and said, 'You're not just beautiful, you are absolutely beautiful. Peggy, can we get the business quickly out of the way?' With that, he was walking through the front door.

'Husbands are like little boys, aren't they?' Marcia said to me.

'Yes, Marcia, I totally agree with you.'

We went into Mr Fredericks' office and sat down. Marcia was standing alongside me, holding my hand. Mr Fredericks was sitting at his desk, his spectacles balancing on the end of his nose.

Ted spoke first. 'Peggy and I have untangled this web of deceit.' He took the first piece of paper out of the envelope and handed it to Mr Fredericks, who read it.

'So, this is the real Lesley Johnson. How did you get this, Ted?'

'Being in the right rank in the police force and having a few good, loyal friends.'

Mr Fredericks nodded at Ted. He sat quietly for a few moments. Marcia's hand squeezed mine tighter. She had an impatient look on her face. Ted then handed him the second piece of paper, the report from the British Navy.

Mr Fredericks' eyes connected with Marcia. 'So, she is not dead! She is still alive!'

I felt the whole of Marcia's body relax, then the tears started to flow. This started me off as well.

Mr Fredericks looked at Ted. 'So, Ted, you've found what you were looking for, or should I say, what they are looking for?'

'Yes, we did.'

I broke in. 'Mr Fredericks, Lesley kept a journal. She recorded everything she did during the war in every detail. It would be very dangerous for those in high places, and please excuse us if we don't tell you where they are; we have to protect you and Marcia.'

Mr Fredericks nodded and appeared to be in deep thought. 'So you and I have a bit of legal work to sort out.'

Mr Fredericks and I talked a lot of mumble-jumble, if this is that, would that be there. That wouldn't be the moral side, the legal side.

Mr Fredericks said he had not lodged any papers, so they could put things back together exactly as they were when we first arrived in the office and put them back in the file. 'We have proof that Lesley Johnson is still alive, so her will goes back into the safe. Thank you for keeping me informed.'

Marcia looked at me, 'Where will you go now Peggy?'

'Ted said the last entry that he read in the logbook for *Daisy May* was Dartmouth, so we thought we'd go down there and see what we can find.'

Marcia squeezed my hand again. She grinned at Ted and let go of my hand, walked over to Ted, and took his hand.

Ted stood up. 'Lunch, Ted?'

Ted nodded, and he and Marcia walked out the door into the hall.

Ted stopped. 'Marcia, I don't want to be forward, but I have a colleague standing out there, and when we came in, it had started to rain again. He works for MI5, but I very much respect him; he once was one of mine. Would you have enough lunch for him, also?'

'Ted, if he is a friend of yours, he is a friend of mine.' She walked over to the window to see a man leaning against an old oak tree, out of the weather. 'Is that him?'

'Yes, his name is Michael.'

Marcia tapped Ted on the shoulder, turned around and took her raincoat off of the hall stand, and disappeared through the kitchen door. Ted stood at the window, watching. Marcia turned up out of nowhere and spoke to the man. Michael turned around sharply and stared at Marcia.

She politely said to him, 'A colleague of yours has invited you to lunch; please follow me.'

He hesitated for a moment. Marcia turned slightly, 'He's a high-ranking police officer!'

Michael shook his head, raised his eyebrows, and said to himself, *here we go again* and followed Marcia.

To Ted's surprise, they walked through the kitchen door. Ted helped Michael off with his coat and helped Marcia with hers. Soon they were all seated at the dining table, but Michael did look a bit out of place.

Ted started the conversation about Australian kangaroos, snakes, and birds, especially the kookaburras that laughed at you.

Marcia served the soup, then the main course. The vegetables were absolutely beautiful, with fresh peas straight out of the garden. More wine was served, along with more chitchat. Then Marcia came in with a ladened tray.

She put one bowl in front of me: rhubarb and apple crumble with custard and cream. Ted's lips started quivering, and his eyes nearly popped out of his head! Marcia put a bowl down in front of her husband

and another in front of Michael. There weren't any more bowls on the tray. Marcia shook her head, 'I'm sorry Ted, there wasn't enough to go around, so I gave it to Michael.'

Michael's eyes widened; I lowered my head. Mr Fredericks stared at him.

Marcia said to Ted, 'I'm sorry Ted, but you invited Michael.'

The look on Ted's face! He was trying to compose himself, but I could see the little boy in his eyes, the disappointment. Marcia shook her head and went back into the kitchen. Everyone at the table was quiet. Then Marcia came back with two bowls; one was heaped up with dessert, you could not get another spoonful on it.

Marcia put hers down and looked at Michael. 'Oh, Michael, I have given you the wrong one.'

Ted could not contain himself. 'No, he is quite happy with the one he's got.' He put out both his hands and took the bowl.

I burst out laughing. 'Somebody else gives you your medicine back.' Marcia and I kept laughing; Michael had his head down, but with a big smile all over his face.

Michael said to Ted, 'If you have trouble Ted, just let me know.'

I watched Michael and Ted as they chatted and drank their wine. Ted needed that time to talk with Michael. He was home.

Ted put his hand on Michael's shoulder, 'If you ever want to come to Australia, Michael.' They stood quietly, looking at each other.

Then Michael said, 'I will give it some thought, Ted.'

Mr Fredericks nodded to the two of them, and they went through to his office. I asked Marcia where they were going.

She replied, 'They are going to do their football pools! They will have their ears glued to the radio for half an hour.'

'One of the last entries in *Daisy May's* log mentioned Dartmouth, so Ted and I are going to get the train to Dartmouth to see what we can find. Maybe we might be able to get more answers.'

We started to clean the dishes up. I picked up Ted's bowl and spoon. 'Marcia, I don't think we need to wash this bowl; it is perfectly clean already.'

Marcia giggled and replied, 'Yes he did lick it when we weren't looking.'

'That's my Ted,' I laughingly replied.

Soon, the men came back out of the office, chatting about football. Michael walked in front of everybody and stood in front of Marcia. 'Thank you for inviting me to dinner, Marcia, and giving me time with Ted. I'm so very grateful to you. Now, I must get back to my post.'

He turned and shook hands with Mr Fredericks. 'Thank you.'

And to Ted, 'Ted you have given me something to think about, especially warm weather.'

He turned and went out through the kitchen door.

Mr Fredericks put his hand on Ted's shoulder. 'A light port in the lounge, Ted?'

We followed him and sat and talked with them both. In the evening, Marcia brought in a big plate of sandwiches. Ted's face lit up again at the sight of more food. We had a very enjoyable evening, and by the time we got back to the flat, it was 2 am!

'Ted, you said the train leaves at 6 am, so we would have to leave here at 5 am, which means we'll only get three hours of sleep! So, you had better set the alarm.'

CHAPTER 11

We found that the train was quite busy, but we had booked a window seat in first class. 'How did you get first class, Ted?'

'I gave him my position in the police force.'

To which I replied with a very serious look, 'Old friend Ted?'

'You could say so, Peggy.'

I cuddled into Ted's shoulder, making myself nice and snug, and comfortable. I closed my eyes and woke to hear a man talking to me. He was dressed in a railway uniform. 'Your ticket, madam.'

I glanced at Ted; he was sound asleep. I nudged him with my elbow. He opened one eye, turned his head, looked at the man, and reached into his inside pocket. He showed the man his card.

The man replied, 'Thank you' and went to the next person.

'Ted, that wasn't a train ticket you showed the man, was it?' I said.

'No, dear, it was my warrant card.' He winked at me. 'We are on official business.'

With that, he closed his eyes. I thought I needed a cup of coffee, so I got up and went to the coffee bar. I bought two coffees and two toasted egg and bacon sandwiches and returned to our seats. I put the coffees on the tray in front of us and put one sandwich down alongside me and started to eat the other. I could see Ted's nose quiver. He opened his eyes. 'What have you got, Peggy?'

I replied, 'A lovely hot, toasted egg and bacon sandwich with a bit of onion.'

There was silence. Ted didn't say anything; he grinned at me. 'Are we playing a little game, dear?'

'What do you mean, Ted?'

He sat up straight and looked on my seat, reached over, and picked up the other sandwich. 'You are a very funny lady, very funny!'

Ted ate his sandwich and drank his coffee. Soon we arrived in Torbay; it was just before 9 am. We transferred to another train for Dartmouth. It was a beautiful ride, very scenic.

Ted pointed to a lovely house perched on a cliff, 'That's where Agatha Christie lived.'

The train climbed up a hill, then started to head down into a cutting. We saw the Dartmouth River. There were many small boats anchored or tied up there. The train continued into the town; the harbour was on our right, the town on our left. We arrived at the station and alighted from the train. It was quite warm, and Ted took off his Mac and put it over his arm. I could sense him thinking.

'I reckon we should go over the river to the other side; the harbour is there,' he said.

We walked down the footpath towards the river. Then we walked under an arch. From there, we could see the river and the ferry. There was a little tug that pushed the ferry back and forth across the river. While we were waiting for the ferry to return to our side, Ted pointed out various points of interest to me.

'Peggy, the Naval Academy is further up the river, and just down there is where the Mayflower first left. She started to take on water in her hull, so they called in to Plymouth for repairs. There is a plaque on the wall on the other side of the river saying that the Mayflower left from there, and the date. On this side, but a little further up, is where they made the D-Day landing barges. At the mouth of the river, there is a fort where Henry VIII had a chain put across the river to stop any unwanted vessels from entering the harbour. On the top of the hill, on this side, there is a tower called the Day Tower. It's a beacon at the entrance to the river, and it's thought that the Romans built it.'

'You should have been a tour guide, Ted.' I nudged his shoulder with my elbow. He just grinned at me.

Soon the ferry arrived on our side of the river, and the cars and trucks were off-loaded. We went aboard. More vehicles were loaded back onto the little ferry, and we started to cross the river. It certainly was hard work for the little tug. We arrived on the other side of the river, between two buildings. They let us off before the vehicles, making sure we were safe. We walked up the ramp between the two buildings, then we turned right into a beautiful street filled with old shops. The upper floor of the shops hung over the road, taking us back in history. I wanted to stop and look in the shop windows, but Ted wouldn't stop; he was on a mission!

'Ted, is that a toilet over there?'

Ted replied, 'Yes, it is.'

I smiled at him and told him to sit and wait. 'I'll be back! That's a good little puppy!' I turned and went straight for the toilet.

Meanwhile, Ted saw a policeman standing next to a corner shop and walked up to him; his sense of humour clicked in again.

'G'day mate, how are you going?'

The policeman's eyes narrowed. Ted handed him his warrant card. The policeman read it and bent his head slightly to one side, looking at Ted, a little puzzled. Ted put his hand out, and the policeman put his hand out, and they shook hands. Ted asked the policeman, 'Constable, were you here during the war years?'

'Yes, I was,' the constable replied.

Ted asked, 'Do you remember a barque sailing clipper by the name of *Daisy May* being here?'

'*Daisy May?*' The constable was a seasoned man who could play the game and the politics. He paused for a while before answering. 'You see that man over there repairing the sails on that two mastered schooner. I would suggest, sir, that you talk to him.'

Ted stared into the constable's eyes for a few moments. He knew that he would have to give him a reasonable explanation for his query. He didn't want the constable talking to his superiors.

'Thank you, Constable, it's just a personal matter.'

Ted walked back to where I had left him. I had returned from the toilet by now.

'Do I get a biscuit now, dear? Or perhaps a little something tonight?' I patted him on his head.

Ted then decided that he also needed to go and made a beeline for the toilets. I couldn't help myself; this was my chance. I went over to look in the window of a little shop. I noticed a policeman looking at me with a puzzled look on his face. I thought it best to ignore him. I was looking at a beautiful pair of earrings when Ted's voice behind me said, 'Would you like them Peggy?'

'Yes, I would, Ted.'

'Then I will buy them for you later, but now we have more work to do. Come on.'

Ted started to walk away, and I followed. He walked up to a man working on a yacht. I was puzzled, but didn't ask any questions.

Ted asked the man, 'Excuse me, are you Michael?'

The man looked at Ted very seriously. In his younger days, he would have been an extremely handsome man, a ladies' man, but now his hair had become grey and thin. He looked straight at me. I saw a smile, and the twinkle in his eyes and in a beautiful voice said, 'You are Peggy!'

He took Ted and me totally by surprise.

'I will just put my tools away.' He turned and put his tools into a bag and put them in the cabin. He stepped off the yacht and walked up to me. I knew he wanted to cuddle and hold me, but he didn't. He just smiled. 'Would you follow me, please?'

We started to walk back the way we had come.

Michael spoke to the policeman. 'Good morning Stephen, how are the pheasants?'

Stephen replied, 'We have had a good NYE this year; everybody should get a good bag! Will you be at the shoot on Sunday?'

'Wouldn't miss it for the world, Stephen.'

Michael put his hand in the air and kept walking. We followed. I asked Ted how he knew his name was Michael. Ted grinned at me, 'When I read the ship's log, there was a Michael. I just put two and two together!'

Instead of walking back towards the ferry, Michael turned right, then left and walked for a little while. He stopped in front of a white house. It was one of those little houses that said 'England', and I fell in love with it.

Michael walked up to the front door. There was a placard on the wall, *Mr Doolan, Solicitor and Financial Accountant.* On the door was a beautiful brass door knocker. Michael knocked three times, and the door was opened by a good-looking and well-dressed lady. I guessed she would have been in her seventies. She looked straight at Michael with a serious look and said to him, 'I don't want any of your fancy cheek! Just come in.' Michael stepped forward and put his arms around her, and cuddled her with so much affection.

Softly, he said to her, 'You are beautiful,' and quickly stepped backwards, but he wasn't quick enough.

She slapped him on the shoulder and said, 'You're a cheeky little boy!' She turned to us. 'So, you are Ted,' she lowered her voice and smiled at me with so much tenderness and said, 'You are Peggy, Lesley's sister.'

She took me totally by surprise. How did Michael know who I was? How did this lady know who Lesley was? And how did she know I was her sister? So many questions.

The lady put her arms out and gestured for us to come in. She led us into the front parlour, a beautiful little sitting room, so very English. It was certainly a women's room, with all the bright colours. There were two ladies sitting on a couch, and an old man sitting in an armchair.

He stood up and put his hand out to me. 'Mr Doolan, Peggy.' Then he extended his hand to Ted, 'Mr Doolan, sir'.

Ted shook his hand. I noticed that hand grip again. One of the boys.

Ted was looking at the two ladies on the couch. He put his hand in his pocket and brought out a card. It was the warrant card he had acquired at the theatre. He looked straight at the first lady, slightly bowed his head, and with a serious look on his face, said to her, 'Good to see you Jackie.'

She just nodded to him. He then looked at the second lady. Still very serious, he handed her the warrant card. 'I believe you lost this at the theatre.' He stared at her for a few moments. 'You disappointed me. I thought you were better than that. You were the best in the busines, Jennifer Howard, but then you were a police officer, not a political tool.'

The lady's head slightly dropped down so she couldn't see Ted's face, but Jackie's eyes were flashing at him.

In a sharp voice, she said to Ted, 'So, you found what we're looking for, that is why you're in Dartmouth?'

With a sharp look on his face, Ted replied to her, 'We're here looking for Peg's sister Lesley, and the truth as to her whereabouts.' He raised his voice and very loudly said, 'And, we're hoping to find the answers here. I am not a politician, I am a policeman, and I want the truth!'

Jackie slowly sat back on the couch. Ted was still looking at her with a very serious look. He could not believe what he was seeing. Jackie started crying. She wiped away the tears with her hands and in a very sad voice, said, 'Lesley was mine; she was the very best we had. She had reached such a high rank, and what she had achieved during the war was absolutely incredible; and she survived it all.

Jacko, Mervyn, and Bill Farquhar had saved her and brought her back to me, then they took her away. They forged her death certificate. I don't know where she is, or what they have done with her.'

Jackie started to shake, and tears were pouring down her cheeks. She looked straight at Peggy. 'The last time I saw her, Peggy, she was on the *Daisy May* with her friends. They were leaving Dartmouth. We stood at the fort and watched them sail away. The only information I have is that the *Daisy May* had been given a cargo of tinned food to deliver to those places that desperately need it, but I cannot find out any more information than that. *Daisy May* has vanished. Where? To the bottom of the sea? Have they silenced Lesley somehow?'

Jackie started to sob again. Mrs Doolan walked around to the back of the couch, lent over, and took Jackie's hands.

'Well, Jackie, you have finally let it go, haven't you? All of this has been tied up in knots inside you, and now you've finally let it go. I think it has been a long time since you last really cried, and now it's all out.'

Jackie got up and put her arms around Mrs Doolan and cried. Ted and I sat down on another couch. Michael sat down on an armchair. We all waited until Jackie could compose herself again, and she sat back down on the other couch.

She looked at Ted. 'What's it like in Australia?'

I put my arm in Ted's arm; he gently touched my hand.

'Australia, it is a mystical world, a long way away,' he said. He smiled and touched my hand again. 'Australia is a land that is fresh and new, made up of many nationalities since the war. They migrated to Australia, looking for a better life, and found it. Yes, they had to work hard to make it work, but they were rewarded for their hard work and the sacrifices they had to make. They knew that their children would have a far better future. If you work hard and save your money, then there is nothing to stop you from rising to the top. There is nothing you can't do. A train driver can become prime minister. There are no aristocrats playing the game for their own ends. They don't care what it costs the country or the people; it is total selfishness. As a policeman, I can do my job properly. There are no politicians to interfere with the truth, there are no aristocrats to bend or twist it. I am free to do my job. If you want freedom and are prepared to stand up for it, then Australia is the place for you. That is why Australians are respected all around the world, and the word is *true blue, fair dinkum* you don't put up with the *drongo* or a galah.'

Mrs Doolan's voice broke in at this point. 'We have prepared some food and drinks for you in the dining room. Mr and Mrs Jones, we have accommodation here for you tonight. You can have one of the front rooms, and Jackie can have the other.'

She looked at Michael, 'You, can have the couch!' She raised her finger and shook it at Michael. 'I don't trust you with single women.' But in saying that she had a beautiful smile on her face.

As we all went into the dining room, Ted put his arm on Michael's shoulder 'So you are single, Michael?'

Michael looked at Ted with sadness in his eyes. 'My wife died five months ago from cancer. We brought the schooner to sail back to Australia together. I'm looking for a companion to sail with me, just a companion, nothing more. I thought my wife and I had at least 15 or 20 years left to take it easy, sailing around the world to Australia, but it wasn't to be. But I'm still going to make the journey.'

It was a most enjoyable evening. I could see Jackie enjoying herself. It was like a weight had been lifted off her shoulders. She could talk without being constantly on guard. Jackie and Michael seem to have found common ground together, and Michael was making Jackie laugh. I don't think she'd done this for quite a long time; the pressure on her had been too great.

CHAPTER 11

The next morning, Mrs Doolan walked into the front parlour and, with a commanding voice, said, 'Get up lazybones. Everybody is waiting for their breakfast. Jump to it, Michael.'

Michael rolled over and looked at Mrs Doolan, and with a cheeky grin and in a husky voice, said to her, 'You are so lovely first thing in the morning.' Mrs Doolan shook her head and grinned at Michael, turned and walked back out the door. The deep friendship between them was something magical, and just what Mrs Doolan needed. They all sat at the breakfast table.

Mr Doolan spoke. 'No matter where *Daisy May* is, she has the number three painted on her bow. She belongs to the British Navy, and I know she comes under the Secrecy Act, and so does Lesley.'

I watched Ted studying Michael. What is my husband up to? Ted laid both his hands gently on the table. I saw his little moustache quiver. The policeman in him is going back to work.

'Michael, there is a crew member on *Daisy May*. His name is Gerard Collins.' I sat back in my chair, surprised. Gerard Collins is one of my best customers; I'm always doing legal work for him in Australia.

Michael studied Ted for a moment, then he looked at Jackie. Ted also looked at Jackie, who gave a deep sigh and said, 'Michael, you signed the Secrecy Act like the rest of the crew, but I believe that is now finished, so I believe you can answer Ted's question.'

My mind is a lawyer's, and it raced forward. Secrecy Act. How dangerous is this?

Jackie said to me, 'I believe it's all right, Peggy, as long as it's a truth.' Jackie must have read my mind!

Michael sat back in the chair and said, 'I won't call him Gerard; he's Jarrett. Back when the war had just begun, *Daisy May's* owner asked Bill Farquhar to take his son to sea and make a man of him. Bill certainly did this. Jarrett was an arrogant little sod, and the Navy made an officer of him. His mind was quick and sharp; he left Dartmouth on the *Daisy May*. That's all I can say.'

Ted thanked Michael and said to me, 'Peggy, there may be an answer. Peggy and I will return to Australia and delve deeper.'

Jackie spoke up. 'And the journals and logbooks?'

Ted glanced at me. 'I believe they are in a very safe place.'

'Yes, Ted, I agree with you, and they will stay where they are. Legally, they are Lesley's, not mine. And Lesley is a Naval Officer, so who will argue with that.'

After breakfast, a car arrived for Jackie and Jennifer, but before they left, they had a private talk with Michael. Afterwards, they were smiling and laughing.

Jackie walked over to Ted and put her hand out to shake his, saying, 'Ted, you are one big headache, but you may have solved a question for my future, and for that, I thank you.'

Ted frowned at her because she had left the question of what, unanswered. We thanked Mr and Mrs Doolan for their hospitality and walked back down to the harbour with Michael, where we said our goodbyes to each other. Michael gave me a big hug and said he hoped we would meet in the future. I certainly hoped so. On the spur of the moment, I asked him a question, 'Michael, did you make Lesley a pair of gloves?'

Michael replied, 'Yes, I did.'

I threw my arms around his neck and said, 'They are a beautiful pair of gloves.' I could see tears welling in his eyes and sadness on his face.

'Peggy, your sister is a beautiful lady, strong, yet gentle and compassionate. I miss her and our hour-long conversations. I will never be comfortable in my mind knowing how they treated her, but that was war!'

He put his hand out and shook Ted's, saying, 'Happy to meet, sorry to part, happy to meet again.'

With that, he turned and started to walk back to his schooner, not looking around.

Ted and I started to walk towards the ferry. Then Ted stopped. 'Peggy, we nearly forgot your earrings.' We walked back to the little shop, and Ted bought me the earrings. I threw my arms around his neck and kissed him on the end of his nose.

'Peggy, I have to go somewhere.' He turned and headed off to the toilet. Typical man, a magic moment, and they go to the toilet. Whilst he was gone, I saw that there was a beautiful silver and gold pen in a small case. I quickly paid for the pen and asked the man to put it into a bag, which I slipped into my pocket.

I watched Ted coming out of the toilet. Men have a typical waddle when they have been to the toilet. They have to allow time for their privates to settle back down. I could see Michael watching us from the schooner. He nodded, and I nodded back.

We returned on the ferry, then transferred to the train. Ted said, 'Well Peg, we are gradually putting the jigsaw together. I think we will find more answers when we get home.'

'Ted, I would like to read through Lesley's journals before we go home; there are some things that I need to know.'

Ted looked at me seriously, 'You would need a full day.'

'*Yes!*'

'Okay. I will arrange our flights back home so in the evening we can see Marcia.'

I replied, 'Yes Ted.'

Ted sat back, pulled his hat down, and closed his eyes. Soon we were back in London, and after a couple of exhausting days, fell into bed.

CHAPTER 12

The next morning at 8 am I walked out of the foyer of the apartment. Ted had given me an old shopping trolley. I was wearing a big, old hat, which was totally out of place, a comfortable, loose dress, and a terrible pair of old shoes. Ted had gotten me these clothes; I don't know where from, but, yuk! Ted was watching me out of the window. Nobody followed me as I went to the Old Lady Bank. I headed for the women's toilets, where I changed my clothes. It was a great relief to put my own shoes on. I went up to the counter and went through the same procedure with the teller as before. The teller said to me, 'madam, would you like to leave that trolley with us?'

'Yes, please, I would certainly like that. Thank you,' I replied.

We went into the security room, where I sat down at the table with the safe deposit box in front of me. For a few minutes, I just stared at it. What was I going to find? Another Lesley I do not know? What did they do to her? How did they use her?

I slowly reached forward and opened the safe deposit box. I took out the pair of gloves and put them to one side, then the pouch with the watch in it. My eyes turned to the gloves again. I had met the man who had made these especially for Lesley; he had obviously been a great part of Lesley's life. The pouch with the watch belonging to my childhood friend, Jacko. They both belonged to me. I took out *Daisy May's* logbook. There was his name, Gerard Collins – Crew. I had worked and socialised with this man. Does he have the answer? Has it been there all the time in front of me, and I didn't know? Did he know who I was? Did he know I was Lesley's sister? Did he come under the Secrecy Act as well?

So many questions. I felt frustrated, annoyed, and angry, and I could feel the tears starting to come. I shook my head to clear my emotions and read further through the logbook. It gave me heaps of information about the voyage from Australia to England, but not what I needed.

I put the logbook to one side and took out Lesley's personal journal. When she arrived back in England, she was transferred to the Naval Academy with Gerard Collins. She trained the officers, so she didn't see much of Mr Collins. Lesley met Bill Farquhar again at the Admiralty in London. She talked of her mixed feelings for Captain Farquhar.

She was given an assignment and a team of commandos to work with, and boarded a warship. She was surprised that the Captain of the ship was Bill Farquhar. Soon, Lesley and her commandos were transferred to a submarine, and they landed on the shores of Germany. They were there to take photos. Lesley described the hardship, the cold, and wet. There were barbed wire fences everywhere, and they got many cuts and bruises. She described many things I didn't understand because they were in military terminology.

Lesley and her commandos returned to England via submarine. She wrote about many of these assignments. After each one, when she had returned to the safety of her flat, she would curl up underneath the bed-clothes, shiver, and cry.

She wrote about how she hated the briefings, as they would bring back the trauma of it all, but as the war continued, she embarked on different assignments. Sometimes, she would be flown to a secret location to meet with German businessmen, and they would discuss the war, where it was going, and how these men could use the war and its circumstances to their own ends. They discussed high-ranking businessmen in England and how the war would affect them.

Lesley was caught up in the high circles of society. She was a *'gopher'* for the aristocrats. She would have meetings with Winston Churchill and others, and talk about the politics of war. Towards the end of the war, Lesley had secret meetings with high-ranking officers in the German army. They were like rats trying to find out how to leave a sinking ship and maintain their wealth and rank. She also had meetings with English high-ranking officers and aristocrats. Even the King was at one meeting where they discussed finances and property protection. Some of the aristocrats were playing the game from both sides. Lesley had put every detail in her journals: names, ranks, business, and what England and America needed from Germany once they had won the war.

The scientists, the engineers, their top advisers, where had all the wealth gone? Lesley had seen the hardship, misery, and despair of the ordinary people in Germany. They didn't create this war, they didn't want it, but they are the ones who are suffering the most. Most of the citizens only had the clothes on their back, no shelter, no warmth.

These journals and the information about certain individuals were both toxic and frightening. It left a cold shiver up my spine. Just how far would they go to have these journals destroyed? I closed the journals and stared at them. If these journals came to light in thirty years' time, how dangerous would they be?

Had Lesley found a place where nobody could find her, hidden away from the world? Do they know that Ted and I have found the journals, and what danger does that put us in? Oh God, I want to get back to Australia with my Ted. I replaced everything back in the safe deposit box. I did think of keeping the gloves, but said to myself *No!* Everything must remain as it is; just one item could give it all away. It's too dangerous.

I went back to the foyer and wondered whether I should put the disguise back on or not. I noticed a young gentleman standing there, dressed in the bank uniform, ready to assist customers. I walked over to him.

'Yes, madam, can I help you?'

'Yes, please. I need to go to the museum. Is there a quick way to go?

'Yes, madam, go through that door over there, down the stairs. When you get to the toilets, turn left. The door says *staff only,* but you are a customer, I believe?'

'Yes, thank you,' I replied. My mind was racing: do I leave the shopping trolley here, or not? No, always clean up after yourself. 'I left my shopping trolley here behind the counter,' I said.

'Yes, madam, I shall get it for you.'

I thanked the young man and went through the door with my shopping trolley, down the stairs, and stopped at the toilets. I need this; my nerves are all tied up in knots, and you know where it affects a woman. I must have sat there for half an hour, composing myself.

Ted would be waiting for me across the road with his brother. I felt that I really needed to be with Ted to feel safe. I went out the back door of the bank with the shopping trolley. I chuckled to myself, how convenient there is a truck picking up the rubbish. I pushed the trolley to the rubbish and nodded to the man. He nodded back, and the trolley was gone. I found the small alley, turned left, and found the restaurant we had gone to before. I went through the door into the kitchen. Sniffy looked up and smiled at me; he nodded his head towards a back door. I went through; there was Ted! I ran towards him and flung my arms around him. He held me for a while.

'Please just hold me tight.' Ted didn't argue.

We sat down in one of the cubicles, and Sniffy, or should I say Peter, brought us coffee nicely laced with something extra. I knew my hands were shaking. Ted looked at me puzzled. 'No Ted, I can't talk about it at the moment. I've got to settle down. Both sides used her; that's why she disappeared! She is too dangerous if she talked!' I shook my head, and Ted reached out and took my hand.

'We are having tea with Marcia, and we fly out tomorrow morning.' I placed my hand on top of Ted's and squeezed it.

Peter sat down with us to have coffee, or was it Scotch? I breathed in with my nose again. Yes, definitely Scotch coffee. Peter looked up at the door and stood up. Ted turned to see what he was looking at and stood up, too. A thin, old lady with a walking stick came in. She slowly walked up to Ted. I could see that Ted's emotions were all tied up in a knot. He put out both his arms and stepped up to her. He put his arms around her. Her head came up to his chest. She had tears in her eyes as she gently pushed him back.

'I didn't think I'd ever see you again Twinkle toes. They said you were living with kangaroos!'

Ted replied with a very husky voice, 'Mum, this is my wife Peggy. Peggy, this is my beautiful mum.'

We all sat down in the cubicle. Ted had his arm around his mother. 'Mum, I apologise for not coming to see you, but we are tied up in something serious, and I didn't want to involve the family.'

I could see Ted's mother looking at me very seriously. 'Margaret, you are a clever one, aren't you, and very sharp. I can see why Ted married you and you married Ted; you keep him grounded. I could never do that; he was always dancing around like a boxer in a ring.'

She talked about Ted and her other five children. 'Thank you, Ted, for sending me money. Sniffy, could you please call me a cab? I am getting a bit tired.'

I started to get up to walk out with her, but Ted stopped me. He shook his head. Sniffy walked to the door with her. She turned and looked at Ted, nodded and went out the door.

Sniffy returned to the table, saying, 'She is having a lot of trouble with her health, but seeing you may have tied up some loose ends for her so she can leave in peace.' Sniffy, Peter put his hand on Ted's shoulder. Ted nodded, stood up, and put his arms around his brother.

'Hope to see you again, brother.'

He put his hand out for mine, and we walked out through the kitchen and through to the back alley. We turned left back up towards the theatre.

We soon reached Marcia's home. Ted held my hand as he reached up with his left hand to knock on the front door.

Marcia opened the door, and when she saw who it was, threw her arms around me. 'Come in, come in.' She looked at Ted and laughed, 'No, you stay out here!'

I don't really think Ted was amused, but he took it in his stride and went in. Mr Fredericks stepped forward from his office and shook Ted's hand.

'Come on in. Tell me what's been going on.'

We both sat down, and Marcia stood alongside me. 'How was Devon, Ted? And Dartmouth.'

Ted raised his eyebrows. 'Very surprising.' Ted filled him in on the events that had happened.

Marcia could not contain herself. 'And Lesley, how about Lesley?'

I answered that we knew Lesley was somewhere safe, but we didn't know where. We hoped to find out more when we returned to Australia.

Marcia had prepared roast pork with crackling, peas, and carrots, which were straight out of her garden, followed by apple pie, custard, whipped cream, and ice cream. I looked at my husband. He was a very contented little boy. Later, we had coffee with a sweet liquor and assorted cheeses. We sat and talked until 1.30 am.

I lent over to Ted, saying, 'We still have to pack our clothes.'

'I've already done it, Peggy.'

'That's a good husband, and to think Marcia was going to leave you outside.'

We said our goodbyes, and we walked down the front steps and as we started to walk down the footpath, Ted stopped and shouted out, 'We're going home now, you can follow us if you wish.' He looked at me and in a low voice said, 'I hope he can fly.'

CHAPTER 13

Sir John was sitting at his desk. He picked up his phone receiver, 'Mrs Evans, would you come into my office, please?'

Jackie Evans knocked on the door and walked in. Sir John, in an arrogant manner, gestured her to a seat. Jackie sat down.

'We have had a meeting and have decided to bring Ted Jones and his wife, Margaret, in for questioning,' Sir John said.

Jackie reached into her pocket and pushed a switch. She wanted to grin, but kept it in. 'That is going to be a little difficult, sir.'

In a very loud, sharp voice, Sir John shouted, 'Why?'

Jackie looked at her watch and, in a mocking voice, said, 'They should be landing in Australia in an hour or so.' She was enjoying this game of chess; it was getting good.

Sir John's eyes seemed to bulge, and his face went red! He slapped both his hands on the desk, sending the phone, pencils, and ashtray flying. He stood up and shouted. 'Jackie, you stupid, incompetent stupid fool! You let them slip through our fingers. You are fired! I want your resignation on my desk. Now get out!'

Jackie smiled at him, thinking, *you have given me exactly what I want, and I do so love playing chess with a loser!*

Sir John saw the grin on her face, and this infuriated him even more. He shouted at her, 'You're fired, you incompetent bitch!'

Jackie rose from her chair and slowly walked towards the door. She opened it, turned to look at Sir John, and thought, *it's over, it is finally all over, I'm free.* She walked out of the door, but didn't close it. She went back to her office, closed the door, and took the tape recorder out of her pocket. She played it back, listening very carefully. She sat for a moment, then burst out laughing. *I have it on tape. I am fired. What a lovely payout, and Ted is still ten steps ahead of you.*

A week later, Sir John walked into Jackie's old office. He spoke to the lady at the desk. 'I want Jackie Evans in my office as soon as possible!'

To which she replied, 'That can't be done Sir John!'

He stared at her for a moment. 'Why not?'

'Well, at the moment, Jackie is on a sailing vessel somewhere at sea; we don't know where,' she replied.

Sir John stared at her again, and walked over to the window and looked out. 'Where is Jennifer Howard?'

'She is at sea with Jackie.'

Sir John's anger started to rise again. He was biting his lip, trying to think, but his anger got the better of him. He shouted at the top of his voice, 'Everybody in this department is totally incompetent, everybody! It's stupid.'

The lady at the desk could not help herself, 'Does that mean you, sir, as well?'

He snapped back at her, 'Do you enjoy working here?'

'No, sir, I don't.'

Sir John snapped back at her again, 'We can take care of that!'

'There is no need to sir, I have already resigned. I start back with the police force on Monday morning.'

Sir John's anger rose again. 'I suppose you are one of Ted Jones's people?'

'Yes, sir, I was trained by him!'

Sir John turned and walked out the door, slammed it shut, and went back into his office. He sat down at his desk. *I am finished; they will replace me. I have totally failed. What is the answer? Retire? I need to get in first to save my reputation and officially retire. I will be like the others, free! Maybe I'll go to Australia and set up a small chicken farm.*

CHAPTER 14

Daisy May was silently gliding down the channel, past the ferry, past where the *Mayflower* had left from all those years ago. We looked at the houses on either side of the channel; the cliffs were getting higher and higher. As we passed the fort, I thought I was seeing things. There was a man wearing a hat. He had hunched shoulders and was smoking a cigar. Alongside him stood Jackie Evans. The man took his hat off and waved it. I saluted him and then slowly walked to the stern.

Had it all been a dream? Would it be a dream that would never go away? The wind was moderate from our starboard side. I shouted out 'Mr Coe, set all her sails.' *Daisy May*'s bow gently rose. She tipped to the waves as she leaned over slightly; there was nothing to obstruct her. Her hull had been cleaned of barnacles and weeds, so there was nothing to hold her back. She was free, and she looked absolutely beautiful. Jacko was at the wheel, and I stood alongside him. I had my arm around Lesley, holding her tightly into my side. Cat was sitting on the bench, on Colin's jacket. Colin's pipe was still on the windowsill.

I watched the rays of the sun glittering on *Daisy May*'s newly varnished decks. It seemed to make the sails white and illuminate them.

What more could a man ask for? I have it all. Then I heard his voice in my head, '*You have made it boy. You have made* Daisy May *come alive!* I saw Cat stand up and stare at me. I thought to myself, '*Yes, Colin's here.*'

Jacko turned around and grinned at me. 'He's always been here!'

'Jacko, you are a very spooky man!' I replied. I looked at Cat; he seemed to be quite contented. I glanced at Jacko. Lesley had gone to get coffee and sticky jam doughnuts. Is life one long dream? Did yesterday really happen? Was it all a dream? I thought of the old man on the train. '*I was once a Captain of a four mastered clipper.*' When he closed his eyes, was he dreaming that dream all over again? Is that what life is all about?

Jacko turned and winked at me and said in his cheeky voice, 'A lot more dreams to come Skipper!'

I shook my head. He would know when I wanted peace before I knew. Standing here, now, in this moment, I have Lesley, Jacko, *Daisy May*, and my crew. You could say I owned *Daisy May*, or we owned *Daisy May*. I could trade cargo as I wanted, and nobody would argue with us. That was my terms with the British government. They would give me assignments of cargo to deliver, but it was my responsibility to keep her correctly loaded. In a matter of words, we were free to do as we wanted.

'Jacko, stay between 50 to 51°E and 180°E. We have to be on our toes; we are off of Worthing, so traffic should get busier. We will alter course and have to watch out for the Queensbury Lighthouse and St Andrews.'

CHAPTER 15

My mind began to wander back to yesterday. The day of our wedding. It felt like stepping into a dream that I never wanted to end. Lesley, radiant in her simple elegance, walked onto the stern of *Daisy May* with a grace that made time seem to slow down. Everything around us felt more vivid, as if the world itself had paused to witness our vows. I looked into her eyes, and in that moment, the weight of all our shared years, the laughter, the struggle, the quiet moments, seemed to settle gently around us like a warm blanket. Standing there with the people we loved around us, I felt like I was exactly where I was meant to be. It wasn't just the start of a new life together; it was the continuation of the journey we had already begun, a journey full of love, trust, and endless possibility.

Les, the cook and the heart of our crew, outdid himself with the wedding cake. He had baked it right here in the *Daisy May*'s small galley. We all gathered around in anticipation when it was brought out. It was simple but heartfelt, just like everything Les touched – rustic layers iced with care, adorned with small seashells and flowers he'd found during our last stop at port. It was more than a cake; it was a piece of the *Daisy May*, born of the same hands that had fed and cared for us during countless voyages. As Lesley and I cut into it, the crew cheered, and the sound of their laughter mixed with the soft lap of the waves. Les had a grin from ear to ear, watching as we took the first bite. It tasted like the sea, like home, like everything that mattered.

CHAPTER 16

Just then, Lesley walked in with coffee and donuts. I didn't get any cheek from Jacko, just that silly grin.

'Food! How's that old bunk of mine? Is it comfortable?'

'Yes, Bill, I now have sheets, a pillowcase, and fluffy blankets; it's extremely comfortable.'

'And my beautiful feather mattress?'

Lesley cuddled into me.

Jacko called out in a squeaky voice, 'Where's my sticky bun?'

Lesley walked over to him, rubbed his hair with her fingers. 'They're not all yours!' She patted his tummy and asked me, 'Your new bunk Bill, is it comfy?'

'Yes, it is, but the ceiling and my head don't agree. But as long as you're underneath me, I don't mind one bit!'

Lesley reached out and took her coffee, not her cup, another one, and two sticky buns, before Jacko could get them.

Lesley and I slowly walked up the deck towards the bow. I was checking everything I could. From the deck to the rigging, checking the hatch covers, anything that might be out of place. I knew Ted had everybody working; I could see smoke coming out of Les's galley kitchen. Anything that Les could burn was important fuel for his stove. Ted was making sure that any rubbish left over from the refit that was burnable was safely stowed away. Trevor was aloft with Margaret; they were checking *Daisy*'s sails and rigging. Dominic and Les were in a deep discussion on how to make salami.

Lesley grinned at me and said, 'This should be interesting,' and licked her lips. I checked the bilge pumps. *Daisy May* had been sitting idle, the suction pads may have deteriorated. I turned around and glanced at Ted, caught his attention, and glanced at the bilge pumps. Ted nodded his head. I knew he would take care of the problem.

Lesley and I kept walking along the deck, and I could feel my emotions start to rise. My throat was tight, and my eyes started to tear up. Oh, how I missed the movement of *Daisy May*'s deck, the feeling of total freedom. I was at one with nature itself. Then I felt *Daisy May* turn slightly to meet the swell. I turned around and looked at the Bridge. Jacko was pointing in the air. I looked aloft and saw that Trevor and Margaret were checking the main royal sail on the mainmast. Jacko had turned *Daisy May* slightly to take the movement of the mainmast. I nodded to Jacko.

Lesley touched me on the arm and asked, 'How did he know, he can't see aloft from the Bridge?'

'Lesley, I've lived with him all my life. I don't know how, but when we were on the Diamantina River, his people would disappear, and we would know there was something wrong. It might have been a dust storm coming or heavy rain, a strong wind, or we were in for a cold snap. They just knew; they are nature itself. You just have to accept you're living with a very spooky man. I wouldn't change him for anything.'

We continued to walk up onto the bow. I studied the bow spread and the jib boom, they carried the sails over the bow.

My mind was now at peace; everything seemed to be in its place. We turned around and started to walk back towards the Bridge. Phillip and

Mervyn were pumping the bilge pump, and Ted was looking over the side to see how much water was being pumped.

I spent the rest of the day filling out my logbook. The barometer was holding steady, but to me, the day had slid past too quickly. We were at Longitude 0, opposite Worthing, and daylight was fading. I estimated we were doing 8 kn, but the next part of the English Channel past Hastings was narrow, and we would not have the tide with us, but against us. The last time I was here was during the war. There were no lights to warn us, but this time, we have the lights with us.

'Ted, bring the crew together.' Ted rang the bell, and all the crew came on deck. I walked out of the Bridge and spoke. 'For those of you who are not familiar with this stretch of the English Channel, we have the tide flowing against us, the wind is holding with us, so the wind is pushing up the surface of the water, we are playing games with the elements. I know all of you will work as a team, so if you carry out the commands—I put my arms around Ted—or *Grumpy's* commands, we will be in good hands!'

Ted pushed me aside and in a mocking voice said, 'Yes sir, no sir, three bags full sir.' He tapped his Captain's badge with his finger, and turned to the crew, 'Take the silly grins off your faces and get back to work.'

Jacko started to do one of his little dances while saying to himself, '*grumpy, grumpy.*' He lowered his voice and said, *grumpy*! Ted shook his head and walked off, but he had a grin all over his face.

I nudged Jacko with my shoulder. 'When you stop dancing, do you think you could possibly alter course to North 140?' I noticed he was already turning the wheel. 'When we reach longitude 2, we will turn due north. This time, Jacko, no big fish to follow us or give us an unwanted present!'

'Ted, could you and Jarrett, and one or two others get some rest?'

Ted nodded and went on his way. I noticed Jacko sniffing the air, then I smelled it: roast pork with baked apple!

'Jacko, would you like to go first, or would you like me to go first?' Jacko snatched my hand and laid it on the wheel, and was gone. I wondered if he would leave anything for me. I could feel *Daisy May* starting to fight the tide, but the wind was still with us, coming from the port side. Do I change sails? What is the pressure on her masts and rigging? I knew that I was using my inner senses, what I could feel on the deck, what I could hear in the rigging. A warship does not have this: buttons, gauges, and levers, no feeling! *Daisy May* is alive. She is talking to me through the deck, the sound of rigging, the movement. I am alive once again. Lesley walked in behind me and put a tray on the bench, beautiful roast pork with apple. I grinned, 'so the greedy little sod left some for me!'

Lesley's voice broke in. 'No, Bill, this is for the cat!'

Cat's ears pricked up. He looked at Lesley, and his ears went down. I think he sensed what I was saying to myself. Lesley took the knife and fork out of her top pocket, put her hand on the wheel, and pushed me to one side.

'Lesley, is this married life?'

'Yes, dear, but you will pay later!' I raised my eyebrows and took my first mouthful of pork. Cat stood up, looked at me, jumped off the bench, and headed for the galley.

I noticed navigation lights in the distance. We should be seeing green to green, but I saw green and red. There was a big vessel some distance ahead, and the law of the sea is, if we are heading towards each other, we put our green light to their green light; that is, our starboard side. I put another mouthful of pork into my mouth. God, it tastes so good. Food on a battleship is good, but not like this. Then Jacko was standing alongside me; he had felt the movement of the props on the other vessel.

'She is the big boss!'

The red light started to fade; we could only see the green. I reached down with my fork for some more pork, but there was none there! I looked around at Jacko; his mouth was full! Lesley burst out laughing.

'You are true blue, Jacko! You live by your tribal laws; nobody owns anything, it belongs to all.' Lesley burst out laughing again at the look on my face.

We started to look up at the vessel coming towards us. I heard Lesley's voice, 'Good God, she is big!' All of her top decks were illuminated in lights; people were looking down at us. Her name was illuminated in lights as well: *Queen Mary*. All the crew were on the starboard side, looking up at her, not talking, just looking. Then, they made their way to the stern until she was just a dim light in the distance.

Trevor burst onto the Bridge; he couldn't contain himself. 'Skipper, I want to be the Captain of one of those big ships!' I stood looking at him with a grin all over my face.

'Well, Trevor, you've got a lot of work to do. I know Margaret will help and support you!' Trevor frowned at me, not quite understanding the implications of what I had said. He turned and left the Bridge.

It was good to see the lights on the shores of England. I could also see the glow of lights from France. I looked at the clock above the wheel and noticed it was on English time, then I looked at my chart; Dover was on our Port side. I opened my logbook and wrote North 30 ° 11.30 pm, barometer steady. *Queen Mary*, starboard side.

'Lesley, I'm just going to check the decks.' I shook my head at Lesley. 'I know I'm not on a battleship; I'm going to check the deck.'

Lesley smiled at me, saying, 'I'm going to put my head down; it has been a long day!'

I nodded to her, turned and walked out of the Bridge. I slowly walked to the stern and put my arms on the bulwark. I thought of Colin. The cancer had become too much for him, and he had ended it all here. I felt something touch my leg and looked down. Cat was leaning up against my leg, 'You miss him too, don't you?' Cat looked up at me, the dim light reflected in his eyes. Before I realised what I had done, I had picked the cat up and was holding him in my arms. He pressed his head into my shoulder. I couldn't remember ever having done this before. He was always my enemy. 'We've been through a lot, haven't we, Cat, and Jacko tells us there's more to come.'

There was another movement at my feet, and a small meow. Whiskey had joined us. I reached down with my right arm and picked her up. What is happening to me? Am I getting soft, or have I missed something all these years? I'd bet that Jacko's laughing his head off.

I turned and slowly walked up the deck with both cats. I found myself talking to them, 'How many rats and mice are aboard? Are you both keeping the numbers down? Just because you've got a friend, Cat, doesn't mean you can take it easy.' When we got to the galley, I gently put them down. Les had already put food out for them.

I kept on walking to the bow, thinking of *Daisy May*'s seaworthy certificate. *Daisy May* had steel ribs, not wood. In the report, there were question marks alongside one or two ribs? Why? *Daisy May* had been partly loaded before I had read the report. Was there a problem, or was somebody playing it safe? You could only see one part of the rib; the other side of the rib was bolted down with brass bolts to the planks of her hull, and they were heavily coated with pitch. I reached the bow, but could see nothing that seemed to be out of place. Her sails were full. By the feeling of her deck, the tide had slackened off, and the wind was coming from our stern. Ted and Jarrett were waiting for me in the Bridge. Ted got stuck into me straight away.

'Could you tell this fuzzy little fella to relinquish command to me before I take my knife and cut all his hair off!'

Jacko suddenly stepped aside, his hands on top of his head. Ted took the wheel, and I winked at him.

'Is there a problem, Captain?'

'No, Captain, it has been resolved.'

'Good to see that you have everything under control.' I winked at him again. 'If you need me, I will be in my quarters, but please knock first;

I could be busy.' I put my thumb in the air and disappeared into my cabin. I lay down on my bunk and fell right off to sleep.

I awoke to find myself looking up at the ceiling, too bloody close. I rolled over to look down at Lesley's bunk, but she wasn't there. The clock said 7 am. Lesley will be working with Les in the galley. I swung my legs over the side of the bunk, bent my head down, took hold of the rope which was suspended above, and slid down to the floor. I managed better this time. I dressed and went onto the Bridge. Jarrett was at the wheel. He grinned at me, 'How's the head this morning Skipper?'

'I learn very quickly, thank you for asking,' I replied.

We were on a northerly course. The wind had increased on our port side. Ted had stowed the topsails, fore royal, and main royal sails.

'Jarrett, I've got a little more work for you to do. Young Trevor wants to be the Skipper of a big ship. He has seen a goal, and he may be useful for you in the future. If you work with him, you'll get to know him and his abilities, and the best place for him, for both of you. You're going to need people around you who you can trust, who know your views, thoughts, and principles. If you work with him one hour per day, I will get Jacko and Ted to do the same. I think Trevor has become an individual, and he needs to do it with you on his own. When he's working with Ted and Jacko, Margaret will be with him.'

'Yes, Bill, I understand. I like Trevor and get on well with him. When I get back to Australia, I know my future; it's already pre-planned, and it does concern me. I will need my own people who understand me, and you have picked me a good colleague. Margaret is a very quick thinker. She is intelligent and extremely trustworthy. I know she is still suffering from the hardships of the war and the way they used her, but in future management, with her experience, she could be very valuable to me. I will never be able to thank you enough for looking after me and my future. I was a selfish, arrogant, spoilt little boy, and with you, Jacko,

Ted, Michael, and the rest of the crew, I grew up. Give me Trevor and Margaret, and I will not fail you.'

I put my hand on Jarrett's shoulder and nodded to him. I put my hand out and shook his. I turned and went down onto the deck to look for Ted, who emerged from the hatch that went down into the hold. He grinned at me. 'The two cats have made themselves a nice little nest, plenty of privacy. They didn't waste any time, did they?' He chuckled to himself. 'There is a rumour going around, but I don't believe a word of it!'

I was automatically on guard; I don't like rumours. Ted chuckled again. 'They say you were seen carrying both cats and having a conversation with them!'

'Ted, when men have idle minds, you hear all sorts of rumours don't you. So I've got to find more work for you to do.'

Ted knew me like the back of his hand and was waiting for what was coming next.

'Ted, I would like you to teach young Trevor and Margaret everything you know about the sea, the unspoken laws, how to be prepared for the unpredictable.'

Ted shook his head. 'I thought you were going to give me something I wouldn't like, but that I would enjoy doing.'

'Thanks Ted. I've been thinking about the weather; last time we were in these waters, it was cold, and we weren't particularly prepared for it.'

'Yes, Skipper, I've been thinking the same thing. In our stores, we have naval woolen jumpers, underwear, trousers, socks, and sturdy wool-lined boots. We have more than we can use.'

'Ted, Foxy put them onboard for the Shetland people.'

'Skipper, we have good oilskins as well!'

'When we were in these waters before, we found that the wave trough was different, we prepared for it.'

'Yes, Skipper, I remember, That's why I took the topsail off.'

'Good man, Ted, good man.'

'Skipper, do you think Jacko would wear a pair of those boots?'

'That is something I'd really like to see,' I replied. 'Now, could you go and get some rest?'

'Aye aye, Skipper.'

Jacko was at the wheel while Jarrett was resting. Lesley brought my breakfast onto the Bridge: fried pork, eggs, onions, and bread. I looked sternly at Jacko, 'All mine Jacko. You stay that end of the Bridge and I will stay this end!'

Lesley put her hand to her mouth and started to giggle. She was looking at Cat, who was looking at my breakfast. I cut a bit of pork off and gave it to Cat. Then I looked at Jacko with a serious expression and ate my breakfast. When I had finished, Lesley took my plate down to the galley.

'Jacko, we've got to keep an eye out for the Dodger mud bank; we are now on the outside of it. As long as we stay on course, due north, we should be in open water, no obstructions. When we get to latitude 65° we will alter course to our destination.' I looked at Jacko and knew there was something wrong. 'What is it, Jacko? What's worrying you?'

Jacko took a deep sigh and said one of his little chants, he would say when he was talking to the witchy. 'Bill, things are not as they seem, There is a big change ahead, a big, big secret, big secret.' He gave one of those little chants again, then he went very quiet. He had given me a warning to be aware. I sat staring at him; he is never wrong.

'What do the gods have in store for us now?'

Jacko looked at me with a serious look and slightly nodded. Lesley walked onto the Bridge. She had a plate of freshly cooked biscuits. The steam and smell were rising off them. Jacko's eyes got even bigger as his hand reached out to take one. Lesley pulled her hand back.

'No, Jacko, you have to promise me a game of chess and play here, not in the desert.'

Jacko's eyes were still big, and he had this grin all over his face. 'We play chess here!'

Lesley put the plate forward so that he could take a biscuit, but he took three, leaving just three on the plate. He looked up. 'Three for me, three for you.'

Lesley gave a small chuckle and handed me the plate. I opened the drawer, took out the chessboard, and laid it on the bench. I took the plate containing the three remaining biscuits and walked back out onto the deck, where I saw Ted.

'Ted, you've got troubles now. Jacko and Lesley are playing chess.'

Ted shook his head. 'Which one of them is going to be grumpy?'

Lesley made the first move. Jacko studied the board, he raised his head, looking at Lesley with a deep, serious look.

'Lesley, they named you Grevillea. You, with the sweet nectar. Bill cannot understand why I left *Daisy May* to find you, but I am the keeper of our people. He does not know why you and Peggy, the blossom of the lily flower are so important to me. Your mother is my oldest sister. You both belong to me; you both belong to our people. I am your protector.'

Tears started to flow down Lesley's cheeks. She stared at him, but she couldn't see him properly with the tears in her eyes. She made a fist with her knuckles and started tapping on the bench: tap, tap, tap. She was back in the desert, back on the Diamantina River, giving Jacko the deepest respect she could. She threw her arms around Jacko's neck.

Ted was looking up at the Bridge. 'I don't know what they're playing at Skipper, but it isn't chess!'

'Ted, Jacko has given me one of those warnings. We have to be on guard. Nothing is what it seems; there is going to be a big change.'

Ted looked at me. Then he said, 'Here we go again, lots of questions, but no answers.'

I shrugged my shoulders. 'Coffee, Ted?' He nodded, and we walked to the galley. As we drank our coffee, we discussed changing course to latitude due north; that would take us closer to Great Yarmouth. We would have to be very wary of mud banks, but we should pass them on a high tide; then we'd be out into the open sea. When we get to Latitude 56, we will alter course to West 70°, that should take us to our destination.

I put my hands in the air and gestured with my shoulders, 'With luck, we shouldn't have any problems. According to the season, the currents should be with us. Where's Jarrett, Ted?'

'With Trevor. They've got Margaret handing out clothing and boots for the crew. Margaret was grumbling because she couldn't find her size in boots, but I think she won in the end.'

Just then, Ted and I felt a small quiver. Ted ran to the mainmast whilst snaring a marlin spike. He looked up, pausing for a moment, then ran to the side of the bulwarks and started tightening a turnbuckle. That tightened a cable that went up to just under the main top galley sail; it had become slack.

Daisy May was Ted's baby; he breathed it, he could taste it, he had a passion for her. *Daisy May* was his dream. Along with Jacko and me, we were in love with her.

Ted put the marlin spike into its socket at the base of the mainmast. We both watched Margaret sorting the warm clothing. She gestured to Lesley to come over to her, and together they picked up a big bundle of clothing and boots. We wondered whether they could see over the bundle as they headed towards the Bridge and disappeared.

Ted and I talked about the cargo that was bound for Lerwick on the Shetland Islands. Then we saw the two women return to the bundle of clothes. Together, they sorted out another bundle, laughing as they did it. They again returned to the Bridge with the bundle of clothes. Lesley gestured to me with her head, then looked at the Bridge.

Ted nudged me. 'You're a married man now, jump to it!' I thought to myself, *I'm the Skipper, not God, but the Captain.*

I stepped inside the Bridge door. Jacko looked at me with a worried look on his face.

Margaret, with a voice of command, said, 'Skipper, could you take the wheel please?'

I looked back at Jacko and winked.

'No, not yet. Jacko, alter course due north. We are at longitude 2, just up from Dover.'

I still had to make a point. I looked at the clock and barometer, then I glanced back at Jacko and raised my eyebrows.

Jacko's voice boomed out, 'Barometer rising sir, all is well.'

'Thank you, Captain Jacko, I will relieve you of your command. Jacko, I believe that the women need you,' and nudged him to one side. I took the wheel and enjoyed watching Jacko; he was like a schoolboy being fitted out with new clothes. The only thing he was happy with was the oilskin jacket lined with sheepskin. Then the women produced underclothes. This was just too much for Jacko! He took off out the door, nearly knocking me over in the process. He jumped to the deck, straight into Les. I raised my eyebrows at Margaret and Lesley, 'Jacko is a very private man, you pushed him too far.'

We heard Les laughing, then Jacko shouted out. 'Women belong here!'

I saw him stuffing sticky jam doughnuts into his mouth, looking at the Bridge. I put my hand outside the Bridge door and put my thumb in the air. He couldn't answer me as his mouth was too full of doughnuts, but the look on his face did answer me.

Later that day, he returned to the Bridge and gave me a lecture on why women should not be in the Bridge. I agreed with him. When he had finished, I asked him, 'Does that mean Jacko, that Lesley cannot come in with sticky buns and hot coffee? And rub her fingernails through your hair, or play chess with you and keep telling you what a funny man you are, with all that love and affection in her voice, and all the respect she has for you?'

He gave me one of those funny little chants of his, shook his head, and nudged me away from the wheel.

Holding the wheel with both hands, he said, 'This is my wheel, mine!'

I was busy filling out my logbook. It was time we altered course. The barometer was holding steady. I was startled by sudden laughing from Jacko; he slapped his hand on the wheel and burst out laughing again. I stood up to see what he was laughing about. Jacko pointed to Ted. Lesley and Margaret were trying to fit him out with new clothes, and he didn't look too happy. Ted liked shirts without sleeves. He liked coloured shirts, not the navy colours. It made Jacko's day.

I went back to the logbook and wrote down Jacko's words. I couldn't get them off my mind. He was never wrong, what a challenge! I thought about the tides, wind strength, and currents at Lowick. I'd only ever been there once before, during the war.

I walked back out onto the deck and saw Jarrett. He was with Phillip and Dominic; they were scrubbing the deck with sandstone blocks. I walked up to them. 'Are you settling in all right?' They all nodded at me.

'There is nothing like a good crew on a sailing vessel,' Dominic said.

'I'm going to take Jarrett off you for a while. He is definitely working too hard, and you both can't keep up his pace. It's too hard for you, so just take it easy!' I replied.

Jarrett followed me back to the Bridge, ignoring the kind words from behind us.

'The last time we went into Lowick, you had naval charts.'

'Yes, they are in the galley,' Jarrett said. He went into the galley and came out with them and handed them to me. He had rolled them up in canvas before he left *Daisy May*.

'Thank you. Come back onto the Bridge.'

We spread the charts on the bench and studied them. The pencil marks were clearly marked from before, so we knew our passage.

'It's a great fishing port; I should imagine they're all back fishing. Last time we were there, we all left with big headaches, we did have a good time,' Jarrett said.

Jacko was doing his funny little dance. 'I hope we enjoy ourselves like we did last time!'

Jarrett nudged him. 'I thought one of those women would have got you then, dangerous place, Jacko!'

CHAPTER 17

Over the coming days, the crew settled down to their routine. The two ladies spent more time with Les. If a man were to enter his space, he would tell them where to go, sharply, but he enjoyed the company of his ladies. I noticed he had a clean apron on every day and his hair was neatly combed, with that beautiful wave on top. You could hear them singing with each other. It gave me a warm feeling. He deserves this; he has always been there for others and played his part, providing hot food, day or night, coffee whenever you wanted it. I frowned. He spends more time with my wife than I do!

The wind dropped to a very gentle breeze, and the sea was calmer. I leaned out of the Bridge and spoke to Ted, 'Could you put the topsail back on her?'

Ted nodded, then he spoke to Tommy O'Hia and Trevor. 'Mainmast tops.' They both nodded and were on their way. 'Phillip and Dominic four mast top sail.'

I noticed Lesley and Mervyn kneeling on the stern, talking to each other. Lesley reached up and touched his shoulder, then she pushed herself up on her toes, put her arms around his neck, pulled him down to her and kissed him on the forehead, cuddling him at the same time. Mervyn gently picked her up in his arms, then he laughed out loud and ran to the bow, turned and ran back to the stern, then did it again. They were both laughing. He ran back with her to the galley and gently put her down. There were tears in her eyes. They had lived a world together during the war, and the memories were still there. They had a deep respect for each other and a very strong friendship.

I saw Ted looking up at the mainmast. I looked up to see what he was looking at. Tommy didn't look too happy; he was having trouble aloft. Ted and I looked at each other, and we mentally agreed. The four men returned to the deck. I nudged Jacko; he turned the wheel and the compass to alter the course to west 70°. We were level with Edinburgh.

I walked up to Tommy, 'How are you Tommy?'

He turned around, his eyes had a sparkle in them, and he had a cheeky smile on his face. 'Good, boss, glad to be back at sea.'

'Tommy, we will keep you on deck now; you are too valuable to lose. It would be very inconvenient for us to turn around and pick you up out of the water.' I winked at him. Tommy is a full blood Maori. In some ways, he's like Jacko. Give them a job and do not interfere with them. If you do, their sense of humour will kick in, and they will only frustrate you and make you look like a fool.

'What did you do in New Zealand, Tommy?'

'I was a schoolteacher. I played rugby and a few other sports.' I asked again, 'How did you become one of Fox's crew?'

'I came from quite an influential family in New Zealand. I was on the team of paddlers in a Waka Taua 40 m decorated war canoe. It sank, and the 20 of us had to swim ashore. They weren't very happy and displayed it with their gestures. The sea was the best place to be.'

'Tommy, if you could spend a little time with Trevor and teach him what he should know for his future, I would really appreciate it.'

Tommy nodded. I gently tapped him on the shoulder and continued walking towards the bow. The young man who owned Whiskey looked up at me. 'All well, lad?'

'No, Skipper, Whiskey has found herself another friend. I don't see much of her anymore. Ted tells me they have made themselves a nice, private, and comfortable nest.'

'You may have more cats to come! Do you have your warm clothing?'

His eyes and face lit up. 'Yes, Skipper, I've never had warm clothing like this before, and fur-lined boots!'

'It is going to get cold, and the wind will be very sharp, so don't hesitate to wear them!'

I looked in the forecastle. Dominic was there, sound asleep, snoring his head off. It's a pity he's not sawing wood; Les would appreciate that! For some reason, I counted the hammocks; five spare. Why did I count them? Was it Jacko's words sharpening me up? I looked at a small pot-belly stove alongside a box full of odds and sods to be burned. I looked at Dominic and, in a soft voice, asked him to fill up the box as well. I left him to his peaceful slumber.

I turned and saw Ted. 'Could you have a man light the pot-belly stove in the forecastle?' I glanced towards the bow. 'I don't believe it's been lit for a long time,' Ted nodded.

I walked through the door onto the Bridge and nudged Jacko. 'Get some sleep, Jacko.'

'Skipper, I think the tide and current are with us; she is moving freely, but the barometer is dropping. Must get some food before sleep,' and he was gone.

The two cats were asleep on the bench, but as soon as Jacko mentioned food, they were up and gone. Lesley came in with a plate of food. She put the plate and coffee down on the bench and put her arms around me. We were there together, with nobody to interfere. We enjoyed the moment and said nothing. The sun was just setting; there was a silver mist on the surface of the water, it was just like frost on the land. Lesley didn't say anything, just squeezed me tighter, watching the beauty of it. The sun slowly sinking into the sea; the colours radiating from it were just magical. Then, the sun disappeared into the sea. I started to eat my tea when Ted walked in.

He looked at me for a moment. 'Do all Captains get room service?'

'No, Ted, just one Captain and one of the crew.'

Ted shook his head. 'I suppose that would be Trevor?'

'What makes you think that, Ted?'

'Because Trevor has Margaret to bring him his meals!'

'Okay, Bill, what are your plans for entering the harbour?'

'I would like to be in just on daylight, so we can see where we are going. Jarrett has the naval charts, and we don't want to get in the way of the fishing fleet. After all, it is their harbour, not ours.'

'Sail changes, Skipper?'

I looked at Ted, thinking the wind hasn't dropped off as I thought it would at dusk. The barometer has dropped, but is holding.

'Leave all her sails on. I would like them to dry, so if there's a frost when we're in port, they won't ice up. We can go into port using our motor.'

'Aye, aye, Bill.' He disappeared.

Lesley had backed away whilst Ted was in the Bridge, but now she had her arms around me again.

'Bill, I have so enjoyed these last couple of days. I don't want it to stop.'

'So far, we've had a good voyage. The crew have sorted themselves out; Ted has established himself as Bosun. Les is happy, and the weather has held with us; the currents have been moderate,' I said.

The winds stayed at the same strength but moved from South to West during the night, so we had to tack our course during the night, changing course three times. We had changed to our original course, west 70°. But when daybreak came, the wind dropped to a slight breeze with misty rain, and it was cold.

Lesley slid the door open and closed it behind her. 'Where is he?'

I pointed under the bench. Jacko was wearing his new coat and was curled up in a ball like a puppy. I took a sip of my coffee, then waved the cup under the bench. A head popped up, or should I say a mop of white hair, saying, 'My coffee?'

Lesley reached down and scratched his head with her fingers. He emerged with the coat wrapped around him and put his hand out for his coffee.

I looked at them both and shook my head. 'Lesley is becoming your mother, and you're getting soft, Jacko.'

'Bill, she is your wife and your mother!'

With that, he left the Bridge with his coffee. Lesley protested when he had gone. I chuckled and smiled at her.

'Don't worry, Lesley, he's just gone to relieve himself!'

The door slid back, and in walked Ted and Jarrett. Ted stared at me for a second. 'It's damn freezing out there.'

I asked Ted how the cadets had been during the night.

'I was proud of them, Bill. Not one of them grumbled; they just did their job.' He grinned at me. 'I never used the whip once!'

Jarrett nudged him. 'It's a bit hard, Ted, when you're on the deck and we are aloft!'

Well, it looks like my plans have changed, mice and men. The wind has dropped during the night and we had to tack, we won't be in port when I wanted to be, if this drizzle should ease off during the day and our sails dry, we can get them off and stowed, then we can motor in. I'm hoping we'll still have daylight.

I stood aside, and Jarrett took the wheel.

'May I take you to breakfast?' I asked Lesley.

'Oh, Bill, I thought you'd never ask. Certainly.' We went to the galley, but you'd never guess who was there first!

After breakfast, I went back to the Bridge and spoke to Jarrett. 'I'm going to go and have a lie down and shut my eyes for a moment so that I can clear my head. There is too much happening at the moment, and I need to think clearly.'

Next thing I knew, Ted woke me up. 'Land on the port side Skipper, the wind has picked up, and the drizzle has gone.'

I was lying on my side, and I looked straight into Ted's eyes. Ted winked at me. 'Not like the old days, boss!'

'Better than a hammock, Ted!'

Ted walked back out onto the Bridge. I stood on my feet, looking at the clothes Lesley had laid out for me. *I'm not as brave as you, Jacko.* I put the clothes on, went outside, and looked up at the sails. I watched the way the black tags were moving; they gave you an indication of how the sails were reacting.

'What do you think Ted, dry enough?'

'Skipper, the way the clouds are moving and the colour of them, we've got no choice.'

'Ted, could you have Tommy start the motor? For some reason, he likes the sound of it.'

Jacko had relieved Jarrett. Lesley had food and coffee for the three of us.

Lesley said, 'Jarrett told us his dad wasn't well; he had blood problems, and it is worrying me. Bill, how does Spooky know? He talked to me on the Bridge, and you would have thought he had read the letter! Jacko told him he would be with his dad again. He will show you how to take over the company, and you will be successful. Once you have taken the weight off his shoulders, he will be better.'

Ted laughed, 'I stopped talking to Jacko a long time ago. Nothing is private; he knows it all.' Ted got up and went out on deck and rang the bell three times. The whole crew came running to the deck. He gave orders, and the team went to work. I heard the big motor start.

Tommy walked back onto the deck and shouted to Jacko. 'Let her warm up a bit; she's cold. Give her ten minutes.' He put his ten fingers up in the air. Jacko nodded.

Lesley leaned on my shoulder. 'There's something about Ted I just can't put my finger on, but I know I can trust him, and I have faith in him.'

I stood at the wheel with Lesley and Jacko. Jacko loved the way Lesley put her arms around him and pulled at his beard. She said in a warm voice, 'It's a lovely harbour with the old stone buildings and the town hall with its clock rising up at the back of it, the green hills behind, protecting the harbour. Beautiful.'

We tied up at the same wharf as before. The air was cold. I could feel it going through my skin.

'Ted, stand down the crew, let them rest. If they want to, they can go ashore. Jarrett will let them know about the headache they could get!'

Ted grinned at me, 'Mine was worse!'

I saw a well-dressed man walking down to the wharf. He had others with him. One had a clipboard and a brown satchel over his shoulder; his hair was snowy white.

'Jacko, Ted, look at the man with the white hair.'

The crew were still lowering the gangplank, but Jacko was off. He bounced, then jumped and landed on the wharf. He slowly walked up to the man with white hair and said, 'You haven't changed colour yet! Snowy white.' They embraced each other.

'Where have you been?' the man asked Jacko.

The first man walked on board. 'I believe I have to ask for permission to come aboard, sir?' He put his hand out. 'Captain Richard Hollis, sir.'

I shook his hand. 'William Farquhar, Skipper of this vessel.'

Captain Hollis replied, 'I once met Captain James, have you been here before?'

'Captain James and I are old friends.'

'His health is not good, so he has retired.'

I nodded and thought, *how far can I go? People know this vessel, and they know my crew?*

'Mr Norde, your man Snowy,' Captain Hollis frowned at me, 'and his colleague will go through your cargo manifest.' *This is a naval vessel. He does not have jurisdiction here, but I have nothing to hide. Now, why did I think that?*

'Yes Captain. Mr Coe will assist you in any way you want.'

Captain Hollis handed me an envelope. I was puzzled. This was a naval envelope. I used to receive these during the war.

'Captain Farquhar, there is a lady in my office who wishes to see you. If you would follow me, please.'

I looked at the envelope. I wanted to look at it first.

'Would you excuse me for a moment, Captain?' I broke the seal on the envelope and took out a piece of paper. *Captain William Farquhar and Commander Lesley Johnson, could you please come and see me now.* No signature. I turned and walked into the galley and handed the letter to Lesley. She read it, turned the piece of paper towards me, and tapped the top of the letter. There was a small mark.

Lesley started to walk towards the gangplank as though she were in total command, and I followed her.

She turned to the Captain on the wharf and, in a cold, commanding voice, said, 'Lead the way Captain.'

Lesley quietly said to me, 'We've got trouble Bill. The mark on the top of the paper,' she hesitated, 'Mrs Henderson!'

If I wasn't cold before, I was definitely cold now. Mrs Henderson was an old colleague from the war, MI6, Lesley's superior. What now?

We went into a beautiful stone building. I had been here before. The Scots really knew how to build a building with class, and to last. There were five soldiers in the foyer; they all had kit bags and firearms. I knew the first man, but couldn't remember from where. He smiled at me with his eyes and tapped his left shoulder. Then I remembered. The man at the gates to the barracks and my pin: Australia. I nodded to him and enjoyed saying G'day to him. I put my thumb up in the air and followed Lesley through the door.

Mrs Henderson was standing, looking out of the window with her back to us. Why do people in command take that pose? Is it to prove they're in command, not taking any garbage?

'Mrs Henderson, you are a long way from home!' She turned around sharply and stared at me.

'William, you are always the Australian, but that just makes you more valuable. Commander Johnson, you're looking well.'

'Yes, madam.'

'Well, Lesley, Bill, let's talk straight. We have a new assignment for you. The destination is in those envelopes.' She pointed to the desk. 'Your cargo is 60 crates, each weighing half a ton of gold bullion.'

Lesley and I raised our eyebrows.

'You have five Navy SEALs, Mervyn, Dominic, and Philip to protect your vessel, and another, who is mine, Tommy O'Hia. He was also on the *Castle* tramp steamer. They had the same cargo as yours. *Daisy May*, for security reasons, must disappear. She never left Melbourne. There isn't any paperwork to say she ever did!'

She looked at Lesley for a moment, 'You do understand Lesley?'

'Yes, I do, Mrs Henderson.'

'Be careful, Lesley. There are those higher up than me, on both sides, who want you to disappear. I promised Winston that I would protect you as much as I could. You are in command, Lesley. William is in command of the *Mary Moore* and her crew. Once you arrive in Cape Town, you can offload some of your stores in our barracks. You can fuel up with anything you need.'

She picked up the phone and, in a commanding voice, said, 'My plane.' Then her voice dropped to a warm and compassionate tone, 'You two take care of yourselves. During the war, I could handle this, but now I'm having trouble!'

She walked forward to Lesley, put both her hands into Lesley's, shook them, then stamped a foot on the floor. 'Take care, Lesley, take care.'

There was a knock at the door. Five men came in and lined up in front of Mrs Henderson. She put her hands behind her back and said to them, 'This is Commodore Johnson, you are under her command, and this is Captain William Farquhar, he is in command of the vessel. Thank you, gentlemen.'

They all turned and filed out of the room. Mrs Henderson shook hands with us. 'My plane is waiting; I must leave.'

Lesley and I stood alone in the office. I walked forward and picked up the envelopes. One was addressed to me; the other two to Lesley. We didn't say anything, just walked back to the *Daisy May* with the five men following us.

Cat and Whiskey were sitting at the top of the gangplank. 'Too cold to play?' I said to them.

Ted walked forward with Jacko and Les behind him. He looked annoyed and frustrated. 'They've changed her name!' Before he could say anymore Lesley put a finger up to her mouth to silence Ted.

'We will talk in the Bridge. Ted, take these five men to the forehead, bed them down. Gentlemen, if you would go with Ted Coe, my Bosun, then to the galley where Les will feed you.'

'We will talk later, thank you, gentlemen!' Lesley added. 'Les could you bring coffee for us to the Bridge and join us there?'

We waited for Ted. 'Yes, Jacko, you were right, as usual. Everything you said has happened, big changes.'

I opened my envelope, and Lesley did the same with hers. In mine were documents for *Mary Moore*. You would think some of them were 40 years old, or even more. We still weighed the same 550tn, same length, same sails, but it didn't mention the motor, just a word *Propulsion*. Everything else was identical, but there was still another envelope. Just then, Ted walked onto the Bridge.

He looked at me, annoyed, and asked why they had changed her name. 'You don't change the name of a vessel!'

Lesley stepped forward and put her arms around him, whilst looking at Jacko and Les.

'Apparently, *Daisy May* never left Australia. There is no written record that she came under the National Security Act. She has to disappear to protect national interests. It is complicated, and I know how much it hurts you all. In private, she is still *Daisy May*, but that is only between us. We now come under the top Secrecy Act. Ted, you are still a Naval Officer; you have not been discharged. Bill is still a Naval Officer, and I am still Commander Johnson. We have a new assignment. Our next cargo is 60 crates of gold ingots, each weighing half a ton. This is top secret. Yes, gentlemen, it took my breath away as well.'

I shook my head at Jacko. 'We will unload our consignment tomorrow. Ted, the five men who came aboard, make sure they have appropriate clothing. I want them to look like ordinary seamen.'

Lesley spoke to Ted, 'Put them to work as regular seamen.'

She finished her coffee, picked up her paperwork, nodded to me, and then went down to the galley. Les followed her. Lesley scanned the five men with her eyes; she knew them all. She looked at Trevor and thought, *he is in the Navy, but not Secret Service, but he's married to Margaret.*

She looked at Margaret. 'Margaret could you ask Phillip, Dominic, and Mervyn to come here, please.'

Les filled up five bowls with what he called Irish stew. He put them on the table, along with five big, fresh bread rolls, and spoons. By the way the men ate their stew, they were definitely very hungry.

Margaret came in the door first; she was laughing. The others were teasing her. When they saw the other five men and recognised them, the chatter started, and the handshakes began.

Lesley, in her best commanding voice, said, 'Could I have your attention please gentlemen.' She glanced at Margaret. 'Trevor, you are not part of this group. They are special forces, but you are in the Navy, and you are Margaret's husband.'

Lesley had a piece of paper in front of her with names. 'Gentlemen, just give me your first name, John? John nodded. Paul? He nodded. Tommy, you are the mechanic? He nodded, 'and you are from New Zealand?' He nodded again. 'Tony,' he had a spoonful of food in his mouth and just gestured. Lesley put her hands behind her back. 'I believe, gentlemen, you have already been briefed by Mrs Henderson. Mervyn, you are the sergeant. Phillip, you are next in command. For those of you who have not been briefed, our assignment is to pick up 60 crates of gold bullion, each weighing half a ton, and deliver it to England. You will act as seamen on this vessel at all times and only use your first names. If you would give Margaret the size of your clothing, she can fit you out. Thank you, gentlemen. Tony, if you want more food, just ask Les.'

I looked at Ted. 'Life wasn't easy before the war; we had our problems, but not like this. Sixty crates of gold bullion, and we don't exist!'

Ted shook his head. 'You are the Skipper, but you're not! I am the Bosun, but I'm not!'

Jacko's voice kicked in. 'I am the helmsman, and I stayed the helmsman. Nice and warm where we go, funny place, never been there before.' He gave one of his funny chants.

Ted looked at him seriously. 'Nobody has told us where we're going! You wouldn't have a bit more information by any chance, Jacko?' He just grinned at him.

'Ted, the amount of crew we have aboard is ridiculous. She was designed for passengers, but a long time ago. If we put a bunk underneath this bench with drawers underneath it for Jacko. Yes, Jacko, you say what you want, however you want to say it. We could use the locker at the stern, under the deck, to put stores and coils of rope. Spare canvas can go alongside the motor. We can put bunks in there for Trevor and Margaret.'

'Skipper, the five men who came aboard all have collapsible beds!' 'Good, Ted, that saves that problem. The best problem I'm going to solve in the morning is a good, hot bath!'

CHAPTER 18

I woke just before daylight. I'd had a bad night's sleep. There wasn't any movement in *Daisy May*'s hull. No sound of the waves or sea, no creaking within her structure; it was unnerving. I rolled over, looking for Lesley, but she was already up. I got dressed and was wondering why I had gotten out of a warm bunk. I looked out of the Bridge. There was Lesley with the five men, and Mervyn, Phillip, and Dominic doing exercises on deck. I looked at the wheel; it seemed strange. There wasn't anybody there. Jacko was curled up underneath the bench, with Cat and Whiskey on top of him. To my surprise, Richard Hollis was sitting talking to Les, with coffee and a sticky doughnut in his hand.

'You are early, Mr Hollis,' I said.

'Big day, William,'

Les was pouring me coffee, and I could smell the bacon and eggs sizzling in the pan.

Les smiled at me, 'You'd better get in first Skipper; that bunch will be in very soon.'

Before I could say another word, Jacko was alongside me. The smell of bacon and eggs wafting through had woken him up.

'Richard, do you have a carpenter available? I need some more bunks made.'

Richard had a clipboard beside him, and Les had already given him a list of things he wanted written down. He added carpenter to the list. Then, he gave me a piece of paper for *Daisy May* to load ambulances and deliver them to Bell, Ireland.

'Richard, who is this from?'

'I don't know Bill, I assumed it was from a government department.'

Just then, Snowy Norde walked in with his satchel and clipboard, with that beautiful smile of his. Before he could say anything, Jacko was into him.

'Where have you been? Why are you here?

Snowy slapped him on the shoulder, 'You're still a big wombat gone grey!'

Jacko laughed at him, 'You're a lost cockatoo!'

Richard had a very confused look on his face.

Snowy laughed, 'We go back a long, long way, Richard.'

'What are you doing here, Snowy?'

'Well, when I last saw you, I was drafted into Navy Ordnance and Supply, the same as I was before the war. Then I found myself in England doing the same thing. After the war ended, I went to several places, checking items that had been left behind, recording them, and sending them back to England.'

Richard gave some paperwork to Snowy, who read it very carefully. 'Yes, there are three ambulances from the airbase.'

He looked at Richard. '*Daisy May*, what vessel is that?'

'Oh, there was a sailing vessel in port before, but it had nothing to do with me. I don't remember its name!' Richard replied.

I love the way Snowy handed the ball back to Richard.

'Yes, I remember it, Snowy, but it wasn't under my jurisdiction. I don't record every fishing craft that comes in and out of port. I wouldn't have enough time in the day.'

'Richard, Snowy, I need more cargo to keep this vessel down in the water. Could you suggest anything?' I said.

Snowy grinned, 'Ambulance, two large generators and all the equipment to go with them?'

Richard put both his hands in the air. 'Nothing to do with me!'

Les, who was serving out eggs and bacon, looked up. Richard said, 'I will sort out your supplies and find you a carpenter.'

He looked at the eggs and bacon. Les didn't say a word but handed him an egg and bacon sandwich, then he laughed, 'It was Jacko's.'

Jacko stared at the sandwich but didn't say a word; everybody else was grinning.

Before Richard could get out of the door, Snowy asked him, 'Do you have somebody who can use a spray gun?'

'Yes, I do.'

'Could he meet me at the base? I believe the port could use the other two. I will put them down as scrap.'

Richard didn't even turn around; he just went out through the door.

Jacko got his bacon and egg sandwich handed to him on a plate. I hadn't seen Jacko eat off a plate for a long time.

I sat down at the bench in the Bridge trying to sort my logbook out. The words came back to me again, *as little as possible, Bill.*

There was a knock at the door, and in came two men carrying boxes and another with bags of tools.

The first man asked me, 'You be the Captain?'

I replied, 'I am.'

'Well, we came to fit the radar.'

I stared at him. I didn't want to appear to be a fool; I am the Captain.

The man continued, 'Where do you want us to fit it?'

My mind went racing back to the vessel I commanded during the war.

'Just a moment, gentlemen.' I opened the drawer and pulled out the plans, read them, and quickly folded them. *Daisy May* was written on the top. I tactfully laid them out on the bench so you couldn't see the name of the vessel. 'I would suggest, gentlemen, on the mizzenmast, just below the gaff topsail.'

I looked at the man's face. 'You are not seamen?'

Just then I spotted Trevor on the deck and shouted, 'Trevor,' I told him of the situation. 'If you could show these gentlemen,' and pointed to the plan, 'they have to fit an instrument; it cannot interfere with the sails or any movement of the rigging.'

Two of the men left with Trevor. The other one walked onto the Bridge and put the box on the bench. I folded up the plans and put them back in the drawer. I had a fair idea what was in the box.

The man looked at me with warmth on his face. 'I am Jimmy. We've met before, during the war. Is that funny man still with you, the Aborigine?'

'Yes, he is. He's just coming out of the galley; he'll be here in a minute.'

Jacko walked onto the Bridge. He looked at the man and shouted, 'You took your time Jimmy! I came a long way to see you.'

He took two handfuls of red beard and shook it. 'But you are a red-head, I will forgive you!'

They shook hands. 'I bought you a present, Jacko.' He looked at the box. Jacko couldn't help himself; he was undoing the wrapping at lightening speed. Inside, there was a radar screen.

I said to Jacko, 'Just tell the man where you want it, Jacko.' I left them to it.

I looked at the gangplank. There were three men coming up. The same three that had worked on the stern. I felt annoyed and frustrated;

she is now the *Mary Moore*. It's not their fault; they're just doing their job.

'Good morning, Skipper, we're here to make some bunks.'

I glanced at the stern. Tommy was there with two others. Ted was busy unloading cargo.

'Follow me, gentlemen, to the bow.' We went into the living quarters. I raised my eyebrows and chuckled. Very neat and tidy. Was this Margaret's work? I walked forward to where it curved into the bow. 'Gentlemen, if you could put a bunk on each side.'

'Skipper, the way it curves and the shape would make it easy for us to put one bunk on top of the other on both sides, and make the sides higher on the top one. Then, you could use it as storage.'

'Good man, good idea. Could you also put some holding brackets on both sides of the bunk? This is probably the most uncomfortable part of the vessel, and I need to tie things down. If you would follow me to the stern.'

As we walked by the galley, I called out to Margaret, who popped her head out of the door. 'Please follow us, Margaret. All shipshape Tommy.' I thought he looked amusing with his fur collar turned up around his head; all you could see was a big ball of black hair and a voice that came out of nowhere.

'If you go down with Margaret, she will tell you where she wants the bunks.' Margaret gave me a surprised look.

'Sorry, Margaret, we have to have married quarters now.' I winked at her. If it's good for us, then it's good for her. 'Privacy, you know.' I winked at her again. 'Now, we've got one more bunk underneath the bench in the Bridge, but if you go and see Jacko, he will tell you what he wants.'

I walked up to the galley door. 'Les, Lesley, could I invite you to a good hot bath?

Les disappeared, went to a drawer, and took out his wash bag and was walking towards the gangplank before I could even blink. Lesley came back from the Bridge with ours. I knew exactly where to go; I had been there before.

Ted was on the wharf; he looked at the three of us coming down the gangplank. Lesley started to laugh, 'Sorry Ted, brass always comes first!'

I gestured to Ted that I was innocent. Les just grinned at him. When we got to the bath house, I stepped slowly into the hot bath, easing my body down. 'Oh, this is so good!' I said.

My shoulders were eventually enveloped in the wonderful hot water. Steam was rising off the water. I realised then that it was salt water. Why couldn't I have one of these on *Daisy May*? I felt a sudden, sharp pain of sadness. She is now *Mary Moore*. I eventually realised the time had come, and I stepped out of the bath. The three of us walked back to the wharf.

'Our voyage will take ninety or so days to return. How much stores do you need?' Lesley asked Les.

'Lesley, let me think about it for a few moments.'

Our cargo had been offloaded. Snowy was back with his clipboard. There was a crowd of people on the wharf watching Jacko doing one of his special dances on the gangplank.

A woman in her 60s put her arms around me. I was startled. 'Captain Bill, Captain Bill, remember me?'

I put my arms around her. 'You arranged all the clothes we made to be sold for you, and we have lots more.'

The lady asked, 'Could we have Jacko for a little while? He is funny and makes us laugh, and we love him. He's like a little puppy dog!'

'Yes, you can spoil him all you like, but don't feed him too much.'

I put my arms around Lesley. 'Don't forget, the puppy dog belongs to Lesley; she must have him back.'

Jacko didn't even wave at us; he just went with them.

Les shook his head, 'Poor Jacko, but poor me. I'm going to have to put up with him chattering non-stop when he gets back.'

Snowy and Richard were measuring the hatch to the hull, writing and drawing on the clipboard. I walked up behind them. 'What are you two up to?'

Richard spoke first. 'The ambulances are mounted on a long chassis of a jeep, too long to go straight down into the hold. We will have to put them in at an angle so that the bonnet goes in first; we can then move it forward and lower it in. We just want to get the angle right.'

Snowy had a big grin on his face. 'We've got to get this right. We should go into the galley, sit down, and work it all out.'

I watched them go into the galley. They pushed the paperwork to one side, then Les put down plates of bread rolls with butter and cheese, curled slices of salmon, coffee, and sticky buns. What could I do? Neither of them came under my jurisdiction. I went onto the Bridge. The carpenters had finished. I looked at the bunk, but there were two, one smaller than the other. I shook my head. Don't ask questions; I know the answer will come in the future.

I went to the stern, glanced up at the men who were still working on the radar. I looked in the hatch. Margaret and Lesley were there; they both had paintbrushes and a big tin of blue paint. 'Where did you get the paint from?'

'From Snowy,' they replied.

The carpenters had done a good, professional job on the side tables. One was beside the top bunk, a fold-down table on the sidewall, shelves with sides on them. I thought Leslie and I had the wrong cabin; it's better than ours. I noticed a pile of mattresses, another present from Snowy.

Richard Hollis walked up the gangplank. 'Bill, your cargo is ready; we load tomorrow. I'm moving the crane up today.' He gave me the cargo list. I put it down on the bench in the Bridge, then started to go over the figures.

One ambulance: 3 ton

One jeep with accessories: 2 ton

Two generators: 5 ton each

20 crates of assorted equipment for generators

10 drums of electrical cable: 1 ton each

2 crates of tools: ½ ton

24 x 44 gallon drums of diesel

Plus the stores we already had on board.

'Richard, I need more weight.'

'Plenty of fish, Bill, cod and smoked herrings,' Richard replied.

'Richard, I will discuss it with Ted.'

I looked at the barometer; it was falling fast. 'Richard, we have bad weather coming, bad weather, I would say late tonight.'

'Then I've got work to do,' replied Richard, and he was on his way off the vessel.

I felt annoyed. Where is Jacko when I need him? He is my personal barometer! I walked up to Ted and put my hand on his shoulder 'Bad weather, Ted, I would say just after dark. I would suggest getting those new men aloft and trying them out, Mervyn as well.'

Ted shouted his orders, 'Close the hatches, batten them down, another bow line, another stern line, two extra springers.' (These stop the vessel from bumping into the wharf). 'Tommy, get those mattresses stowed away and those bundles from the people; bad weather coming.'

Lesley walked past us, looking quite content with herself. She had blue paint on her face. She walked into the galley.

I went back onto the Bridge and looked at the radar. I hoped it wouldn't interfere with the compass; anything with metal or magnets can alter the compass several degrees if they are too close.

I saw Lesley handing a piece of paper to Ted. 'Lesley, we have to get something straight right now!' he said. They walked onto the Bridge. 'Bill, I respectfully say to you and Lesley, as Bosun on this vessel, you Bill are the Captain, Lesley is Commander Johnson, where is my jurisdiction? What about the crew and the new men aboard?'

Lesley spoke first. 'Everyone on board this vessel comes under the Captain; he can use them as he will to sail his vessel. My jurisdiction is to discuss all my business with the Captain, who will give the commands.'

Ted gave Lesley back the piece of paper, who, in turn, handed it to Bill. 'This is the list of stores that Les needs.'

Lesley put both of her hands in the air. 'Ted, I just work under Les, but Ted, give me any trouble and Margaret and I will give you a bath with scrubbing brushes!' She winked at him.

'No, no, no. I've got work to do,' Ted said, and was gone.

He walked up to the five men who had been helping with the bow lines 'We're in for bad weather, so we want to see how you can handle the rigging and mast, but first, where's Mervyn?' A head appeared out of the hatch. 'To the mainmast, Mervyn. You three to starboard, and you three to port. Climb the rigging as far as you can go and come down the other side.'

It was like they were in a race, climbing each side of the mast. They were fit, they will be good when they get back down on deck. Ted instructed them to climb the mast to the second yardarm, 'Go to the end of the yardarm, then go to the opposite end of the yardarm, back down the mast.'

This time, they had to work as a team. The men all came back down onto the deck and stood at attention.

'Gentlemen do not stand to attention; you are seamen, not military men, whilst on board this vessel. Trevor will teach you how to fold and unfold the sails, and how to reef them.'

I was watching them. One of the men, John, said to me, 'We've had training sir.'

I said to them all, 'You call me Captain, Skipper, my name is Bill, you may have had training, but not on this vessel. The sails are Trevor's responsibility; you will take your orders from him.' I grinned at them. 'We will make seamen of you, won't we, Ted?'

I turned towards the galley and saw Lesley grinning at me. The three men who had come aboard to install the radar equipment were coming out of the galley.

'All finished, gentlemen?'

'Yes, Captain,'

'How does it affect my compass?'

'It doesn't Captain, your compass is on due north. Some time in the future, I believe, we will be using magnetic north. There is a 10° difference, but not yet. This radar only tells you where land or objects are. I have left the instructions on the bench; they are quite simple.'

'Thank you, gentlemen.'

'Captain, will you be at the party tonight?'

'No, there is quite a bad blow coming over, and I need to be on my vessel, but my Bosun, Ted, will be, and one or two of the others. Thank you for your work.'

I turned slightly so that nobody on the wharf could see that I had handed him an envelope. 'Have a drink on me, lads.'

They nodded and left. I felt the breeze pick up; it certainly was cold and biting. I didn't like it. The fishing boats had returned to port, and the wharf had become very busy. Ted and I walked down the deck, looking for anything that needed to be stowed. I noticed a small trickle of blue smoke from the stern. Ted said with a chuckle, 'Snowy has found a nice little stove for Trevor and Margaret.'

'Ted, I've got the wrong cabin and can't do a thing about it!'

Ted burst out laughing. 'That's what happens, Skipper, when you get soft; they take advantage.'

'Ted, do you think I should go to the party tonight and you stay on board?'

'Skipper, you're a married man!' He disappeared into the galley. I walked onto the Bridge, and Cat stood up and looked at me. 'No, Cat, I don't think he'll be home tonight. We're both married, so we will stay on board. No trouble here.' I reached under Colin's coat. Cat didn't stop me. Whiskey didn't move. I took out the envelope, which contained my instructions. I couldn't think of a safer place to hide it!

Daylight was starting to fade, and it was getting colder. I noticed a man walking up the gangplank. He was tall and wearing a well-fitting black overcoat. He had a ginger beard; his hair was well groomed, and he carried a walking cane, which appeared to be embossed with silver. I slid back the Bridge door and gestured him to come inside. He waved his cane, walked inside, and closed the door.

'Captain Farquhar?'

'Yes, I am.'

'I'm Gibby McKay.' He shook my hand. I was totally surprised, as nobody had shaken my hand like this for a long time. He said some words, and without thinking, I said some words back to him.

My mind went racing back through time. Walter Wright had installed words into my mind over and over and over until I could repeat every line to him. When we entered Sydney Harbour and tied up at the wharf, he took me to an impressive building with a square and compass on the front of it, and I was installed into Freemasonry. Each time we entered a port, we would go to a Freemasons Lodge. Since I had been Skipper of this vessel, I had not been to Lodge.

'William, our meeting is tomorrow afternoon. I am the Master of the Lodge.' He hesitated, then said, 'I would like to invite you to the Lodge.'

'Yes, it will be a pleasure to attend the Lodge,' I replied.

'Good, I will have somebody here to escort you.' He gave me a grin, letting me know he was playing games. 'William, you will need firewood.'

'Yes, Gibby, how much and what size? Let's talk to Les; he looks after the galley.'

I slid the papers back underneath Colin's coat, and we walked out of the Bridge. Gibby talked to Les whilst eating jam doughnuts. I watched him go down the gangplank. How did he know I was a Freemason? Somebody must have informed him, but who? Then I saw the first snowflakes. Did Gibby cover himself by asking if we needed firewood? Anyone else would think that was the reason he was on board. I reached under the coat and took out the papers and spread them on the bench. I started to read them.

Destination Bangladesh, Calcutta. Longitude 90, latitude 20. Call into Cape Town to unload some stores, to the barracks. Report to Captain George Sharmon, then proceed to your destination. A vessel will meet you with three red flags on its mast. If it has four, then beware. Six of the crew will disembark. We leave the course to your destination up to you. Maintain strict radio silence. Code 3.

There were other papers relating to *Mary Moore*. They definitely looked original, going by their colour and the rest of the paperwork appeared to be in order. There was another piece of paper, which really hurt me. It said to dispose of all paperwork relating to *Daisy May*. I stared at it. She is my mother, no, she has been my mother and I must let her go. No, she will always be *Daisy May* to me, no matter what. No matter what happens to me or where I go, *Daisy May* is my mother.

I noticed the deck and rigging were turning white from the snow. I wondered what Jacko was going to think of this. Just then, Lesley walked in with coffee.

'That man who came on board Bill, that wasn't just for firewood, was it?'

'No, I've been invited to the Freemasons Lodge tomorrow afternoon.'

Lesley raised her eyebrows. We talked about the voyage, the six men, and other matters; we saw the crew returning to the vessel.

'I'm glad we're not sailing tomorrow; I don't think the crew would be too happy. Lesley, how about we sleep in the new bunks in the fore-castle? It has heating.'

'No, Bill, how about we sleep in one bunk together with a hot water bottle?'

'Good suggestion, Commander Johnson. I will carry out your orders.'

The next day was a complete loss, with a very strong wind and cold.

Trevor and Margaret slept in the forecastle. The paint was not yet dry, but the little stove had kept it warm all night. First thing this morning, Margaret was down there making it more cosy.

'That's Margaret's home; it is hers,' Lesley said to me.

I was a little concerned that Jacko had not yet returned. 'Did you see Jacko last night?' I asked Ted.

'Yes, we did. The women were all over him, and he did a beautiful job of entertaining them. I think he's going to break a few hearts when we sail.'

Ted kept the men busy sorting out the hull. I told Ted that we would be stopping at Cape Town, and the stores for Cape Town would be our first. The stores Les needed to feed us could be evenly spread throughout the hull. With that, the day wasn't really wasted. But in my mind, we had been in port too long.

CHAPTER 19

The next morning, when I opened my eyes, Lesley was warm and comfortable, and I felt good with my arms around her, but my back was cold. If we did this at sea, I would be on the floor by now. Stop grumbling and enjoy the moment, I told myself.

I felt the pressure rising. I would have to get up shortly and relieve myself, but not just yet. There was a knock at the door. I got up, and Lesley said to tell them to go away we were busy, but I ignored her and opened the door to the Bridge.

Ted was standing there. He did not look too healthy. 'Bill, please don't talk loudly; it's my head.'

'Ted, if you were a married man, you wouldn't have that problem, would you?'

Ted grumbled back, 'Bill, shut up, it's too painful. They moved the crane up and are starting to load. I've got the crew clearing the snow.'

He turned around slowly and started to walk out of the Bridge. He looked like he had six dozen eggs on his head and didn't want to break them. Everything is a memory, but the moments with Lesley were the best, I thought.

I walked past Tommy. 'What a beautiful morning, makes you feel like singing, doesn't it?'

Tommy looked at me with a very sad look in his eyes. He handed me the shovel he had been clearing the snow away with, made his way to the side of the vessel, and put his head over the rail. I patted him on the shoulder. 'Good man, Tommy, no alcohol on board.'

I started to clear the snow from the hatch covers, being careful not to damage them. Eventually, Tommy's hand took the shovel from me. 'My shovel, Bill, not yours. I don't know what they put in the whiskey, but it's good. When I get my head back on, it will be better still.'

By 12.30 pm, the major part of our cargo had been loaded and lashed down. Ted put chocks on either side of all the wheels, rocked the vehicles backward and forward to make sure that the ropes were tight.

I went back to my cabin. Les had pressed my uniform, and Lesley had laid it out on my bunk. I stood, staring at it. Did I really want to wear it? What sort of statement would it make? Is it sending the wrong message?

A voice came from behind me, 'Wear it Bill!' It was a commanding voice; I couldn't argue. I looked in the mirror, thinking I never wanted to wear this again, but I am still a Navy officer. I put my finger up and touched the little clip that said Australia and my medal. There was a lot of noise on the wharf; people were laughing and shouting.

Ted was standing by the door. 'You've got to see this, Bill.' He was pointing at the wharf. I could hear bagpipes playing. There was a man walking down the wharf dressed in a Scottish uniform: jacket, kilt, socks, and shoes. He had a blanket draped over his shoulder with a big pin, and a sporran on his waist with a sword by his side. There was a dirk in his sock. He was the perfect Scotsman, proud and majestic, walking to the sound of bagpipes.

'I don't believe it, Ted, it's Jacko! They had even trimmed his beard. Ted, you're right, he'll break a few hearts. I must admit that he looks really good. Somebody must have a camera. There was a man on the wharf taking photos. I quickly went down the gangplank and told Ted to stand alongside me. Ted was quick off the mark. He had ordered the crew to do the same thing. As Jacko walked up the gangplank, Ted gave the order, and we all saluted. I now knew I was dressed appropriately. But Jacko looked far better than I did.

He stopped opposite me. 'Captain Jacko, sir, permission to take up my duties again.'

'You have my permission, Captain Jacko. Report to Captain Ted Coe.'

He stepped to one side so that he was facing Ted. 'Permission to resume my duty, sir.'

It was all Ted could do to stop himself from laughing. Lesley was laughing, and so was the rest of the crew, except for the five newcomers, who all looked totally confused.

Jacko bounced up onto the handrail of the ship's bulwark. He started to do a little Scottish dance, one hand above his head, one hand on his side. The crowd roared with laughter.

I leaned over and motioned to Ted, 'I leave you in command Ted. I'm sure you can handle the situation. We set sail at daylight tomorrow morning.' I winked at Ted. 'But speak to Captain Jacko first.'

I saluted Ted, but couldn't get the grin off my face. I walked down the gangplank, where there was a car waiting to pick me up and take me to the Freemasons meeting. As I got into the car, Ted was looking at me, shaking his finger and saying something. I pointed to the crowd and pointed to my ears, then got into the car. We drove off.

The Freemasons Lodge building was very impressive. There were columns at the steps. 'I do not have an apron,' I said to the Tyler.

'We have one for you, sir,' he replied. He put it on me and tied the tape behind me. We talked for a while, mainly about Jacko and the way he fascinated people. There was movement at the door, and I entered, I was greeted into the Lodge. I knew that if you wanted to learn anything about Freemasonry you have to be invited. I was very impressed with the service and their work. Being Scottish, they do everything to perfection.

The Lodge was closed in Peace and Harmony. We went into what could be the *South* for refreshments. There certainly was plenty of food and drink. I declined the alcohol. I don't think they really understood, but I had my set rules.

Eventually, everybody left. Gibby McKay asked me to sit down at a table with two other gentlemen. He put two envelopes in front of me. 'William, in this envelope is your accreditation. Your dues have been paid for and you have been vouched for by the craft, meaning all of Freemasonry, the circle. You have proven yourself to be an outstanding person. In the other envelope are the names of gentlemen you will meet at your destination. Use the secrets of Freemasonry wisely, it will protect you. Yes, William, it is far bigger than you have realised. Lean on Tommy O'Hia; he belongs to her, and he belongs to us.'

I was confused, but knew I couldn't ask any questions.

A car took me back to the vessel. I shook the driver's hand and said thank you. When I reached the top of the gangplank, Tommy was standing there. It was snowing, and he must have been there for quite a while, as the snow was quite thick on his shoulders. With the half-light illuminating him, he looked quite spiritual. He nodded his head at me but didn't say a word, just turned and went to the forecastle. I stood watching him. He had acknowledged that I was back. Was he my keeper? Was he here to protect me? But why? From what?

I walked into the galley and felt the warm air. Snowy was sitting there with a cup of coffee and donuts. I sat down alongside him, lost in my thoughts for a moment.

Snowy chuckled and handed me a piece of paper. It was his discharge papers. He chuckled again, saying, 'I put in for a discharge, put my position down as a storekeeper. People sitting at desks know that they no longer need storekeepers now that the war is over. They didn't question what I did with the stores. I am free. Would you have a place for me onboard?'

Les put his hand on my shoulder. Lesley's hand was on my other shoulder. They both answered for me, 'YES! We do!'

'But where do we put you to sleep? With all the stores, you have a problem,' I replied.

Lesley shook my shoulder, and Les shook the other one.

'I cannot go over the Captain's head; if he doesn't want you, I do!' Lesley said.

I looked at Snowy very seriously. 'How do I protect you? You have been a friend for a long time.' I put my hand on his shoulder. 'I couldn't do that to you Snowy, I have to protect you from Lesley.' I paused for a moment, then raised my voice. 'I am the Captain of this vessel, so you are one of my crew. Please get me another cup of coffee.'

Snowy laughed. 'Yes, Captain, straight away.'

I thought before the war it wasn't as complicated as this on the dreadnought. Everything was done for me, but now I'm married, have I gone soft? I thought of the Lodge, very confusing. Tommy O'Hia, 60 ton of gold, a voyage to Bangladesh, no-man's-land for me. Then I thought of Jacko in his kilt. What next?

Then the young man Whiskey belonged to said in a loud voice, 'Whiskey's got four kittens! Cat is a dad!'

Les and Lesley burst out laughing. I shook my head and quietly drank my coffee. I looked down at my uniform. You are the Captain, Bill, but of what?

Lesley got two hot water bottles, and we walked onto the Bridge, closed the door, and listened to Jacko snoring. Lesley took one of the water bottles and put it into Jacko's fur coat, which he had wrapped around himself. We went to bed with the other bottle.

CHAPTER 20

Lesley and I got up well before daylight. The clouds had cleared, and we could see millions of stars in the dark sky. The barometer was rising; there was a gentle but cold breeze, just what I needed. Cat and Whiskey weren't on the bench, nor were they on Collin's coat. The Scottish clothing was neatly folded, and the sword was on top of it. We went down for coffee, but Les had already prepared bacon and eggs for us. As we sat down to eat, Ted walked in. 'Warm weather on the horizon, Bill?'

'Yes, Ted.'

Ted sat down alongside Lesley. Margaret brought him his bacon, eggs, and coffee. She kissed him on the forehead. He grinned at her. 'Thank you, Margaret, thank you. You're the daughter I always wanted.'

Margaret winked at me and said, 'Are you getting soft, Ted?' She was off before Ted could answer.

I grinned at him. 'Ted, we will motor out of the port. Once we get around the headland, we will raise the sails. Which ones, I don't know yet; we'll just wait and see what the weather is like.

Jacko walked in, twitching his nose; he had smelled breakfast.

'Jacko, we're leaving at daylight; we are going out using the motor.'

Jacko nodded to me.

'Jacko, have you got a headache?'

Jacko nodded again.

Tommy walked in. 'Good morning, Tommy. Before you have breakfast, would you start the motor?' Tommy raised his eyebrows. 'Margaret is here, Tommy.'

Margaret burst out laughing. 'Could I, could I please start the motor? That will get Trevor out of bed.' She laughed again. 'Not his head, but his body! I told him to stop drinking, and I didn't like what he said to me. Please, Tommy, please.'

They both walked off towards the stern. Soon I heard the little motor start. It had to build up air pressure to start the big Gardner motor. We heard the big motor turning over and over, then it fired, but didn't start. It turned over and over again, then it fired on all cylinders. It had come to life, purring away. It sounded much louder in that cold air. Ted didn't have to call the crew; they were all awake.

Margaret trotted into the galley with a big, cheeky grin on her face. She went straight back to work with Les, acting so innocent.

All the crew came into the galley, which made it a tight fit, but they all squeezed in.

I stood up and addressed the crew. 'We will be leaving the port during daylight. 'We will use the motor until we get out to sea. Stow everything away; no loose items. I want the sea air on the rigging to take away the ice before we unfold the sails. Those of you who have bad headaches, go and see Les. I'm sure he has a concoction that will help you. Please note, if I find any alcohol on this vessel, may God help you. We have a long voyage down to our first destination, Cape Town. We will be heading out to the Atlantic Ocean, down past Ireland. It could get a little rough. Work as a team, do not argue with Ted, just do as he tells you instantly, if not quicker. If somebody is having trouble, help them; do not hesitate to lash them to the mast or yardarms until they are safe.'

I glanced at Ted; he stood up alongside me and nodded, and then said, 'Jacko, Bridge. He bowed his head to Lesley. Margaret, Lesley, galley. Tommy, look out forehead. Trevor, inform our crew of what you want aloft. Our rigging and canvas are frozen and must be treated with respect. If I ask you to stand down and rest, do so. I don't tell you how to rest, but rest. I want you to be at your best. Trevor, how is your head? Margaret was so worried.' A couple of us started to chuckle.

'I'm innocent. I never touched the little lever on top of the motor, did I, Margaret?' Tommy said.

Margaret had her hands on her hips and was scowling at Tommy.

'Enjoy your breakfast, lads.' I beckoned to Lesley and Jacko, then poured three cups of coffee. Les broke an egg into one. The neck of a bottle came out from under his apron, and he poured some of it into that same coffee cup. A little of the hair of the dog that bit him.

I looked Les in the eyes, letting him know that I didn't approve, and shook my finger at him. 'We'll talk later!'

I picked up the three coffees and walked out of the galley. Lesley and Jacko followed me onto the Bridge.

'Lesley, I thought we could sail this course to our destination. If we were going to Cape Town, they would expect us to go down the English Channel. If we head out into the Atlantic Ocean, they would be confused. Then we could head down to Cape Town. I have informed the crew deliberately of our destination and course. If there is anybody aboard who cannot be trusted, we will find out and be on guard. First, Jacko, sail due South, then West West 260°, then longitude nine; then we'll see how the weather holds.'

Richard Hollis appeared on the gangplank. I slid back the door and waved to him; he came onto the Bridge.

'Good morning, Bill, Lesley, Jacko. They gave you clothes; why aren't you wearing them?'

'Because they are itchy.'

'Bill, have you seen Snowy?'

'No, not this morning.'

'Bill, the town hall is full of stores, and he has put paperwork on my desk. I need to talk to him.'

I looked at Lesley. 'Do you know where he is.'

'Yes, I do; he's in my old quarters,' Lesley replied.

I went to Lesley's old cabin and knocked on the door. No answer. I opened the door and walked in. There was Snowy curled up on the bunk. A voice from under the blankets said, 'Whoever you are, go away.'

'Snowy, you signed on as one of my crew, now get up!' A head appeared from under the blankets. 'If you would please come onto the Bridge now!' I left him.

Jacko was drinking his coffee; he didn't look too good. 'What's the witchy saying, Jacko?'

'He says I piss into the wind, not a wise thing to do. I don't like the way he looks at me.'

Snowy walked in. He picked up a coffee without asking whose it was and started to drink it. His eyes widened. 'What's this supposed to be?'

Jacko grabbed the coffee. 'That's my coffee, Snowy.'

'That's not coffee.'

'You'll get used to it, Snowy,' I said.

Richard then spoke. 'Snowy, could you explain to me all the stores and paperwork on my desk?'

Snowy's eyes were a little bloodshot. 'My orders were to tidy up the store and dispose of everything. The people who sit at the desks just wanted it all to disappear so they no longer have a problem, and they can close the file. I have disposed of everything. If you could give them to the public who need them most, I would be grateful. All the other stores are aboard a naval vessel. Nobody is going to argue with that, are they, Commander?'

Richard looked at Snowy for a minute. 'Snowy, I don't quite know what to think of you, but I would like to shake your hand and say thank you on behalf of the people of Lowick. I will take care of the paperwork, but I'll leave the rest to Gibby McKay; he knows the people better than I do.'

He stood at attention and put his hand forward. 'Goodbye, Captain Farquhar.' He shook my hand as a friend would. He nodded to Lesley, stood straight, and said, 'Commander.' Lesley nodded back.

He stepped forward to Jacko, put both of his hands on Jacko's shoulders, and shook him. 'You come back, Jacko, any time you want. You gave these people what they needed; you gave them yourself. You made them laugh, but not just laugh; you took away the problems they had because of the war. You entertained them like no other man could. Thank you, Captain Jacko.'

He looked at me and looked at Lesley, then Richard put his hand out and shook Ted's, 'if I ever go to sea, it will be with you.' He turned and walked out of the Bridge.

'Ted, could you raise the gangplank, please?' Daylight was just starting to come.

I heard Ted shout, 'raise the gangplank, remove the springers.' He opened the galley door and shouted, 'Land lovers on deck!'

I pushed the 'On' switch, and the radar came to life. It was then that I realised Cat wasn't on the bench. I looked towards the gangplank, but Les was feeding both him and Whiskey.

'Jacko, where is Cat sleeping?'

'Margaret has them by the fire. The kittens are doing well.'

I nudged Jacko with my shoulder. 'I thought Cat was your friend!'

'Too many females aboard, Skipper.'

Lesley nudged his other shoulder. 'Keep an eye on us, Jacko.'

'Lesley, we have quite a number of crew. I think the best way is to command as a naval vessel. That way, we can keep the crew busy. Snowy, when we get out to sea, you and I will go through our cargo, then I will know what mischief you have been up to.'

I tapped Jacko on his shoulder and nodded at Ted, who boomed out, 'Let the bowline go.'

He nodded to me. 'Bowline was freed and stowed away.'

Jacko put the gear stick into astern. She gently moved astern, and Jacko turned the wheel to port, and the bow moved away from the wharf. She gently tightened up on the stern line, and the bow came out further and further. She was now at near right angles to the wharf. Jacko put the gear stick into neutral.

I nodded to Ted, whose voice once again boomed out, 'Let the stern line go.' He nodded to me, letting me know this had been done. The stern line was now stowed aboard and would not foul the prop. I tapped Jacko on the shoulder. He put the gear stick into forward, he turned the wheel to starboard. We were now on our way. I tapped Jacko's shoulder and thought, *she is still Daisy May!*

Jacko moved his head slightly towards me, 'Yes, she will always be our mother.'

'Lesley, could you ask Jarrett to come and see me, please?'

'Yes, sir.'

And she was gone. She returned soon after with Jarrett.

'Good morning, Jarrett, how would you put the last three days into a logbook?'

'Well, Skipper, I just wrote it down as it came, but when I read it back to myself, I get confused. There is one piece of information I don't have, Skipper.'

'What's that, Jarrett?'

'Well, what did Jacko wear underneath his kilt?'

Jacko's voice boomed out, 'That is personal and private!'

'Jarrett, I would like you to resume your normal duties as the navigator, radio operator, and radar operator, but you can't use the radio until

I give you the command.' I raised my eyebrows at him. 'And maintain your log, and take the wheel when Jacko's resting.'

'Yes sir. We have one thing missing, Captain.'

'Yes, I know, that big, comfortable chair.'

I stood aside and pointed to the chart. 'This is the course for the day. I want to avoid the shallows here; we will alter course just before. These are very dangerous waters. The wind blows from the west, they will blow you into Ireland. This is where the Spanish and Norwegians came unstuck. They sailed too close to shore and could not tack in the strong wind. I feel a lot safer now that we have plenty of diesel on board.'

Just then, Ted walked in. Jacko's voice boomed out, 'Captain on the Bridge!'

Ted nudged him. 'Whatever Les gave you, Jacko, it worked! But I liked you the way you were, quiet!'

'Snowy,' I said, 'with due respect to you, Jarrett Collins is a Captain in His Majesty's Navy. He is now on the Bridge so the small cabin is his by right. There are bunks in the forehead, but I would suggest you use a hammock. Ted, is Michael's hammock available?'

'Yes, I stowed it away,' Ted said.

'The choice is yours, Snowy. Have a look at Ted's hammock, which Michael made for him; it's extra special. Ted, do you want to know about the sails?'

'Yes, Skipper.'

'I don't want to put any more weight on top of the masts; they already have ice all over them: outer jib, inner jib for lower topsail, mainmast, lower topsail, mainsail, gaff topsail, spinnaker. We'll see how she likes that.'

Snowy walked out behind Ted. 'Lesley, could you ask Les to see me, please? Jacko, we referred to this as the Bridge but we'll still use first names.'

'Does Ted have to call me sir? Jacko asked.'

'You're a cheeky sod. Only if you call him, sir.'

I looked at my logbook. Jarrett had the right advice. Fill it out; don't read it back to yourself. I felt a slight movement in the *Mary Moore*; the sails were being unfolded, and they were picking up a slight breeze.

Jacko commented, 'We are now where we belong!' Les walked in with 3 cups of coffee and his legendary sticky buns. He put them down in front of Jacko, whose eyes lit up.

'Les, do you have any of that substance called *the hair of the dog*?' I asked.

'Yes, I do, but for medical purposes only. For sterilising my instruments. I have just one bottle left.'

'Could you open the door, then stand outside, facing me.' I winked at him, despite my raised voice. I shouted, 'Do we have that clear Les? No alcohol aboard this vessel. You, of all people, should know my rules.'

Les put his hands in front of him and lowered his head. Nearly all the crew were looking up at the Bridge. Jacko was trying to keep a straight face; Ted had his mouth wide open. 'Now come onto the Bridge.' Les came back onto the Bridge.

Jacko said in a soft voice, 'Naughty boy.'

Les clipped him around his ear.

'Thanks Les. How are you coping with the women?'

'It annoys me when they keep fussing over me, but I will miss it when they're gone. We have a large crew, Skipper. Could we do the meals in two sittings?'

'Les, we will have a night crew and a day crew. That should split the meals up. Use Lesley all the time in the galley; Margaret, whenever you need her; but go through Ted first. Jarrett is assigned to the Bridge.' I pointed to the floor and winked again. 'Les, when you come onto the Bridge, seek permission from Captain Jacko first.'

Jacko did one of his little dances; Les winked at me. 'I'll bring my big wooden spoon with me.'

'Les, you run the galley. I won't interfere, but I do want you to have more rest.' I put my hand up to stop him from arguing. 'Jacko gets more rest than you; he does 12 hours, you do 16 hours or more. We have more crew than we need, and I need to keep them all busy. I will assign Tommy O'Hia to you after each sitting to assist. No, Les, you will not argue with me when it comes to your welfare. Remember this: I have two women on my side.' I had to change the subject. 'How are the kittens doing, Les?'

A beautiful smile came over his face. 'Bill, you do change the subject, but I'm still annoyed. Ask Jacko about the kittens. Margaret and he are like possessive parents.' He turned and walked out of the Bridge.

'He knows you love him, Bill, and it's all in his best interests,' Jacko said.'

Jarrett had been sitting quietly, reading the charts. 'Jacko, or should I say, sir Jacko, but the Captain's on the Bridge. Permission to alter course, sir?'

'Give sir Jacko your orders.'

'West to 260.'

I slid back the door and shouted, 'Coming about west.'

Ted was shouting his orders. He had been waiting. The position of the yardarms was changed, and she swung around to face the west, her sails full of wind again.

I stood, looking at the sails. Ted came onto the Bridge. He already had a man aloft, and we both watched him. Then, he waved to say everything was well. 'Put the rest of the canvas on her, Ted.' Ted was already shouting orders before he left the Bridge. Jacko put the gear stick into neutral, and Ted had instructed Tommy to shut the motor down and take Margaret with him. She knew how to start the motor; now, she had to learn how to stop it and shut the seacock off to the water that cooled the motor. I picked up my pencil, crew on board.

Ted   - Bosun
Jacko   - Helmsman
Jarrett - Navigator
Les   - Cook
Tommy O'Hia
Young George with Whiskey the Cat
Trevor and Margaret
Lesley and Snowy
and Mervyn?
Add five more
Witchy says *lose 2, gain more*,' Jacko said.

'Ask Jacko questions. He won't have the answer straight away, but just remember what he says, just remember. Jarrett, the vessel is doing well; we must have a strong current pushing us.'

'I'll take the ordinance before the light goes.' Jarrett picked up the sexton. It wasn't my sexton, it was far better than mine, much more complicated.

He saw me looking at it, 'Not mine, Skipper, belongs to the Navy, but they don't know I've got it. As Snowy says, too much paperwork.' He stepped into the daylight.

I walked out onto the deck, thinking of what Jacko said lose 2, gain more. He had warned me of big changes, but again, he couldn't tell me how big or what. I walked past George and stopped.

'How are the kittens, George?'

'They're doing very well, Skipper. Margaret is looking after them; they're in the warmest place on the vessel and are very safe.'

'George, we must talk. I don't know anything about you; we will have coffee together later.' I saw tears in his eyes. 'Coffee later, George.' Lesley saw me and came out of the galley.

'All well, Bill?'

'Yes, all is well. The barometer is dropping slightly, but we haven't had to change course or tack. Just at dusk, we'll alter course to miss the banks.'

'I don't know anything about them.'

'If you have a minute, come up to the Bridge, Lesley.'

'I'll just let Les know.' She walked onto the Bridge practically behind me.

I showed her my piece of paper. 'This is my crew. I tapped Mervyn's name with my finger.'

She looked at me, deep in thought. 'I wish he were one of your crew; he would be safe, but no, he is one of the five. The sixth member.'

I stared at her for a moment. 'Lesley, you are not part of this, are you?'

'No Bill.' I breathed in deeply, then let go of my fear of losing her. When the five came aboard, I hadn't any answers. I worried about Lesley. I walked forward and put my arms around her. She pressed her head into my shoulder, then she kissed me on the lips. 'Bill, I've got work to do.'

Jacko said very softly, 'Witchy says six leave, not seven.'

Jacko always talks in riddles.

I walked up to Ted. 'Coffee Ted?' We walked into the galley.

I got two coffees and sat down. 'We've got 10 crew, 11 with Mervyn, and five Marines. So, we split them into two sections: day shift and night shift. Choose them as you will, Ted. Lesley works with Les. I want him to have more rest. He does more hours than any of us. Have Tommy in the galley after meals.' I looked at my watch. 'I'll be back in a minute.'

I walked out onto the deck. Jarrett was standing outside the Bridge, waiting for me. I nodded to him and heard him say to Jacko, 'South 220.'

With the wind in that direction, nothing needed to change. Our sails were still full. I beckoned to George; he followed me into the galley, and I gestured for him to sit down by Ted. I made him a coffee.

'George, you first came aboard my vessel with Jack Fox. He had all your paperwork in order. Where do you come from?'

'From the streets of Melbourne,' he replied

'Your parents?'

'I don't know.'

'So that's why there's no birth certificate. So, how did you meet Jack Fox?'

'I was in a gang loading wool bales on the Castle, and I asked him for a job on board.'

'So, they picked you up from Helford store?'

'Yes, Skipper.'

'That's how Jacko and I started, just like you, on this vessel,' I said.

George's eyes widened.

'But you are a Captain in His Majesty's Navy, and so is Jacko.'

'So, George, there is a goal for you if you want it. Jarrett will work with you.'

'You are a good man. You follow orders, you don't argue, and you have a quick brain. Can you read, write?' Ted added.

'Just a little.'

'Then let's see if we can give you a future.'

Les turned up with three meals and put them down in front of us. 'Bill he reads well and writes well.' Les said and returned to the galley.

'Skipper, Tommy has been helping me.' Tears started to flow from George's eyes. 'Skipper, I've never had a family, but since I've been aboard, I have found everybody here is family. You look after everybody; I've never known it before. Nobody criticizes or tells you that you are useless, or to go away. They just want to help you and let you be part of the family. You are not the Captain; you are the father. On the warship, you were the Captain. They called you God! Don't get on the wrong side of God! they'd say.'

'George, I hated being God. When you are God, you've always got to be right; you are in total command. But, as you said, this is a family. Now, if you will excuse me, gentlemen, I must rest.'

As I walked out, I patted George on the shoulder. I returned to my quarters. Yes, George is right, the crew is my family, and it gave me a warm feeling. I think I was asleep before my head hit the pillow.

I felt somebody pushing a hot water bottle into my back and next to my feet, and it wasn't Jacko.

CHAPTER 21

Four o'clock in the morning, Lesley was waking me.

'Rise and shine,' she said.

I got up and checked the chart. We had to tack during the night, but it was to our advantage, south 200°. We had a moderate sea. The vessel was heading into the swell at a slight angle, easing the pressure off her bow. Tommy was at the wheel. 'Good morning, Tommy.'

'Skipper, I wondered why Cat wasn't on the bench, then I heard you snoring!'

'Wise Cat.'

Lesley walked in with three coffees. Tommy picked up one, I picked up the other.

'Tell me, Tommy, did Ted put you at the wheel so he could sleep? Nobody snoring?'

'Something like that, Skipper.' His big eyes shone.

'Apparently, you've been doing a good job with George. They say his reading and writing are good.'

'He's a good student, Skipper, just needed somebody to have faith in him. He's good with figures as well. He's teaching Trevor his figures;

136

they work well together. Margaret made me laugh when the big motor fired and made that noise. Margaret's head nearly touched the deck. Her little joke on Trevor backfired.'

'Thanks, Tommy, I'll take over the wheel now,' I said. Lesley picked up the mugs, and they went down to the galley.

The day passed quite quickly. Everybody seemed to get into their routine, and I'd got my paperwork finished.

Jacko was quiet. What mischief was he getting up to, or what problems did he have? Five? I'm going to have to work it out for the best of all concerned.

'You just leave it with me, Bill.'

'You worry me, Jacko, especially when you're thinking about other people's welfare.'

Jarrett walked onto the Bridge. He had been taking the bearings with his sexton.

'Jacko, take a break, get some food,' I said. That magic word, food, he was gone as quick as lightening.

Jarrett looked at me. 'What's wrong with Jacko?

'I don't know Jarrett. When he's like this, I know I've got problems.'

'Skipper, we're at longitude 15; we're heading due south.'

I turned the wheel due south. He was doing the figures in his head now; he's good. I need to get him home. He is now the man his father needs to run the business and take the weight off his father's shoulders. He certainly would be proud of his son now.

Jacko's words were in the back of my mind. Big changes, six, not seven. I've got a problem, Skipper, but I've got to solve it. He always leaves me up in the air, with no real answers.

Jarrett brought me back from my thoughts. 'Skipper, you do not want to see land until we get to Cape Town?'

'That's right, Jarrett, the fewer eyes that see us, the better. I know it's a puzzle for you, Jarrett, but I will explain later.'

CHAPTER 22

Once again, Lesley was waking me.

'It's four o'clock, Bill.'

I threw my legs over the bunk and slid down onto the floor. There was movement in the vessel. Tommy was at the wheel again; Jacko was asleep in his bunk. 'Good morning, Tommy.' Those big eyes with the sparkle in them stared back at me in the half-light.

'A few whitecaps, Skipper, but nothing breaking over the deck.'

'We didn't tack during the night?'

'No, Skipper, it was a good night.'

'You get some rest now, Tommy.' I opened the door for him, but Lesley was just about to walk in. Tommy stood aside.

'Thank you, Tommy, you are a gentleman,' she said.

'Anything for you, Lesley.' With a grin, he winked one of his big eyes at me.

'Lesley, I'm enjoying you spoiling me with a hot water bottle for the night and waking me at four; I'm getting used to it.'

We watched the daylight start together. 'I've always thought this is the best time of day at sea.' We could smell bacon and eggs, but didn't want to spoil the moment. Then this head appeared from under the bench, its nose twitching. I slid back the door, and he partly crawled, partly walked out of the Bridge and down to the galley. I slid the door back.

'Bill, were his eyes open or closed?'

'I think he was moving by smell, not sight.'

'I'll go and get you some breakfast, Bill,' and she was gone.

Ted walked in the door, holding a cup of coffee. 'Good morning, Skipper.'

'Good morning, Ted.'

'It's good to be back at sea, Skipper. Less problems.'

'Yes, Ted. At the moment, but Jacko's got me puzzled.'

Ted grinned and gave a little chuckle. 'He is quiet, isn't he?'

'Yes, that has got me concerned.'

Ted grinned again. 'It can't be too serious; he's putting the food down.'

'I know, Ted. He doesn't like sleeping under the bunk; he likes the fresh air, but at the moment it is too cold, and he doesn't like wearing too many clothes. But that isn't it.'

'Bill, I hope we don't find out when it's too late to do anything about it. I don't want to see him hurt. He is a very special soul.'

'Ted, I would like to give Margaret training at the helm so that we have another ace up our sleeve if we need it. We're on a straight course, so it's the best time to teach her to concentrate on the course.'

'I remember, Bill, you sitting on top of the mainmast.'

'Yes, old Walter let you know the seriousness of keeping on course.' We chatted more about the old days and the total teamwork of the crew. There was more pressure on the Captain to get his cargo from A to B. Time was money for the owners, but steam and oil had taken over, and the trade routes had changed.

I looked at the clock. 'Where is Jacko?'

I was just about to ask Ted to find him when he walked in the Bridge door. He didn't say a word, just nudged me to one side. I looked at the radar; it was picking up the coast of Ireland, but on its outer limits. It was very reassuring to know. Jacko had left the door open. Ted patted his tummy and walked out of the Bridge. I followed him.

I found Snowy in the galley doing paperwork. I got two coffees and two sticky buns and sat down alongside him. He slowly put his papers in his satchel.

'Good morning, Bill. I took your advice. The hammock is comfortable, but in the mornings, you have to be very careful getting out.'

'Yes, Snowy, I learned the hard way.'

'At least, Bill, it's getting a bit warmer.'

'Yes, Jacko's left the door open. I want to go through the rest of the stores with you. The stores that we don't have!'

Snowy picked up his clipboard and looked at it, took a sip of coffee and a mouthful of bun. Snowy was what you would call a very cool man; his facts and figures had to be right, his morals and principles had to be on the square.

'Bill, paperwork, people want me to clean up the Air Force Base; they didn't want to take on any responsibility. I have done the job, but it doesn't sit right with me. The general public has lost everything because of the war. If we could give something back to them to help them survive, I know I would sleep better at night.

'The straight and undivided line of conduct, Snowy.'

He grinned at me, 'Yes Bill, something like that.'

We finished our coffee and sticky buns, then picked up two of those funny new torches and went to the hatch. The hull had narrow pathways running through the cargo. We went to the bow. Tinned food for our return trip was stacked up in the crest of the bow, then the jeep. Cable drums were stacked around it with spare canvas; the ambulance was locked in with cable drums for the generators. I noticed the back door to the ambulance was slightly open. I couldn't fully open it because of the cable drums, so I reached over and closed it. But why was it open?

Two generators were stacked behind each other. Drums of wire and crates of equipment were all stacked and lashed together. There was tinned food where Les could easily get at it, sacks of vegetables, potatoes, smoked meats, and eggs.

I noticed two plates and two cups. What were they doing there? Drums of diesel that had been covered with canvas, drums of fish in brine, other drums and smoked fish. Stacked on top of all of this, there were Navy supplies right up to the deck: shirts, jumpers, socks, trousers, coats. All the clothing you could imagine, including boots and shoes. Then I noticed a small movement.

Snowy had seen it as well. He asked, 'What would children be doing down here?'

'Wait there, Snowy, don't move. I'll be back in a minute.'

I went back to the ambulance and shone my torch in the window. Somebody had been sleeping in there. Jacko was behaving funny, having plenty of food, two plates, two cups. I went back up on deck.

'Ted, it looks like I've solved one problem and found another. Could you get Margaret to relieve Jacko with Tommy?'

I walked up to the Bridge. I was a bit surprised to see Cat sitting on the bench in his rightful place. 'Hello Dad, how are you and the children doing? Well? Is Whiskey okay?' Cat just stared at me.

Margaret and Tommy walked in. 'Margaret, I want to give you some training at the helm. Take the wheel from Jacko. Let her have the wheel Jacko, we've got a problem of yours to sort out. Follow me.'

He knew that I knew, and instead of following me, he headed towards Les, where he felt he would be safe. I didn't even look back.

'No, Jacko, follow me.'

I stopped by the stairs and ushered him to go first. He slid down the stairs. I had to climb down. I pointed to the two plates, then beckoned him to follow me. Snowy was waiting. He put the torch to his face and grinned.

'Snowy and I will go back on deck, then you, Jacko, can bring them,' I pointed to where we had seen them, 'to the galley where Les can feed them properly.'

Snowy and I went on deck. I walked over to the galley. 'Les, it appears we have more on board. They are friends of Jacko.'

The crew seemed to have turned up from nowhere, knowing there was something going on. You can't keep secrets aboard a ship. Jacko appeared first from the hatch, then two children slowly walked onto the deck. They both covered their eyes from the light. The older one had a violin case. They were both wearing Air Force jumpers, but on looking closer, they appeared to be wearing two. They had two or three pairs of socks on their feet and were wearing big, floppy boots.

The crew was fascinated. Lesley and Les were staring at me. Margaret, who was on the Bridge, standing behind the wheel, couldn't believe what she was seeing. She shouted at Tommy to take over the wheel and headed for the door to be with the children. I saw her, and I understood, but I'm the Captain; this vessel comes first. I shouted at her to go back to the helm. She stopped. I shouted again, but slowed my words down 'get…back…to…the…helm.'

Margaret hesitated; she saw Ted scowling at her. She went back to the helm and took over the wheel from Tommy. She looked into Tommy's eyes. They told her that he was disappointed in her.

'Jacko, take the children into the galley and Les will feed them.' I turned and went up onto the Bridge. 'Tommy, take the helm. Margaret, look at me! That wheel is the most important part of this vessel; it must be maintained at all times, no matter what the circumstances. You cannot walk away from it. You may be relieved, but by Ted or myself, other than that, it's where you stay. Let this vessel have her head, and we will have torn sails, broken yardarms or worse. I only know of one time Jacko had left this helm to me, and that was when Trevor was having trouble in the rigging. It was a life-or-death situation. I thought you were the one person I could totally rely on. I let the Captain down once, and I learned the hard way. How do I make the point to you? Take the helm until Jacko returns.'

I turned and went back to the galley. I glanced up when I stopped at the galley door. I could see Margaret through the glass of the Bridge. I could see the expression on her face. What have I done? I felt annoyed and frustrated. Children aboard! I still could not get this clear in my mind. What am I going to do with two children? Where did they come from? How did they get aboard? Looking at Margaret gave me a pain I had never felt before. I saw Tommy hand her a piece of cloth, which she put to her eyes. I knew Tommy was consoling her.

'Margaret, he did not chastise you as a Captain. He chastised you as a father, you let him down, you put yourself first. This vessel comes first at all times, and you know that, Margaret. We all know that you want children, and there they were. He knows that, Margaret.' She turned to face Tommy; the tears started to flow. She took the rag from him to wipe away the tears.

'Tommy, he has never spoken to me like that before.'

'But you know, Margaret, he was right. You owe him an apology. He is not the Captain he was before the war. He has seen and experienced too much. To me, he is a far better man. He has more compassion and understanding, and Margaret, he is your father because he loves you like a father.'

Margaret was wiping the tears from her eyes when Jacko and Jarrett walked in. They were laughing about the events that had just happened in the galley.

Jacko said to Margaret, 'Bossi wants to see you in the galley.'

I walked into the galley to see the two children surrounded by the crew. The children had plates of food in front of them and were busily eating. 'Now, lads, you've got work to do. Go back to your stations.'

I leaned over to Ted. 'Are you getting soft now, Ted?' He grinned at me, then glanced at the children.

'Yes, Skipper, yes.' Ted's voice then boomed out to the crew. 'Back to work; those of you who should be resting, do so now the barometer is falling.'

I sat down with the children. Jacko sat down with me, and Snowy went to get some coffee. The boy appeared to be about 12 years old, and the girl, I would guess, six. 'It is quite clear where you have come from, but why are you aboard this vessel?'

'We have nowhere else to go. Our parents were Jacobite's and we're not wanted,' the boy replied.

'Where are your parents, boy?'

'They're dead, sir.'

'Do you know how they died?'

'Our father was a pilot in the Air Force, he didn't come back one day. Our mum got very sick. They said she died of pneumonia.'

'Did anybody look after you?'

'They took my sister from me. I found her, and we've been living on the streets.'

'How have you been surviving?' Lesley asked?

The little girl, with a mouth full of food, said, 'By playing my violin for money. Our mum played the violin.'

'What is your name, little girl?

'Daisy.'

We all looked at each other in surprise. The boy said his name was Robbie McGregor, and his sister was Daisy McGregor.

Les could not contain himself. 'Robbie, could you play the violin for us?'

Robbie didn't hesitate. He put the violin case on the table, opened it and took out a beautiful violin. Daisy said the violin was his mum's. The two children looked at each other; I could see the sadness in their eyes. Robbie put the violin to his shoulder and looked at Daisy. She got up and walked to his side, putting an arm around him; then he started to play.

It brought tears to my eyes. Les was wiping his eyes with his apron, so was Lesley, Snowy was just staring and listening. We sat there mesmerized, listening to the beautiful sound. This young man was very talented. Just then, Margaret walked through the door with Tommy. They stood staring at the children and listening to Robbie playing the violin.

Margaret walked up to me and leaned on my back, 'I'm sorry Bill.'

'We'll say no more, Margaret, but your penance is,' I hesitated, 'you have to take care of these children.' I saw a big grin come over Les's face. Lesley just shook her head.

'Now, as Ted said, the barometer is dropping. We've got work to do. The children have been sleeping in the ambulance, and I feel this is the best place for them. It's nearly midship; less movement. Tommy, there is a cable drum stopping the door from opening. Could you move it before the seas get rough? Snowy and I will finish what we started. Margaret, come down below. I'm sure Les wants to hear some more music.'

We all went below. 'Margaret, I think you should pad out that ambulance to protect the children. Snowy has plenty of blankets and pillows. Snowy, what are these four boxes?'

'They belong to the five who recently came aboard, one has ammunition, one has firearms, in the other two there are bazookas, and one has explosives.'

'Now, Snowy, I really wanted to know that!' I stood staring at the boxes. This would come under Lesley's jurisdiction, but explosives on my vessel? I should have been informed. 'Snowy, have you recorded explosives on the vessel?'

'No, Skipper, I haven't.'

I thought for a moment. Do these come under the Security Act? This is a naval vessel, and so comes under Lesley. There appeared to be a bundle of something under the canvas. 'What's this, Snowy?'

He pulled back the canvas. My eyes lit up as I shone the torch on it so that I could see better. 'Where did these come from?'

'They were in the offices at the base.'

'Would one of them be mine?'

'I'm sure it could be Skipper.'

I shouted out to Tommy. He was standing behind me straight away. 'Tommy, take one of these beautiful leather chairs up to the Bridge and put a sign CAPTAIN on it.'

Tommy winked at Snowy. 'With all due respect, Skipper, there are politics here.'

I saw the two of them grinning at each other.

'What's the problem?' I asked.

'Commander Johnson,' Snowy replied.

It's good to have two rogues watching your back.

'Tommy, could you put both of these chairs in the Bridge?'

'Yes, Skipper, straight away.'

Before I could even blink, Margaret was in one of the chairs. She cradled her arms as if she were holding a baby. 'Skipper, Mummy needs a good chair.'

'Then we will leave them down here for you. Tommy, lash them down so they can't move. So, Snowy, we have 40 drums of diesel, that is 3 to a ton, 50 drums of assorted fish, clothing from the Port of Lerwick, pillows, blankets, mattresses, socks, shirts, trousers, boots, jumpers and hats.'

'There are also pocket knives, belts, notebooks, and pencils, six light office chairs for desks; the others were too heavy,' Snowy said.

'The others were too heavy?' I replied in a mocking voice, 'Well, that's a pity isn't it? There are also 12 boxes of cigars.'

'But I don't smoke, Skipper.'

'Snowy, that's a pity, isn't it! Kitchen sink, Snowy?'

'No, Skipper, they were all bolted down.'

'Four wall clocks and one barometer. Are you sure that's all, Snowy?'

'There might be some other small things, but they're not important.'

'Thank you, Snowy, thank you.' I turned around and went back to the ambulance, glancing at the military boxes. Margaret had done a good job. The children will be well protected against any movement of the vessel. I noticed a bucket to one side. I pointed to it. 'Margaret, leave that there.'

I went up onto the Bridge, and there were the two comfortable office chairs. Jarrett was sitting in one of them.

Jacko, in an annoyed voice, said, 'Can't put them behind the wheel.'

I pointed to the one Jarrett was sitting in. 'That is Commander Lesley's, and this one is mine, Captain; no room for any more.'

I turned towards Jarrett and winked at him. He sat back in the chair. I put one hand on the wheel and one on Jacko's shoulder, 'I thought there was an understanding on this vessel: no secrets from the Captain. Is that correct, my brother?

Margaret is doing her penance, so you have to do yours. You will empty the bucket below every day. Ted thinks I'm getting too soft as Captain, so I have to do something about that, don't I, my brother?'

Jacko raised his eyebrows and went below to empty the 'pee bucket.' Jarrett and I heard the children laughing and giggling. I looked at Jarrett. 'Why would I be getting soft here, Jarrett?'

He grinned at me. 'It is written, Skipper, that on a sailing vessel you should not have women, as they soften the Captain, and children remind him that he is just a mortal man. Coffee Captain?'

'Yes please, Jarrett.'

He returned with the coffee. 'The children are having a bath. Lesley and Margaret are soaked through. Ted was standing outside, listening. He told me that he was on guard at the door. I asked him whether he was getting soft, and he told me to shut up. He said that I had been mixing with Jacko too much.'

'If we stay on Longitude 11 due south, tomorrow at 12 pm we should be just past the British Isles. I'm expecting the wind to increase. It normally blows in from the west and curls around southern England into the English Channel, so we'll have to watch what it's going to do at Latitude 49,' I said.

Just then, Ted walked in, looking troubled.

'Ted, by the looks of the barometer, we should shorten the sails.'

'Bill, I remember coming through these waters before. We need to take off her top sails and the upper main sails.'

'Yes, Ted, you've got a good memory.'

'The sea never lets you forget her rules, Skipper.'

As Ted left, Jacko walked in with two sticky buns in his hands. 'That Snowy is a good man, Skipper. He gave me a wooden seat for the bucket.'

I thought of what Snowy said, *bits and pieces he can't remember*. Then I heard Ted shouting his orders.

Jarrett squeezed past us. 'Excuse me, Skipper, I've got work to do.'

We were now prepared for the storm. Les had his galley prepared, hot soup broth and fresh bread. Margaret was taking the children below to their little cubby. Ted put Jarrett and George on the pumps. I walked the deck with Ted; we were checking everything. Then, we felt a change in the wind. We saw the whitecaps on the water. She rose her bow up to meet the waves; she had become alive. The first spray came up over the bow. She gently slid down the other side of the wave, ready to meet the next one. You would think that she loved it. She was built for this. You could hear the creaking of her timbers; they had been designed to meet this pressure. You could hear the whistle in her rigging as if she were singing to herself. Ted went into the galley, and I went to the Bridge. Jacko grinned as I got there. '*Daisy May* is happy now.'

'Yes, Jacko, she sure is.' Colin's jacket was on the bench, and so was Cat. I gently put my hand on Cat's back. He didn't move. I was waiting to move my hand quickly out of the way. 'It's good to see you back. Now Jacko has his best friend to talk to.'

'Cat isn't happy. Ted and Margaret have taken the kittens below with Whiskey for the children to play with,' Jacko said.

'Well, I expect him to be at work shortly, catching mice,' I answered.

CHAPTER 23

Every now and again, you could feel a thump as a wave came side on, and hit the side of her hull. To her, it was the same as when you patted a dog on its side; she loved it. I went to my cabin to get some sleep and awoke at 2 am, slid out of my nice, warm bed to go and relieve Jacko. We were still meeting a heavy swell.

'Coffee Jacko?'

I noticed Ted had relieved the two men on the pumps. I started to walk into the galley, but thought of the children. I made my way below; both children were cuddled up to Margaret. They looked happy and content. Then I saw the twinkle of two cat's eyes, then the twinkle of eight kittens' eyes. I thought, I asked myself a question a while ago: Is this a dream? Is it really happening? I am a logical man. I see things practically. On this vessel, there is yes or no; there's no in between. But what I'm looking at now has never been in my rule book. What's in store now?

I went back to the galley. Les was re-stacking his stove with wood, preparing it for breakfast.

'Good morning, Bill, do you think the wind will slacken off at daylight?'

'Yes, Les. I think it will turn to the stern, but I haven't consulted with Jacko yet.'

I went back to the Bridge with two cups of coffee. 'Jacko, what's the wind going to do?'

'Change to our stern, Bill.'

I sat down in my new, comfortable chair with my coffee. I certainly was spoiled in the Navy. I should have gotten a chair like this years ago. Then I heard Lesley's voice behind me.

'You just sit there, Bill, in your comfortable chair, and I will get myself a cup of tea.'

Jacko did one of his little chants. 'Shut up, Jacko.'

'I'm sorry, Lesley. I thought you were asleep. Sit down in your chair, and I will get it for you now.'

I got up quickly before she could argue with me. When I got to the galley, Les was ready for me and handed me her cup of tea, which was in my cup. I went back up onto the Bridge and handed Lesley her tea. 'I'll take the wheel, Jacko. To Jacko, that meant food, and he vanished. 'Lesley, I wish you had told me there were explosives on board.'

'Then, my dear, we are even. You didn't get my tea!' Lesley gave me a cheeky grin.

'Lesley, we cannot go into Cape Town as a trading vessel when we have ammunition and arms aboard. So, Commander Johnson, it becomes very complicated. We will have to declare them. Then they'll ask where are they bound for, and for what? So, we have to go into port as a naval vessel, but I also have cargo to trade. Commander Johnson, this comes under your jurisdiction. What do you suggest? We can talk more after breakfast, as I believe Les needs you at the moment.'

'Certainly, Captain Farquhar.'

'Lesley, before you leave, Ted has Phillip and Dominic on the bilge pumps. I haven't seen much of them; they are not exercising with the others. Is there a problem?'

'Bill, as you know, they trained as naval commandos, so they come under my jurisdiction, but they are your crew and therefore not under my command, but I will have a talk with them.'

'Thank you, Lesley.'

Lesley went down to the galley. I noticed Ted changing the men on the pumps, Phillip and Dominic went into the galley for their breakfast.

The wind had changed to the stern. Ted had put more sails aloft. *Daisy* seemed to be happy. I had not recorded *Daisy* in the logbook; she was listed as *Mary Moore*. I had also not recorded the children in the logbook, but I had made a note in the column on the side. I wrote Daisy and Robbie in pencil.

Jacko and Jarrett returned to the Bridge. Jarrett picked up his sexton and went outside to take his bearings. Jacko grinned at me and looked at the barometer, 'She's happy Bill, she likes the waves pushing her stern.'

'I'm going to get some breakfast. Are you saving your breakfast for later, Jacko?'

'No, Bill, why should I save my breakfast?'

I laughed. 'Because Jacko, half of it is in your beard!'

I went out through the door and down to the galley where Les had my breakfast ready with my coffee. I sat down next to Phillip and Dominic. 'You two are staying very quiet.' I grinned at them. 'Don't you like the cool weather?'

Phillip shook his head. 'I certainly don't! Dominic said we should leave the cold weather where it is. I was born in Australia, where it is lovely and warm.'

'I have the feeling you two are not happy.'

Phillip gave a small cough. 'It isn't that we're not happy; it's just that we want to get back to Australia. We've had enough of war; we've seen too much, and we've lost a good mate. The five that came aboard are professional soldiers; you could call them mercenaries, but I respectfully say that they have an important job to do. Will they ever return?'

'They've lost too many mates during the war and don't know why they've survived. Something has happened to them inside, and they must keep on fighting. We don't want to end up like that! We still have family in Australia; they have nobody left to go home to!'

'I understand. As far as I'm concerned, you are a part of my crew, Australia.' I lifted my hand up looking for the little emblem, but it was on my uniform. As I started to eat my breakfast, I could hear the sound of a violin. The sound was so magical here at sea, it seemed to soothe my very soul and leave a part of my mind at peace. Phillip and Dominic finished their breakfast and got up. They nodded to me and went outside. I ate the rest of my breakfast and listened to the violin. When I had finished, I put my plate in the sink.

Les smiled at me, saying, 'He certainly is good, isn't he?'

I went back onto the Bridge. Daisy was dancing alongside her brother. This is what they must have done to earn enough money to survive. Ted and the rest of the crew were standing or sitting, listening and watching, then I saw Whiskey and the four kittens seeking attention from them. I had never seen anything like this on board *Daisy May* before.

Jacko nudged me. 'Have we been missing something, Bill?'

'Yes, I think so, Jacko.'

Young Robbie didn't seem to get tired; he just kept playing his violin. I could see Margaret. She had taken something out of his violin case and was reading it. Cat stood up. I thought he was staring at the kittens, but then he looked straight at Jacko. Jacko was looking at him. I knew they were talking together. Was it trouble? What were their senses telling them?

Jacko turned to me. 'We think your problem, Bill, with the children, has been solved. Good things for the children ahead!'

Another warning, or a good message with no answer, but I knew I had to wait. Something will happen. I have been told; I have been warned!

Robbie stopped playing his violin and went to put it back in its case, but stopped. He was looking straight at Margaret, who was holding a piece of paper in her hand. She spoke softly to him. I couldn't hear what she was saying.

Jacko looked at me and said, 'She's asking his permission to read the letter.' I saw Robbie nodding his head. Margaret started to read the letter, and I went back to my chair.

'What is happening, Jacko?'

'Good things, good things happening.'

Lesley came out of the galley and shouted, 'Bath time you two, bath time.'

Robbie put the violin back in the case and closed it. He took it with him to the galley, but he left the letter with Margaret, who was still reading it. After she finished, she looked up at me and seemed to be crying. She came up onto the Bridge and handed me the letter. She leaned against Jacko, who put his arm around her and held her tightly. Trevor turned up. He knew there was something wrong with Margaret. I started to read the letter.

Dear Jane,

I'm sorry to hear that we have lost him. You say that his plane went down somewhere over the sea and that they have not found him. It makes things a lot harder. I wish I were there with you to support you. I hope the children are well. I will try to get you to Cape Town, but the war has been a great toll on us. I cannot buy stores for my shop, and we have been selling things to survive. I have sold my father's sword to a Scottish friend who said I could buy it back when I have the money. I will send the money to you, as it rightfully belongs to my older brother. The children are so important to us because we cannot have

our own and they are the future of our family. You say that you've had
a bad cough and hope it will go soon. Everybody seems to have it. My
thoughts are with you. Please keep writing. I will do everything I can
to get you here.
Love to you and the children.
Henry

I looked at Margaret and saw the tears in her eyes. She slowly turned and looked at Jacko. 'You knew, didn't you, Jacko? That's why you brought them on board. You knew they had family who would love and care for them. They say you are a very spooky man.'

She threw her arms around his neck and cuddled him, and said in a whisper, 'That's why I love you so much. Why can't we all be like you and see into the future.'

Margaret turned around to Trevor and pushed him away, saying, 'You are going to give me children, do you hear me? A girl and a boy!' They both walked off, and she said again to him, 'Don't you argue with me.'

Trevor turned to me and winked. He replied to Margaret, 'Yes dear, I will try my hardest.' He gave one of Jacko's little dances.

Margaret went back to the galley and helped Lesley with the children. I turned the envelope over and looked at the back. Fortunately, there was a return address. That makes things a little easier, I thought.

I put the letter back into the envelope and placed it in my logbook. Jacko was standing there, waiting for me to say something. 'When we get to Cape Town, we will visit their uncle, and you will wear your Scottish regalia. Margaret will cut your hair and trim your beard, do you hear me, my brother? You started it, you finish it!'

I looked down at the smaller bunk he had made under the bench. 'If you have something else you haven't told me about, keep it to yourself for a while. I'm too busy at the moment to worry. Coffee Jacko?'

'Sticky buns, Bill.'

'I wonder, Jacko, do we have enough stores aboard to feed you and the crew?'

I glanced around the deck. Lesley was there on the stern; she was talking to Phillip and Dominic. I went into the galley.

Lesley put both her hands out and held Dominic's and Phillip's hands. 'You both belong to me; you will always belong to me. We did so much together, and achieved so much, that nobody else will ever know about. Bill is concerned about the two of you. You have signed on as crew, although you still belong to the British Navy. This is a British naval vessel; you are paid by the British Navy as crew, not as British commandos. Your final destination will be Australia. When, I don't know. As you joined the Navy in Melbourne, you have to be returned to your home port.'

Phillip stared into Lesley's eyes for a moment. He had tears in his eyes. 'Thank you for being straight with us, Lesley. Dominic said we started aboard this vessel and would like to finish aboard this vessel. Bill has spoken with us, and we both feel a lot better.'

Lesley squeezed both of their hands. Phillip spoke again, 'You're worried about leaving Mervyn aren't you?'

'Yes, I am. He also belongs to me, but I can't do anything about it, as it's not within my jurisdiction.'

They saw Ted looking at them, with his hands on his hips. He pointed to the pumps. I had three cups of coffee in one hand and a plate of sticky jam doughnuts in the other. With my head, I gestured to Lesley to follow me. I put the coffee down alongside Jacko, then went to the other end of the Bridge. Jacko couldn't contain himself. 'Cat doesn't eat doughnuts.' I kept my back to Jacko, took out a piece of meat from under the plate, and gave it to Cat.

'Are they good doughnuts, Cat? Would you like another one?' Out of the corner of my eye I could see Jacko trying to keep the vessel on course. I gave Cat another piece of meat. 'Les said you've been missing out; the other cats are getting to the food before you, and you've been letting them do it, so he is going to feed you here, or should I say Jacko is.'

Then I turned around and handed Jacko the plate of doughnuts. I took two and handed one to Lesley, who was standing in the doorway, grinning. When we had finished our coffee and doughnuts, I handed Lesley the letter. 'Margaret found this in the music case.' She looked at me, then looked at the letter, and started to read it.

'Bill, have you entered them in your logbook?'

'No, I haven't.'

She turned and looked at Jacko, who was standing at the wheel looking oh-so-innocent. Speaking very softly, Lesley said, 'Jacko,' and shook her finger at him. 'Yes, Jacko, the witchy would have told you, but I wouldn't take that to court. Bill, I have thought about our problem. We go in as a cargo vessel. If anybody official comes on board and asks the wrong questions, I will be dressed in my uniform.' She gave Jacko a very stern look. 'And Jacko will be dressed in his Scottish uniform. Is that clear, Captain Jacko? You are a British officer, but you don't have a British officer's uniform; you have a Scottish one. Good afternoon, gentlemen.'

'Does that mean I get to wear my medal as well, Bill?'

'You heard the Commander, Jacko. You're a British officer.'

Just then, Ted walked in, looking very frustrated. 'What's wrong, Ted?'

'You have women aboard, then you have children aboard with cats and entertainment, which I will not criticise, but it's very hard to do my job. No respect at all.'

'Are you handling it all, Ted?'

'Yes, Skipper.'

Jacko cheekily looked around Ted's head. 'Bill, there's steam coming out of his ears.'

'Yes, I did notice Jacko. Quite extraordinary, isn't it?'

Ted put his hands in the air. 'No respect here, either!'

'Ted, we will be going into Cape Town as a cargo vessel. I know that we have ammunition, arms, and explosives aboard, but if anybody should ask questions, Commander Johnson will handle the situation. Our berth is #16; we've been there before. The children have relations in Cape Town, so we believe they will be staying in Cape Town.'

Ted didn't look too happy. 'What's wrong, Ted?'

'It's easy to get attached to the children. You try really hard not to, but when we were changing sails to alter course, Margaret was sitting with the children where they were safe; and couldn't get in the way. After we finished, Daisy walked up to me, put her hands on her hips, and said *Teddy, you are very bossy, aren't you*. She went back to Margaret. I don't think she would make a good crew member; she would have my job!' He turned around to Jacko. 'Steam coming out of my ears? Jacko, you are just a big troublemaker. It's good you're here, out of my way. You stay here, I will stay out there,' and he left.

'He's not very respectful to me, Bill,' Jacko said. I had my head down, looking at the charts, and didn't answer him.

'This time tomorrow, we should be entering Cape Town Harbour.' I glanced at the barometer; it was falling slightly. I looked up at the sky.

Jacko spoke. 'We've got wind coming, Bill, not bad wind, but wind.'

'That, along with the current, changes quickly at the Cape. So, you had to be on your guard.' I checked the radar and could just see land in the far distance.

Jacko spoke again. 'Birds looking good, feeding well, not far from land.'

Just then, Jarrett walked in, picked up his sexton, and went back out on the deck. Ted had a man aloft as a lookout and a man on the bow. Jarrett came back in and wrote down his figures and marked in the chart.

'Jarrett, we should be entering port tomorrow morning; we berth at #16. Do your calculations match mine?'

'No, Skipper. I was one wave out.'

'Soon, you will be the big boss, and people will have to be tactful with you. How bigger a wave was it, Jarrett?' He just grinned at me. 'We are entering port as a cargo vessel. If you have any problems, Commander Johnson will sort them out. The children have relations there.' I winked at Jarrett. 'Jacko is officially a Scottish Captain.'

Jarrett winked back at me and said to Jacko, 'You will look very impressive, Jacko, in your new uniform back in port. I will never forget it. I'm going down for my tea, Skipper, before I relieve Jacko. Food, Jacko, glorious food! Nothing like it, glorious food.' He slapped Jacko on the back and disappeared.

Lesley walked in, looking for dirty dishes. 'Jacko, Margaret is waiting for you with a big pair of scissors to trim your hair. We can't have you looking like a scrappy Scottish man, can we?' She widened her eyes and grinned at him, and put two fingers in the air with a scissor-like motion, moving them backwards and forwards.

Jacko hunched his shoulders.

'Lesley, I am the Captain; Margaret is not!'

'But Jacko, Les is going to help. Do you want to argue with him?'

'Lesley, we play chess, and I will beat you!'

'Jacko, you have a date.'

I was looking through my paperwork. Lesley lent on my shoulder. 'Lesley, they do know we are coming, don't they? I've never tied up at that berth before. It's normally reserved for bigger vessels. Do they know we are a naval vessel? It says here we are to put our bow to the south. It sounds like orders from a naval command. Everything tied up with a nice bow.'

'Bill, I talked to Phillip and Reno. They seem to be happy now. I know you talked to them earlier.'

'Yes, all they want is to get home. They are your big brothers, aren't they, Lesley?'

'Yes, they are, Bill.'

'Lesley, could you ask Les to have a list of stores that he needs and get Snowy to write it down on official Navy forms.'

I saw Cat sit up and look at Jacko. They both stared at each other. 'What's wrong now?' Jacko didn't answer. We both kept watching him; he wasn't happy. He was looking out of the window.

Then he shouted, 'Strong wind on the horizon, strong wind.'

CHAPTER 24

I rushed past him and rang the bell. Ted looked up at me. I glanced at the horizon.

Ted started to shout his orders. 'Reef the mainsail, reef the lower topsail, take off all optional and other sails.'

Men were removing any loose items off the deck and making sure everything was lashed down. Margaret took the children below. I shouted out to Margaret to stay with the children. Ted had two men putting shutters on the windows. I went to help them.

Jacko was turning her into the wind to meet the incoming swell. Jarrett and John were on the pumps and lashing themselves down. Les made sure his stove was off. I knew he was stacking dishes away so that they wouldn't get broken. Tommy had started the big motor and was coming back out of the hatch. Cat had disappeared. I looked towards the bow. The first big waves were coming with the wind, which was driving them forward. Lesley came out of the galley with food and water.

'Come up onto the Bridge, Lesley, get yourself into Jacko's bunk underneath the bench and wedge yourself down with blankets.'

I went back into our cabin, snatched the blankets off the bunks, and gave them to Lesley. I saw the bow starting to rise up and looked over the deck to see where everybody was. Ted was lashed to the mainmast as usual. Two men were on the pumps, then I saw Tommy running to the hatch, which hadn't been closed. Shutting the door tight, he lent against it to protect himself from the onslaught of the first wave coming over the bow. I didn't like the way the bow was rising up and up.

'Here we go,' Jacko shouted. Then we were looking at dark green water as we were going down the other side of the wave. Her bow crashed into the next incoming wave, and she started to rise again. Water was splashing all over the decks as she started to rise up again. We could see the sky; it was blue once again. We hit the next crest of the wave, then started to go down the other side. We could see that dirty, dark green water again, and the white foam. We crashed into the next wave; the hull creaked and groaned, but she was designed for this. Water was again splashing over the decks. I looked over to see where Tommy was, but he wasn't there. The water had washed him to the stern. The bow rose up again to meet the next wave. Tommy used this break to throw himself into Trevor and Margaret's cabin.

Jacko laughed, 'She's not going to get pregnant with him there.'

'Jacko, keep your mind on your job.'

Then Jacko gave one of his little dances and chanted some words in his native language. I knew there was trouble. I looked up to see another wave, much, much bigger, coming towards us.

'Jacko, when we get down in the trough, give her full throttle on the motor. Lesley, hold on tight.'

'Why Bill?'

'Just hold on tight!'

We went down into the trough of the wave, and Jacko gave her full throttle as we started to climb up the next wave. We could hear the sound of the roaring sea; it was the devil himself. The shutters on the windows were also adding to the noise. We started to rise up and up; we could just see the crest of the wave with white foam on top. The wind was blowing it away in streaks. We reached the top of the wave; the vessel shook and vibrated as the prop came out of the water. Jacko eased back on the throttle. I rushed forward to help with the wheel as we started to slide down the other side of a wave, but the crest was bigger. Although the vessel seemed to handle it better as she rose up to meet the next wave, it was easier, not so violent, Jacko said that the worst of it had gone. We pushed into a heavy sea for the next hour before it started to calm.

The warm currents were hitting the cold currents, creating the turbulence. I slid back the door and went out onto the deck. Ted had already changed into dry clothes and was waiting for my orders.

'As soon as the crew are alright, Ted, get sail back on her.' Ted started to walk away. 'Ted, are you alright?'

'Yes, Bill, but could you ask Jacko to give us more warning in the future? He is getting slack.'

Ted changed the men on the pumps, who both went into the galley, totally exhausted. I went to the stern and lifted up the hatch. 'Are you all okay, Tommy?'

'Yes, Skipper, just a couple of bruises.'

'Tommy, go and get yourself some coffee.'

I went below to see how Margaret and the children were. 'Everything alright, Margaret?'

'Yes, Skipper, the children have gone to sleep, and so have the cats.' There was Cat curled up next to Whiskey.

'Margaret, you had better thank Tommy for looking after Trevor.' I winked at her, picked up the bucket, and went back on deck and discreetly emptied the bucket and washed it out. I saw Trevor starting to go below to see Margaret and tossed the bucket to him. 'Tommy, could you please go and relieve Jacko?' He nodded, and I went into the galley.

I got the strong impression he thought there was something in the bucket, by the way he stepped back as he caught it at arm's length. He shook his head and grinned at me. I grinned back.

I saw Jarrett and asked him to take the bearings, then go for a rest. I walked up to the forecastle, looking for Phillip. I found him in his hammock, sound asleep on his back, snoring away. I picked up a blanket and covered him. Phillip and John had a hard day, just trying to stand upright and keep on pumping.

From there, I went into the galley. George was sitting on the table, and Lesley was binding his ankle up with bandages. She looked up at me. 'I think it's just a sprained ankle.'

I grinned at George and winked. 'Anything to get attention from the women. Well, George, I've got bad news for you. You are peeling potatoes for a little while.'

Just then, the two children came in with Margaret, and Les disappeared to get their breakfast—bacon, eggs, baked beans on toast, all nicely cut up into squares. Jacko walked into the galley and looked at their breakfast.

'You don't cut it up for me like that, Les,' he said.

Les scowled at him. 'Sit down, Jacko. I might be able to find you something to eat. Will cold toast be alright?'

Margaret handed me a letter, and I opened the envelope. There were two birth certificates in it; they belonged to the children. I glanced up at Margaret.

'They were in the violin case, Skipper. There wasn't anything else.'

'That should make things easier, Margaret.'

She smiled at me. 'Skipper, Trevor has deep trauma.'

I frowned at her. 'Margaret?'

'He woke up from a deep sleep and put his arms around me and said some nice words.'

I saw Tommy's face; he didn't look amused.

Margaret walked away to get her coffee. Jacko found it very funny. Daisy had finished her meal.

She looked at Ted very seriously. 'Totty, why was the sea so angry?'

'Oh, I think you should ask a higher authority than me. Jacko, why was the sea so angry?'

Jacko lifted her up and sat her on the table. Her feet couldn't quite touch the seat. He gave her a cheeky smile and said, 'There are two witchys, one is a cold current the other is a warm current, they are not happy together, and when they meet, the wind, he likes to play his funny games with them. They make the big waves and play very selfishly and don't think of us, but the big mumma wave comes and tells them off. *You are very silly currents, stop playing with the wind; you cause too much trouble.* Then, they have to behave themselves. Big mumma is too big to argue with, that's right, isn't it, Totty?'

'I wouldn't argue with you, Jacko, or add to it.'

Les put Jacko's breakfast in front of him. 'Jacko, we've cooked bacon and eggs. It's late in the day, I know, but it's the easiest thing to cook after a storm. Would you like a small meal later on, like a roast?' He turned and walked off.

Ted grinned at him. 'I think you will be sound asleep, Jacko.'

Margaret's voice broke in. 'Ted, food first, sleep later. That's right, isn't it, Jacko?'

Jacko never even looked up; he just kept on eating. I walked out on deck and watched the setting sun. All the beautiful red and gold colours, so calm and so peaceful. I thought nobody rules the sea, she keeps telling you. *I control, I'm in command here. Take me for granted, ignore me, do not respect me, and you will feel my wrath. Be on guard at all times, keep watching, keep listening, keep watching, those of you who live on the sea and in the sea. Respect us all the time.* The last of the sun slid down below the horizon; darkness once again was coming. I could hear the violin. It was a soothing sound that touched my very soul.

Every voyage is different, but I'd never had children aboard before this voyage. It has been a totally different voyage. In Ted's words, *have we missed something, Skipper*? I turned around and looked towards the galley, listening to the beautiful sounds of the violin, Ted.

I went back onto the Bridge. Jarrett was doing the last of his calculations, looking weary and tired. 'Go to sleep, Jarrett.'

'Yes, Skipper, see you in the morning.'

'Jarrett, be here at 2.30 am.'

'Aye, aye, Skipper.' And he went to his cabin.

Ted walked in, tapped Tommy on his shoulder, and took over the wheel.

'Tommy, be back on deck at 2.30 am.'

'Yes Skipper. I hope the wind stays as it is.'

'Ted, we've got to be on guard now, as you know. The warm and cold currents, the tides, and the winds, they all seem to love the Cape. Too many vessels are lost. We should see the lighthouse about 2.30 am Ted, and I want Jarrett to see this for his future knowledge. I'm going to shut my eyes for a while. When Lesley comes in, wake me. Who have you got on deck?'

'Young Trevor's on watch.'

'So, Margaret will be with him.'

'No, Skipper, she's with the children.'

'I couldn't argue with her.'

'I understand Ted.' I sat back in my chair.

Next thing I knew, I woke up with Lesley's head resting against mine. She had coffee and food, but my head was still a little thick. I didn't want to wake up, but this wasn't the time to play games; these are very dangerous waters. 'Thank you, Lesley.' I took the coffee. This certainly was good coffee to wake me up.

I stood up, holding my coffee with one hand and taking the wheel with the other. 'See you at 2.30 am, Ted.'

'Bill, you certainly snore better nowadays!'

He was gone before I could think of a reply. Lesley sat down in her chair, closed her eyes, and fell asleep.

We had a full sail on the vessel, and she was pulling against the rudder. I wanted to get Lesley a blanket, but I couldn't let the wheel go. Just then, Cat sat up and looked at me. I could hear Colin's voice in my head *'Look after him, Bill, teach him all that you know. Fair winds to you.'*

Cat sat down, and I heard Jacko mumbling in his sleep. Teach who? But Colin had gone. I looked at Jacko asleep. What are you two up to now? Another loose end. I looked at the smaller bunk. Why did Jacko have that built? Lesley made a small sound in her sleep and rolled over in the armchair. Whatever the future has in store, I certainly have found the right partner; I will not be alone. I glanced back at Jacko. You are a part of me, like another arm. I grinned. If only our mum could have seen him in that Scottish regalia, she would have been so proud.

Then, in the darkness, there was a flash, then another, very faint, then another. We were at the Cape of Good Hope.

Just then, Jarrett walked in with Ted. I looked at the clock; not quite 2.30.

'Ted, could you please gently wake Jacko up without waking Lesley?'

Ted went down on his knees, put his head next to Jacko, and whispered in his ear, 'food, bacon and eggs, sticky jam doughnuts, chocolate slice, honey on bread.'

Jacko's head raised up, nearly knocking Ted over. He blinked twice. 'Where's my food?'

I put my finger up to my mouth to say *silence*. He looked straight at me, then stood up.

'Jarrett, there is the Cape Lighthouse. It's known as the new lighthouse and was built in 1919. There is another lighthouse on the point; it is called the Roman Rock. It guards the entrance to the naval dockyard. If there is fog or low cloud you will see it. This is a very dangerous stretch of water. There are many lighthouses; they are staggered on the mainland so that you can only see one at a time. The Flying Dutchman is a good lighthouse; it is perched high up on the land. Jarrett, you haven't as yet had the opportunity to come in from this direction, so I would like you to study these lighthouses, the Roman Rock, Danger Point, Cape Augusta, Port Elizabeth East, London Durban Naval base, Simon's Town Cape, and Relieve Lighthouse Danger Point, which is where the Lusitania was lost. Yes, the original one. I want you, Jarrett, and Jacko on the Bridge. Your food will be brought to you. Ted, if you could get somebody aloft and somebody on the bow as a look-out, in one hour we will stow the sails and start the motor. Tommy, oil and water.'

Lesley's voice boomed out. 'What are all you people doing waking me up at this time of the morning?'

I knew my team was working well. We all pointed at Jacko. He shouted *'Food'* and was gone.

Lesley smiled and said, 'This means work Bill, doesn't it?' She headed off to the galley.

'Ted, get Trevor to look after the children, and have Margaret come on deck. Jarrett, I'm going to shut my eyes for two hours.'

I glanced at the barometer; it was holding steady. I lay down on my bunk, but it was Lesley's bunk, with fluffy blankets, fluffy pillows, and it smelled of her.

Next thing I woke and was looking straight into Lesley's face. She knelt down, her arms were folded, and she was looking straight at me.

'Time to get up, my darling.' I stood up, my mind was racing: How much sail? How close are we to land? Have there been any problems? I put my arms around Lesley and kissed her on her forehead.

I went onto the Bridge and checked the chart. Jarrett had recorded everything in meticulous detail. The barometer was still holding steady.

I tapped Jarrett on the shoulder. 'Good man, Jarrett, good man. Has Jacko been giving you any trouble?'

'Skipper, Jacko is Jacko, always giving me trouble.'

I walked past Jacko and nudged him on the shoulder. 'Food, Jacko?'

'Very funny Bill, yes food.'

'Jacko, Mum taught you manners. Yes, please, Bill.'

I kept on walking; through the darkness, I could see flashes from the lighthouses. They were getting stronger as we neared them. I could just make out flashes from the Roman Rock Lighthouse. I looked up to see what canvas Ted still had aloft. He certainly makes my job easier, always on the mark. I saw young Robbie McGregor, 'How are you, Robbie?'

'Very excited. I've never seen anything like these lighthouses.'

'Yes, Robbie. I don't know how the old seamen in the past did without them; they are our eyes in the dark. We will be entering port just at daylight. Could you do a very important job for me?'

'Yes, what is it you want me to do?'

'Well, if you get yourself something to eat and something for Tommy, also a cup of coffee for Tommy, could you take it to the bow and stay with him? It is a very important position on a vessel going into port. Could you do that for me, please, Robbie?'

'Yes, Captain, yes.'

'Good lad.' Off he went to the galley. I followed him and got two cups of coffee. Les had two plates of bubble and squeak, bacon and eggs, and toast. There's nothing like freshly baked bread, toasted.

He smiled at me. 'I've never been able to fill him. Where he puts it all, I don't know!'

I grinned back at him. 'Les, as long as he stays at the helm and keeps warning me, keep feeding him!'

I walked back onto the Bridge and gave Jacko his breakfast. I saw the grin on his face. Mum used to enjoy seeing that grin. I gave Jarrett his breakfast. 'If you have trouble eating all your breakfast, Jarrett, Jacko will help you.'

Jarrett replied, laughing, 'Do you want the plate back? He will eat that, too.'

I raised my eyebrows, shook my head, and left them to it.

Margaret was on deck, coiling rope. 'Good morning, Margaret, how is Daisy?'

'Sound asleep with Trevor, one cat, and four kittens in my nice, warm, and comfortable bed.'

'Robbie is on the bow with Tommy, filling their faces with food. You can't understand a word they're saying. Have you thought about what's going to happen when we reach port, Margaret?'

'Yes, Skipper. I have to let them go. Trevor and I have talked about it, and he promises me a Daisy and Robert.'

'Don't work him too hard, Margaret, or he is no good to me in the mornings. He's all tired and weary.'

Margaret giggled. 'He is not doing too badly at the moment, Skipper.'

'Coffee, Margaret?'

'Yes, please.' We both went into the galley.

Ted was talking to one of the crew. I walked up alongside him. 'Excuse me, Ted, I'm going up to the bow to relieve Tommy for a moment. I want him to start the motor. Make sure Margaret is with him so she can do the job in an emergency. The breeze had turned a little colder, so I picked up two jackets and took them to the bow, and handed one to young Robbie and put on the other. 'Tommy, could you start the motor?'

Young Robbie's voice boomed out, 'Could I go with him please? I've never seen the big motor.'

I put both my hands on my hips, saying, 'Robbie, I am the Captain of this vessel. I gave you a job to do; that is your responsibility.' He put his head down. 'To stay here as a lookout, is that correct? If you don't carry out orders on a vessel like this, what happens? You could hit something, and the vessel would sink. Good man, and because you're a passenger on this vessel, you can go with Tommy, but when Tommy returns, you have to stay with him. He will be relying on you.'

Tommy, with his big eyes, winked at me. He turned and beckoned Robbie to go with him. I stood there watching the lights, was I too hard on the young lad, or was it a good lesson for him? Hopefully, it was the second. He's a good lad. He's done a good job looking after his sister, and he has talent.

I saw the first glimpse of daylight, then the sound of the motor. What's in store for us now? What did Colin do when we left the Cape and entered the Indian Ocean, the unpredictable ocean? Just then, I heard Robbie's voice talking so quickly in his Scottish accent. I knew he was talking about the big motor and the noise. I turned around; Tommy was frowning at me. I tapped him on the shoulder, 'Ted will have you relieved shortly Tommy.' I walked back to the galley; Ted wasn't there. 'Right lads, finish your meal, go on deck, and stay sharp.' Just then Daisy and Trevor walked into the galley. 'Good morning, did you sleep well?'

She pointed at Trevor. 'He snores!' She walked over to Les. 'Les, Trevor is very hungry; he worked last night, then he looked after me and the cats.'

I left the galley, grinning. If she were aboard for six months, she would be Captain. I went back to the Bridge. I knew never to interfere with Jacko when we were entering a port. His concentration was so deep when he was working. He peered out of the door, looking at the sails. I saw him glance at Ted, who nodded and shouted his orders. The crew sprang to work; the man aloft shouted out and pointed to our port side. There was a small fishing boat just a bit too close. Tommy pointed to the starboard, and Jacko turned the wheel slightly to starboard. The man aloft pointed straight to the bow. Tommy stopped, pointing to starboard, meaning our passage was clear, and we were entering port. The law of the sea is that powered vessels give the right of way to sailboats.

I wanted to steer, but I knew not to interfere with Jacko. He was in his element, back in the desert, using all his senses. He was watching the seagulls flying high, swerving and diving, using the wind to play their games. The ripples on the surface told him where the currents were flowing and their strengths. I watched him with a sense of deep pride. We were coming closer to Wharf 16, where we were to berth. Ted walked up alongside me; he didn't say a word. He also knew not to interfere with Jacko.

'Port side.' Ted was back out on deck, giving his orders. Jacko was watching the wind, and its strength. He knew how to bring the vessel alongside the wharf, and for the vessel to kiss it, like the touch of a feather. We started to turn broadside to the wharf. Ted had her bow lines ready; they had a length of rope tied to them with a seaman's knot on one end, which they could throw to a man on the wharf.

I said to myself, *here we go* Daisy May, *you are beautiful. Jacko certainly loves you,* Daisy May.

Jacko gently put the gear stick into reverse, and she came to a stop just touching the wharf. He put the gear stick into neutral, turned and looked at me with a cheesy grin on his face. I couldn't help myself. 'One day, Jacko, you will get it right!'

He did one of those little dances and said a few words in his native language. I thought I was the only person that understood what he had said, but I heard Lesley answer him in native language, and she burst out laughing. Jarrett looked totally confused. I shook my head, 'Jarrett you wouldn't want to know what they said. It is just about 7.30 am, please enter it in the log.'

Jacko had gone; he just disappeared. Ted had the gangplank secured.

CHAPTER 25

A big black car pulled up on the wharf. The driver got out and very discreetly opened the back door, a man got out. He was dressed in a dark suit, and was carrying a briefcase. I went down to the gangplank and waited at the top.

The man stopped and stared at me for a moment, and in a commanding voice said, 'Captain Farquhar?'

'Yes, I am.'

'I've been told that I have to ask permission to come on board, sir.'

'You have my permission.'

His eyes flashed around to make sure that nobody was listening. 'I have business with Commander Johnson.'

'Follow me to the Bridge, sir.'

This man had to know that I am the Captain, but first of all I had to ask, 'Who are you, sir?' He handed me his business card. It read Commander Walter Simpson. I didn't bother reading the rest, I just escorted him to the Bridge.

Lesley stepped out of our quarters and spoke to the man. 'Wally, how are you?'

He looked at her very seriously. 'Lesley, could you get that uniform off and look like an ordinary seaman.' His eyes were flashing his command.

Lesley put her head to one side as though she didn't want to argue, but wanted to know why. 'Excuse me, gentlemen, for just a moment.' She disappeared into our quarters.

Wally put his briefcase on the bench, turned and put his hand out. I shook his hand. He had a strong grip. 'Captain.'

'Call me Bill.'

'Yes, Bill, the least people who know I'm here the better. If we had taken you into the naval yard, there would have been too many questions. As you are here as a merchant vessel, I have arranged for fuel and water, six 44 gallon drums of water. We think you may need more. I would like a list of any other stores you require.'

Just then, Lesley walked out. 'That looks a lot more comfortable, Lesley. We have heard a rumour that there are those who are looking for you. You are in a very dangerous position politically, so you know why you should stay a seaman on this vessel, and you must keep your men under control. They are not to disembark. Mrs Henderson is very concerned. Your mission is extremely important. We don't want any loose tongues wagging.' His eyes flickered to Jarrett. 'Good morning Captain Collins, enjoying your holiday?'

Jarrett smiled. 'Yes sir, very much.'

'I have been informed by British authorities to get you home as soon as we can. After this mission, we will get you home.'

'Thank you sir, I would appreciate that.'

'Enjoy your holiday. You have a big job to do when you get home. Lesley, is there any more that I can do for you?'

'Yes, there is. Strictly off the record.' Wally smiled at Lesley.

'Lesley, you outrank me, so it's off the record.'

'Thank you Wally. Three days out to sea, we found that we had two children aboard.' Wally put his head back and frowned at her. 'They are homeless and came on board during the night. How they got on board is another question. We have found that they have relatives here in Cape Town. Their father died during the war and their mother died of pneumonia. Their father's brother lives here.' Lesley reached out and Jarrett put the letter in her hand. She handed it to Wally.

Wally read the letter and raised his eyebrows. 'Yes, I know Mr McGregor. He is one of the most respected men here. During the war, he just about sent himself bankrupt by looking after others. I must admit they were Scotsmen and Freemasons. He was true to the craft.'

I raised my eyebrows and glanced at Lesley. Wally continued, 'He owns the biggest clothing store here in Cape Town and has two or three warehouses trading in whatever he can trade. I know him well.'

Lesley put her hands in her lap. I know that some women do this when they are playing their games with men. 'Could you arrange for him to come down to see us and meet the children? We have their birth certificates.'

'Lesley, a friend of mine told me not to play chess with you, or a man called Jacko! I will go and ring him now,' Wally answered.

Just then, Lesley saw Jacko walking up the deck in his full Scottish regalia, including his sword and a dirk. 'Wally, have you ever met Captain Jacko?' she asked.

'Yes, I have. I was one of the team who gave him his ticket at Dartmouth, aboard this very vessel.'

'Well, Wally, he has changed a lot since then. In fact, he is just coming through the door.'

Wally stepped back. His eyes widened as he blinked. Margaret had trimmed Jacko's hair and beard, and his clothes were freshly pressed. Jacko stared at Wally and put one hand on the hilt of his sword, and stood erect. He boomed out, 'I know you! You were at Dartmouth. I had to explain the questions to you, as you didn't know them.'

Words couldn't come out of Wally's mouth. He was totally shocked and surprised, then he burst out laughing. 'This makes my day. Children aboard a naval vessel and a Scottish Captain from Australia! And Indigenous! I think I have seen everything now. Don't you take that regalia off, you will make my friend's day. I remember you so well. You have more knowledge of the sea than any naval officer.'

Lesley's voice broke in. 'Please don't tell him all that Wally, we have to live with him aboard this vessel.'

Wally turned to Jacko. 'Any time you want to join my crew, just let me know.' He left to make his phone call.

Lesley walked out behind him. She wanted to know how the children were. She knew she was going to miss them. She wiped a tear away with her sleeve before entering the galley. Robbie was just getting his violin out to play. Tommy had lifted Daisy up onto the table so that she could dance. Les asked Lesley if Jacko had made an impression on the visiting gentleman.

'He certainly did. The man who had come aboard was totally shocked. He is now contacting the children's uncle.'

Just then, Ted walked in. He went to say something but stopped and got himself a coffee. He knew this would be the last time he would hear the violin and see the children. He wouldn't be able to have conversations with little Daisy. Something deep down inside him was lost. He didn't want to admit the answer.

Robbie started to play the violin, and everybody sat and listened. Daisy started to dance like a little fairy, so perfect, so gentle, they certainly could mesmerise anybody. Three quarters of an hour had passed in just one second.

Ted spun around to see a lady crying at the door, with a man wearing a red beard alongside her. The lady had a lace handkerchief and was wiping her eyes. She slowly walked towards the children. She was one of those warm, compassionate people. I could sense it straight away. She put her arms out to the children. 'I am your auntie and this is your uncle; he is your father's brother. We are going to protect and look after you both.'

She stood up straight and looked around at the people in the galley. She was sobbing and wiping tears away. 'My husband and I would like to thank all of you for keeping our family safe and bringing them to us. We were lost. We couldn't find out what had happened to the children, or where they were, and now you have brought them here to us.'

She went back to the children and put her arms out to them. They both stepped into her arms. We knew the children were home.

The man with the red beard stepped forward. He was definitely a Scotsman. 'Robbie, my boy, we will find you the best tutor we can find to help you with your violin studies. You have a marvelous talent. Both your parents could play musical instruments as well. I will take you fishing. We will walk in the hills with you. The mountain at the back of the Cape is like Scotland, so you will feel at home.'

Ted's voice broke in. 'I'm sorry to break this up, lads, but we've got work to do. Hatch covers off, yardarm to be stowed and rigging prepared.'

Each one of the crew slowly walked past the two children and said their goodbyes.

As they left, Daisy turned towards her uncle saying, 'This is Totty. He is very bossy, but I like him. He is my friend, aren't you Totty?'

Ted was trying to keep his emotions locked in. 'Daisy, you and I will be friends until the end of time, and I do hope to see you again soon. I must go now as I have a job to do.'

'Yes Totty,' Daisy replied. She walked to the end of the table and put her arms out and cuddled him. He gently cuddled her back and slowly let her go. He walked out the door, closing it behind him. He stood outside the door for a moment, trying to control the pain in his chest, trying to cope with the lump in his throat. Then he pulled himself together and started shouting his orders to the crew to prepare the vessel for leaving port.

Daisy turned to her aunt. 'This is Margaret, and this is Lesley. They have been mummies to us. I don't want to go, but Robbie tells me they have a job to do and they must do it and not complain.'

Les walked out of the galley and went to the stern. He couldn't take it anymore. He had fallen in love with the two children and the pain of losing his own children was back. He had locked them away in his heart where they couldn't hurt him. He needed time to himself.

The lady sat down and the gentleman sat down alongside her. 'I am Henry McGregor,' he stated, 'and this is my wife, Margaret. We can't have children of our own and you have brought us a daughter and a son that belong to us. They are our family. We cannot thank you enough.'

Lesley sighed deeply. 'Well, I think you ought to thank Jacko, he is responsible for the children coming aboard. We don't want the authorities to know there would be too many questions.'

Just then, Jacko, the Commander, and I walked into the galley. Henry McGregor stood up. He was totally surprised. He walked towards Jacko and shook his hand. I thought Jacko's arm was going to fall off. Lesley said, 'May I present Captain Jacko Farquhar and Captain William Farquhar, or I should say Bill? He is the Captain of this vessel.

Henry looked totally surprised. He put his hand on Jacko's shoulder. 'I really do not know what to say, Captain Jacko, but my wife and I are truly grateful to you.'

He took out a small flask from his jacket pocket, he unscrewed the top and handed it to Jacko, who took a sip and handed it back. Henry put it back in his pocket.

Daisy's voice boomed out, 'there is a big mummy wave and a big daddy wave. Jacko is the big daddy wave who looks after everybody on the ship.'

Some of the crew were grinning, others were laughing. I put my hand out and shook Henry's. Henry's eyes widened. I nodded.

'I believe we can do business together, Henry. I have cargo aboard you may be interested in. If I can get you to sit down with Snowy, he will go over the paperwork with you, so that you fully understand the cargo. The man who can vouch for me is Mr Gibby McKay.'

Henry's eyes had a smile in them. 'Yes, I went to school with him. I grew up with Gibby.'

'So Henry, our trade will be done through him.'

Snowy and Henry sat down with the very impressive-looking Jacko. The ladies started to chatter. Les walked back to the galley. I nodded to him to come back out on deck. Wally went back out the door.

'Les, how is George's ankle?' I asked.

'I looked at it this morning, Bill. I don't really like the colour, it's blue. I was going to talk to you about it. I think he needs to go to a hospital.'

I glanced at Wally, who replied, 'I'll take him to the naval hospital myself. If they give him morphine, he might talk, and others could ask questions. Les, do you have the list of stores you require?'

'Yes, I will get it from Snowy.' He walked off into the galley.

'Bill, I had thought the war was over and all the politics would end, but they had started all over again. Paperwork everywhere, politicians getting the credit, never the blame,' he sighed. 'I envy you being at sea where they can't get at you.'

Just then Les walked in with his list and handed it to Wally.

I beckoned to Ted. 'Could you have two men get the stretcher. George is going to the hospital.'

Ted shook his head. 'Couldn't you get somebody else Bill? George is one of my best men.'

'Yes Ted, I understand perfectly.'

With frustration in his voice, Ted shouted at two men, and a stretcher appeared. Wally sighed. 'Bill, high tide is at 5 pm tomorrow. Do you think you'd be ready to sail by then?'

'Yes,' I replied.

Cat was sitting at the gangplank. Wally stopped and stared at him. 'Don't argue with the Cat, Wally. He's the best security officer we've got!'

Wally walked around him, George followed, being carried on his stretcher.

Ted's voice boomed out. 'You two, back on deck.'

They grinned at him. No pub today.

I went back into the galley and sat down alongside Snowy. Henry McGregor said with a big chuckle, 'The best cargo I've had for a long time, Scottish fish, the best of Scottish clothing, all made by the best Scotland has. They'll be sold before I've even got them on the counter, and the price is right.'

I raised my eyebrows. I'd never talked to Henry about the price, but the deal had been done.

Snowy started to speak, but paused. 'Bill, I don't know what you think about this, but Wally has quite a number of barrels of wine that were produced during the war, but there wasn't a market for them. He bought them from a friend to help him out. You need a cargo, you need weight in the hull. I know your policy on alcohol, but you would get a good price for this cargo. With the weight we are discharging and the weight of the wine, they would balance each other out.'

I clamped my teeth together. I needed weight, and I needed it now, but the crew bringing alcohol aboard is different? Am I just justifying it? No! I have to have weight. I put my hand out and shook Henry's hand.

'You send the money for the cargo you have bought to Gibby McKay, and I will pay for the wine.'

Henry shook his head. 'No, we are in a partnership. Whatever you sell it for, we split 50/50.'

'We have a deal.' I shook his hand.

Snowy commented, 'So our paperwork, Bill, will say 140 barrels of assorted wines, red and white. Year 1945 or younger.'

'It's a very bonny day today, it has been marvelous. We now have two children. Margaret is now a mother, and I have stores which will tickle the fancy of my customers,' Henry said.

Everybody walked out to leave. Les had parcels of food for them. Margaret had their clothes. The crew had stopped working and joined in saying goodbye. They got to the bottom of the gangplank. Jacko was following them. He started to get into the back of the car.

'Where do you think you're going, Jacko?'

'Bill, we Scots have to stick together. I'm going out to have dinner with some Scottish friends. I'll be staying onshore tonight.'

I stepped back. I couldn't think of anything to say. Ted was standing there with his mouth wide open, but no words coming out. Les just shook his head.

Just then, the children ran up to Margaret and Lesley and cuddled them both. Robbie went to Les and put his hand out and shook Les's hand and nodded very politely. Daisy ran to Ted and wrapped her arms around his legs. Ted reached down and picked her up and cuddled her. He whispered to her, 'you're my little angel, and I will always be with you.' He kissed her on the forehead and walked her to the car, put her in the seat next to Jacko, and stepped back. I knew he had his teeth gritted together to keep his emotions locked in.

The car drove off, everybody waved, and they were gone. Everyone just stood there. Then in a low voice, Ted said, 'Come on lads, back to work.' He turned and walked back up the gangplank and came face-to-face with Les. There were 1000 works spoken silently between them. Ted put his hand on Les's shoulder and kept walking up the gangplank.

Lesley slipped her arm in mine and we walked up the gangplank together. Les put his arm around Margaret. She pressed into his side, sobbing. We had coffee, but somehow we couldn't eat the sticky buns.

Les shook his head. 'When he gets back, I'm going to ring his neck. Everywhere we go, he is number one. He doesn't know his own charm, the cheeky little sod. If you were to send a photo of him now to his people, what would they say?' He walked off, shaking his head and mumbling to himself.

Just then, a truck turned up to pick up the cargo. Others were bringing wine in big barrels. It was hard work for the crew, but Mervyn and his colleagues seemed to love it. It was much better than their exercises.

I saw Lesley looking ashore, but she was doing it very discreetly. She walked up behind Mervyn and spoke to him. Mervyn looked like he was joking with her, and he turned around like a ballet dancer and faced Lesley again.

I watched Mervyn very quietly talking to his five colleagues. He was pointing to this barrel and that barrel. They all laughed. One of them nudged Mervyn, and Mervyn nudged him back. Lesley walked up to Ted and was talking to him. Ted walked up to the six of them and said in a loud voice, 'Go ashore and roll those barrels out of the way.'

I wanted to go out on the deck to see what was going on, but something stopped me. These are Lesley's men. What was happening? The five men went ashore and started to move the barrels, but why?

I knew Ted had to be careful reloading the vessel, making sure the weight was evenly spread along the keel. They had to remove some, replace some, but this didn't fit. I watched the men, they had spread out, then I noticed another man standing in a doorway, watching the vessel. He was dressed very neatly and was wearing a hat. Then I realised three of Lesley's men could not be seen. Where were they?

Mervyn and the other two started to argue over the barrels, causing a scene. The man in the doorway was watching them very carefully. All of a sudden, the man was lying flat on the ground. Three of Lesley's men were on top of him, pinning him down. Mervyn and the other two ran over to help them. They lifted him to his feet, they had his hands behind his back, somebody's belt was wrapped around his arms and pulled tight.

Lesley ran down the gangplank towards them. When she got there Mervyn stood in front of her, protecting her. The other men had given the strange man a thorough body search, slipping his coat over his shoulders and down to his hands. One of Lesley's men had a pistol, and it looked like it had a silencer on it. Another one was holding a knife. It appeared to be a switchblade.

They pushed the man back into the doorway. Lesley went over to the phone and rang someone. I couldn't hear what she was saying. She hung up the phone and went back to the doorway. I went to walk out of the Bridge, but stopped. I wanted to know what was happening, but I couldn't do it. It was out of my jurisdiction. I am the Captain of this vessel, not the wharf.

I saw Ted shaking his head, as if to say *no* to me. Twenty minutes passed, then two black cars turned up, and the man was ushered into the back seat of one of the cars. They had put chains on his ankles.

Wally got out of the other car. They gave him the man's revolver and other items. They all got into the car and drove off.

Lesley walked back up the gangplank, and the others followed her. They went into the galley and I followed them. Ted had beaten me there and was holding the door open for me. I walked into the galley and looked at Lesley. I raised my eyebrows and titled my head slightly. She looked at me very seriously. 'Bill, thank you for not interfering. Ted, you played the game very well. Bill, that man was a high ranking German Gestapo agent. He is known as *The Assassin*. He is wanted by Nuremberg for war crimes and is now being taken straight to the airport. His destination is Nuremberg. Mervyn and I met him twice in Germany when we were having secret meetings with high-ranking officials. He's a totally cold man. We will never know what atrocities he has committed.

The rest of the day went by quickly. Unloading and loading, each barrel contained 100 gallons, so the crew certainly got some exercise. Soon it was evening. Ted had the crew covering the hatch for the night. I walked up to Ted and we talked about the cargo. 'Do we need anything more to secure the load?'

'No Skipper, the top row will be up against the side of the hull wedging them in. The 44 gallon drums of water are next to the water tanks, so far the plimsoll line is even.'

Just then Mervyn and the rest of the crew walked past us. With a chuckle Mervyn said, 'The best day we've had Skipper, putting our talents to work and getting some good exercise.'

'Ted, I'll ask Lesley to put some of her crew on guard tonight.'

Ted gave a loud chuckle. 'That'll calm him down, Skipper!'

I went into the galley and looked at Les. He wasn't himself. He was dropping pans in the sink and mumbling to himself. I looked at Margaret, she just hunched her shoulders, letting me know she didn't know. I walked up behind him. 'What's wrong Les?'

He turned around, his eyes flashed at mine. 'It's Jacko, what is he doing, where is he, what will they do with him?'

'Les, he got the children aboard, he brought them home, they are very grateful to him. The Scottish people gave him the highest honours they could, and that was the regalia he was wearing. That is his accreditation to the Scottish people. Let him have his moment, he certainly deserves it. Les, you have to let your son go sometimes. He's all grown up. Even the Captain of this port respects him for his knowledge of the sea. He has made his mark. Let him enjoy it, Les.'

I put my hands on his shoulders. 'We can still worry. He is ours and we both love him, but we must let him have his time.'

CHAPTER 26

Lesley and I had our tea and turned in early for the night. We were both sitting on the bunk, very tired and weary. 'Bill, we both have to get up at daylight tomorrow, and I will be dressing up in my Navy uniform when we leave the Bridge. I will say some words to you, rather sharply. Please don't argue with me, just accept what I'm doing. Everything will take its course.' She put her arms around my neck. 'And don't let anybody know I love you.'

She lay down on her bunk and seemed to be sound asleep. I climbed up onto my bunk and lay there thinking, what do I put in my logbook? What would make sense? What was Lesley up to? Just let things take their course. What's Jacko doing? I don't want Les to get upset. The children leaving brought back pain to him.

Lesley was up before me, dressing in her uniform. I lay on my bunk, looking down at her. She looked up at me. 'Lesley, I am enjoying this.'

'You are a typical man, Bill! I hope you're not to be trusted later on. Now, come on, get up.'

Daylight was well upon us as we walked out of the Bridge. Lesley stood for a moment outside the door where she could be seen, winked at me, then said, 'Bill, I am a naval officer, when I'm given a command I carry it out, so don't argue, and please don't talk to me like that. I have to go.' She turned and walked down to the galley, and I followed her. She reminded me of my mum and the way she spoke to Jacko and me when we were little.

We both walked into the galley. There was another woman in there. I didn't know what I was looking at. I looked at Lesley, then I looked at the other lady. There were two Lesleys. Margaret was trimming the other lady's hair. My Lesley walked over to the other Lesley and shook her hand. 'Thank you for volunteering.' She turned to Les, 'Have you fed him well?'

'Yes Lesley, I have.' He looked totally out of control.

The word *him* kept going around in my mind, it just didn't compute.

Just then, the door opened and Commander Wally walked in. He looked at both women and chuckled to himself. 'Would the real Lesley Johnson please step forward?' Humour stepped in and they both stepped forward. Wally grinned, 'I know you are the real Lesley. You're wearing the right grade on your uniform, and I can't mistake that nose.'

'Wally, you did a good match. Do you think I should change over my braid?'

'No Lesley, everything will happen so quickly. You will drive straight to the airport.' He winked at Lesley and realised what he'd said. 'Board a naval aircraft and take off straight away.' He turned to the other Lesley. 'Are you ready, Lesley?'

In a deep manly voice, the other Lesley answered, 'Yes sir.' He picked up an overnight bag and followed Wally out the door. I followed them, still a little confused. I stood at the top of the gangplank. Lesley stood there for a moment, turned to Mervyn and shook his hand, gently resting her head on his shoulder. Mervyn didn't look happy, but played along. He, she, he turned to me, threw both his arms around my shoulder and kissed me full on the lips, then turned and walked down the gangplank. I looked at Mervyn in total shock. Letting him know with my eyes, don't laugh.

Lesley's double got to the back door of the car. A man opened it for her. She turned and saluted me. I saluted back and then the car sped off to the airport. I stood there for a while, trying to sort out my thoughts. An ambulance turned up. It was George being returned. He was taken into the galley. Then three more trucks turned up.

The car that Lesley's double was taken away in pulled up alongside an aircraft, which was waiting on the runway. Lesley's double got out of the back seat and stood there talking to Wally for a few minutes. She slowly walked up the steps into the plane. At the top of the stairs, she turned and saluted Wally, who saluted back. She entered the aircraft, the door closed, the steps were removed, and she started taking off the female navy officer's clothing, and put on his pilot's uniform. He removed the wig and wiped his face with a towel to remove all the make up. He went through to the cockpit and sat down in the pilot's seat.

'Radio through to control tower, 1456 ready for takeoff.'

'Control tower, you have permission to take off. Wind coming from the east 10 km.'

Within minutes, the plane took off. When it eventually landed in England, the three pilots disembarked. A well-dressed man asked them if there were any passengers aboard, to which one of the pilots replied, 'No sir, we are a cargo plane, not a passenger plane.'

The man asked where they had come from.

'This is a naval plane, not a civilian plane. That information is classified.' The pilots kept on walking. They did mention the man to their superior officer.

CHAPTER 27

Back at the dock, I went into the galley to check on George. I thanked the ambulance drivers. George's ankle had a plaster cast on it. 'Well, George, what was the problem?

A badly twisted ankle, bruising and ruptured ligaments.'

He handed me some papers from the hospital. It was, as George had said, a badly sprained ankle, plaster to remain on for two weeks.

'Well George, I've got some bad news for you.'

George had a very serious look on his face.

'You are replacing Colin, peeling potatoes for the next three weeks, and any other little tasks Les can give you. I'll have one of the good chairs brought up from below for you.'

I glanced out of the window. Cat was sitting at the top of the gangplank. That only meant one thing: Jacko was coming back. I glanced at my watch: 11 am. A car pulled up and Jacko climbed out of the back seat. Two men got out and shook his hand. They got back into the car and drove off. Jacko, still in his full Scottish regalia, stopped at the top of the gangplank, knelt down to Cat. Anybody that was watching them would not know what Jacko was saying to Cat. He picked up Cat and walked towards the galley.

When he got inside, Margaret was there with both hands on her hips. She looked annoyed and said, 'Where are they?'

Jacko looked at Cat saying, 'You tell me off. Now Margaret is going to tell me off, then I will have to face Whiskey and George. And to Margaret, he replied, 'The coat you gave the children had very big pockets. Daisy has one kitten and Robbie has the other. Could you find a better home for them?'

He put Cat down on the floor and stood up with both his hands on his hips and in a very cheeky manner said again, 'Could you find a better home for them, Margaret?'

Just then, Cat gave a big meow and went to the door. Jacko gave a small laugh and chanted some words in his native language. 'So, he is here'. Cat and Jacko went out of the door. Everybody was confused.

CHAPTER 28

'Who is here?' Les said. With the exception of Lesley, who remained inconspicuously hidden in the back of the galley, they followed Jacko and Cat out of the door. Jacko and Cat walked down the gangplank and met with a woman who had two children with her, a boy about 15 years of age and a girl a little younger. I was watching from the Bridge and so was Jarrett. Jacko invited them up the gangplank. Ted was standing there puzzled, but not wanting to interfere. Jacko took the visitors to the galley. He looked up at me and beckoned me to come down to the galley. I did so and Jarrett followed me. Jacko also beckoned to Ted.

The lady was sitting at the table. Les was sitting with her, holding one of her hands, and talking to her. 'We lost Colin, he had severe cancer in his chest. He decided to end the pain himself. Yes, he was the Bosun of this vessel. He was also my best friend.' There were tears in his eyes.

The lady took some paperwork out of her bag. I reached forward and took the papers and read the first one. It was a marriage certificate between Colin Garland and Tracey Newton. There were also two birth certificates, one for the boy, Colin Garland, and for the girl, Juliette

Garland. I glanced at Jacko and shook my head. Now I knew why he had a smaller bunk made in the Bridge.

The lady, Tracey, had a very sad look on her face. 'I checked every sailing vessel that came into port, but it was always the wrong name. I was looking for *Daisy May*, and when this vessel came into port, I thought I was wrong again. But, nobody can change the name of this vessel because I knew it so well. Colin, Ted, and I met quite a number of years ago. I was just a young girl working anywhere I could make money to survive. Colin was a man who seemed to know the hardships, disappointments, and despair of life. He said I was a girl not to be used by others, and we were married. He bought a small coffee shop and said that it was now mine, but it was ours.'

Tracey took some more documents out of her bag and handed them to me. 'These are the documents for the coffee shop.' There were other documents saying that she owned both the shops on either side. 'I don't need the money, but I do need to get my son away from here. He has got himself into trouble. He needs to become a man like his father.'

Young Colin was sitting on the bench and Cat jumped up onto his lap. Colin put his hands around the cat and held him. 'If he stays here, I don't know what's going to happen to him.' Tears started to flow down her cheeks.

Jacko glanced at both Ted and me. He stood behind Les and spoke up loud and clear. 'He is Colin's son, so he is now our son.' I nodded in agreement. So did Ted, Les and Jarrett.

'Young Colin Garland, do you want to go to sea on this vessel? I said, 'It is your right if you wish to do so.'

'Yes, sir.'

'Good, then I will enter you name into the logbook. Your mother must sign her name underneath it. You have a brother in England. He also served on this vessel and became a man. It's going to be hard work, and you have to earn the right to be a man on this vessel. Give me your word.' I put my hand forward and shook his hand. 'I also shook the hand of the Captain of this vessel many years ago, so did your father. He was a man amongst men. Shake the hand of Ted Coe.' Ted stepped forward. 'Do everything this man tells you to do. Do not argue with him or cause him any problems. If you don't understand something, then ask a question straight, but if this vessel is in a storm or gale, or a rising sea, carry out his orders instantly,' I told the boy.

I gestured to Jacko. 'This man is Jacko and because of his regalia, he is a very influential man. He is the helmsman and he will teach you everything about the sea, and I mean everything. You must take a note of everything. Do you write and can you spell?

'Yes sir.'

His mother spoke out, 'He did well at school, until just recently.'

'Good. Then you will be given a logbook by this gentleman.' I gestured to Jarrett. 'Fill in that logbook every day. Jarrett Collins will show you how to do it. Each one of these men are Captains.' I softened my voice. 'If we have problems, we talk to this man, Les. He will feed you and look after your sores and bruises, and you will respect him at all times.' I winked at his mother to ease anything that may be in her mind.

'Ted, is our cargo stowed away?' I asked.

'Yes, Captain.'

'Is there anything else to come aboard?'

'Just Les's firewood, it's being unloaded now.'

I looked at my watch. 4 pm, one hour to go.

'Young Colin, Cat belonged to your father. Tracey, would you stop and have a meal with us?'

'I would very much enjoy that. Thank you gentlemen,' she answered.

We all nodded to her. I glanced over at Lesley before leaving and she nodded to me.

Ted glanced at young Colin and said, 'Stay here with your mother and sister until we leave port, then go to the Bridge with Jacko, and just watch what's happening.'

Ted and I walked ashore. Ted looked at me with a half-hearted laugh. 'What else does that spooky little man have in store for us?'

We looked at the plimsoll line, then walked about 20 paces away from the vessel, looking for anything we didn't like. The vessel was sitting square in the water, everything seemed to be shipshape. We went back aboard and I beckoned to Jarrett and Snowy. 'Come below with us, check everything, make sure you're happy with it. We're going into waters that I don't have very much knowledge of, and I'm looking for the worst-case scenario. If anything needs another wedge to stop it moving, or needs to be lashed down tight, let Ted know.'

Soon, we were saying goodbye to Tracey and her daughter. Young Colin was standing there, crying. Margaret walked up to one side of him and Ted the other. Cat was in Colin's arms.

I nodded to Ted and he shouted his orders to stow the gangplank. The big motor started. A black car turned up at the wharf, Commander Wally Simpson got out of the car, stood and saluted me, I saluted back. I nodded to Ted again. He knew I'd given him orders to cast off, and he was shouting out his orders.

Another car turned up on the wharf. A man and a lady got out with two children. We gently pulled away from the wharf and headed out into the harbour. The crew were already putting canvas on her. I put my hand on Jacko's shoulder and whispered, '*Daisy May* is back out to sea again and Colin is aboard.'

Just then Cat stood up and got off Colin's jacket, he stretched himself and settled back on the jacket. Jacko turned to the young man saying, 'I think you father wants you to wear his jacket. If you reach down to your bunk there is a spare blanket, you can put it on the bench for Cat. Yes, young man, that was your father's jacket, wear it with pride. I've a question for you how did your mother know this was really the *Daisy May* not *Mary Moore*?'

'She knew by the ladies head on the bow!'

CHAPTER 29

We were now in open sea. Though there was a gentle breeze, the swell was quite high, but *Daisy May* rose to meet it. Her cargo was loaded well, and she seemed to enjoy being back out to sea. All her sails were set.

Ted walked in and smiled at young Colin. 'Well lad, school starts now. Follow me.'

They both walked back down the deck to where Trevor and Margaret were sitting on the hatch. Trevor had canvas over his knees and Margaret was holding it up for him. The two kittens were playing behind Margaret and Whiskey was lying on her back, catching the sun.

'Colin, this is Trevor, and Margaret his wife. Trevor is the sailmaker and rigging master. He will teach you the sails and the rigging. He's now making a funnel to catch rainwater and feed it into a barrel. Water from now on is very precious, don't waste it. You are going to have some problems. You've never left home before, have you?'

'No, sir.'

'My name is Ted. When you feel homesick, come and talk to Margaret. When you're on the Bridge with Jacko, talk to him, but don't tell him I told you so.'

Ted winked at Margaret. 'Stand up, Margaret!' Margaret stood straight up. 'As you can see, Margaret didn't ask me why, what, when or how, because she knows not to argue. Everyone's life depends on everyone else, everyone depends on the next person to carry out that command straight away, because their life depends on you! Bill saw something in you straight away. You are an intelligent lad, that's why the Captain has asked you to fill out a logbook. You are also very strong in personality, that's why you've got yourself into trouble in the past, but you are your father's son, and that's what we could see straight away. Now Margaret is an incredible lady. What she had achieved during the war was absolutely incredible. If Margaret shouted out to me *flat on deck,* I would flatten myself on the deck because I know there would be a sound and logical reason why, maybe a pulley had come loose or something else is whipping in the air. Other crew members will give you a command when you're aloft or on deck.'

Just then, Tommy walked past. Ted shouted out, '*hit the deck Tommy.*' Tommy fell flat on the deck, rolled over and stared at Ted, waiting for an answer. 'Sorry Tommy, I was just making a point to the young lad.' Tommy got up looking annoyed, and kept on walking. Ted continued, 'Now young Colin, if anybody aboard this vessel does that to you without a really sound reason, he or she will sit on top of the mast for three days in a gale!'

Ted gestured to young Colin to sit down. He did so and reached out to touch one of the kittens. Ted shouted, 'Stand up Colin!' He stood up immediately. 'Go and get three coffees, bring them back here, then go and get three more coffees and take them to the Bridge, then come back here. If you were to try to bring six coffees all at once, without your sea legs, you would spill all six. When you've got your sea legs, we will get you aloft with Trevor and Margaret.'

Colin walked off to get the coffee. 'What do you think of him, Margaret?' Ted asked.

'He certainly has a lot of potential,' she answered.

'I was watching his movements and his eyes. He took it all in. I think he will be a little homesick Margaret, he might need a mother.'

Margaret gave a small laugh. 'Well, don't you bully him for a while.'

Ted smiled at her. You're already a mother, Margaret.' He turned and went to the Bridge to talk.

I was filling out my logbook, discussing it with Jarrett. For diplomatic reasons, we could not mention the children. This was a naval vessel, but if we jotted their names down in the margin, we agreed it would not be official.

Ted walked onto the Bridge and started to laugh. 'Bill, who's this at the wheel? I thought we had a Scotsman.'

Jacko stared at him.

'Jacko,' Ted went on, 'you said the other day, *I stay at the helm, you stay on deck.*'

I turned to Jarrett. 'The children are back, Jarrett!'

Jarrett raised his eyebrows. 'Do you think we need earplugs, Skipper?'

'Yes Jarrett, we certainly do. Jarrett if you would like to take Jacko with you to the galley so Les can feed him.' Ted took the helm. 'Ted, you never told me you had long conversations with Daisy?' He didn't answer for a few moments. He seemed to stare into space.

'No, Bill, it was something private. Margaret and I just sat and listened to her. She is so perfect, so innocent and so wise. No small talk, straight as it comes. No-one has tampered with her mind, it is hers.' He paused for a moment. 'I didn't want her to leave this vessel. She was so precious, she was perfect, I just wanted to protect her.' He paused again. 'Is this what it's like when you have your own children? I've been at sea all my life, and never experienced anything like Daisy. It hurts deep down because I will never experience it again, and because it hurts so much, I won't let it happen again!'

He saw young Colin walking up the deck with the coffee and closed the sliding door. Young Colin knocked on the door and Ted slid the door back. 'Come in lad.' Colin handed one coffee to me, then one to Ted. He looked a little confused. 'Yes lad, that one's Jacko's.' He put it on the bench. 'You go and have yours.'

Ted and I talked about the last few weeks. We found them very confusing, but in another sense, very sharp in our minds.

CHAPTER 30

The days seemed to slide past. The crew were back into their routine, exercises in the morning, and then on deck. The deck had been scrubbed down to keep the green slime off. Colin was doing well with the logbook. He was a quick learner and seemed to take life aboard as though it was just natural. He talked to Les and Ted about his father. I had told him about his brother and the farm in England, and why his father had gone to sea. I didn't know he had married again to a lady in Cape Town. I told him of the high principles and ethics his father lived by, and that he had told me when I was 15 a man must be a man and be responsible for himself, live by his standards and be responsible for his own passing. Never ask anybody to do something you couldn't do for yourself.

Jarrett and young Colin seemed to have bonded and Jarrett had taken him under his wing. I wondered if Jarrett had plans for this young man. I would talk to Jacko.

We were now in the Indian Ocean. If we followed longitude 55, we would miss Saint Denis Island, Mascarene Islands and another island further north, near the tip of Madagascar, called Tromeln. We needed to be careful of the treacherous waters. The wind was from our stern and all was well, smooth sailing and it was getting warmer. Jacko was now sleeping on top of the Bridge and was quite content. Phillip and Dominic were still keeping to themselves. There didn't appear to be any problems. George's plaster had been taken off his leg, and he threw it over the side. Everything seemed to be going smoothly. Lesley, Ted, Jacko and I had a meeting on the Bridge. The one thing that concerned us was piracy. We were a good target. Lesley suggested she keep her crew on guard, and I said I would put a man on the mast. Ted would keep a man aloft.

The days slid past. The winds were warm, sometimes very gentle, other times quite strong. We hadn't had to tackle very many times. We were now approaching the Seychelle Islands, and I wanted to avoid them. We could just make them out on the radar. I'd noticed Jacko watching the birds and their movements. His radar was also working very well. He leaned out of the Bridge and nodded to Ted, moving his head slightly to starboard. He had everybody ready. Margaret, Lesley and young Colin on the whip lines that worked the pulleys, starboard north east 040.

Everything was working like clockwork. The sails were full of wind and the yardarms all braced. I saw Ted looking at young Colin. Then I realised what he was looking at. I was annoyed with myself. I should have known better and so should Ted, but at sea everything happens at once and your mind is fixed on the sails. You want them to stay intact. One wrong move and you snap a yardarm. Young Colin was making a slight fist with his hands. Ted asked him to open his hands. They were red and looked sore. Ted and young Colin walked into the galley. Ted came back and came onto the Bridge. He leaned on Jacko, pushing him slightly forward as he reached around the back of the wheel and took a pair of gloves. He said softly to Jacko, 'When it is snowing and very cold, what do you wear under your kilt?'

Jacko pushed him back with his shoulders. 'Do you want me to take my trousers down and show you, Totty?'

Jarrett's voice boomed out. 'No. No, I couldn't take it. I would be violently ill.'

Ted went back into the galley. Les was putting mutton fat on young Colin's hands and rubbing it in. Les flashed his eyes at Ted. 'Nice job, Ted. He needs three days.' He looked at the young man with compassion. 'We will put more mutton fat onto your hands tonight and in the morning.' He snatched the gloves from Ted and gave them to Colin and said, 'sit down and I'll feed you.' Les turned to Ted and said, 'I think you have work to do.'

Ted left and went up to the Bridge, He looked straight at me and raised his eyebrows. 'When Les is annoyed with you, he really lets you know and what's worse, he was right. I should have known.'

Ted put his finger up to Jacko and told him to shut up. Jacko did a little dance.

'Ted, have a break. I'll get coffee and some sticky buns.' I put my hand on Jacko's shoulder and said, 'that should keep your mouth full.'

When I got to the galley, I looked at young Colin's hands and smiled at him. 'We will toughen your hands up. Spend the next three days with Jacko and Jarrett.'

I filled up four cups of coffee. I held the handles in one hand and picked up a plate of sticky buns with the other and went back to the Bridge. I put the sticky buns in front of Jacko and gave a coffee to Ted and Jarrett. 'Has anyone seen Lesley?' I asked.

'Yes, she is with Margaret at the stern,' Ted replied.

I went to the stern and called for Lesley. 'Just a minute, Bill,' she replied immediately.

'Could you come to the Bridge please?'

'Yes, Bill.'

I walked back to the Bridge and saw George walking very carefully down the deck. 'Good morning George, is the ankle doing well?'

'Yes Skipper. Peeling spuds has a good healing effect on me, Skipper.'

'Good, but I don't think Tommy is going to be pleased with you healing so quickly.'

I went into the galley and sat down with my coffee. I wondered why Lesley and Margaret were having a private conversation.

Lesley walked in. 'Would you like a cup of coffee, Lesley?'

'No thank you, Bill.'

Jarrett got out of her chair and she sat down.

'Now, our destination is Burma, a place called Sittwe. We will be met and guided in. If the vessel has four flags on it, we don't take any notice. We must wait for the one with only three white flags on the mast. The biggest problem at the moment is the magnetic mines. We have proven this hull is made of 10 inch or more teak planks, so shouldn't set them off. I'm pleased we have wooden barrels aboard, but we do have copper wire and they say that copper should not be a problem. The growth on the mines of weeds, barnacles and other crustaceans are attracting fish, so the fishermen know where they are. There is nothing better than local knowledge. I don't have any more answers. Other than this course we're on should take us straight there. Is there anything you wish to add?'

'But we have steel ribs, not wood,' Jacko commented.

'Yes Jacko, that's true, and is a concern. But we just have to live with that.'

Jacko gave one of his native dances.

'What now?' exclaimed Ted.

'Margaret has two babies,' Jacko blurted out.

Lesley sprung up out of her chair 'That is Margaret's business. There are some things you always seem to know before anyone else, but you shouldn't have said anything!'

Jacko stood up straight. His face seemed to change shape. 'We have to protect Margaret. If we don't all know, how can we protect her?

Because you don't know, do you send her aloft in a gale, do you have her scrubbing decks, do you leave her on deck when the seas are rough? No, you know the babies come first. I am the protector of my people, and she is one of mine, and you, Lesley, are the daughter of my older sister, and I will protect you with my life.' His face changed back to normal. We all stared at him. I thought, he is right, if we didn't know, what would we have her doing. She is good at everything.'

Lesley stared at Jacko. She looked very serious and confused. 'What did you say, Jacko?'

He gave her a warm smile. 'Yes Lesley, you are the daughter of my oldest sister. I am the Peacemaker, the Protector. That's why I'm here, and you have known since you came on board.' He spoke to Lesley in his native language, and she understood perfectly.

She walked over to him, stood before him with her head slightly bowed. 'Is that how you knew me?'

'Lesley, you have traveled far in your career. It is because you have my senses, your mother's senses. You can see over the horizon as well, but the white man's laws have clouded you. Learn to push the clouds away and be at one with yourself.'

I already knew that Jarrett was writing this down for his future reference. Ted was shaking his head. 'Bill, does that mean we have two Jackos aboard?'

'Ted, we've had two Jackos aboard for quite some time,' I answered.

Lesley spoke to Jacko. 'Come and have a coffee with me and talk about my mum.'

Jarrett walked over and took over the wheel. Jacko and Lesley walked off to get a coffee. Ted was still shaking his head as he walked back out on deck.

'Tell me more about the Peacemaker and the Protector,' Jarrett said.

'As you know, we were both born on the Diamantina River in the Channel Country. You know my mum was the cook after Jacko's mother died during childbirth. His father was the head of his people, he was the Peacemaker and Protector. He gave Jacko to my mother, and she brought us up together, and so we are brothers. One night, Jacko's father passed away, and Jacko took his place. We didn't really know how many Aborigines there were in the Channel Country until Jacko took his father's place. They all walked into the desert. My mother told me to stay away, not to go with them, but Jacko was my brother and curiosity got the better of me. I followed them. I crawled up a bank and slid under a bush to watch. They were all in a large circle that had a clearing in the centre, and a small fire with gum leaf smoke rising from it. The elders were sitting in a row. Jacko was standing in front of them. They were all tapping their tapping sticks together. They stopped suddenly and stared at the bush I was hiding under. All the bushes started to move around me as a Whirly Whirly had come. I got up and ran home. Anyone would have thought the devil was after me. The next morning, my mother tore strips off me with her tongue for not respecting Jacko's people and their customs.'

Jarrett was writing all of this down.

'Bill, Jacko has fascinated me all the time I've been with him. We live in one world and he lives in a different world. When he tells Lesley to remove the cloud so that she will see better. I would like to understand that world better, it will help me in the future for the tasks I've got to take on with my father's company. Everything Jacko has told me I have written down so that I won't forget.'

I looked out of the window at Jacko and Lesley. They were talking to Margaret. She put her arms around Jacko's neck and cuddled him. Margaret then turned around and walked over to Trevor and talked to him. Trevor put his arms around her and kept cuddling her. Then they both walked off to the galley. Lesley and Jacko followed. Jarrett laughed. 'I thinking they're going to tell Les. Look at Ted trying to stay out of the way, but still keeping an eye on them.'

I was filling out my logbook and Jarrett said, 'Look at this Skipper.' Trevor and Margaret were walking out of the galley, heading towards Ted. Margaret whispered something to Ted, who put his arms around her and cuddled her. He then shook Trevor's hand. 'Are we next, Bill?'

'I hope so.'

'They are coming this way, Bill,' I went back to my logbook and grinned to myself. Do I put this in the logbook? This is a navy vessel. What other Captain would have put this in his logbook? But I'm certainly going to do it!

Margaret and Trevor walked in the door. Trevor couldn't contain himself. 'Skipper, we're going to have twins.'

I spun around in my chair, trying to look surprised. 'Trevor, that creates a big problem.' They both frowned at me. 'What am I going to put in the navy logbook? I will have to enter the marriage certificate, which I performed and, of course, I'll have to put your name in the logbook. We could both get court martialled, but I'm going to write it in there right now, because I'm a godfather.' I got up and put my arms around Margaret. 'Congratulations.' I was still cuddling Margaret and put my hand out to shake Trevor's hand. A memory flashed through my mind of when I first met him on the train coming back from Bairnsdale in Gippsland.

Jarrett cuddled Margaret and shook hands with Trevor. 'Trevor, where do you think I could find a woman just like Margaret?' he said.

'Jarrett, they are very rare. I had to come right around the world and find mine, and I met her in a very strange place.'

Jarrett gave a big sigh. 'Yes, I remember it well. Next time I will stay sharp and on my toes, but I think I might have found her back home. We have been writing letters to each other. She works for my dad. Who knows what may come?'

I winked at Jarrett. 'Keeping secrets from us all, Jarrett?'

'Yes, Skipper.' He winked back at me.

With a Commander's voice, I spoke to Margaret. 'You will spend more time on the Bridge at the wheel from now on.' She frowned at me. I thought, *be careful Bill, word it right.* 'We have to take care of the baby now.'

'No Bill. Babies, two babies, twins.'

'Then would you make Ted a godfather too?'

'Yes, Skipper!' Trevor replied.

CHAPTER 31

We pushed on in a moderate sea. The air was now a lot warmer, but a little more humid. I knew Jacko wasn't happy. There weren't any birds or migrating fish to talk to him. Dark clouds formed in the sky but the breeze was holding steady, then Jacko shouted, 'Good rain!'

Ted heard him and Trevor was already putting up the canvas shroud to catch the rain for Les's empty water barrels. Everyone was washing themselves down in the heavy rain. Cat, Whiskey and the kittens were nowhere to be seen. Lesley and Margaret were washing their hair, giggling and laughing like schoolgirls. Others were doing their washing. The rain continued for a good three hours. Ted and I checked the rigging. We did need water on the ropes to keep them tight, but this was a good soaking, and ropes tend to shrink with too much water. Some of the rigging needed to be slackened off. Trevor was on the ball, loosening this one and telling others to loosen this one off and that one off.

'I might as well go and sit down for a while Bill, Trevor seems to have everything shipshape,' Ted laughed.

Two days after that rain storm we were heading into a big roll. She would lift her bow, then go down the other side, then rise up again.

It was a gentle rhythm. Ted was looking aloft at the tops of the two masts. The top section appeared to be whipping back and forwards. Ted shouted his orders. I looked up and saw what he was looking at. Trevor was on the mainmast, pushing young Colin up. 'It's all happening. Let's go.'

Jarrett had taken off and was on the forward mast. The rest of the crew had followed. Others were on the whip lines. Margaret started to climb the shrouds to be with Trevor, but Ted shouted at her, 'No!' He pointed to the Bridge, she didn't argue, but did as she was told although she did make a small protest by sticking her tongue out at Ted, who just shook his head.

Jacko was looking a bit concerned, and I took the wheel from him. 'Go and look after young Colin.' I couldn't work out whether he flew up or climbed up, but he was stowing the sail with young Colin.

'Margaret, take the helm.' She did so without any hesitation.

Jacko walked in the door. He grinned at Margaret. 'Do you play chess, Margaret?'

'Yes, Jacko,' she answered.

'Then we will play chess, Margaret.' He took out the board from a drawer.' I thought I'm not needed here and went out to the galley.

Ted and Jarrett were sitting together, talking as they were eating their meal. I poured myself a cup of coffee and nearly spilt it as we moved over the next wave. I heard Les grumbling as his pots and pans slid down the stove. Fortunately they stopped at the guardrail. His other pots and pans were hanging on their hooks. Lesley was trying to wash dishes with her water slopping in the sink. She turned around and glanced at the three of us.

'Les, do you think we need a break and leave the dishes and cook-ing to them?'

We didn't say a word, just got up and left as quickly as we could. 'We've got a problem. We can't go back in the galley, and we can't go up to the Bridge. Jacko and Margaret are playing chess,' I said.

Ted laughed. 'Do you think that spooky little fella will get into her head?'

'This will be interesting. It's worth waiting to see, but I think we'd better to and check the cargo,' Jarrett grinned. When we got below, we found that Snowy had made a little office for himself in the ambulance. He had made himself a bed and was sitting there with his pencils and paper. He was quite happy with himself.

'Snowy, we thought we'd come down and hide with you.'

'No, no, no. I'm safe here from the women. They will find me if you don't go away. Bill, I've been checking the cargo and everything seems to be intact, but I don't like all the creaking and cracking in her hull.'

'Snowy, all wooden vessels creak and crack. That's the movement of the hull. If you didn't have it, that would mean the hull was too rigid and the timbers would snap. They must move like a tree in the wind, but I can hear water moving back and forwards in her hull, so we'll need to get the pumps working. We always need some water in there to keep the timbers right though.' We walked down the hull and checked everything we could see. We couldn't find any problems.

Back on deck, young Colin asked me why the waves were like this when there wasn't any wind.

'Well, there are certain currents that move around the world. They keep the temperature of the sea stable. When these tides meet another one moving in the opposite direction, it causes waves. In about an hour and a half, these waves will die down because the tide will be coming back the other way,' I told him. 'Does that make sense to you?'

Ted and Jarrett, both being funny, said together, 'No, Skipper, but did you understand that young Colin?'

'Yes sir, I did. We were taught at school about the world currents and how they cool the world down, and how the migrating fish use them to travel around the world, but I didn't know the tides made a difference too. I will put that down in my logbook.'

'If you have any questions, ask Jacko. He understands Mother Nature better than I do. You did extremely well in an emergency, being aloft and holding onto a mast with the vessel moving like that. Good man!'

He nodded to me and walked away. I turned around to Ted and Jarrett. 'Is there something you wanted to say? Education is a marvelous thing, if it's used the right way.'

I walked off, back to the galley, and sat down at the table. Lesley brought my tea and a coffee. She got her own and came and sat down beside me.

'Lesley, Les has always fascinated me. He always comes up with a good meal, no matter what the circumstances. I've left Jacko and Margaret playing chess.'

Lesley's eyes widened, and smiling, she said, 'That will be interesting, Bill!'

'Yes,' I said. 'I've never known them to play chess before. Margaret played chess with me during the war and she was very good.'

The sea had started to calm down. We could see that Les was a lot happier, and that settled my mind quite a lot. Lesley saw me watching Les. 'You worry a lot about him, don't you, Bill?'

I turned and looked at Lesley. Emotions were running through my mind. 'I have been with him for a very long time. He's like Ted. They are both a part of me. So, yes Lesley, I do.'

'Bill, this voyage is nothing like he's ever known before. The crew is different. *Daisy May* is not *Daisy May* anymore. She is the *Mary Moore*. Something that was very precious to him has been taken away. Scotland and Cape Town have confused him, nothing is straightforward, he can't work out whether we are a trading vessel or a Navy vessel. We are a Navy vessel one minute, then a trading vessel the next. We talk military strict, straight to the point, then the next minute we are happy go lucky, as a family.'

'Yes Lesley, I know, and I don't know what to do. You and Margaret have helped him a lot, but the children brought back memories for him, and I don't think those memories are going to go away this time. I saw him looking at the photos.' I sniffed the air. 'Come out on deck.' We both went out on the deck. 'Sniff the air, what do you smell?'

'Perfume, Bill.'

'Come up onto the Bridge.' Jacko and Margaret were still playing their game of chess.

Jacko grinned at Bill. 'Land Bill, fresh flowers, cups of tea, wood-smoke smells good, sweet smell. The birds are feeding, fish are moving on the surface of the water. I think we are about 20 miles from Ceylon.'

'We won't be going into Colombo, we will stay on this course,' I said.

'I like Colombo. Good, honest people,' Jacko replied.

Lesley was studying the chessboard. She leaned over to me and in a quiet voice said, 'I think we'd better leave them alone a little longer.' She was smiling. I thought, *does that mean Margaret's doing well?* We left them alone and stood on the stern talking. 'Bill, I have to get my people together. I want them to train more. They need more exercises. I want them to get their arms out and have them at the ready.'

'Well Lesley, we are entering new waters. We have been lucky so far, we haven't tacked too many times, but soon we will be in different waters, in the Bay of Bengal and winds move in strange ways, so I believe we will be tacking many more times. That will keep your men busy. These will be finicky waters for a sailing vessel, and with a bit of luck, we will be out before the monsoons.' We went back to the Bridge. Margaret was at the wheel, steering straight ahead, looking very angry and frustrated.

'What's wrong Margaret?' Lesley asked.

All of a sudden Margaret shouted, 'He set me up! I don't know how he did it, but he set me up and like a fool, and I played straight into it. He won't do that to me again.'

Jacko looked so innocent. 'So, we play, tomorrow?'

Margaret, in a sharp voice, replied, 'Yes Jacko. Why don't you go and get yourself something to eat?'

I looked at Lesley. 'Do you think that Trevor will understand why she's so grumpy? She's normally totally in control, and I think Jacko has upset the balance.'

A few minutes later Jarrett walked in the door. 'Have they finished playing their game?'

'No, it continues tomorrow,' Lesley laughed.

'Then tomorrow I'll take my paperwork somewhere else and not interfere.' Jarrett pointed to the radar, and we all saw land. Jarrett gave a small chuckle. 'I've never seen Burma on the radar. Another one for the logbook.'

The next day, we had calm seas and a gentle breeze. Margaret and Jacko were playing chess again, so we were all staying away from the Bridge, but Lesley just couldn't contain herself. She took some sticky buns and coffee up to them. Neither of them said a word. Jacko was concentrating on the compass and the chess board, and Margaret had both her elbows on the bench. Her hands were on her face and she was in deep concentration. Lesley glanced at the chessboard, then slid the plate onto the bench, along with the two coffees. She tiptoed out of the Bridge and walked over to Ted and me.

'What's spooky up to?' Ted asked.

'I don't know Ted, but I do know that Margaret is giving him trouble!' I would like to have sat and watched, but I would be interfering, Lesley thought. Ted had two of Lesley's men on the pumps, the other four were practising self defense on the deck, laughing and joking with each other. Lesley glanced at me, nodded and said, 'Ted, could I have my six men back? I need to talk to them, and they have to prepare themselves for where we are going, or should I say, where they're going, but they're still yours when you need them.'

I knew Ted didn't like what she was saying. There were too many questions without any answers, and he couldn't interfere. His eyes met mine. 'Yes Ted, we are reaching our destination. I don't know the reason for this voyage, or what exactly is going to happen when we reach the next port, or even where it is! I've only been told if we see a vessel with four red flags on its mast, we are to ignore it, but if we see a vessel with three white flags on its mast, we are to welcome a man on board,' I said.

'Bill, those two on the pumps seem to think it's a game. The way they pump it up and down, we will have to change the leather washers on the pumps when we reach the shore,' Ted said. He walked over to the two men. They both looked at Lesley, who nodded to them. She glanced at the others, then turned and walked towards the galley. All six men followed her into the galley. A few minutes later, Les walked out, wiping his hands on his apron. Jarrett followed him with two cups of coffee. Ted had put George and Colin on the pumps. 'Now you two, just do it slowly. Let the pump fill with water, just a gentle and slow rhythm.'

Back in the galley, all six men knew Lesley was now serious. They stood at attention. Mervyn instructed them to stand at ease, then Lesley said, 'Sit down, gentlemen. We are now nearing our destination and you have been briefed on your mission. When we reach our destination, Captain Mervyn Nelis is in command, not me. You will disembark immediately and discreetly. In the next few days, check your weapons, check everything three or four times. If Ted Coe requires you for this vessel, carry out his orders, but gentlemen, sharpen up, do your exercises any way you think fit. I don't need to say any more. You are all professionals, the best of the best. I hope you've enjoyed your short holiday.' She saluted them and they saluted back. We watched Lesley come out of the galley. She walked over to Les and Jarrett and thanked them for giving her privacy.

'Ted, I think I should go back on the Bridge,' I said.

'Do you want my hat?' Ted laughed.

I frowned at him.

'Skipper, throw my hat in the door and see how it comes back.'

'Ted, it's too valuable. I will find something else. How about sticky buns?'

'Good idea, Skipper.'

I went to the galley and got three cups of coffee and a plate of sticky buns and biscuits, and walked onto the Bridge. Margaret wasn't exactly happy, but she was composed as she stood at the helm. 'Having a good day, Margaret?' I asked.

'Yes and no, Skipper.'

'Who won?'

'Jacko did, by a hair.'

'Will you be playing tomorrow?'

'Yes Skipper, I will play him and I will beat him.'

'Well, Margaret, at the moment, we have time on our side. Are you hungry?'

She took the whole plate and held it so Jacko couldn't get any. Jacko looked up with those big eyes and gave her a pleading look.

'No, I'm having a baby and I need nourishing food!' Margaret replied.

With that, Jacko moved behind my back and was on his way down to the galley. Jarrett walked in the door and squeezed behind me and picked up his sexton and said, 'Who won? I saw Jacko fly to the galley.'

'Jarrett, he thinks he's won, but look at the plate!' Jarrett burst out laughing and went back out the door with his sexton, pencil and paper. I stood at the helm with a grin on my face. So she beat him with food.

The next day, I saw Lesley's men practising on deck. Young Colin and Trevor were watching too, but they didn't join in because it was now getting serious. There wasn't any laughing or joking. This was no longer a game. Lesley was standing alongside me. 'Bill, I'm no longer joining in. It's too dangerous and I'm too old for it.'

'Lesley, you're not past your prime. You have gained new skills,' I said.

'Bill, I'll show you tonight. We need more practice. It's not quite to perfection.' She saw Jarrett coming back with his sexton and gently touched my backside in a very suggestive manner, and went out to help Les.

I saw Ted glancing up towards me. 'We need to tack more to catch more wind,' he said.

I nodded to him.

Ted shouted, 'Tacking to port.' Everything went like clockwork.

The *Mary Moore* settled down. She had a good breeze in her sails and the crew went back to their normal duties. The five commandos were climbing the shrouds as fast as they could, looking at Ted. He wasn't happy. In his mind, there was a fine line. Anything aloft was his; don't play games with it. He glanced up at me, and by the look on his face, he knew that I wouldn't do a thing about it. Just then Mervyn walked in, he looked at me very seriously, 'May I have a word with you, sir?'

'Mervyn, a long time ago I told you not to call me sir. To you, my name is Bill.'

Mervyn looked sad, and he was standing at attention. 'Bill, we're going back to war. My colleagues and I must sharpen up, our lives depend on it. Protocol is a part of sharpening up.' He paused for a moment, the sadness still in his eyes. 'I am in command, and I want to bring my colleagues back alive.' He didn't finish the sentence, but I knew what he meant.

'Then how can I help you?' I asked.

'We will be having firearms practice this afternoon, and out of respect to your crew, sir, they should be warned.'

'Yes, I will warn them and tell them to keep out of the way.'

'Thank you, sir.' He looked at Margaret and bowed his head in respect, but he looked puzzled.

'Mervyn, if you can't win a game of chess one way, you can win in another!' She pulled the plate tighter to herself and grinned. Mervyn slightly raised his eyebrows and nodded, acknowledging he understood, and left. I beckoned to Margaret to take the wheel again.

'Skipper, what about the kittens? Where are they?'

'Margaret, they're on deck with Whiskey.' My mind raced back to my naval training and why you do not have pets aboard a naval vessel. 'Jacko will take care of Cat.'

Jarrett walked in the door with his sexton and notebook. I winked at him. 'Margaret, could you keep an eye on things? I'll be back shortly.'

I wanted to find Ted. I found him with Tommy checking the rigging to the mizzen mast on the stern. He was tapping it with a marlin spike, listening to the sound. It told him whether it needed tightening or loosening. 'Ted, could you warn the crew that there will be firearms practice this afternoon, and to please stay out of their way? Tommy, does that mean you practice as well?'

Tommy looked straight into my eyes. 'Yes, Bill.'

Ted looked at us both, a little confused. 'Ted, Tommy belongs to MI6. He will not be going with the others but will be staying on board as one of your crew. He will not interfere with you. He belongs to Lesley. Before the war, we had a mission. Lesley was on board *Daisy May*, Tommy was on the *Castle*, and they both had the same duties.' I put my hand on Ted's shoulder. 'It all gets very confusing, doesn't it, Ted?'

Ted gave a sarcastic laugh. 'The Navy never wants you to get bored. It's like playing chess with Jacko.'

I left the two of them and went into the galley to speak with Les. I told him what was going to happen in the afternoon. I knew he didn't like firearms. He gave me a look of disapproval.

George was in the galley having his break. I made myself a cup of coffee, picked up two biscuits, and sat down next to him. George had changed since I first met him when we picked him up from the tramp steamer, the *Castle*, that had been torpedoed. He was one of Jack's crew.

Jack was the Captain of the *Castle*. George was a little timid. He was one of my crew during the war, when we were on the battleship. He was very good at his job, very meticulous and extremely trustworthy, but now that he was no longer timid, he would say what he thought, and usually it would be very practical. I wouldn't question him because I knew he would be right, and he always did as I asked. Whiskey was his cat, his best friend. He had the cat when he came on board *Daisy May*.

'George, how's your leg and ankle now?'

'It's doing very well, Skip, just a bit of tightness every now and then. Les has some cream that fixes it.'

'George, there will be firearms practice this afternoon. Margaret is worried about the kittens and Whiskey. Could you put them in a container of some sort and put them in the Bridge with Jacko, Cat and Margaret?'

'Yes, Skipper.'

I took a bite out of my biscuit. 'George, I think Les is getting better at making biscuits. I'll get some more before Jacko gets them.' I got up, picked up some more biscuits and my coffee, and went back to the Bridge. I was about to take a step through the door when I asked Jarrett if he had seen Jacko. Jarrett pointed up, and Jacko's head peered over the top and was looking down at me.

He said very excitedly, 'biscuits!'

'Jacko, go and get your own. These are mine!'

He bounced off the roof and headed towards the galley.

'Margaret, George will be getting a box or some sort of container and bringing Whiskey and the two kittens here,' I said.

I noticed Trevor heading for the galley. 'Why don't you go and join him, Margaret?'

I took a spoke of the wheel from her and handed Jarrett a biscuit. As Margaret passed me, she patted my tummy saying, 'they're both doing very well!' She giggled, then took off for the galley.

I watched the men bring crates up on deck. They took the weapons out, dismantled and lubricated them, and put them back together. They then laid them out on the hatches.

George came onto the Bridge with one of Lesley's containers, the two kittens and Whiskey were inside. Cat stood up quickly. Clearly he wasn't amused. George put the box on the bench next to Cat. Him and Whiskey sniffed each other's noses. They seemed to be communicating. Jacko turned up with coffee, a big plate of biscuits, and two big sandwiches.

George looked at the plate, then looked at Jacko and pointed to his tummy. 'Jacko, how's that all going to fit in there?'

Jarrett spoke to George. 'I have to watch this every day, and I get more confused every time!' Jacko took no notice of them. He just took the wheel from me and started munching.

'Jarrett, why don't you go and get yourself something to eat and some coffee before the music starts?'

'Yes Skipper, I might get a biscuit and a cup of coffee if there's any more left.'

They both left, and I sat down to check my figures of our ordinance with those of Jarrett. One day he's going to be wrong, I thought. I opened my logbook and started to fill it out. I got to where George's leg was doing well, no problem. I sat back in my chair. What do I put next?

I jumped in the chair as a loud crack sounded. Jacko was laughing at me. He had watched it all start to happen. I stood up and peered out of the window. Three of Lesley's men were aiming their rifles over the baulk works with telescopic sights, but they had fired all together, not one second apart. Then they fired another round. I saw an object fly to pieces in the distance, then they all put a cylinder on the end of their rifles, took aim and fired again. No sounds this time, just a light thud. I looked at the bullets. I'd seen bullets before, but not like these. The men walked to the stern. Mervyn had an old coffee tin which had a line attached to it. There was a reel on the other end. He threw the tin over-board, and it started to drift away from the stern. The reel in his hand was peeling off line. It told Mervyn how many yards were reeling off. The three men loaded their weapons with the strange bullets, put the rifles to their shoulders, and stood at attention. The reel still kept wind-ing out.

I was having trouble seeing the tin, so turned around and took out the telescope from the top drawer. With this, I could still see the tin. It went further and further out. I thought that the line must have broken, but Mervyn was still looking at his hand. He put his thumb down on the reel. I didn't hear Mervyn say anything, but within the blink of an eye, the three riflemen took aim and fired together. Through the tele-scope I could see the tin explode. You would have thought the tin had explosives in it, but it was from the bullets. The tin was too far away to do any damage to the vessel. I had seen explosions during the war, but not from shells that small.

Mervyn retrieved his line, and they all seemed to be satisfied. All four of them went back and lay their weapons down on the hatch cover. They picked up other weapons and gave small bursts of bullets over the side. The weapons appeared to have many other features that could be attached to them, but the bazookas were still below with the explosives. Mervyn and Lesley were satisfied, but I didn't like seeing the coldness in Mervyn or Lesley. I had left the coldness of the military way of life behind, but they had brought it back. The men were putting their weap-ons away. They were all ready for action.

Mervyn nodded to me that they had finished their firing practice. Now they were practising falling and protecting themselves, bouncing upright or kneeling down, ready for action. Thank God, I will never have to face them in action.

Tomorrow we should be at our destination if the wind holds with us. It was perfect, but I was waiting for Jacko to say something, to warn me, or give me some information, but he was too quiet. That puzzled me. Was he trying to tell me something? Every now and then, he and Cat would stare at each other. Why?

Just then, Margaret came out of the galley carrying a plate and three coffees. She came up to the Bridge and walked in. Jacko had also seen her and had a big grin all over his face, but before he could say anything, she said, 'No Jacko, they are mine and Bill's.' She saw the sad look on Jacko's face. That satisfied her, and she put the plate down in front of him. 'We play chess Jacko.'

I took two biscuits off the plate, picked up my coffee, and sat down in my chair. I have to watch this, but my thoughts drifted away from them, back to my own problems. I was looking for answers so that I would be prepared. A vessel with four red flags, another vessel with three white flags. I was to take no notice of the vessel with the red flags. Why not? What does that mean? No answers yet. My papers tell me that there are magnetic mines at the entrance. Should I put the women into a lifeboat and tow them a fair distance behind, where they would be safe? I will have the lifeboats prepared to be ready. The last time we had a problem with magnetic mines, we didn't use the prop to propel. We have 10–12 inches of teak timber in our hull, under the generators and jeeps. We have 10 inch planks under them for support. Is it going to be enough protection? Les and Trevor would go in the lifeboat as well. Nothing else that I can think of at the moment.

I was brought back sharply from my thoughts by Margaret shouting at Jacko. 'That's my biscuit. You have had more than me to start.'

I stared at Jacko. I'm trying to keep this vessel afloat, I'm trying to protect my crew. I don't know what's going to happen and these two idiots are arguing about a biscuit! I stood up, went up to Jacko, took the biscuit out of his hand and broke it into two, gave them half each, and left them to it.

I met Jarrett on deck. 'Is it safe to go back and do my logbook Skipper?'

I let my frustrations go and put my hand on his shoulder. 'If you are a very brave man, go. I think somebody needs to be there as a referee. Good luck Jarrett.'

I found Ted. 'They tell us there's magnetic mines where we're going. I'm thinking of putting the two women and Trevor and Les in the lifeboat and towing them well clear of us,' I said.

'Trevor needs to take care of his wife, but do you think you will get Lesley in a lifeboat away from you?'

'Ted, just have it ready. There will be a vessel coming, one with four red flags, which we must ignore. Come on, we'll go and have a coffee together. I would suggest we both have an early night and get up early in the morning to prepare for the unpredictable.'

Les sat down with us and had a coffee too, before he served the evening meal.

'Les, we are preparing the lifeboat for the unpredictable tomorrow. Could you put together a small hamper and have hot water ready, just in case>'

He gave me a serious look and nodded.

'Jacko and Margaret are playing chess and it's got serious. She could win. Jacko might need you to counsel him.'

Ted laughed, 'Could I be here? I would love to give him pity.'

Lesley walked over. 'What are you three up to?'

'Margaret could win!' Ted answered with a chuckle.

Les said quietly, 'be careful Ted, women stick together!' He got up and went back to his galley, where he was safe. I knew he was preparing food for Jacko, just in case.

Ted and I went back out on deck. We could see Margaret on the Bridge, she was dancing and singing.

'Ted, I think we'd better go and rescue Jacko.'

'I'm going to enjoy this,' Ted said.

'Ted, we are supposed to be going to rescue Jacko!'

He gave me a sheepish look. 'Yes, sir.' We walked in.

'Jacko, take a break. Les is waiting for you.'

Ted couldn't help himself. 'Did you win, Margaret?'

'Yes Ted, by this much.' She put two fingers slight apart.

Jacko walked slowly out of the Bridge, mumbling, 'You won't next time,' and he was gone.

'You made my day, Margaret, you are beautiful. I think you need a break,' Ted said to Margaret.

She walked off with a cheeky wiggle.

'Ted, I think young Colin could go with the women tomorrow.'

'Yes Bill, I agree with that.'

'Time to get some rest Ted. I think it's going to be a big day tomorrow.'

CHAPTER 32

Everyone who wasn't on night duty turned in early. I woke at 3 am. There was very little movement. I slid the door aside, not wanting to wake Lesley, but she did wake up.

'What time is it, Bill?'

'3 am Lesley.'

I closed the door again, hoping she'd sleep a little longer, but I really knew that wouldn't happen. She would be worrying about Les.

'What's happening, Jacko?' I asked.

'The wind is from our stern, slightly starboard, our yardarms are braced to pick up all the breeze, but it is dropping.'

I checked the radar. I could just make out land. Should I start the motor or wait a little longer? I wondered. She is still moving well in the water.

'Wait a little longer,' Jacko said.

'Jacko, I wish sometimes my thoughts would be my own and you would stay out of my head! I'm going to get some coffee. You wouldn't like anything to eat, would you?' I left.

When I returned, Lesley was standing next to Jacko. I heard her say, 'Did Margaret win yesterday, Jacko? She told me she had won by a hair. I know you too well, Jacko.' She reached out and took a coffee from me. Jacko took the other and Jacko gave me that hurt look.

'Jacko, Les is cooking you breakfast. I want you at the helm today, sharp. If there is anything you don't like, let me know.'

'Cat doesn't like dogs,' he said.

'What does that mean, Jacko? Cat doesn't like dogs!' I shook my head. Too much happening to worry about dogs. 'Just drink your coffee and go and get your breakfast. Then come back here.'

'Bill,' Lesley spoke, and I turned around. 'Bill, the commando's mission is to destroy an Omega communications tower, it is 300 ft high. MI6 sent in commandos to do the job, but somebody talked and it had to be aborted. The British built it so they had communications with their aircraft and ships, but the government we are friendly with, want it to go, but there is another government that has control of it. We have been hiding their commandos for this mission.'

I felt annoyed and used again. 'Lesley, we are just pawns on the chessboard. Will you and I ever be free?'

'One day, I hope so, Bill.'

Jacko came out of the galley and climbed the mainmast to the very top, and sat there looking towards the land.

Ted walked in. 'What's he up to, Bill?' he asked.

I looked at the radar and could just make out a blip ahead of us. Just then Jarrett walked in and looked at the radar. 'There is a vessel coming towards us with a fair bit of speed.'

Lesley ran on to the deck. The six commandos were already there. They had been waiting in the shadows with all their gear and arms ready. Lesley shouted in her best commanding voice, 'Go and get your breakfast and be at the ready!'

'There is another vessel coming. It is a fair way behind,' Jarrett said.

Jacko came down from the mainmast and popped his head through the door. 'They are both coming very fast, Bill.'

Dawn was breaking. 'Jacko, take the helm. Jarrett, stay with Jacko. Ted, could you get Colin and bring him here? He's to stay here with Jacko and Jarrett.' I thought *I don't have to worry about the rest of the crew. They've had training during the war.*

We were gently gliding through the water. There weren't any swells to hinder her and her sails were still full of wind. I picked up the telescope and focused it on the first vessel coming towards us. I saw that she was flying four red flags. They were only small, but they were there. It is a wooden boat, I would guess a fishing boat. It was passing us on the starboard side about 300 ft away. I visually followed it, then I saw Lesley on the stern. She had her hand up to her forehead showing just three fingers. All is well. The vessel turned and went down our port side, heading back to where it had come from. It passed the other vessel. 'Turn her into the wind, Jacko, and bring her to a stop,' I said.

Ted opened the baulk works starboard and lowered the rope ladder. The second vessel was slightly smaller and looked a little shabby. She tied up alongside of us. Two men came on board. One I recognised, but I couldn't remember from where.

Lesley walked up behind me, 'Mrs Henderson picks her men, doesn't she?' she said.

'Yes Commander, she's a hard task master. How are you, Bill?' He could see the puzzled look on my face. 'Bill, we met a long time ago at the beginning of the war. We got your uniform and I was there when they presented you with the medal.'

'Well, I never! I remember you now, we had coffee together. I was grateful to you for getting me out of the way where people couldn't ask questions.'

'Bill, could you remove her sails so that she doesn't stand out and use your motor for propulsion? Commander Johnson, could you have your Commandos board now with their equipment?'

I noticed Ted was already ordering sail off and stowed away. The commandos were lined up, ready to disembark with their bags and equipment.

Mervyn nodded to them. Each man dropped his kit bag over the side and carried his weapons down with him. The last one to go was Mervyn.

Lesley walked up to him. 'Stand to attention when you address me,' she said. Mervyn did so. 'You will return here in one piece.' She stamped her foot on the deck. Do you hear me Mervyn Nelis? Or I will have to come and find you and carry you home!' Tears were pouring from her eyes. 'Now go!' Mervyn disappeared through the hatch.

'I will leave my man with you. He will guide you to your destination. Have total faith in him,' James said. Then he, too, disappeared through the hatch. Soon, they were speeding away. For an older vessel, it certainly had some speed.

I turned to the gentleman who was left behind, our guide. I put my hand out, 'William Farquhar and Lesley Johnson.' He shook my hand and then Lesley's.

'You will have to excuse me, sir, for security reasons I am unable to give you my name.'

'Well, we will offer you some breakfast.'

He smiled. 'I can smell bacon. I haven't had that for a very long time.' He followed us into the galley. I heard a noise and smelled diesel smoke, then I saw Margaret's head appear out of the hatch. She had a big grin all over her face. She had started the motor!

I asked the man what course we should take. He told me to continue on as we were. I looked up at the Bridge and nodded to Jacko and gave him a small hand signal. He knew what I was saying. Tommy's head appeared out of the hatch following Margaret. He put up five fingers to ask Jacko to allow the motor to warm up. We all sat around the table. Les brought us plates of bacon and eggs. Margaret and Tommy walked in. She was grinning from ear to ear, but when she saw the visitor, her face went pale. I could see and feel the pain in it. The man's face remained blank. He put his finger up to his lips and shook his head. Margaret nodded. She had understood what he was meaning. She turned around and left. We were all very puzzled. Who was this man, and where had he come from? He got up without finishing his breakfast and followed Margaret out of the door.

We could see through the windows that Margaret was waiting for him. The man slowly walked up to Margaret and stood in front of her. Then he put his arms up to her, she walked into his arms. They embraced each other. We knew there were tears between them. The man took a handkerchief out of his pocket and gently put it to her eyes and wiped away her tears. They talked for a little while before coming back into the galley.

Margaret got herself some coffee and breakfast. The man sat down and finished his breakfast. He stood up and turned to Les and said, 'Thank you, I haven't had a breakfast like that since I left England.' He turned to me saying, 'Captain, I have to go to the Bridge now.'

We both left the galley and went to the Bridge.

'Jacko, this is the guide to our destination.'

Jacko's eyes widened, then narrowed. Was he seeing something in this man that I didn't see? Lesley and Margaret walked in. They had two coffees and a plate of food that made Jacko's eyes widen. Lesley gave Jarrett his coffee and handed him the plate of food. Jarrett took some food off the plate and Lesley handed it to Jacko. I was puzzled by the way Lesley was looking at this man.

'Captain, have you heard of all the magnetic mines we have in the area?'

'Yes, I have,' he answered.

'Well, they have been exaggerated over time. That's what protects this little harbour. You are an Australian Captain, so you understand the channel into Melbourne with markers and buoys. You stray out of that channel and you will hit mud banks or reefs. So, it's the same here, Captain. The channel is not marked on any chart that we know of, so Jacko, just follow my instructions and you will be okay. Turn to port, straight ahead.'

Margaret put her hand on his shoulder. 'You can trust these people. They are our people, so they can know your name. This gentleman is Angus McKenzie. We were both in the same jail in Germany. We could see and talk to each other, so every time they would torture and question us, we would consult each other afterwards, knowing they were listening. Without Angus, I would not have mentally survived.'

'Nor would I, Margaret. If I hadn't had you talking to me,' Angus said. 'Commander Johnson was negotiating with the Germans to get us out. She did a swap for a German spy in England, but they only swapped me. And it was Bill who did that exchange.'

Lesley interrupted. 'But it was the Russians who helped us. They did a swap as well and they got Angus out, then he assisted us with the Russians. Angus and I have the same problem. We know too much. I knew they had hidden Angus, but I didn't know where. Angus, you're still working for her?'

'I've got no choice, Commander Johnson. Bring her back to starboard, that's enough, Jacko, straighten her up. Jacko, can you see the bamboo poles coming out of the water? They are the channel markers. Keep them on your Port side. Crustaceans have built up on the mines and the fish feed off them. The local fishermen know where they are. They're all marked, but in different ways, to keep them away from unwanted eyes.'

I saw Ted looking puzzled and went out to talk with him. I explained what was happening. He followed me back to the Bridge. Jacko was handling the helm well, he knew what to look for.

Angus spoke to Jacko, 'They tell me you're a very spooky man. They advised me not to play chess with you because you would get into my mind, but be aware, there are many ways to play chess.'

'Whoever said that was very wise,' Jarrett commented.

'Now Jacko,' Angus continued, 'there is a small island just off shore. We are to head slightly away from it, then turn and head behind it. This creates an optical illusion. You will just disappear from anybody looking from the sea. The illusion was worked out probably 2000 years ago or more.'

I looked on the radar. There was an island, and it had a channel running behind it. There was also something else too, but I just couldn't make out what it was. Jarrett was leaning over my shoulder. 'Skipper, if they were timber, we wouldn't see them.'

'Yes, Captain Collins, this little harbour is all stone. It's ancient, we don't know exactly how old. How old are the pyramids?' Angus replied. 'Now Jacko, see the last bamboo pole? Turn to starboard. We are already quite close to the island. Now Jacko be ready, we waiting for a few moments, but it seemed much longer.

'Now Captain Jacko, hard to port. Head behind the island, so anyone watching you from the sea would no longer be able to see you. One minute you're here, the next you're gone! You have actually turned back on yourself and the island has hidden you. You will see on your starboard side a stone wall with houses behind it. You will be tying up, or should I say berthing, at the end of that wall. Don't worry about the fishing boats. Put your port side to the wall so that you're facing back out the way you've come. That will make it hard for anybody to read her name on the stern.'

Jacko looked at Angus with narrowed eyes. 'How did you know I was a Captain?'

'We know a lot about you, Jacko. Tonight you will put on your Scottish regalia and William will put on his naval uniform. This will be the first time I've ever met an Aboriginal Scotsman!'

Jacko pointed to his hand. 'That ring you and the other man were wearing, what does it mean?'

'Jacko, I think you already know!'

We were now swinging around to berth. Ted had lowered the fenders to protect her sides against the rock walls of the wharf. It was as if we had stepped back in time. This was a very ancient harbour with houses made of beautiful stone masonry. Men were coming down to see us with their wives and children. They seemed to be fascinated by what they saw.

Jacko brought her to a gentle stop. She gently kissed the wharf. Ted had her moored securely. He swung his head around towards me, asking for permission to lower her gangplank. I nodded. The crew were then busy lowering the gangplank and releasing the tie downs to the hatches.

Jacko had gone into our cabin and came back with a book. He opened it to a page with a picture of a knight in armour, with a white cape and red a cross on it. He put it on the bench and pointed to the picture.

'Yes, you're right, Jacko,' Angus said, 'but all will be explained to you shortly. Bill, do you have Alan Norde on board?'

'Yes I do,' I answered.

'Good. Could you bring him to me please?'

Jacko went off to find him.

'Angus, he is known here as Snowy,' I said.

Jacko came back with Snowy and he and Angus shook hands. 'Yes, Snowy, I'm the voice on the other end of the phone. I believe you have some nice presents for our people aboard? We will arrange to get them unloaded.'

I glanced at Lesley, shaking my head. 'Snowy, if you could see Ted, he will take care of the unloading for you. As you know, he has to be careful to protect her hull. I will need to find out about her new cargo.'

Angus stepped in. 'May I call you Lesley?'

'Yes, you may.'

'Lesley, Bill, Jacko and Ted, would you please come with me?'

As we went down the gangplank, I noticed railway lines going down to the wharf. They didn't appear to be what I would call a permanent fixture. The sleepers underneath them were spread out further than usual, and there were two hand trolleys on the railway lines. We walked along the side of the rail lines to a big overhanging cliff with vegetation hanging down all over it. Then we noticed something strange. There seemed to be a castle made from the hanging cliff, but it seemed to change as you got closer and closer. It was a very old structure. I had seen buildings in India, and this seemed to be much the same with the columns and statues.

Angus noticed me staring. 'Yes Bill, we don't know how old it is,' he said. 'The Germans found it, but I think an archaeologist originally found it.'

We followed him through a big archway. The railway lines kept going into the building. Angus showed us cubicles, beautifully made stonework that had crates made of timber stacked in them.

Angus gave a sigh. 'In each of these crates, there is half a ton of gold. There are 60 crates, 30 tons of gold. The destination for these crates is Australia.' Lesley and I glanced at each other, puzzled. 'Yes,' Angus continued, 'we thought we had better keep that bit quiet. In the other rooms there are a total of 30 tons of gold bound for England, but your first destination is Melbourne, Australia, then onto Britain. Yes, Captain, 60 ton of gold on your vessel. If you'd follow me please.'

We walked through a beautifully carved door into a large room. It took my breath away. The décor, the furniture, the beautiful ceiling of the heavens above, with the stars, planets, and gods.

There were five men sitting at a table, and two more were standing. They all stood up when Angus entered. 'Please sit down, brothers.' They sat down. 'Bill, Lesley, Jacko and Ted, please be seated. Refreshments are coming.' A man came out of the shadows. He was dressed in a white cape which had a red cross on it.

The man, whose name was James, said in a quiet, unassuming voice, 'Good morning. I'm sorry my last meeting was so brief, but I had to get the commandos on their way to their mission.' He smiled at them. 'Yes, I am a Knights Templar. All of these gentlemen are also Knights Templar. You are a Freemason Bill, so you are sworn to an oath like we are. We are all part of the same circle. To whom do we put our faith? To God, the supreme being. Near the end of the war there were Satanic Knights, formed by Himmler. They were nothing to do with us. They realised that they could not win the war, so the wealth they had acquired from others, they had to hide. This was one of the hiding places. We are the Knights Templar, we were formed to protect the Holy lands and the birth place of Jesus Christ, not to own, not to possess, not to stand in the way of people wanting to visit or worship God, no matter whom they are. It is the right of all men to believe in his God, without the wrath of others, or the control of others for their own greed. Every time a Lord, Earl, King or Queen or any religion wanted to plunder from the travelers, or put high taxes on them, we were there to protect them, to keep the road open and safe. So, we were a political society. Many rumours were started to destroy us. We started the first banking system. We gave people credit, so they didn't have to carry their wealth around with them. We were considered a dangerous political society, so we had to go, but we went underground. We are still carrying out the work, in our way, to protect others. If Australia is given 30 ton of gold, it is like, you say, taking bread to a bakery. The greatest percentage of gold that comes out of the ground goes out of Australia. It is not government owned, so we have to give it back to the people it came from.

'People from Europe who lost everything during the war migrated to Australia, and we have to provide them with support, so having 30 ton of gold as collateral will help Australia to build dams that will create power stations, Bridges, roads and other structures that will provide wages, housing and a future for their children. That is the only way we know how to give it back to those it belongs to.

'Britain has the same problem. A large percentage of cities in England do not exist any more. Britain has also taken in migrants. The Americans found a cave full of gold and silver and many other valuable artefacts. It managed to pay back their national debt for the war. The gold we have here is still in ingots, the Americans' gold was fillings from peoples teeth, and a mixture of gold bits and pieces that had been broken up and it made it easier to transport, as it wasn't melted down into ingots.

'Now Captain, if we unload all of your cargo we can put a layer of 12 inches by 12 and 18 feet long timbers in your hull, layer them with crates of gold, then another layer of timber on top of them. Another layer of gold crates which will be bound for England, and another layer of timber, then more crates followed by as much timber as we can get on top of them, but we must watch her Plimsoll line. Then load your wine. Anybody looking would think your cargo is timber and wine. We also want to remove the rail line so nobody knows we've been here. If you can't take them, then we will dispose of them, but first we will need them to move the generators into their new home.'

Some food was brought in. Jacko was in his element. There was a lot of fruit, which he really enjoyed but didn't get much of at sea.

We were shown around the building and taken up to the top floors. It had been a marvelous palace at one stage. You could see over the entire island and well out to sea. It was a perfect place to hide and protect.

As we were enjoying the scenery, James said, 'Angus and I will be staying here. I'm 78 years old and Angus has a young family here. The people are wonderful. The outside world hasn't tempered with them, they are totally at peace with themselves. The five men will return with you to Australia and go their separate ways. They will be part of your crew on the way. This town doesn't have an electric lighting system, so that's what the generators are useful for. The ambulance and the jeep will be put to good use as well. The locals can make a substitute diesel from cooking oil to use as fuel. Well, we'll have to return to your vessel. We have a lot of work to do.'

At the gangplank, James handed the paperwork to me. 'I think everything you need is here. I will see you and Jacko tonight.'

James turned to his people and told them that the generators and ambulance were here, and they would remove all the timber to the wharf. He then disappeared amongst the small crowd.

I went back on deck with the others, then joined Ted in the galley. Jarrett was behind me; Lesley was leaning up against Ted. I knew it was her way of trying to give him warmth and comfort as a close friend, and he was enjoying every minute of it. I spread the papers out on the table. The loading plans were there and Ted was studying them. He pointed out certain areas that would have to have extra bracing to take the load evenly. Jarrett agreed with him. First of all, we needed to unload the generators and the transport. If we unloaded some of the barrels first, we have a plan.

'Bill, what do we unload the generators with? We can use our own rigging for the barrels, but not the generators, they're too heavy.'

Jacko walked in the door. 'Come and have a look at this.' We followed him out on deck and stood watching in amazement at a monstrosity moving down the wharf.

Jarrett laughed. 'I've seen these in books. They were used to build castles and churches, but this is the real thing.'

It was a crane, made out of wood, used to lift blocks of stone. It was just what we needed. The five men we had met earlier were there. They just blended in. Lesley said that she and Margaret were going for a walk into town and shouldn't be too long. She laughed and said that neither of them could help. I winked at her and asked her if she would like to take her puppy dog with her, but she declined, saying that he had found the food that was ordered for the lifeboat, so was busy. I noticed the two ladies talking to one of the local ladies on the wharf, then they walked off into the town.

They found the building they were looking for and walked in. It was a hairdresser. A beautiful lady with straight, long blonde hair walked up to them. She looked like a lady from a mystical story found in a children's book. She had a look of disbelief on her face, as if she didn't believe what she was looking at. There was no-one else in the room.

'Yes Lisa, it is us.' Her full name was Lisa Seamer. 'Mrs Henderson has told us to get you out. You have been here for seven years, along with your husband. Is he well?'

'Yes ma'am.'

'My name is Lesley. The war is over. If you put your radio equipment together, I will have a man pick it up for you. Disguise it and try to leave here as if you had never been here. I know it will be hard, but we will get you home.'

Lisa's shoulders slumped down, her body started to shake, and the tears came. Margaret stepped forward and put her arms around her. Lesley put her hand on Lisa's shoulder. They waited for a minute for her to compose herself. She excused herself, turned and went through a door and called her husband, not by the name we knew him, but she called him John. He came to the door.

'Yes? I have a patient with me.' He looked up and saw Lesley and Margaret. His face went white, as though he didn't believe what he was seeing. He turned around and closed the door. Lisa walked up to him and flung her arms around his neck and started to cry again.

'We're going home, John!' John just stared at Lisa.

'Yes John, they want you out of here while they have a chance, but we have to be quiet and discreet. We know that you are the doctor here. Is there another doctor?'

'Yes, there is,' he said.

'Good,' Lesley replied, that solves the problem. We hope to be ready to sail in two days' time.'

Lisa said that they had a dog, and she didn't want to leave him behind. She asked if they could take him. Lesley's mind went back to Jacko *Cat doesn't like dogs!* So he'd been talking to Cat, and just gave us what Cat said. He didn't have the answers. That's Jacko.

'Yes Lisa, we know about the dog.'

'How do you know about the dog?'

'We have a member of our crew. His name is Cat. He talks to our helmsmen, Jacko. It will explain itself when you get onboard. Tommy O'Hia will pick up the radio and there will be others to pick up your luggage. The password is "Cat" and, if I could impose upon you, we would both love to have a real haircut.'

Back at the wharf, Bill said they were glad they had left the slings on the ambulance and generators. It would make them much easier to move. The jeep came out first. The people on the wharf started clapping when the ambulance was moved up to where the jeep had been, but wasn't unloaded as yet.

They then unloaded one generator from the front hatch. The audience on the wharf clapped louder and cheered when Ted unloaded some of the wine, but he left some on the deck. The second generator was unloaded, and the crowd roared again. Some of the crates were unloaded, then the ambulance. The crowd was in party mode, shouting, singing and dancing. I looked at Jacko. If I didn't let him go ashore, it would be too cruel. 'Jacko, go ashore. But remember, we are going out tonight.'

Lesley and Margaret returned from town. Lesley put her arm on my shoulder. I glanced quickly at her. 'Has Jacko got weevils in his pants?' she asked.

I glanced back at her. I was just about to say something when I noticed her hair. When I had seen her and Margaret on the wharf, it didn't register. The women had had their hair done.

'Your hair looks very nice dear, I like it short like that.'

Margaret nudged me on the other shoulder. 'Do you like my hair, Skipper?'

I deliberately tried to look surprised and startled. 'Margaret, what have they done to your hair? Margaret turned around and looked at me. I winked at her. 'It looks absolutely beautiful, Margaret.'

Lesley asked me to walk with her to the Bridge because she wanted to discuss something with me. She raised her eyebrows. 'Bill, we have another married couple coming aboard.' I stared at her, waiting for the rest to come. 'The British and Australian government have had people stationed here to report anything unusual. They have done a remarkable job, but now they want them out, and we have provided them with the perfect opportunity. I apologize to you, Bill, but I didn't notice they were in my paperwork. Whoever put my papers together had done it very discreetly. It was written on the back of other paperwork. Lisa Seamer is a highly intelligent and well-trained lady. Her husband is a doctor, so he was very helpful at the end of the war.'

Margaret stepped in to the Bridge. She started to stroke Cat. 'Cat, we are very sorry.' Cat raised himself up on his front paws and made a funny sound. 'Yes, you're right, we have a dog coming aboard.' Cat jumped down off the bench. We knew he was going down to Les.

I shook my head and followed Cat. I could see the timber coming down to the wharf and being unloaded. I could see another problem and called Jarrett. 'We have another small problem, Jarrett.'

James was standing next to a barrel, looking at the label, tapping his hands on the top of it. 'Skipper, will we lose one barrel or two?'

'I hope no more than that. I will leave that problem to you, Jarrett. Remember, that's my pocket money!'

There were crates coming from one hold, and wine from the other. I was watching James. His eyes seemed to get bigger and bigger. The first layer of timber was being spread out in the hull. I went down with

Ted to make sure the hull was being supported, and that we had made a good deck to keep my mind at ease when we meet unpredictable seas and strong winds that could make the hull lean over to one side and when the bow crashed into high waves. We discussed the 60 crates and how they'd fit. Ted had a tape measure and a piece of white chalk and marked out the sizes of the crates on the deck. We were satisfied that they would all fit in nice and neatly, and that nobody would know that they were there.

'Time for coffee, Ted.' We stepped back out on the deck. The light was starting to fade, and I knew that the working day had finished. We had our coffee, then I went and washed and changed into my uniform that Lesley had pressed for me. I noticed she had also pressed Jacko's Scottish regalia. While I had been washing and changing, Jacko had come back onboard. Lesley had seen him. He was now sitting on a chair in the galley while Lesley and Margaret trimmed his hair and beard. Then, with hot soapy water, they washed his hair and beard and fussed over him. Les was enjoying every moment of it, listening to Jacko's protests.

Lesley said to Jacko, 'There are clean undergarments and your fancy shirt has been washed and ironed. Your other fancy clothes have all been pressed. Now, go and change.'

There were at least six very well-dressed gentlemen waiting for us on the wharf. We followed them. Jacko didn't say a word. We walked up into the village and saw a building which had two columns in front and above them was the square and compass. I turned and stared at Jacko. He punched my shoulders, and we followed the other men. Upon entering the foyer, we were required to sign a visitors' book. Then we went into the main lodge room. About 10 pm we came out of the lodge and went into what they called the *South*, which is a room used for refreshments. They served us a very tasty supper.

'Didn't you know that Jacko had done his first and second degree?' James said to me. 'He did his first in Scotland and his second in Cape

Town. He is now a Master Mason, and Bill, by the looks of him, he is thoroughly enjoying it.'

I didn't want to show my feelings, so I just grinned and nodded. Later we were escorted back to the wharf and the *Mary Moore*. We thanked everyone, said our goodbyes and went back on board. Jacko had a big grin all over his face.

'You enjoyed keeping that secret from me, didn't you, Jacko? You are the big man of your people, you are a sea Captain, and now you are a Master Mason. What's next, Jacko? I do know this. Our mum would have been extremely proud of you. Coffee before we turn in for the night?'

In the galley, Les was waiting for us. He wanted to know that Jacko had been fed.

CHAPTER 33

The next morning, just on daylight, the first crates turned up and were being loaded onboard. Ted was below with Jacko, Tommy, Phillip and Dominic. Trevor and George were on deck supervising the lowering of the crates into the hull. James was giving orders to Angus and the other five men on loading crates onto the trolleys. They were using the jeep to tow them to the wharf. Lesley, Margaret and Les were kept busy feeding them all. Snowy, Colin, and I were busy on the wharf. By 8 pm that night, all the crates were aboard, and we had loaded some of the timber. We spread the timbers on top of the crates, making it look like another deck. We were all exhausted and slept very well that night.

We were up at daybreak the next morning and finished the deck we had started laying on top of the crates. Then we were able to load more crates. This continued for the next couple of days, laying timber, then loading crates on top of them. Finally, the railway line went on top and then the barrels of wine. It wasn't exactly easy—there was little room between our cargo of timber and the deck—but we did have plenty of labour to help.

I stood with a coffee in one hand and a bacon and egg roll in the other, watching Jarrett talking to James on the wharf. They were discussing the barrels of wine. Jarrett didn't mention that we didn't have any more spare, only the two barrels. He put his hand on James' shoulder. 'Why don't you talk to your colleague in Cape Town about the two barrels of wine, one red and one white? Would that satisfy you?'

James replied with big eyes, 'I think I can work something out with him.' They shook hands; the deal was done.

We all discussed a 3.30 am departure for the next day, which was when the next high tide was, so prying eyes would not see the *Mary Moore* leave the harbour.

When it was dark, Lesley went with Tommy, Phillip and Dominic to fetch Lisa, her husband and their dog. The least amount of people who knew what was going on, the better. I spoke with Jarrett. 'I have a problem. We have another married couple coming aboard. If I put them in the two bunks in the bow and it gets rough, they are going to be very sick, and they will want their privacy.'

'Skipper, you want my cabin, and it's midships.'

'Yes, I do Jarrett.'

'Well, Skipper, those two barrels of wine. If James can't do a deal with the Scotsman, they will come from your share.'

'If you were not a Captain, Jarrett. And if you didn't have access to the market, and you didn't play chess with Jacko, I would have the ace card. It's a deal!' We shook hands as friends.

'What about the second sleeping arrangements?'

'Lesley has already worked that one out. She has had a second bunk made up to go on top of your bunk. Would you say Jarrett she has the ace card before you?'

We saw George coming aboard with a young lady. George asked if he could have a word.

'Yes, George, how can I help you?' I said.

'Skipper, you know I come from the streets and I don't know who my parents are, but being here I have found a family that wants me and a partner which whom I have fallen in love with.' He put his arm around the young lady. She looked towards the wharf where her family were all standing, waiting. 'I want to stay here, Skipper, and have what I've always wanted, a family.'

'You were with Jack Fox George. You went through the war with me. What you have now found is rightfully yours. I can't stand in your way. You have my utmost respect, and I could say you've carried out your duties aboard this vessel to perfection. I know Jack would be very proud of you George, we owe you some money, wait here for a minute.' I went to the Bridge and got my purse out, took some money out, and took some more, put it in an envelope, then back to George and his friend, gave George the envelope.

'Skipper, could you say goodbyes for me?' The tears were flowing down his cheeks. He wiped them away with his sleeve.

Jarrett and I watched them walk up the wharf and disappear between the houses. Jarrett didn't say anything. He turned and went to collect his belongings. I stood there trying to collect my thoughts and put everything into perspective.

George returned. 'I forgot something, Skipper,' he said. He ran into the forecastle and returned with a bulge under his jumper. He nodded to me and went back ashore. I knew that he had collected his cat, Whiskey and her remaining kittens. They were the only thing that he had which were actually his.

Lesley returned with Lisa, her husband and some others carrying their belongings. The gentleman had a dog on a lead. I thought Cat doesn't like dogs, and shook my head. What else do they know and I don't? I met them at the top of the gangplank. 'Welcome aboard Lisa.'

'Bill, this is my husband, Matthew. He is a doctor, and this is our dog, Jester.'

I looked at the dog. We somehow knew about the dog, didn't we, Lesley?' Our spooky helmsman has already told us about the dog.

'Yes, Bill, but that is Jacko's little problem,' Lesley said.

She turned to Lisa and Matthew. 'I'll show you to your cabin. It is a bit tight, but you'll only sleep in it.'

'Lesley has arranged for another bunk. Put your belongings down there. We'll all have coffee first.'

I noticed Jacko's legs hanging over the ledge of the Bridge, or is it the Bridge? Cat was sitting alongside him; his eyes blinking in the moonlight. The dog stopped abruptly and looked up at Cat. Doc patted him and led him away.

By the time Les had fed all of us, Lisa and Matthew's cabin was ready and young Colin and I brought the gangplank in. We all turned in for the night.

CHAPTER 34

I awoke at two in the morning and gently nudged Lesley.

'No Bill, it's too early.'

'I know, dear, but duty calls. I know Jacko's on the roof. A pair of legs dangled in front of our window, then he jumped down.

'Jacko, check on Ted and get the rest of the crew up on deck. I walked into the galley. Les was there with hot coffee and freshly baked biscuits. We nodded to each other. 'We've lost George; he is staying ashore.'

'Yes Bill, I expected that. He has been talking to me. He found something he desperately needed and he won't be lonely anymore.'

I drank my coffee and ate the biscuits. The crew started to appear on deck and came into the galley. The dog pushed past them. He had smelled the biscuits and was wagging his tail in front of Les. 'I've got something better than biscuits for you. How about a nice bone with meat still on it?' Les gave him the bone. 'That should keep him busy.'

Jacko's voice boomed out, 'That was my bone!'

'Why don't you ask the dog to share it with you,' Les replied and gave Jacko a mocking grin. 'Don't you talk to dogs, Jacko?' He left with Jacko standing there watching the dog eat his bone.

Ted put a hand on Jacko's shoulder. 'You are going to have to sharpen up now Jacko, you've got competition.'

Jacko replied in a gruff voice, 'Cat doesn't like dogs!'

Angus walked into the galley. 'Good morning, William, Lesley, Jacko.' He nodded to Ted. 'Can we leave quietly under sail, then start the motor when we get to the entrance to the channel?'

'Yes, we can.' Ted started shouting his orders. 'Flying jib sail, and outer jib sail, main royal topsail.' He looked at me, I nodded, he nodded at the four men to let the bow line go. A light breeze caught the sails, and the bow moved out from the wharf. Satisfied, Ted gave the order for the stern lines to be stowed, others were lifting in the bollards, and *Mary Moore* was gently moving down the channel.

Margaret had gone to the back hatch and was waiting. *Mary Moore* was moving very gently and quietly. We came to the end of the island and Ted nodded to Margaret. She disappeared below. Soon we heard the roar of the big motor start. I turned to Jacko, 'let her idle for a moment Jacko, the least noise, the better.'

Angus nodded to Jacko, and he put the gear lever into forward. 'Hard to starboard,' Angus said. We could see a small fishing boat, which only had a very faint light. Angus again said to Jacko, 'keep your starboard to the very faint lights and you'll be in the channel.' We passed the fishing boat with the faint lights, then Angus said, 'You're free, you're out of the channel, turn slightly to your port. Bill, could you shut the motor down?'

Angus gave the instructions to Jacko and put both his hands on Jacko's shoulders, 'You are a remarkable man. I've never met anybody like you.' He put his hand into his pocket and took out two small boxes. He opened the first one, and took out a small pin which was white with a red cross on it. 'Brother Jacko Farquhar, this is the highest order we can bestow upon you as Knights of the Templar.' He stepped forward and pinned it on Jacko's jacket, and stepped back three paces. 'Brother Jacko Farquhar, I now present you with the pin of the Master Mason.

Wear it with pride, for it will never fail you. Jacko Farquhar, you are closer to the great Creator than we will ever be'. He took three paces back and bowed his head three times in respect.

I automatically put my hand up in the sign of fidelity. Jacko is my brother and I'm so proud of him. I wiped away the tears in my eyes. I knew the crew didn't understand what had just happened, and I didn't know how I was going to explain it.

Just then, we heard the sound of an approaching boat. It pulled up alongside us. Mervyn came aboard first, helping another man aboard. The man's shoulder was covered in blood and his arm was in a sling. The doctor pushed past us and Mervyn laid the man on the hatch covers.

'Ted, do you have a litter? The next man is badly injured.' Ted sprung to work straight away. Trevor, Dominic and Phillip hastily made a litter out of a couple of jackets, poles and some rope. They lowered it over the side. Lisa had brought out the doctor's bag and opened it. The doctor asked, 'Bill, do you have any plasma?'

'Yes, we do,' Lesley replied, and quickly went to fetch it.

Les had buckets of hot water ready as Lisa started to clean the blood away while Margaret was removing the man's clothing. The doctor had a syringe of morphine and was injecting it into the man's arm. He looked up at Ted, 'You hold this.' He handed him the plasma, and before you could blink, he had the needle in the back of the man's hand, then he turned around and walked to the other man who was being brought onboard. There was blood all over his stomach and leg. The doctor said to take him directly into the galley and to lay him on the table. Nobody hesitated. They were all trained, and did just as they were instructed. Another man appeared on deck. Although he had blood on him, he was not hurt, just exhausted.

'I'm in the way here,' Angus said to me. 'Thank you, gentlemen. Perhaps we might meet again someday.' He went towards the hatchway, where small boxes and firearms had been brought aboard. He turned, nodded his head in respect, and disappeared over the side. The small craft quickly disappeared into the darkness.

Lesley and I went into the galley. The doctor was working on the man on the table. He had a scalpel in his hand and was making an incision. 'Lisa, swab please.' She dabbed it on the wound, removing some of the blood. The doctor had a pair of tongs in his hands and was probing into the wound. He brought out a bullet and dropped it into a bowl, then very gently moved his fingers around the wound. 'I don't think there are any more bullets in there.' He turned to Les, 'do you have any alcohol here?' Les had a bottle of brandy behind his back in the ready and handed it to the doctor. 'Could you take the top off please, Les? My hands are too slippery.' Les did so and handed the bottle to him. He poured it over the wound and Lisa gently swabbed it again, then she started to stitch the wound. They were a great team. They had obviously seen many wounds. The doctor examined the man's leg wound. The bullet had gone straight through. He poured some of the alcohol on the wound. 'Lisa, this has bled well. I think we'll just stitch it up.'

The doctor went back to the man with the bottle and his instruments, and worked on his shoulder, removing another bullet, which had luckily missed the bones. He stitched it and bandaged it up tightly. The man was put to rest in the forecastle. The doctor went back into the galley. He took the man's pulse. He was still out cold with the morphine. They had cleaned him up.

The doctor looked at me. 'This gut wound is serious, but I don't think it's broken any major blood vessels, or damaged any serious organs, but I would prefer he's not moved for at least three days. I'll keep monitoring him. I don't know the full extent of the wounds just yet. Lesley, do you have any more plasma?'

'Unfortunately doctor, no, we don't,' Lesley replied.

'Do you have any coconuts aboard?'

Les spoke up. 'Yes, we do, doctor.'

The doctor looked straight at Lisa. She nodded, then asked Les to show her the coconuts. She picked out the ones she wanted. The doctor had a clean bowl and wiped it out with the alcohol, and placed a clean tea towel over the top of it. Meanwhile, Lisa had cleaned the top of the coconuts and punched a hole in them. She poured the coconut water onto the tea towel, straining the water.

'Coconut water is a good substitute for plasma,' the doctor said. 'I would like to examine the other two men now.'

He looked straight at Mervyn. 'Remove your shirt and trousers.' Mervyn raised his eyebrows and looked annoyed, but he lowered his eyebrows and with a groan, took his boots off and removed his clothing. He had dark bruises on his legs, shoulders and arms, plus a few abrasions. 'You've been in a good fight, haven't you? Martial arts?'

'You could say that, doc.'

The doctor frowned. 'You obviously won.'

With a grin, Mervyn said, 'he was a good man, a good fighter, but he wasn't prepared for a good Aussie punch to the chin, but he will be now.'

'Mervyn, you are physically exhausted. I want you to rest for three days, but keep moving every now and again so that your muscles don't tighten up. You know what I mean?'

'Yes doc, I do.'

Lesley had a bucket of hot, soapy water. 'Follow me, Mr Nelis.' They both went out on deck.

The other man was examined. He needed some stitches in his arm for a cut. The doctor asked him, 'knife wound?'

'Yes,' the man replied.

'We will clean it up for you and stitch it, give you a wash down and strap your arm to your chest, because it is a deep wound and is close to the main muscle. It will need time.'

Margaret had another bucket of hot, soapy water waiting.

I saw the look on the man's face. 'Don't argue with her. She's a professional just like you,' I said.

Lisa stitched his arm. It was very neat and perfect. I thought of my own duties. Got to get *Mary Moore* back on her way. I walked back on to the deck and saw that Ted and Jacko already had her sails up and she was back on course. I looked at Ted. He nodded. He knew I wanted every piece of canvas on her.

Okay now, it's the Captain's responsibility to keep the logbook up to date, but put in as little as possible. I went back onto the Bridge, gently touched Jacko on the shoulder, 'What does Cat think of the dog now?'

'It isn't the dog he's concerned about, it is the bird!' I looked at Jacko with a puzzled look, then I looked at Cat, then back at Jacko. I waited for a few seconds, then raised my eyebrows, waiting for an answer. Just then Cat got up and jumped down off the bench, went to the door and sat down, looking back and forwards. The dog started to run up and down the deck, barking and yelping. Lisa and Doc came out of the galley. The dog stopped and rolled over onto his back, then a parrot landed on his chest. You would swear they were embracing each other. The parrot's wings were cuddling the dog's chest, and the dog was licking the parrot's face. Lisa and Doc walked up to the dog and parrot. The parrot flew onto Doc's arm. We were all slightly puzzled.

'We thought you'd be better off on land with your own kind, but we were apparently wrong,' Doc said to the parrot.

Lesley, Ted and Tommy walked up alongside them and looked at the beautiful parrot. It was green, with light blue, gray, yellow and green on its back. It had yellow tips on its underside and was quite big for a parrot.

'It is an Alexandria parrot,' Doc said. 'I found it on the ground, it had no feathers. We fed it with an eyedropper. Jester was a lonely puppy then, so they grew up together. We never put parrot in a cage, so he used to fly off and return at will to be with Jester. We didn't know what to do about the parrot, but he solved that problem himself. He's part of our family.'

'Jacko, could you sort them out? They need to be part of the team on board,' I said.

I sat down, opened my logbook. Just what do I put in it? I couldn't mention the 60 ton of gold, or the soldiers on board, or, for that matter, Lisa and Doc. As far as the records were concerned, none of them ever existed. I wrote down the time and date. We have picked up a consignment of teak timber. 'Jacko, would you say there is 200 ton in the cargo?'

'By the look of the plimsoll line, Bill, I would say that's about right.'

So I wrote down 210 ton. I thought it sounded better. A 50 ton consignment of wine. We disembarked one crew member, George. That was the only name we had.

We were now passing through the Bay of Bengal, course due south, altering course at the islands of Andaman. Jarrett walked in with three coffees and a plate of biscuits. Jacko's eyes widened and Jarrett handed him the plate and put the coffees down on the bench. I pointed to my logbook. Jarrett read it and nodded. Ted walked in with a cup of coffee, he took four biscuits off the plate and walked to the other end of the Bridge. Jacko gave him a stern look. 'He who laughs last, laughs best. Those four biscuits were Bill's.'

Ted handed me two of the biscuits. He gave a sigh. 'What happened to the days before the war? We had our problems, but not like the ones we have now. I'm getting too old for this, but I've got no choice. As long as the deck is under my feet, the wind fills the canvas and the sea surrounds me, I'm at home.'

'Yes Ted, I understand what you're saying. The sea is our master.'

The wind stayed with us. For the next three days, everybody seemed to settle down. Doc sat with his patient, taking his pulse every now and then. Lisa was busy cutting hair, but I don't really think the crew wanted their hair cut. They just wanted Lisa's company. She had a sweet, gentle way of talking to them, and they just wanted to listen. They were seamen, and they missed the woman's touch. Jester and the parrot had a truce with Cat. You stay out of the Bridge, it's mine!

CHAPTER 35

The afternoon of the next day I was watching Jacko. There was something wrong, he was uneasy. I could see him gently touching the deck with his feet, and he would keep looking towards the horizon. 'What's wrong, Jacko?'

'I don't know, Bill, but something is wrong with the sea, not the vessel, but the sea.'

'Is there a storm coming?'

'No, not a storm as we know it, but something different. We'll just have to wait.'

I checked the barometer, it was holding steady. Jacko had warned me, and I knew it was coming. But what?

I left my logbook open and went out to see Ted. 'Ted, Jacko is spooked. He said there is something wrong with the sea, but the barometers are holding well. He has given us a warning, and he is seldom wrong. Rig for storm warning, and have the big motor ready.'

I went into the galley and looked at the man on the table. 'Doctor, we may have trouble shortly. Don't ask me what, just take care of your patient and be prepared. Les, Jacko knows something; be prepared to shut your stove down.' Les gave me that knowing look. We didn't argue with Jacko.

'Do we need to move that man from the table to the floor?' Les asked.

'Yes, it's better to be safe than sorry, Les. I will get a mattress. Tommy, Colin, get a mattress and bring it to the galley.'

'Lisa, Doc, I have a mattress coming. Put your patient on the floor and wedge him in tight. No doc, don't argue. I fully understand the circumstances.'

I walked up to the bow, looking at the horizon. I couldn't see anything out of the ordinary. According to the charts, the sea in this area was 1000 ft deep. What has Jacko sensed? He's totally in tune with nature. I went back to the galley. The mattress had been put up against the wall, blankets had been rolled up, ready. The men were standing around, ready to put the blanket under the patient. They very carefully picked up the man in the blanket and gently laid him down on the mattress. Lisa tucked in the rolled up blankets alongside him so he couldn't move. The doctor took his pulse again. I went back to the Bridge. The light was starting to fade, darkness was on its way again. Tonight there would be a full moon. I saw Ted walking down the deck, checking everything. Jacko was reading a book on the bench. It was all about the sea, its moods, and the unpredictable.

Tommy walked in. 'Move aside, Jacko, my watch!'

Jacko didn't say a word. He picked up his book and went down to the galley.

'Tommy, I'm going to shut my eyes for a while. Wake me if there are any problems.'

I didn't sleep well. I was half awake, half asleep. I knew Lesley had come to bed.

I woke with a start. The ship's bell was ringing. Everybody appeared up on deck. 'What's wrong, Jacko?'

'The sea, it's called an uprising. It's when a current and the tide move up the valley at the bottom of the sea and can't escape. It comes boiling up to the surface. It's like water boiling in a saucepan, and it can suck vessels to the bottom of the sea!'

Ted had the big motor ready. Daylight had just started to come, and you could see the sea boiling. All of a sudden, a huge bubble appeared in the front of our bow. We crashed into it, throwing sea water all over the decks and soaking everything. We could feel her hull shake and vibrate, then we could see the whirlpool directly ahead. Jacko gave the motor full power to have more control over the vessel. I glanced down at young Colin in his bunk. 'Stay there lad, stay in your bunk.'

Jacko had eased the vessel to one side of the whirlpool, but it was still trying to suck us into the centre. I stepped forward to give Jacko a hand with the wheel. The pressure on the rudder was trying to force us to port into the whirlpool. We fought hard to hold the wheel firm. We just managed to pull clear, then we hit another boiling bubble, this time slightly on our starboard side. It was pushing us over to the Port. *Mary Moore* laid over on her port side. Water was gushing through her gunnels. Once again, she vibrated and groaned like a boxer who had received a bad punch. She righted herself again. It gave us a chance to see ahead, looking for a way out.

Jacko pointed to our starboard side. 'Look at the birds and dolphins, they are feeding on fish that have been stunned by the uprising, there must be calm water there. Once again, Jacko was at one with nature, playing the elements. He gently eased her to port, trying to miss the next whirlpool, but it was bigger than the one before. It spun us around and around. Jacko and I fought the wheel. Jacko shouted some indigenous words. I knew he was calling for the witchy to help. The vessel came out of the whirlpool and we were heading for calm water, but were still being tossed around. I looked up at the rigging, masts and yardarm, but everything seemed to be right. I noticed Ted was doing the same as I was. We nodded to each other.

'Jacko, I'm going to kiss the big motor. She certainly got us out of trouble, and you, Jacko, thank the witchy for me.'

The dolphins, porpoises and birds were all busy feeding on the stunned fish. Even killer whales were there for the grand feast. It was a sight to behold. I went down into the galley. Lisa and the doctor were there with Lesley, lying down alongside the injured man to protect him. Les was in the corner, where he knew he would be safe in a storm. I started to count heads and went back outside. Trevor and Margaret were coming out of the hatch of their quarters. I counted them. Ted, Colin, Phillip and Dominic. I went to the forecastle and counted the others. One was missing; it was Snowy. I went back on deck and shouted at Ted, 'Where's Snowy?' He glanced at the exit to the hull.

We went down into the hull and saw Snowy lying on a mattress, snoring his head off, and he was still holding on to a mug. Ted took the mug and sniffed it, then he looked at the barrel. 'Skipper, he is drunk!'

I felt anger rise up inside me and looked at the silly grin on his face. I had put temptation in front of him, and he will not remember anything that has happened. We could have sunk, and he would still have been a happy man.

'Check the barrel, Ted. From now on Snowy sleeps in the forecastle.'

I checked the cargo, ropes, and lashings. Everything seemed to be in order. We went back on deck. I walked over to the starboard side and could still see the water boiling in the distance. Huge, great bubbles were coming up to the surface and bursting. I've always admired the drawings old seaman had put on charts of sinking ships, sea monsters, serpents, Neptune and huge fish. These were the places they had recorded. Beware of these places, as they had no answers, so the seamen of old gave them answers.

I could see smoke coming out of the galley chimney. I went in and nodded to Les, letting him know that all was well. Lesley was sitting at the table with Lisa and Doc. I put my hands on Lesley's shoulders, just to be close to her, letting her know how much I cared. The doctor looked up at me with half a grin, 'What else do you do when you get bored, Bill?'

'Doc, Jacko and I will think of something. The last incident was a little tame!' I scratched my head and went to get three coffees. I came back with the coffees and some biscuits, winked at the doc and went back to the Bridge. I gave the biscuits and coffee to Jacko. I knew that food would steady his nerves. Then I handed Jarrett a coffee. He still looked uneasy as he tapped the logbook with his fingers.

'You haven't recorded the trolleys or the railway lines as cargo. How much weight would there be in them?'

'Five ton.'

He stared at me for a few moments. I could see his body start to relax. He nodded. We all express our fear and frustration in different ways.

'Skipper, I hope we never have to go through that again,' Jarrett said.

Jacko boomed out, 'We've heard about them, but never actually experienced one. It was interesting, wasn't it?' He grinned at Jarrett.

'I don't have anything to describe it with at the moment, Jacko, but interesting to me isn't the word.'

'Jacko, pull back on the throttle. We will put full sail on her.' Jacko turned the motor off.

Back on deck I said to Ted, 'I want to put full sail back on her, but I first I want to check the yardarms, rigging on the mainmast and the four masts. If you do the four mast, I will do the mainmast.'

I started to climb the shroud. Trevor was following me and Margaret started to follow as well.

'Ted!' Jacko's voice boomed out. 'No Margaret!' He patted his tummy. Margaret turned and poked her tongue out at Jacko, but she stopped climbing. Young Colin followed Ted up the shroud. I wasn't happy with the yardarm on the lower main topsail.

'Trevor, we will have to whip the yardarm with lashing here, and do the same on the other side. It should give the yardarm more strength. Young Colin can help you and learn.'

Ted and I got back together on deck. 'Everything seems to be in place, Bill,' he said.

'One of the yardarms needs whipping on the mainmast. Could you have young Colin give Trevor a hand?'

Ted started shouting his orders to get full sail back on her.

'Ted, we need to talk to Snowy. We went into the galley and saw Snowy drinking coffee. I had to let all my frustrations go, and I shouted at the top of my voice, 'How is your headache, Snowy? Can I make it any worse?'

To which Snowy replied, 'You're doing a good job already, Skipper.'

I slapped my hand down on the table. 'On deck, now Snowy!' I turned and walked back out on deck. Snowy got up and followed me. Ted and I walked to the stern. I turned around and Snowy was behind me. 'Snowy, Ted and I are the only ones who know you were drunk on board my vessel. As you know, I have strict rules aboard my vessel and you have broken the main one. You could have been down in Davy Jones's locker by now, the happiest man I know. Snowy, I've known you a long time, and I've the upmost respect for you. The way you did your job on the wharf was excellent. You are not actually one of my crew, and you have done a remarkable job in making this voyage successful. Ted and I feel you should sit on the top of the mast for three days, but that wouldn't sit too well with our respect for you, so you can put your mattress in the forecastle and sleep there.'

I walked off, leaving Ted and Snowy together. Ted put his hand on Snowy's shoulder. 'You know the biggest crime, don't you, Snowy?'

'Yes Ted, I got caught. But Ted, it's damn good wine!'

Ted grinned, saying, 'I wonder what Bill's got in store for you, Snowy.' He turned and walked away.

I went back to the Bridge and watched Trevor and young Colin lashing the yardarm. I wondered what the future offered Trevor and Margaret. Margaret is pregnant. The babies should be due by the time we reach Melbourne. Their sea days will be over. Trevor's parents live in Bairnsdale, in Gippsland, Victoria.

'He will make a good father, and they will have many more children,' Jacko said.

'Jacko, you have always been able to get into my head ever since we were children. Sometimes it's very frustrating. I'm going to get a coffee now, but you already know that!'

He just grinned at me. 'Sticky buns with jam.'

I walked off, glancing at the main masts, and then went into the galley. 'Les any problems?'

'No Skipper, supplies are good, fresh water is holding out, but we won't have much left by the time we reach Melbourne.'

'I'll go and speak with Ted, Les, get the canvas ready just in case we reach a rainstorm, and have the empty barrels ready.' I touched Les gently on the shoulder, letting him know I understood. I walked over to Snowy. 'I have a little job for you.'

'Yes, Skipper, Ted did say you would have.'

'Tommy has been working with young Colin to improve his education. We have plenty of crew aboard at the moment, so if you could spend seven hours a day with him to further his education and prepare him for the world and its unpredictable problems.' I winked at him. 'Including any knowledge you have about women and sexual relationships, then I won't need to kill you!' I smiled at him and gave a chuckle.

Snowy whispered to himself, '*three days on the main masts!*'

'No Snowy, this is more fun.' I turned and walked back out on deck with the two coffees and sticky buns, and went back to the Bridge.

To my surprise, the parrot was sitting on Jacko's shoulder. The dog was lying down on the floor next to him and Cat was lying on the bench, looking down at the dog. Should I interfere? I hesitated for a moment, but Jacko had already smelled the sticky buns, so had the parrot. I put the coffee down on the bench with the sticky buns, took one, and sat down. I opened my logbook and read through it, picked up my sexton and took the bearings and ordinances, and went back to finish my coffee. I wrote down the date, time and course bearings. What else can I write? We experienced an uprising caused by currents deep down in the sea, whirlpools and what could be described as boiling water, don't want to experience it again, no problems with the *Mary Moore*, but did need to re-whip and latch the lower topsail yardarm.

CHAPTER 36

It was incredible. The wind stayed with us for the next seven days. We were averaging 200 nautical miles a day, and had covered 1400 miles. The doctor's patients were doing well. Mervyn was doing his exercises on deck with the others. Still no rain. I wanted rain to tighten the rigging and replenish our freshwater. I sat with Jarrett, checking the charts. 'I want to alter course when we reach longitude 110, latitude 15, which should then take us straight down the coast of Australia, missing any land. South 175, so that should be in the morning, by my calculations. Got that Jacko?'

'Aye, aye Skipper. South 175 in the morning.'

'Jacko, thank the witchy for the wind, but a bit of rain would be nice.'

Jacko grinned and did one of his funny little dances. The parrot on his shoulder didn't quite know what to make of it, but stayed there. The dog just rolled over and seemed to be annoyed that Jacko woke him up.

Jarrett sighed. 'Bill, sadly enough, the days of sailing are coming to an end. When we get back to Melbourne, there will be changes. My duty lies with my father's company and I know that I will need experienced sea personnel with me, Trevor, Margaret, young Colin, Phillip, Dominic and Tommy. Mervyn will make his own future. That's his nature. What are your thoughts, Bill?'

I stared at him. He was right. The days of sailing were coming to an end and the younger generation must move on. Trevor had the knowledge to get his Masters' ticket, so had Tommy, but I didn't want to lose Tommy, he was my right hand. 'Yes Jarrett, I don't really know what's going to happen when we reach Melbourne, but I'm quite sure the powers that be have a plan for the *Mary Moore*. If you can give the lads,' I grinned, 'and lassies a future, please do it. They all have the skills you need and I know they would be your people, your crew.'

I felt sad. It would mean my days at sea would end. What does the future have in store for me; only Jacko knows. But I do have Lesley, the future will not be lonely.

The next morning we altered course and set sail down the west coast of Australia, in the Indian Ocean. It will be 6-7 days before we need to alter course again to go around the West Cape, then across the gulf to Melbourne. I thought of Trevor. I first met him on the train in Bairnsdale, when we were heading back to Melbourne. He was just 15 years old, and he was taking full responsibility for his life, looking for work and somewhere to live. I offered him a job, and he took it on and became a man. He is a great asset to himself and anybody who employed him. I had met Margaret in the fjords of Norway. She worked for MI5, and had taken a lot of hard knocks. She met Trevor, and the romance blossomed. Now they were married and had twins on the way. She has recovered well. She is a little older than Trevor, but the chemistry between them seems to work.

Next morning we altered course for Perth. We had a good, steady breeze from the stern. The south trade winds kept our sails full. We were making good time. I could see Phillip and Dominic talking to the man with the injured stomach. They were sitting on the hatch cover. It gave me a warm feeling and a sense of satisfaction that he was doing well.

I had noticed the other men were assisting him where they could, and were doing the exercises with Mervyn. Lisa and her husband seemed to be enjoying a holiday together. Ted had a little grumble every now and then, I told him he was getting old, he would growl at me, but I knew he was enjoying the company, as he would often say *Not like the old days Skipper,* with a grin on his face and shaking his head.

CHAPTER 37

The following day went well, although in the afternoon it got humid, very humid. Lisa was sitting in the shade with the dog, who was panting very heavily. The parrot was sitting in the rigging, with its wings spread open, trying to catch a cool breeze.

Jacko said, 'I don't like this Bill, don't like it at all. The hot air and cold air don't mix, witchy doesn't like it.'

I glanced at the barometer; it had dropped slightly. 'When, Jacko?'

'In the morning Bill.' I put my hand on Jacko's shoulder and squeezed tightly, then went to find Ted, who was in the galley, drinking coffee and talking to Lesley. I walked up behind them, not wanting to interfere with their conversation. Ted turned around and looked at me.

'Jacko has warned me bad weather is coming in the morning, cold and hot air mixing.'

Ted shook his head. 'That is not what we want, hurricanes and tornadoes. Mother Nature having tantrums!'

'Ted, we still need water. Could you be ready?' He gave me that look. 'I think we'll rig for storm warning about 11 pm.' I walked over to Les. 'The new passengers looking after you, Les?'

He smiled. 'They are keeping me busy, but they're very easy to get along with. They'll do anything I ask them to do.'

'The great one has informed me we're expecting bad weather in the morning.'

'Well Bill, I'll have his food prepared.'

'We hope this will give us a chance to replenish the water, which will take the worry off your mind, my dear friend.'

I picked up a hot, freshly made biscuit off the plate and tossed it from hand to hand. I heard Les chuckle. 'A little bit hot, Bill?'

I walked over to Snowy and young Colin, put the biscuits down in front of Colin. 'Bit hot! Snowy, bad weather coming tomorrow, stay in here, both of you.'

I left and went to find Lisa and Doc. 'We're expecting bad weather tomorrow. Could you keep the dog and parrot in a safe place? I'm more worried about the parrot, your dog will most probably stay with Jacko. They seem to have made good friends, but as long as he is inside. Your parrot is a cheeky little sod, isn't he?' He had found Les's biscuits. 'I have to get them red hot, get them straight out of the oven while they're still hot. Are you comfortable in your quarters?'

'Yes, we are Bill. Could you confine my patients to their quarters tomorrow, Bill, so they don't stretch their stitches open.'

'Follow me, doc.' We walked up to the first man, who was sitting with Mervyn. 'We don't call you by name, because you're not really here on this vessel. Tomorrow you will stay in your quarters, tightly wrapped in your bunk. I would prefer hammocks. If you were to fall out, we would have bigger problems. Remember, bad weather tomorrow. Do you hear me?'

'Yes, sir.'

Sergeant Nelis and I winked at him. 'You can take care of Lesley tomorrow; she hasn't played chess for quite a while. Now, where's the other gentleman?'

'Trevor and the other gentleman have been asked by Ted to lash down the bow line rope.'

I saw Trevor and asked, 'Trevor, could you ask Margaret to stay in her cabin tomorrow. You know why.'

He put both his hands up in the air and stood up. 'Beg your pardon Captain, but isn't that a perilous job to give to me? I thought that was the Captain's responsibility.'

'Yes, it was once Trevor, but I discovered that in the navy the Captain's job was to delegate the jobs. I found it such an easy way out and I don't end up with bruises. Sorry Trevor.' He sank down to his knees.

I looked at the other gentleman. 'How's your knife wound doing?'

'It's healing up well, Skipper.'

'Could you let the doc have a look at the wound?' The doctor glanced at me with a serious look.

He looked back at the man. 'Have you been feeling all right?' he asked.

'Just a bit hot and sweaty with the humidity.'

Doc replied, 'I don't like the colour of it. If it's going to be rough tomorrow, I want to open it up now. It looks like a little infection. Could you please come down to the galley now?'

As we walked back down to the galley, the doc said, 'Bill, these men are tough. I don't know whether it was sweat on his forehead or a fever, but you knew something, didn't you? Some things rub on you from Jacko.'

'He is so much more in tune than I ever could be.' The doctor glanced at Lisa and raised his hand. She knew that he needed his bag. The doctor went to the galley.

'Les, could you have a saucepan full of boiling water please?'

'I can have it whenever you want it.'

'I need to operate on this man again. Could you also boil some tea towels and my instruments?' Mervyn walked in the door. 'Mervyn, could you get me a bucket of sea water and another empty bucket?' Mervyn didn't hesitate. Les was already scrubbing down the table and drying it. Lisa came in with the doc's bag and put the instruments into the boiling water. A clean sheet was spread on the table and the man was lifted up onto the table, and before he could blink, a morphine needle had been injected into his arm. He started to argue and protest, but his words were slurred and before long, he was out cold. We rolled him onto his side and lifted his arm. Mervyn and Lesley held him down.

The doctor quietly said, 'you see this yellow on one side of the wound, that is the infection. I will need to lance it first. Could you hold that towel here?' He took out his scalpel and slowly pressed it to the yellow point. Yellow fluid eased out of the wound, which was swabbed down with the towel. 'I'm going to make an incision down here.' He took the scalpel, rinsed it in the hot water, then opened the wound. More foul fluid eased out. He took his syringe, filled it with water, and flushed out the wound. 'Ah, here is the culprit. This is a piece of his shirt and it has infected the wound. I thought because it bled so well, it was clean. We will wash it out and stitch it back up.'

Imagine, just a fragment of material could do that! This time his arm was well bandaged to his side. The man slowly opened his eyes and continued his protest, not even knowing he'd been unconscious. We all laughed and slowly left the galley. Lisa and the doctor helped the man off the table. 'You had a piece of material left in the wound, which is why it had become infected.'

Lisa said to the man, 'Next time the doctor asks you a question, answer him straight and truthfully, because it is your life in his hands. I want you to sit up in your bunk for the next three days.'

I went and stood next to Jacko at the helm. He nudged me with his elbow. 'Would you like to get the coffee, William, from the galley which you have just come from?'

'Jacko, you are like a nagging, chattering kookaburra.'

I went back down to the galley for his coffee, biscuits and dough-nuts. I returned and placed them on the bench. 'Is there anything else that sir requires?'

I took my sexton out on deck and took my bearings, went back and recorded them in the logbook: time, date, course, sea calm, humidity 2, extreme, very high, expecting weather change by the morning. I went back out on deck and spoke with Lisa. 'Could you put the parrot some-where where he is safe? We expect a bit of a blow tomorrow, your quar-ters would be sufficient. If you want to put the dog with the parrot, that's okay, but you can leave him with Jacko if you want. Ted, could you relieve Jacko at dusk. Let him rest; he'll have a big day tomorrow. At 12 am rig for storm weather, we'll see what it's like to catch fresh water. Is the diesel tank full?'

'Yes, Bill, and I'll have safety ropes on deck.' Just then, we heard a cheer from the stern. Trevor had a long line out with a red jig and had caught himself a tuna. That will keep Les happy, fresh fish for supper. I stood with Jacko, watching the sunset. There was an ominous yellow glow around the setting sun. Mother Nature was using all her colours, absolutely majestic, but Jacko didn't like it. He didn't say a word, and that's what worried me.

CHAPTER 38

Darkness had crept in, the moon rose, Tommy had taken the helm. Jacko was watching the moon. It had a silvery glow around it, ice crystals in the upper atmosphere. 'Yes Jacko, I see it. Talk to the witchy Jacko, then get some rest, you've got a big day tomorrow.' He nodded and went into the galley.

The air was still humid, I heard Lesley's voice. 'Your supper Bill,' I went into the galley. Most of the crew were there getting food while they could and hot coffee.

Lisa smiled at me 'our parrot is sulking. He has pushed himself into a corner of the bunk and won't come out'

Jacko said, 'When they know a storm is coming, they will crawl into a tree hollow where they are safe. The dog is on my bunk; it is my bunk, not his.' I put my hand on his shoulder.

'But he is our guest Jacko, and you know Mum's rules. Treat your guest with the upmost of respect.' I turned around, went back to the Bridge, and sat down in my comfortable chair. Tommy and I talked for a while. 'Tommy, Jarrett tells me the days of sail are coming to an end.

How long, we don't know. Profit and loss will decide our future. What would you do Tommy when we have to retire?'

'Bill, I would like a small farm and some cows, and a cuddly woman, in my bed it's getting lonely and I need somebody to love, getting too old for all the other stuff, but it would be nice, in a manner of speaking Bill, I need what you've got, a companion, a friend, somebody who I can talk to and will understand me.' We talked a little more, then I dozed off to sleep. I knew Lesley had come to bed, but she didn't disturb me. When I did wake up, I could hear Ted giving his orders to rig *Mary Moore* for storm weather. It was still very humid, but somehow your senses warned you that something was different. Jacko had already taken the helm, he chuckled to himself 'I told dog he can sleep in your bunk because you're not using it! Remember, Mum's rule, Bill look to the bow, starboard side,' every now and again I could see a faint flash, but couldn't hear any thunder, it was too far away, over the horizon.

Ted came onto the Bridge with young Colin 'Bill I don't like it; it looks like a cyclone.'

'Yes Ted, that concerns me as well, but you see those flashes of lightening, I'm hoping we're going to miss it and go down one side of it, young Colin, this time you're one of the crew, so you must be part of the team, get yourself a bucket, you will experience fear, but remember fear is in your mind and you must control it, for yourself, now go down with the lads and be part of the crew.'

Lesley came out of the cabin. 'You're a noisy lot. Bill, you looked so handsome and inviting this morning, that I kissed you on the end of your nose, then I realised it was the dog!' Jacko burst out laughing. Ted and Jarrett looked confused. Lesley lent up against Jacko. 'I'll get you some breakfast and coffee and get dog something. You are both my little puppies!' and off she went.

Ted started to leave the Bridge, but lent up against Jacko, raised his voice slightly and said, 'you're my little puppies, I will go and get you a nice breakfast.' He walked out of the Bridge. Jacko said to himself, *he's jealous!* But said it in his own indigenous language.

'You could be right Jacko,' I said to him. Jarrett looked a little confused. 'Jarrett, could you make sure the two injured men in the galley are wedged up against the bulkhead with mattresses around them?'

'Yes, Skipper, straight away.'

Jacko and I watched the lightening over the horizon. Jacko looked at the Cat; they stared into each other's eyes. That was a warning to me. Lesley came back with two breakfasts and 2 cups of coffee. Margaret followed her with two more plates. Lesley put one plate and coffee in front of Jacko and one plate in front of me. Margaret put one of her plates in front of the Cat and went into our cabin and put the other plate in front of the dog.'

'Lesley, how did the dog get up into my bunk?'

Lesley lent up against Jacko. 'We wouldn't know, would we Jacko?' he grinned at me with his cheeky grin and left.

'Margaret, could you stay on the Bridge and curl yourself up in Lesley's bunk? Then I won't have to worry about the babies, but I would suggest you get yourself some food and water.' I spun around and looked at Jacko. The humidity had gone.

Jacko said 'here it comes!'

Daylight was just starting to come and we could see the white caps on the small waves coming towards us from our starboard quarter, the *Mary Moore* pushed her way through them, I lent out of the Bridge and shouted to Ted 'have Tommy start the big motor,' but Tommy was already on his way, I glanced up, Ted already knew that I wanted to brace the yardarm so the sails could catch the winds. I went back onto the Bridge to have my breakfast, then went into the galley with the empty plates and cups. 'Jarrett, could you please stay with Jacko' Jarrett got two coffees and some biscuits and disappeared back onto the Bridge. 'Lisa, doc, it will be too rough for you. Stay here in the galley. It's quiet now so get anything now that you might need. I felt the first thump of a good wave and nodded to Les, he knew to shut his stove down, I glanced around the galley, everything appeared to be shipshape, Ted had the men putting the shutters on the windows, I followed Margaret back on to the Bridge. Lisa was coming out of her cabin and locking the door. The big motor roared back into life, black smoke belched out. We were prepared.

I looked towards the bow and saw the black sky and a huge wave coming towards us. I rang the bell three times and braced myself for what was coming. I could see Ted lashing himself to the mainmast. Two men were on the pumps. Jacko had lashed himself to the helm with a rope and Jarrett was ready to help him. I watched the menacing-looking wave curling in front of us, it would have been 45 feet high. The *Mary Moore* plunged into the wave then rose up in the air to meet it, throwing water up over herself, out over her sides and vibrating with the impact. She prepared herself to meet the next wave, crashing into it again, throwing water even higher. It was good knowing we had a good weight cargo, which would keep her steady and stable. She didn't seem to roll very much and she was meeting the waves the right way, or was it because we now had a propeller to give us more thrust? She rose up again and again to meet new waves. They were a menacing dark green, black waves, straight out of hell. There were flashes of yellow and red from the lightening and white caps on the waves. Every now and then a wave would curl over the top of the bow and go crashing down her decks. I kept looking for Ted and the two men on the pumps. Every now and then I would be able to see them, but the noise, the roaring and howling of the wind in the rigging, it was menacing. I called out to Margaret to check that she was all right. She replied she was. I wondered how Lesley was, but the waves started to move more around to our starboard side, so we altered course slightly to our port so that we were catching the waves on our starboard quarter, we had plenty of distance between us and the coast, so we should be safe during the night.

CHAPTER 39

It was morning! The wind had swung around to our stern, port side quarter, we altered course back to starboard and our original course. The squall was now pushing us and it very slowly depleted over the next 12 hours.

Ted and Tommy checked the cargo. Everything was right. I talked to everyone of the crew, and everybody seemed to be intact, no broken bones, just some bad bruises.

Les had the stove burning again, and he was serving hot food along with Lesley, Margaret and Lisa. He enjoyed the women's company.

The Doctor was busy checking out the crew's bruises and attending to his patients. I sat down and opened my logbook and recorded everything about the storm. We seemed to be making good time. The last part of the storm coming from the stern had helped us.

Something touched my shoulder. I looked around expecting to see Lesley, but it was the parrot 'Good day to you parrot. How did you weather the storm?' It just made a chirping noise and nibbled my ear. I put my finger up and stroked under its beak; it seemed to enjoy it. I gave it some biscuit; that went down well too, but I noticed Cat was looking at me. 'I'm sorry Cat, I don't have any tuna, just biscuits.'

Jarrett walked in behind Jacko and nudged him. He put a plate of sticky buns down in front of him, and Jacko rewarded him with one of his big cheeky grins. 'So the parrot is working on you Skipper, he does that to anyone who's got food.'

Jarrett picked up his sexton and went back out to take his readings. For his naval ticket, he must know all the questions and the answers, but for now, he needs to put them in the right places and order. 'Jarrett, Trevor is now your man, but in my mind,' and I put my hand on Trevor's shoulder, 'he will always be one of my crew. You are one of the best lad, and I know Ted will miss you.'

The next two days went smoothly. I had taken my bearings with the sexton and entered them in the logbook: date, time, ordinance and bearings, barometer is dropping, altering course to due east, the last leg to Melbourne. I underlined Melbourne. Without thinking, I put home.

I glanced at Jacko. 'Yes Bill, we both miss the desert. We had a longing for home.'

'Now Jacko, tell me what the course is.'

Jacko grinned, 'Due east, Bill, and you're going to get two cups of coffee.'

I didn't say a word, closed my logbook and went to get the coffee. I poured out three coffees. Trevor was just finishing his breakfast. I started to walk out the door. 'Trevor, to the Bridge. I've got your coffee.'

Margaret looked up with a frown and a puzzled look on her face. We left the galley and went to the Bridge. 'Trevor, if you want to write anything down, use this pen and paper. He's all yours Jacko.'

I sat down in my chair and started to drink my coffee. I looked up at the barometer. It was falling to where it said 'rain'. I glanced at the horizon and could just make out some clouds in the distance. I listened to Jacko talking about entrances to harbours and channel marks, but I had finished my coffee and was thinking about filling up the barrels with fresh rain water. I got up and went down to the galley with my cup. I met Margaret on the deck. She was waiting for me.

She looked at me very seriously, put both her hands on her hips. 'What are you doing with my husband?'

'Margaret, I believe both you and Trevor are going to work with Jarrett when we reach Melbourne. I want Trevor to be prepared for what Jarrett has in store for him. Now Margaret, say thank you, Captain!'

Margaret gave a small curtsy and said, 'thank you Captain.'

'Margaret, when the babies are born you can call me granddad, and Lesley grandma. I put my hand out. She took it and pushed it to one side and threw her arms around my neck.

'Captain, you've always been my granddad, from the first day we met.'

'Yes, I remember a skinny little girl coming through the hatch in the baulk works in Norway.'

'Yes, you've always been there when I needed you. Now, the Commander sent me to tell you that you haven't had your breakfast yet. Would you please follow me, sir.'

'I didn't realise granddaughters were so polite.' We went into the galley. Ted was just finishing his breakfast. 'Ted, there is a rain squall ahead of us, and we need fresh water.' He nodded and finished his breakfast. Then Ted nodded to Mervyn and young Colin and they followed him back out on deck. The wind had picked up slightly and then the rain started. Philip and Dominic were slacking off the whip and guide lines, as the rain would cause them to tighten. The rest of the crew were having a good wash in the fresh water and doing their washing. It rained all day and part of the night. The water barrels were full.

The next day we had a stiff breeze from the stern quarter starboard side, we were making good time. We had a big swell. One minute we were on top of the wave, the next we were in the trough, looking up at them on either side of us. We were in the gulf, waves were coming up from the South Pole. This continued for the next three days, fortunately the barometer stayed steady.

On the fourth day Jacko shouted, 'Whales port side.' We could see their waterspouts and their tails rising high in the air. There were also dolphins, porpoises and migrating fish. We were in the gulf stream that runs the down right side of Australia. We had to tack backwards and forwards. The wind stayed with us, making good time.

Jarrett was working with Trevor, taking bearings and working out how to take ordinance. I took my sexton and did the same. All three of us put our figures together, and low and behold, they all came out the same! Jacko winked at Trevor and nodded.

Tonight we should see the flashes from the lighthouse on Kangaroo Island, South Australia, but it will only be very faint. It is the only working square lighthouse in the world. The Boyd lighthouse was never commissioned. We should see Cape Nelson lighthouse in the early morning, then, if the wind stays with us, Cape Otway in the early morning.

I looked at Cat and thought of Colin. Memories came flashing through my mind of the years gone by. Soon, we will be where he wanted to be, where his spirit could see the ships entering and leaving port. *Colin, we're in far better shape now than last time we entered Port Melbourne.* In my mind I heard a voice, *'Bill, you're both home and your mum knows your home. My boys are home again!'* I turned and looked straight at Jacko. He was grinning at me and nodded. Cat was staring at both of us. 'Coffee Jacko?'

'Yes, and something to nibble on.'

'Jacko, I can never understand why you're not 18 stone instead of just a broom handle!' I started to leave the Bridge and saw Jarrett coming towards me carrying coffee and food. I thought he would make a good waiter carrying plates on a moving vessel. I stepped back onto the Bridge. 'Jacko, the waiter is coming.' I sat sipping my coffee and watching Jacko stuffing food into his mouth. When you are standing at the wheel, you are the helmsman. Your mind is constantly on your course, your body is constantly working, moving the wheel from port to starboard. The minute you lose concentration, you're off course. I believe it is the most responsible job aboard, and Jacko does it extremely well. Just then, Lesley walked in and sat down in my chair.

'Bill, if I had a chair like this in the galley, I wouldn't get any work done!'

I thought, *is she making a suggestion?* Lesley nudged me on my leg with her foot.

I looked at Jacko, Jarrett, and Lesley. I raised my voice slightly. 'I cannot understand how this old sailing vessel and its crew were given the task of deceiving the Germans with a cargo of uranium. Now she has been given the task of deceiving the world with a cargo of 60 ton of gold. We've nearly pulled it off, we should go down in history, but we won't. It's all one big secret and who would believe us?'

Jarrett chuckled to himself, 'Bill, nobody will know what we're smiling at, because it is our secret and we share it together.'

Just then, Trevor walked in through the door. 'School time?' Jacko asked.

'I'll leave you three together.'

Trevor's voice boomed out, 'Bill, not all three together?'

'Sorry lad, it is what it is. Jarrett wants the best out of you, he has a lot in store for you.' I winked at him, 'and it's a secret!'

I left them to it and went into the galley. 'How's everything Les?'

'Good Bill, plenty of fresh water.'

'How are those two in the corner?'

'I think Snowy is in a bit of trouble. Young Colin is quick and sharp. He is also very streetwise. That young lad needs to go to university.'

'How would we get him into a university?'

'Lesley and yourself have a high standing in the British Navy, he comes from Cape Town. I believe he would make a good officer and a good seaman.'

'Do you think Snowy has taught him all he can?'

'Yes Bill.'

'Good, then we will move him up a class, to the Bridge.'

I slowly walked over to Snowy and young Colin. 'Do you want a break, Snowy? If so, we will move this young man to the Bridge.'

Snowy smiled at me. Then his face went very serious. 'Bill, what do you have in store for me now?'

'Next I would like you to get with Jarrett and ensure that all the paperwork is in order for the wine. It doesn't belong to the Navy, it belongs to us.' I headed towards the stern, nodding to Ted and young Colin. We went to the Bridge. I nodded to Jacko, and he joined us. Jarrett took the wheel.

As we all stood at the stern, something touched my leg. I looked down, and there was Cat. I picked him up and put him on my shoulder. 'Colin, we are near the quadrants where your father was laid to rest by his own hand, it is where he wanted to be, your father was our brother, he taught us our trade, now you go back to the galley and fetch Les.'

We waited quietly, then watched as Les and young Colin walked together. 'This is what our brother Colin would have wanted. His best friend and his son together.'

Les put both his hands on young Colin's shoulders and looked straight into his eyes. We could see the tears in his eyes. 'Young man, your father was my best friend; we had lived a lifetime together. I know your father would have wanted us to give you the best chance in life that we could, and we will use all our resources to give you that in this voyage, you have proved yourself a man, your father would have been so proud of you, or should I say,' Les was looking at Cat, 'he is very proud of you.'

We all looked over the stern. Les stood behind young Colin with his hands on his shoulders. The rays of the setting sun over the sea shone on all of us and illuminated the sails and rigging. We all stood there for the next half an hour, thinking of Colin. Finally, Jacko did one of his little dances and said a few words in his language. We all went back to the galley.

'Young Colin, you are on the Bridge tomorrow studying. We don't have much time left for you to learn all that you need to know.'

Jacko was back on the Bridge. Jarrett was having his supper. Lesley and I sat together. 'Lesley, Jacko tells me there are big changes coming, but he doesn't have the answers.'

I have a big crew. They all seem to work so well together. Everything is happening just like clockwork. It was easier for Ted. Les enjoyed being with the women, their laughter and chitchat, the way they treated him like a granddad, and he liked listening to their little problems. The Doctor and Lisa were sitting there together, with their dog. To them, it was the holiday they so badly needed. They could be themselves and not hide. I've never had a crew with their hair so neatly trimmed!

'Lesley, I'm going to shut my eyes for a while.' I went up to the Bridge; Jacko and Ted were there. Jacko looked at me with big sad eyes, 'Yes Jacko, Lesley will feed you. Ted, go and get some rest. Get Tommy to relieve you. Wake me the minute you see the Cape Otway Lighthouse.' Ted nodded, and I went into my cabin.

I woke with a start. There was a hand on my shoulder. 'The lighthouse, Skipper. We can just make out the flashes of light.'

A muffled voice below me said, 'will you two shut up. I've got another two hours sleep, so you two little boys can run away and play.'

Ted gave a little chuckle. 'Excuse me madam, didn't mean to wake you, but I had no-one to play with!' He put his hand on my hand and shook it. 'Get up, Skipper!'

I swung my legs over the bunk. 'Ted, get Jarrett to relieve Jacko.' Ted turned and faced Lesley and gave a little bow, but her head was buried in the blankets. I got dressed and went onto the Bridge, glanced at the barometer, it was holding steady. We had all sails set and a good breeze to fill them. I slid the door back into the cabin so we wouldn't wake Lesley again. I was watching the flashes of light from the lighthouse. This was one of the most important lighthouses in Australia. We turned sharply to port and headed down the Victorian coast to Melbourne. Miss this and you're headed to King Island, Wilson's Promontory or one of the many small islands in Bass Strait. The sequence of the flashing lights was three flashes, 50 seconds, then another three flashes, 50 seconds, then a third three flashes, 50 seconds. We were right on course. We were heading for the dreaded Eye of the Needle. This is crucial for a sailing vessel, but this time I had an ace up my sleeve, my beautiful Gardner motor.

Jarrett entered the Bridge without a word being spoken. Jacko was off to the galley. 'Good morning, Skipper.'

His voice broke my train of thought. 'Good morning Jarrett. It looks like it's going to be a good day. The light from the lighthouse is bright and strong, no fog or cloud to interfere with it. I think the wind will be coming from the east, when we alter course around Cape Otway and pass Apollo Bay. This is not what we really need, as it will try to push us into the rugged cliffs along the coast. When the lighthouse is over our stern quarter, we will alter course North East 62° and head for the rip. I'm going to get something to eat. Jarrett, have you had your breakfast yet?'

'No, Skipper.'

I started to walk past him and put my hand on his shoulder. 'I'm going to miss you, Jarrett. You have been with me through the worst of it.' I sighed deeply. 'You've always been there Jarrett, my right arm, you never questioned me, just did as I asked. A Captain couldn't ask for more. I don't have a son of my own, but somehow you've taken that place inside me.'

'Skipper, when I'm sitting at my desk surrounded with paperwork, my mind will be on this Bridge, with *Daisy May*, Jacko and the rest of the crew. You have taught me what I need to know to go forth into the future. I will not fail you, or my father.' He nudged me and smiled. 'I'll just do a funny little dance and chant a few funny little words and it will all work out!'

I took another deep sigh and fought back the tears, nodded to Jarrett, and went down for my breakfast.

'Les, I don't think Jarrett is going to have another one of your breakfasts for a very long time. Could you pile his plate up so he never forgets?'

Les looked at me with a sad look and nodded. He went back into his kitchen and went to work on the breakfast plate. I sat down next to Mervyn and his men. 'How are your wounds, gentlemen?'

The man with the knife wound said, 'The doc's fixed mine well. He was the right man in the right place, at the right time.'

I looked at the other man, 'how are you doing?'

'Doing well, Skipper, but Doc said I will need an x-ray to make sure. I'm walking around well, so things must be getting a lot better.'

I saw Les walking out of the galley with a plate and a cloth over the top of it, with two mugs to keep it warm. Jacko couldn't take his eyes off it. Les walked onto the Bridge and put the plate on the bench with the coffee. He knocked on the cabin door and gave Lesley her tea.

'Lesley, the galley is going to get busy. I need you, my dear daughter.' He turned around and walked back onto the Bridge and closed the door. 'Jarrett, enjoy your breakfast. Time is catching up with us and we're going to lose you. We will all miss you. You have become a man amongst men, now always walk tall.' He put his hand out and shook Jarrett's hand.

'Les, I couldn't have had a better teacher or a better friend. If there is anything I can do for you, no matter what, please let me know.'

Jarrett couldn't stop the tears flowing. Les turned and went back to the galley so Jarrett wouldn't see his tears.

I got my breakfast and walked over to Tommy O'Hia, put my plate down on the table, and sat down beside him. I looked at his big fuzzy black hair. 'Tommy, it looks like Lisa has missed you. Your hair is still intact!'

Those big eyes shone and that contagious grin came over his face 'No, Skipper. I'm next off the rack. I have an English lady waiting for me in Melbourne and Lisa has said I might frighten the life out of her. She said whether I liked it or not, she's going to trim my hair and shave my beard off. When I started to protest, she said doctor's orders.'

I saw Lisa scowling at me. I know you can't fight three aces in the deck!'

'So what are you going to do in Melbourne, Tommy?'

'We're going to head up the coast and breed cattle.'

'You have certainly earned that right, Tommy. I wish you well for the future. Perhaps you will meet Foxy again and talk over old times.'

I finished my breakfast. Lesley was walking through the door. I got up, walked over and kissed her on the forehead. 'Good morning dear, they tell me the early bird catches the worm!'

She glanced at Jacko and nodded. 'I think he's already eaten them.'

I went back onto the Bridge. Ted was there with Jarrett. I glanced at both of them and nodded. I reached up, took the rope for the bell, and rang it three times. The crew all appeared on deck, but I heard Jacko laughing. Jarrett said to me, 'Look at Snowy!' There was Snowy wearing a white dressing gown and slippers. I had never before seen this on a vessel, it was quite amusing.

'Well lads, this is the last leg of this voyage. We will now turn north-east, and head down the Eye of the Needle. The yardarms have to be braced, then when we enter the rip, the yardarms will be braced again. Wait for Ted's command. We have to be sharp and on the ball. Ted will put half of you to rest. Rest doesn't necessarily mean sleep!'

Ted walked past me and went on deck. I put my hand on Jarrett's shoulder and nodded at Ted. 'North East 60° Jarrett.' The working half of the crew went to work. Yardarms were braced again to catch the wind. Though Ted had given the command, it just happened that the vessel lent over to her port side and settled back down again.

I shouted out, 'Margaret, start the motor.'

She looked at me with a puzzled look, turned and headed towards the stern.

'Walk Margaret, don't run!'

She turned her head slightly to me and patted her tummy, and walked to the stern. Tommy walked over to the side and looked over. I heard the little donkey motor start, then we heard the big motor turn over and come to life. Tommy looked at me, he lifted both his hands in the air, raising his thumb up to me, he was just making sure Margaret had turned the sea cock on, so that the water could cool the motor, she returned to the deck with a beautiful grin.

'Coffee Jarrett?'

'No, Skipper. Could you make it tea with two sugars? I'm starting to worry about my kidneys. How much coffee can they take?'

Jacko was sitting in the galley talking to young Colin. He was making good work of a plate of fresh biscuits. 'Jacko, come and talk to me.' He got up and walked over. 'What do you think about letting Jarrett take her into Melbourne? You take over just before Williamstown. I will stand behind him.'

'Yes, Bill, that would be a good idea. This will be his day. He will never do it again.'

'Yes, Jacko, they say this is one of the worst ports to enter in the world.'

'No, Bill, you just have to know what you're doing and frighten the witchy out of the fishermen who get in the way.'

I got Jarrett's tea, my coffee and biscuits. Jacko did the same: coffee, biscuits and biscuits. We went up onto the Bridge. After a while, we saw Jarrett fighting the wheel towards starboard. Jacko got up and walked over to him and took the wheel. Jarrett didn't argue. 'Bill, we have a strong current coming towards us and the wind is pushing us to port, not good.' To Jarrett he said, 'put the gear lever into gear.' He did so, 'push the throttle up a little, a little more, a little more, now she's happy.'

Jacko stepped back from the wheel and Jarrett took over again. He found the pressure had gone from the starboard side. Jarrett nudged Jacko with his shoulder and winked at him.

'I knew what the problem was all the time, but I thought it would make you look good fixing it.'

Jacko put his arms in the air and turned around to face me. At the same time Jarrett stole three of his biscuits. 'Jacko, you do these little jokes on other people and they get to do them back.'

Jacko looked like a sad little puppy. I could see Mervyn and Lesley standing on the port side looking towards land. Daylight was glowing over the land; the sea was still dark. 'We've come a long way Mervyn, and it's hard to prepare yourself for what's going to happen when we reach port,' Lesley said.

Mervyn replied, 'Yes, Lesley. Since I first met Bill, I've had no control over my life. Whatever my orders were, I did. I lost two men, they were the best. We've destroyed the communication towers now. I ask myself, why? That communication tower had been out of commission for a long time, the buildings were all overgrown with creepers climbing up the tower, the support cables were covered in creeping vines, the communications building was empty and obviously nobody had been there for a very long time, it wasn't a threat to anybody, it was all political, not military. How did they know we were coming? They were there waiting for us. They were good, but we had the advantage of modern weapons, but I lost two men. Why? I've been writing everything down from when I first met Bill, everything we did together, where we went, who we saw. I've got dates and places. Losing Reno, a little girl's hero. I'm going back there one day with a good bottle of wine. When I've finished, I'm going to put all the information into the National Archives in Canberra so nobody will be able to read them for 30 years.'

Lesley put her hand on his shoulder. 'You may have solved the problem for me, Mervyn. Mrs Henderson could be very helpful. She owes both of us a big favour. I've got to get back to Les. See you later.' She gave me a cuddle and walked back to the galley.

Mary Moore held her course well. The early morning light is with us now. I could see the birds flying out to sea to feed. The wind had dropped to a gentle breeze, all our sails were full.

A head popped out from underneath the bench. Young Colin asked, 'how does it take the pressure off the wheel?'

Jacko and I glanced at each other and smiled. I said, 'Well, Colin, the wind filling our sails, that is pushing us forward, it is also trying to push us to port,' I put my left hand up, 'if this vessel from my elbow to my fingertips,' I put my hand at a slight angle, crossed my arm, 'the wind is coming from this angle, it is filling the sails, pushing us forward, but also pushing us sideways to port. The tide is pushing us from the starboard side so Jarrett has to push the rudder to our starboard to compensate, putting more pressure on the rudder, but because the propeller is behind the rudder it puts more water into the rudder, so that means Jarrett doesn't have to turn the rudder so far, easing the pressure off the wheel. Does that make sense, Colin?'

'Yes, Skipper.' His head went back under the blankets. 'No young Colin, time for you to get your breakfast. You've got learning to do. We should be at the heads by 1.30 pm.'

I picked up my tide guide. High tide is at 2 pm. Jarrett take an hour's break, then fill out your logbook, then go and see Snowy and sort out your cargo papers. You need two copies, one for you and one for us, then return here.'

I took my bearings with the sexton, just for the logbook, and started to fill it out. By the time we had rounded the Cape, my expected arrival time at Port Phillip heads, Queenscliff, wind strength and direction of the high tide at Port Phillip heads.

I could see Jacko was shivering and not quite himself. 'What's wrong, Jacko?'

'Take the wheel.' I didn't argue with him. He went outside and jumped on top of the Bridge, looking towards the stern. After a minute or so, he came down. 'We're being followed again, but a long way away, to our stern, he took the wheel. I got my telescope out and looked towards the stern. It was a long way off, but I knew what it was straightaway—a submarine. When you think you're alone, you're not. I went back to my logbook, wrote down time and submarine at our stern. If it wasn't for Jacko, I wouldn't have known. The radar is showing us land, but nothing else. We were just passing Lorne on our port side, on our starboard side we could see Cape Schanck.

Jarrett turned up with one cup of tea and took a sip. Jacko stared at him. 'Sorry Jacko, no food.'

'Jarrett, I have to be good. I need food. You didn't see the submarine, did you?'

'What submarine?'

Jacko pointed to the stern. I handed Jarrett the telescope. He put his cup down and went out of the Bridge, then came back in.

'How long has that been there, Jacko?'

'Since Adelaide.'

But I had to be sure. 'Jacko, would you say you first sighted or sensed it?'

'I sensed it, then sighted it with the telescope.'

I went back to my logbook and wrote down submarine first sighted off of Adelaide, but I couldn't write down the coordinates because I didn't know. I went down to the galley. 'Lesley, we have had a submarine following us, according to Jacko, since Adelaide.'

Ted walked into the galley. 'I believe there is a pilot boat coming to meet us.'

I went back up onto the Bridge, Jacko had already spotted it. 'Bill, it is a far better boat than when we were here before. Look at the speed, it passed on our starboard side, turned and came up to our port side, where it was better protected.'

Ted had everything prepared. A man in a naval uniform came aboard. I was going down to greet him, but Ted brought him up to the Bridge. he gave me a very arrogant look. 'I'm your pilot. My name is Peter Connolly.'

'And I am Captain William Farquhar, of his Majesty's Navy. Is there something you have forgotten?'

He looked at me for a moment, then said, 'Permission to come aboard, sir.' He saluted me.

I saluted him back. 'You have my permission, Mr Connolly.'

He took a large envelope from his briefcase and handed it to me. There was nothing written on the front of the envelope. I opened it and took out the envelope inside; it was a naval envelope. 'Captain William Farquhar.' I opened it. Inside there was another envelope and some papers. I took out the other envelope. It had 'Mrs Farquhar' written on the front. I gave it to Ted. 'This is for Mrs Farquhar.' Ted nodded and disappeared. I took the papers out and read the first one.

Captain William Farquhar, welcome home. All on board who have uniforms will be required to wear them when entering port. You will be berthing at Williamstown Naval Dockyard. Have all passengers ready to disembark.

It was signed by Admiral French.

The rest of the papers were just normal procedure. 'Mr Connolly, take the wheel.'

'I don't normally do that, Captain.'

'While I'm Captain, you will!'

He took the wheel. 'So there's course on the compass. Jacko, put on your fancy duds. Jarrett put on your uniform and your medals.'

I shouted out, 'Ted.' He was there alongside me in a second. 'Have all the crew with uniforms, put them on, and you put yours on, along with all your medals.'

I went to my cabin and put my uniform on. I touched my clip that said *Australia*. As I started to leave the Bridge, I thought of Margaret. How would she put her uniform on with that baby bump? I saw her walking down to the stern. 'Margaret, could you come up to the Bridge and stand next to Mr Connolly? Mr Connolly, this lady outranks you.'

Then I went down to the galley and sat down next to Lesley. She handed me a piece of paper. 'So, Mrs Farquhar, you are one of the crew.' I smiled at her. 'Lesley, you are a galley slave for Les. I did see Lesley Johnson leave Cape Town.'

'Bill, I have papers here for Jarrett and Tommy. They are discharge papers. I cannot sign them as I don't exist.'

She put the papers in front of me and handed me the pen. I held the pen in my hand. I had felt these emotions before when I was aboard the battleship and lost so many of my crew. These two men were mine! We've been to hell and back! How do I just let them go with the stroke of a pen? I know I had tears in my eyes. I turned and looked at Lesley.

'Yes, Bill, I know that you have to let them go, but they have the right to live free and have a life for themselves. Bill, a father has to let his children go and not stand in their way.'

I looked down at the documents. I had trouble seeing where to sign because of the tears in my eyes, but I signed them.

'There are two more, but you can't sign them yet.'

I knew who was standing behind me. I knew whose hands were on my shoulders. Les didn't say a thing, just gently squeezed my shoulders, then I heard his soft words, 'They will always be yours, Bill, they are your family.'

I put my hand on his and squeezed it. 'If you would both excuse me, I must be on the Bridge.' I stood up and gently kissed Lesley on the forehead, and nodded to Les. I went back to the Bridge.

'Margaret, you and Trevor stay on board. If you want to put your uniform on, that's up to you.' I looked down at her tummy.

'Granddad it would look good in a photo, wouldn't it?' She patted her tummy.

Mr Connolly looked totally out of control. Margaret left the Bridge. Mr Connolly spoke very hesitantly, 'Captain, could you take all the sails off please. I have never taken a sailing ship into port before.'

I smiled. 'Then, Mr Connolly, it will be a good experience for you. We will leave the sails on.'

'But I am the pilot, sir.'

Just then Jarrett walked in, with Ted following him.

'Mr Connolly, relinquish the helm to Captain Collins.'

He did so and took three steps back. He looked like he'd seen the devil himself, for there was Jacko in his full Scottish regalia, along with a sword and dirk. 'Mr Connolly, would you argue with four Captains?'

'No, sir.'

'Is there something you forgot, Mr Connolly?' He looked puzzled for a moment, then turned and saluted. We all saluted back. 'Captain Jacko, there is time for Mr Connolly to have a good breakfast before we enter the Rip. If you would speak to my wife, I'm sure she will feed you.' I nodded to Jacko and Lesley. Jacko returned to the Bridge and stood behind Jarrett. Ted went back down onto the deck.

Jacko gave one of his funny little dances. 'We're back in the Navy God Save the King.'

We were right on course to the Rip, for we had just passed the fare-well Bell. We could quite clearly see the Point Lonsdale Lighthouse overlooking the Rip. With the early morning sunlight illuminating it, you would have thought it had been freshly painted white with its observation deck going around the base. This lighthouse is one of the few left that is staffed and records kept on all shipping entering and leaving the channel. Its light beam flashes every 15 seconds. Its range is 12 nautical miles. It certainly looks tall and majestic. She is a perfect lady looking after shipping. I could quite clearly see the green and red lights guiding us into the channel.

Mr Connolly had turned up on to the Bridge. He certainly doesn't take any time eating his breakfast. I don't think he wanted to miss anything.

'Captain Farquhar, is your radio switched on?'

'No, it isn't.'

'Where is it?'

'Just around the corner, there.'

He picked up the mike and turned it on. 'His Majesty's vessel No. Three, permission to enter the Rip.'

A voice came back. 'The channel is clear. You have permission.' Mr Connolly never even looked at me. He just put his hands behind his back. I thought that he thought he was totally in control.

'Mr Connolly, this is a sailing vessel, of which you apparently have no knowledge of sails. If Captain Collins asks you a question, talk straight to the point. He will have to make quick decisions.'

Jarrett glanced at me and I moved my hand to my side, pushing it back and forwards. I saw the grin in his eyes.

'Captain Jacko put the gear stick into neutral.' I could see the crew in position, waiting. They were eager for this moment. I saw the doctor walk up to the man with bullet wounds. He was holding a whip line, he was ready with the others, the doc tapped him on the shoulder and said, 'No!' He took the line from him, but Lisa had already walked forward and took the soldier's ear in between her fingers and led him away. Ted put his arm around Margaret and I thought he was stopping her from taking the whip on. He said something to her. She was half grinning and half chuckling.

We started to enter the Rip. I could feel the current pushing us. It was the last of the high tide and we had to be quick to alter course and enter the main channel, so it didn't push us aside. I thought of the motor, but decided not to use it. She'll turn sharper under sail. One would not be fighting the other. I could see Ted, and he could see me. I leaned over to Mr Connolly, 'East 3°.'

He stuttered at first then said 'Helmsman East 3°.'

I raised my hand, then I heard Margaret shout, 'Brace the yardarms!'

Mr Connolly's eyes were wide open watching the spas that held the sails, turn to face the wind, but it worked like clock work. Every one of the yardarms turned at exactly the same time.

The *Mary Moore* heeled over slightly to port then turned west, down the south channel and she had free passage, no other vessels were coming towards her. Ted was preparing the crew to embrace the yardarms again, when they got to Hovels Pile. The end of the channel would be on our port side. We could see the Chinaman's hat, it marked the edge of the channel on our port side, on our starboard side we could see the quarantine station. We glided down the channel. There was no movement of water to hinder her. We were on high tide, slack water, the breeze was in our favour. We passed Sorrento on our starboard side, then the south channel. We were nearly up to Hovels Pile. I put my hand on Mr Connolly's shoulder, 'Just hold this course a little bit longer.' We were under sail, and could see the green buoy getting closer on our starboard side. I then said to Mr Connolly in a low voice, 'North 1°.'

Mr Connolly shouted, 'North 1° helmsman.'

I started to lift my arm to Ted, but he had already spoken to Margaret who shouted out, 'Brace the yardarms.'

The crew knew exactly what to do. Ted didn't want them fully braced, only half. *Mary Moore* leaned slightly over to the starboard side, then settled down. We headed straight to Melbourne in Port Phillip Bay, and could see people ashore stopping what they were doing to stare at us in wonder. *Mary Moore* was indeed so beautiful, with all her sails or without. Small boats started to come near us, people were taking photos, or just looking to admire her.

Then Mervyn shouted, 'Those in uniform stand to order and line up, half of you face the starboard side the other half face the port side.'

Mr Connolly picked up the radio mike. 'Naval vessel number three clear of channel.'

I wondered why he didn't just give the name of the vessel, or the type of vessel, does this ship exist or not? Another question without an answer.

We could just make out a passenger ship coming out of Hobsons Bay. The channel split into two just before Williamstown. One went straight into Hobsons Bay, the other one went up the Yarra River. We should meet the other vessel off of Brighton, on our starboard side. I walked out of the Bridge, 'Mr Nelis, permission to use your men?'

'You have my permission, sir.'

Ted and Margaret were watching me. Ted said something to Margaret, and she shouted, 'Stow all canvas.'

They all went to work, some going aloft, some pulling lines. Jacko had already put the motor into gear to give her more power. The sails seemed to disappear as they were stowed away. Having more crew made it so much easier.

'Captain Jacko take the wheel. Mr Collins finish your logbook.'

Jarrett couldn't help himself, 'Jacko would you like me to take your sword, it could get in the way.' Jacko's eyes said it all.

CHAPTER 40

The Captain of the passenger ship was disappointed. He wanted to see the other vessel with all her sails on, but he understood why they weren't. He had once been a Captain of a sailing vessel. He wiped a tear away. This particular sailing vessel left him with many memories. A voice from behind brought him back to the present. 'Captain Fox, your coffee, sir.' He thought back again for just a moment. Is it like tar?

'Thank you.' He took the mug from the man. He wanted to leave the Bridge, but he couldn't, because he was the Captain. He reached forward and put his hand on a button, pressed it, and the horn gave one loud blast. He pushed it again, another loud blast. He pushed it a third time.

Lesley hadn't seen the passenger ship as she was busy in the galley, but on hearing the three blasts, she spun around and looked at the passenger ship coming up the channel. Jacko, Ted and Jarrett also watched the approaching ship. Jacko reached up and pulled the chain to the foghorn three times. I thought, whoever is on the Bridge of that passenger ship would have known who we were. I walked out of the Bridge and went to the starboard side and looked up at the ship as she passed. As

293

I walked back onto the Bridge, I saw Tommy and Mervyn looking at me. I hunched my shoulders. Jacko said, with a big grin all over his face 'That was Foxy.'

'Did the witchy tell you?'

'No Bill, it was the way he blew the three blasts.'

At the beginning of the war we had picked him and his crew up in lifeboats. Their tramp steamer had been torpedoed. He had been a seaman aboard this vessel a very long time before.

Mervyn had his men turning to order with their kit bags alongside them.

'Jacko, put her stern in first.'

We tied up on the starboard side. Mr Connolly never said a word, he just watched. The doctor and Lisa walked up to us. Lisa put her arms around Jacko's neck, cuddled him, and kissed him gently on the end of his nose. 'If I wasn't happily married, I would marry you. Take care Jacko.' She shook hands with all of us and said thank you. The doctor did the same. Jacko was making a fuss over the dog, who was in a cage.

The doctor handed me some papers. 'These are the reports on the injured men. My name isn't on them, and I haven't signed them. Lisa and I don't exist. You do understand.'

'Yes, I do.'

Three uniformed men came aboard. I walked to the gangplank. The first man saluted me. It took me by surprise, as he was an admiral in the British Navy. 'Permission to come aboard sir?' I am Admiral French. I'm here to see a certain lady aboard.' He discreetly showed me three fingers.

'If you would like to go into the galley, sir.'

He nodded, turned and walked away to the galley. The second man walked up to me and saluted. I saluted back. 'I'm from the Ministry of Supply and Defence. My name is Paul Smith.' He handed me his papers. I read them briefly and turned and nodded to Ted.

'Ted, this is Mr Paul Smith from the Ministry of Supply and Defence. I handed Ted the papers.'

The third man didn't salute me. He did, however, give me the sign of vitality. I did the same and shook his hand. 'I have come for my brothers.'

'You have my permission to come aboard.'

The man smiled at me. 'Is it possible to meet Jacko?'

'Yes, he is in the galley. You won't miss him!'

I noticed a black car had arrived on the wharf. Admiral French, Lisa and the doctor had walked out of the galley and were walking towards the gangplank. Lisa stopped, turned around and threw her arms around my neck and cuddled me. I cuddled her back. In her soft, warm voice she said, 'thank you for bringing us home.' I saw the tears in her eyes, they were falling down her cheeks.

'Lisa, no matter what the purpose of our voyage was, you made it all worthwhile.'

She pressed her head against my chest, then turned to join her husband. I watched Admiral French saying goodbye to them, then their car slowly drove off.

Admiral French returned aboard. 'Bill, if I may call you Bill.'

'Certainly.'

'My name is Martin.' We shook hands. 'I'm returning to England to all the pomp and ceremony. I'm going to miss Australia, the warmth and friendliness of the people, but, back to work. That car is taking them to Government House. I believe they are going to be awarded the St. George Medal. Now Bill, you outrank me; Lesley outranks me.'

Just then Mervyn and his men started to walk towards us. They saluted us, we both saluted them back.

'Mr Nelis.' I handed him an envelope. 'If you could give this to the medical staff. In it, there is a report. The doctor would like your man to have an X-ray, as he is not happy with the way his wound is healing.'

'Captain, he is more concerned that a lady led him away by his ear, and how he's going to live it down amongst all his colleagues!'

Mervyn and I shook hands. I said to him, 'Happy to meet, sorry to part, happy to meet again,' and they were off to a waiting bus.

The next man to walk up with his kit bag was Tommy. I looked at him, surprised, but I had a grin on my face. 'That lady certainly did a good job on you. Your hair and beard look really great. I wouldn't have recognised you.'

'Bill, I have been discharged from the Navy. All I have to do now is pick up my pay. I have had enough trouble with Jacko, so please don't give me any more trouble.'

Those big, wide eyes twinkled at me. 'Tommy, enjoy your new companion and your cows. Mr French said to take these papers.' I reached into my inside pocket and handed him an envelope. 'You are booked into this hotel, and you are summoned to Government House at 11 am tomorrow. A Government car will pick you up.'

Admiral French winked at him and with a grin said, 'the room is booked for two!'

Tommy shook my hand and walked down the gangplank. He didn't look back.

Mr Connolly was the next one to go ashore. I put my hand out and shook his. 'Thank you, Mr Connolly, for your services.'

'It is I who should thank you Captain, I was warned before I came aboard not to interfere with you or your crew. It is something I wouldn't have missed for all the world. I've read about it, and now I've experienced it. Thank you, Captain.'

Admiral French said to him, 'Remember what we said. None of this happened!'

Mr Connolly nodded to him, turned and walked off down the gangplank.

This is another part of the loose end. No answers, yet! I thought.

'Coffee Martin? We walked off towards the galley. The brother-hood had just finished talking to Jacko. They stood up and bowed their heads to him. Jacko did the same to them. They turned and left the galley and walked down the gangplank. They just seemed to disappear.

Lesley walked up to us with two plates of bacon and eggs. Les had coffee. 'Martin, may I present my wife, Lesley.'

Martin shook her hand, and with a grin all over his face said, 'I once met a lady by the name of Lesley. She was a writer for a magazine. A friend of mine in England wants to make sure the magazine ends up in the right place. I must talk to Mr Collins.'

I nodded to Jarrett. He walked over to us. Martin put his hand out and shook Jarrett's hand.

'My launch is waiting alongside to take you to Spencer Street. I need you to dispose of the wine barrels as quickly as possible. That much wine aboard a naval vessel would cause too many embarrassing questions. I haven't informed your father that you're home, but for the record, you did arrive home on a naval vessel, but not this one.' He pointed to a submarine. He stepped back and saluted Jarrett, and said, 'it has been a privilege to meet you.'

Jarrett saluted back and walked over to Lesley. He put his arms around her, and with a grin, he winked at her. 'I've got no idea who you are, but you certainly are beautiful.' He turned to Jacko and saluted him, then he gave one of Jacko's funny little dances and said, 'Witchy says you looked very funny.'

Jarrett turned and faced Les, walked up to him, and put his arms around him. 'Les, if there is anything you want in the future, please come and see me. Let me know. I am a son, and very, very proud of my father. Yes, the word would be love.' He turned to face Ted, stood straight, and saluted him. 'Captain Coe, it has been an honour to serve under you.' He turned and walked out of the galley and down the gangplank.

Admiral French turned to me 'Bill, Paul Smith will have the men here today.'

Just then, a man walked into the galley. He was dressed in working clothes and was one of those men you liked when you first met him. He was warm and friendly and you knew he would be totally 100% reliable.

Paul Smith walked over to him, shook his hand, then they walked over to us. He nodded to the Admiral. 'Captain, this is my man,' he put his hand on his shoulder. 'Mr Billy Barlow. He and his men will unload and reload the vessel, according to Captain Coe's orders.' Just then, I noticed Ted walking out of the galley. 'We will unload the wine first, then the railway line, loose timbers and then the top layer of timber. Tonight we will unload the crates,' he looked at me very seriously, 'of detonators.' I looked at Ted, then Lesley.

In a soft voice, Lesley said, 'that should keep people away.'

Paul Smith continued. 'There will be more timber arriving. It is mahogany and will give you a full load. These men will keep people away. There will also be four divers checking your hull, making sure everything is in place. Now, I believe you have a man aboard by the name of Snowy Norde. There is nothing wrong. I just want him to sign some paperwork regarding disposal of stores.'

I saw the look on Admiral French's face and glanced at Ted. 'I don't think he's aboard, Ted.'

'He was just a passenger, so he has disembarked,' Jacko's voice boomed out.

Admiral French commented, 'I believe he's been discharged from the forces, hasn't he?'

I replied, 'Yes, he has. I've got a copy of his paperwork. I was told to return him to his home port.' Then I swallowed deeply, as he was in the corner of the galley.

Paul Smith replied, 'Well, I just wanted to tie up some loose ends with the paperwork.' I could see that he had his teeth gritted, but he took a cigarette out of the packet, and put it in his mouth, took a lighter out of his pocket.

'Mr Smith, I said that we have detonators aboard!'

'Oh yes.' He put the cigarettes back in his pocket. 'If there are any problems ring me.' He gave me his card and left. He didn't look around, but said in a loud voice, 'I'm so disappointed. I wanted to meet him, but if he's not here.'

I called Trevor over.

'Admiral, I would like you to meet Trevor Evans. He has completed all his questions in front of three Captains and a Commander of the fleet, to become a Captain. Is it possible for you to arrange the paperwork?'

He looked at Trevor for a few moments. 'Trevor Evans, do you abide by the rules of the sea?'

In a low voice, Jacko prompted Trevor, 'say I do.'

'Do you abide by the written laws?'

'I do.'

'And do you solemnly swear, at all times, to put your vessel before yourself and not fail to discharge your duties to your crew and treat them equally without malice?'

'I do.'

'Bill, I'm just trying to find fancy words here because I forget the right ones! It is a long time since I've done this. I will have the paperwork for you in the morning. Trevor Evans, let me be the first to congratulate you on becoming a Captain, you have had the best tutors any Captain could have. Now, my problem is to word it right on your papers.'

Margaret walked up alongside Trevor. Admiral French stared at her for a moment, then he saluted her. She didn't salute back.

'Good morning Uncle, you look a bit surprised.'

'Margaret, I knew you were aboard, but didn't know you were pregnant!'

'I am now Mrs Margaret Evans.'

'Margaret I have tried to keep your secret from your parents, as to where you have been, what you have done, if I could tell them, I would, they would be so proud of you, but I can't because of the damn Secrecy Act. They live with immense pain, not knowing whether you are alive or dead. They don't know what type of life you're living. I have been summoned back to England. Can I please talk to them?'

Margaret stared at him. She took Trevor's hand and squeezed it. 'Yes, you can. You are the only person who can tell them. Lesley and I shared the same secrets, which we cannot divulge. We both live with the devil within us. Lesley has found her rock to lean on, and now I have found mine. If you could let them know that, then something in me can be at peace.'

'Margaret, you have to be at Government House tomorrow at 12 noon. My launch has returned, so will you all excuse me? I have much work to do.' He saluted me, saluted Lesley and Jacko, turned, and he was gone.

Ted was busy giving his orders to take the hatch covers off, and to brace the spas out of the way. I noticed one man discreetly undoing the hatch covers and walked over to him.

'They tell me, Snowy, that paperwork always catches up with you. Paul Smith is no fool. He could smell something is wrong.'

I walked over to the side of the baulkworks. Admiral French's launch was still lying alongside and tied up. I nodded to Snowy. He discreetly walked across the deck and climbed down into the launch. I dropped his bag down to him, then I walked over to Ted. 'You had better go and shake hands with Trevor, he is now Captain.'

Ted nudged my shoulder. 'Haven't we got enough Captains, Skipper?' He went off to the galley.

I watched Billy Barlow and his crew. They were certainly very professional. Just a nod, a wave of the hand, they all knew exactly what each other was doing, and the crane they were using made the job so much easier.

Jarrett climbed down to the launch, two men saluted him. He returned the salute. 'Could you come into the cabin, sir.' Jarrett sat down, and the launch was on its way. He was very impressed with the speed and performance. They were soon at Flinders Street and Spencer Street. He stepped off the launch onto a small jetty. The launch headed back to Williamstown dockyard. Jarrett stood there for a few minutes, trying to take it all in. *I'm back in Melbourne! And more than a bit confused, nothing seems to have changed. It is exactly as how I left it.* He shook himself. *It's going to be a very emotional day, now to put it all together!*

As he walked up Spencer Street, flashes of the past raced through his mind. He got to where his father's business was and looked up at the steps. *Well, here we go. I'm a Captain now and I must act like one.* He went up the steps and entered the foyer, went to the lifts, and pressed the third floor button. When he arrived, he walked out of the lift and went up to the lady sitting at the Reception desk.

'May I help you, sir?'

'Yes, you can have dinner with me tonight, Helen.'

She looked up at his face with a start. She looked at his uniform with the Captain's insignia and all the braids. 'I don't believe it. I've just been reading your last letter, and now you're here!' She went around the desk to him and Jarrett put his arms around her and kissed her. He just wanted to hold her tightly to him. Then Helen realised she was standing on her tiptoes. He wasn't this tall when she remembered him.

'7 pm for dinner. You live in the same house?'

'Yes, I do.'

'Could you ring my father and tell him there's a Captain here to see him?'

'Yes, sir, I will.'

Jarrett started to walk through the glass door into a small foyer. He looked back at Helen and winked, then continued to walk through the door. There was another door, a beautiful, panelled timber. He didn't knock, just walked in. He saw his father looking out of the window with his hands behind his back. Many of the Captains of the vessels he owned would see him this way. This was the way you showed a man that you were in command. He slowly turned around. 'Put your papers on the table.'

'I do not have any papers.' Jarrett took his hat off and put it under his arm. His father just stared at him. This is his son's face, but he's wearing a Captain's uniform with full military honours. Tears started to flow down his cheeks. His hands were shaking. Jarrett walked up to him, put his arms around him. His father put his head on Jarrett's chest.

Then his father said, 'Thank God you're back home, safe and sound.'

'Father, I'm home to stay!'

'Jarrett, I so badly need you.' It was becoming all too much for this old man. He stepped back, composed himself, picked up his phone, dialed a number and said, 'My son is back, yes, in my office.' He gave a small smile and chuckled, 'Yes, in my office.'

Jarrett's father's partner burst through the door, stopped and stared at Jarrett for a moment, then put his hand out and shook his. 'This means a celebration dinner and a few good drinks.'

His father picked the phone up and rang another number. 'Yes dear, it's me. Hold on to something dear, your son is home. Yes, he's here with me. We'll meet you at the restaurant, yes dear.' He put the phone down, then picked it up again. 'Helen, would you ring the restaurant and book for lunch please. There will be four of us.'

'Father, before we go to the restaurant, there are barrels of wine in the naval dockyard,' Jarrett handed him the papers, and he quickly glanced over them. 'Could you have them picked up as soon as possible, like now?' He looked at his father's face. 'Yes, Dad, you taught me to wheel and deal. We don't want prying eyes seeing them.'

His father picked up the phone again and rang a number. A voice answered. 'Shut up and listen. I want six semi-trailers to go to the Williamstown dockyard. Everything has been organized. Take the goods back to the store.' He was looking straight at Jarrett. 'The paperwork will be at the gate. I will have Fred there looking after it. I want them there now! If not sooner. No, I don't want to know your problems, just do it! So I owe you another one, yes, favours for favours.' He put the phone down, took the paperwork, and went out of the office.

Jarrett's dad's partner said, 'Your dad hasn't been well lately. The doctors have told him to slow down, but you know your dad.'

He tapped the braids on his uniform. 'I will take care of that.' His dad returned, and they started to head off to the restaurant. Jarrett just wanted to see his mum.

As we walked through the foyer, his father said to Helen, 'my son's home, we won't be back today. Why don't you go home early?'

Jarrett discreetly put his thumb in the air. Helen smiled. They arrived at the restaurant. His mother was there waiting. He quickly walked up to her and put his arms around her. Her head came to just under his head. She had put a little bit of weight on. He smelled her hair. When he was a child and his dad had gone to the office, he used to get into bed with her and snuggle close in beside her, and press his head into her hair. She always kept it long, and in the day it was always in a bun.

She stopped crying and stood back. 'What have they been feeding you? You have grown so tall and so handsome. You are certainly not the little boy who went to sea without saying goodbye.'

'Mum, you wouldn't have let me go.'

'Well Jarrett, that's a matter between your father and I.'

They sat down to lunch and bombarded Jarrett with questions: where have you been? What have you been doing? He tried to answers the questions tactfully. Finally, he said that he was under the Secrecy Act, and couldn't answer some of their questions. He told them, ' I have been to sea and have been to war. I've seen men die. I've laughed and I've cried. You speak of hell and the devil. Well, I've been there. You speak of God, you think of everything good in men, I have seen it, the courageous, the brave, the true blue.'

His father changed the subject. 'Jarrett, there are big changes for the future. There is a new type of cargo vessel. Containerization is big. There are bigger vessels with a new type of loading and unloading. We haven't ordered any new vessels yet, we are waiting until we know the infrastructure has been set up for the big changes. We have been keeping it quiet because it's going to change the whole workforce; the way of working on the docks. There is going to be trouble with our labour, but it is the future, it is your future. We will just become grumpy directors. Helen, our secretary, has been marvellous. She was sent from heaven, nothing is too much trouble for her. I know we take her for granted sometimes, but we try to show her our appreciation.'

Jarrett had so much to do, and the day was sliding past too quickly. Once lunch was over, he said to his parents, 'if you would excuse me, I've got things to do.'

His mother said in soft protest, 'I thought you were coming home with me. I was going to run a hot bath for you and buy you some new clothes.'

'Mum, I have been running my own life in the Navy for a long time now. I won't be home until late. We can talk over breakfast.'

'Why won't you be home until late?'

'I'm taking Helen out for dinner. We have much to talk about.'

His mother stood up from her chair. 'Jarrett, I'm your mother, and I haven't seen you for so long. Why would you want to see her before me?'

His dad glanced at his partner and smiled. They knew and totally approved.

The first place Jarrett went to was a jeweller. There was a well -dressed man just inside the glass door. He approached Jarrett. 'May I help you, sir?' He had summed Jarrett up and put him in a little box in his mind.

'Yes, I wish to buy a ring.'

'What type of ring, sir?'

'An engagement ring. A good quality ring.' Jarrett realised that he knew nothing about rings. A ring is just something you put on your finger.

'If sir would like to go up those stairs, turn to your right and go straight through to the far counter. One of our best assistants will help you.'

'Thank you.' When Jarrett got to the top of the stairs, he very quickly realised he had been sent to a special part of the store. He turned right and went straight through to the far counter, where a well-dressed sales assistant met him.

'May I help you sir?'

'Yes, I wish to buy an engagement ring. I only want the best.'

'Well sir, we have a large range of engagement rings. What type would you like?'

'I don't know. I've been at sea for a very long time and don't understand what women like.'

'Yes sir, I understand perfectly. Is your girlfriend a person who likes to be in the public eye?'

'No, she is very straight, business-like, and very professional. She likes everything to be in its place.'

'Yes sir. If you would like to come to the other end of this counter and have a look at these rings.' He took a tray of rings out from under the glass counter, looked at them for a moment, and returned them. 'I don't think these would be the right ones for your friend. Sir, if you would excuse me for a moment, I think that I may have something in the back which you will like.'

He went out through a door marked 'staff only' and came back with two trays, which he placed on the counter.

Jarrett studied them, but the more he looked the more confused he became. If I like it, will she like it? 'sir, may I suggest this one?' He took a ring from the tray and put it on a felt pad and handed it to Jarrett, then gave him a magnifying glass. 'The personality you described to me fits this ring perfectly. If you notice the band is strong, it is 18 carat gold. The diamond in the centre has been perfectly cut to catch the light. The two baguette diamonds on either side complement it perfectly. If it doesn't fit, we can alter it for you at no charge.'

Jarrett hesitated for a moment, thinking to himself *I'm a Captain, I have been trained to make big decisions, but not like this.* 'Yes, I'll take this ring.'

'Thank you, sir.' He put it into a dark red velvet box.

The second stop was to John McCoy's Men's clothing store, where he bought some suits, new underclothes, shirts, ties, socks, shoes and cuff links. He changed into one of the suits. Which tie do I wear? he asked himself. He stepped out of the cubicle and asked the gentleman at the counter, 'which one of these ties goes with this suit?'

'Is it for business, sir, or for a lady?'

'I'm going to ask a lady to marry me.'

'Then this one would be appropriate, sir, and if I could be so bold, you will need some handkerchiefs and maybe some of this 'Old Spice' cologne. You would also need to purchase a bunch of red roses.'

'Thank you for your suggestions. I will take them up. Could you have the clothes and my uniform delivered to this address, please?' He wrote down his parents' address. 'Thank you.'

CHAPTER 41

The semi-trailers had turned up and were waiting in line. Then they started to load the barrels of wine and left. The men on the forklifts had not messed about. The teak timber was now coming out of the hold and was being stacked on the wharf. Everything was prepared for the crates to be unloaded. I noticed the armed men move a little closer to us, but discreetly. Just at dusk the trucks turned up for the crates. Billy Barlow was giving his men orders, but with a little more authority. They took out the hydraulic trolleys from the trucks and brought them on board, and went to work. Generators were brought on board and lights were plugged into them. Jacko came out of the galley with a cup of coffee for me and a roast beef sandwich. I took the coffee from him and held out my hand for the sandwich. 'Bill, if you don't want it, I could eat it.' I snatched it out of his hand.

'Funny day tomorrow Bill, you could be grumpy with the new crew,' Jacko said. He went back into the galley,

I shook my head. I'm the Captain and he knows more than me. I bit into my sandwich to ease my frustration. I stood there for quite a while watching the men unload the crates. When I finished my sandwich,

I walked over to Ted. 'Why don't you go and get something to eat Ted and have a break? I'll keep an eye on things here.'

Billy Barlow and his crew certainly knew their job.

Soon Ted turned up alongside me. 'I've had some lunch, so I'll take over Skipper.' I knew not to argue with him.

I walked up to Billy Barlow. 'When do you want your men to have a break? There will be food in the galley.'

He looked at his watch and scanned the crates. 'In an hour,' he said.

'Right Billy, I will let my man know.' I went to the galley and spoke with Les, and he started to move pots and pans around on his stove. He nodded at Lesley, and they started to go to work.

Margaret was washing dishes. She saw me and threw a tea towel at me and threw one to Jacko, and said, 'get to work.'

I started to dry the dishes and asked here where Trevor was. 'We got sick of him telling us he was a Captain and the responsibilities that go along with being a Captain, so we sent him to bed.'

Just on daylight, Billy Barlow walked into the galley. 'My men have all left. I want to thank you for the meal. We won't forget it. We are going to have a long busy day at the Treasury.' He winked at me. 'Why would they want detonators!' He turned and left.

I took my papers back onto the Bridge and sat down in my chair. Before I knew it, I was asleep. The pressure of the cargo in my mind had gone.

I awoke with a start. There was a hand on my shoulder. It was Lesley. 'Admiral French's launch is just pulling up alongside us.'

I still felt a bit groggy. I wanted to look at the sails and feel the deck under my feet. I glanced at the barometer, but we weren't at sea. 'Come and have some breakfast, Bill, before the day gets busy.'

I picked up Billy Barlow's papers and followed Lesley into the galley. I noticed the four men on guard, they were the same four men from yesterday. I walked down the gangplank. 'Have you men been fed?'

'Not really, Captain.'

'Two of you stay, two of you come aboard. You can still do your job aboard.'

'Beg you pardon, Captain, but we come under Admiral French.'

'I outrank him. Men cannot be their best on an empty stomach.'

Just as we got to the galley, Admiral French stepped aboard. The men looked a bit concerned. I spoke to Admiral French. 'My ship, my command,' and I shoved the two men through the door. 'You are the man I want to see, privately. Could you wait here for a moment? I opened the door to the galley and waved to Lesley, then thought, we have been trying to hide Lesley, and keep her off the deck. If the three of us were seen talking together on deck by the wrong people… 'Lesley, we are going to the Bridge in 20 minutes.'

I nodded to Martin, and he followed me to the Bridge. 'You're looking tired, Bill,' he said.

'Yes, I fell into a deep sleep in that chair. How is Snowy Norde?'

'Bill, I would rather say I had never met him and I wouldn't get tied up with all this paperwork!'

'Martin, we have a young lad aboard. His name is Colin Garland. He is the son of one of our crew, who is deceased.' Just then Lesley walked in with our breakfast. Martin's eyes lit up.

'This bacon is absolutely delicious. What makes it so good?'

'It is smoked and hung. We don't have refrigerators on this vessel.'

'That's something I should have realised.'

'So, the lad I'm talking about is extremely intelligent and has a very quick mind. He is a good seaman. He doesn't argue, he just does his job, then asks the questions, intelligent questions. We were wondering whether we could get him into the Academy at Dartmouth.'

He looked at Lesley, then at me, then put another fork full of breakfast into his mouth. I could see him thinking. We waited while he put another forkful of food into his mouth.

'Bill, that brings us to the next part of your command. We had thought of unloading all of your precious cargo and transporting it to England in another way, but the powers that be thought it was getting too complicated and it would change hands too many times. If you have a beautiful sponge cake, everybody wants a piece, so we've decided to leave it on board, and this vessel will become a Naval Training Vessel. You will have ten young men training to be officers and you will take the soft edges off of them and turn them into men.

We would suggest that you use your motor whenever you think fit, to shorten the time of your voyage. There will be carpenters coming aboard to do some small alterations to make accommodations for your new crew, but with your approval, you will be having one more woman brought on board. Naval regulations state that we have to have a Medical Officer aboard.'

Just then, young Colin walked in. I quickly said, 'Salute the Admiral.' He did so, and the Admiral saluted back.

'So you are Colin Garland?'

'I am, sir.'

'And you want to be an officer in the British Navy?'

Young Colin's eyes flashed to Lesley, then to me. Lesley said to him, 'It's your life Colin, if that is what you want, say yes, or no, but it must be what you want.'

'Yes, sir.'

'Then I will have to ask you a few questions, to which you will answer with candour.'

Colin answered all his questions without hesitation. He asked Colin to add some figures together, then subtract and then multiply. We were all totally surprised how quickly Colin did this in his mind. The Admiral picked up a pencil and wrote the figures down on a piece of paper, did his calculations, then looked at Lesley. 'This young lad worries me. He could have my command in six months. Just wait for a moment while I finish my delicious breakfast.' He finished it and washed it down with his tea, but he was looking at my coffee. 'How do you drink that tar?'

'It's an acquired taste which goes with this vessel.'

He looked at me, shook his head, slightly raised his eyebrows, then said, 'here are the papers for Trevor Evans. He is now a Captain in the British Navy. He has been to war and has been discharged in his home port, therefore he is entitled to everything that goes along with the title.'

I nodded.

Then he said, 'Margaret will have a car to pick her up with Trevor to take them to Government House. With Margaret belonging to Special Forces, she is not under my jurisdiction, but I believe they are going to present her with the recognition of services in the forces.'

I saw his eyes looking out of the window to the wharf. 'Bill, that tray truck on the wharf that they are loading teak timber onto. Do you know anything about it?'

'No, I don't,' I answered.

'Young Colin, wait in the galley for me.'

We both walked down the gangplank and walked over to the tray truck. Admiral French said to one of the men, 'Good morning, I am Admiral French. Do you have any paperwork for these timbers?'

'Yes we do, yes we do.' The man looked very suspicious to him. It was his English accent.

'May I see it, please?'

The man went to the cabin of the tray truck and came back with a clipboard. He handed it to the Admiral.

The Admiral read through the paperwork. I saw his eyes flit around the wharf. Then he took a notepad out of his pocket and started to copy things down. The delivery address, phone number and a few other particulars, then he asked the man, 'You work for a hire company?'

'Yes, we just got a customer asking us to pick these timbers up. This paperwork came from our office.'

Admiral French looked at him for a few moments. 'Well, there's been a mistake. You see that stack of timber over there. They are the timbers you are supposed to pick up. They were a pile of timber gluts, which is what you put under a load so that a forklift can pick them up.'

The two men started to laugh, and one of them said, 'Thank God for that mate, these are too bloody heavy.'

'I'll get you a forklift to load the others. They slid the teak timbers off of the tray truck, then the forklift loaded the gluts. When they had finished chaining down the load, the Admiral signed the papers, but he just signed as Martin French, no rank. He tore off the carbon copy and gave the clipboard back to the driver. They took off.

We saw two guards coming down the gangplank, they looked quite content with themselves. The other two were ready to walk up. 'Well, Bill, we may have some answers. We have an address, and it says chicken farm. We have a phone number, but we have a few unanswered questions. When you were in Scotland, somebody sent you paperwork to deliver an ambulance to Bell, Ireland. How did they know? It was supposed to be top secret.

'When you were in Cape Town, how did the German assassin know you would be there? When the aircraft from Cape Town arrived in Britain, a man asked the Captain about the passenger, the same man asked the staff if the aircraft had landed in Europe to refuel. Nobody gave him any answers. On this paper, it says six teak timbers for verandah posts. How did they know about the teak? We won't do anything about this until you reach England. Then we will do some enquiries, but by the time you get to England, whoever it is here will feel safe and will be off guard.

'Now Bill, the mahogany timber will not arrive for three days. I didn't rush the order, so it wouldn't look suspicious. I just told them we want the best. It is for building ships that will give you time to work with your new crew. Now, how about a nice cup of tea?'

We went back to the galley. Les walked over to Admiral French and said, 'Thank you for looking after our son. His father was my best friend, and everything is in its right place now. I have just taken out some biscuits and sticky buns from the oven. Would you like some?'

Admiral French grinned and said, 'Yes, please.' He took his notepad out of his pocket and studied it for a moment. 'Bill, somebody told me something about a chicken farm, but who?' He looked at his watch. 'The crew should be here now to load the rest of the teak, then it will be out of harm's way.'

Les put a plate of biscuits and sticky buns in front of the Admiral, along with a cup of tea. I wondered where he was going to put it all after his big breakfast. Les put another plate in front of young Colin and said to him, 'What you don't eat I'll put in another bag for you. Do you have all your belongings packed in the rucksack?'

'Yes Les, I do.'

Les patted him on the shoulder. 'Your father would be very proud of you.' He turned and walked back to his kitchen.

Ted and the crew were busy loading the rest of the timber. Four men came aboard with some tools. I stepped forward, 'Good morning gentlemen, my name is Bill. I'm the Captain of this vessel.' We all shook hands. One of the men gave me all of his paperwork. I glanced down at it and looked up at the *Mary Moore*. I sighed. She won't be the same.

One of the men stepped forward. 'I am the plumber, Bill. They told me you only have one toilet. I have to put in another three, plus showers.'

I thought about that for a minute and thought about hot showers. Cold showers would make men out of these boys. 'Are you putting hot and cold water showers in?'

'I just assumed that I would be.'

'No, make it cold water. This is a timber vessel. There could be problems with heating for hot showers. The first cabin is for the ship's nurse. I'm sure you'll know what to do. There is a cabin at the stern. If you could fit a toilet in there, it would be good. Now to the forecastle at the bow, but if you would excuse me for just a moment, I will get some further advice.'

I called Lesley to follow us. 'Lesley, these gentlemen are here to fit out with a few luxuries. Where would you put showers and toilets? We have 10 hammocks in here.'

Lesley thought for a moment, then she just took over. One of the men said to me in a low voice, 'You act like you're married!'

'We are!'

'That makes sense. I've got one at home the same.' Nobody else heard him.

I asked one man to step aside with me. I pointed up to the yardarm that had been whipped with rope.

'Are you also a shipwright?'

'We are Bill.'

'Could you have a look at that for me as well?'

'I will arrange for the right people to do it. We have been instructed to do anything you want in the Bridge.'

'I'm quite sure my wife will want something changed.'

Lesley had finished her discussions with the men. 'If you would come with me and I'll introduce you to the right person who can help you. Ted walked over to us. 'This is Ted or Captain Coe, if you want anything, ask him. His cabin is at the stern. He'll tell you what he wants. I hope he doesn't want it painted.' I winked at Ted.

I shouted at Jacko, 'Could you take the whipping off the spa?' Jacko bowed to me.

Ted said, 'that is our entertainment officer.' He put his hand on one of the men's shoulders and said, 'come with me.'

They both walked to the stern. 'When it is time for you to have a break, gentlemen, go into the galley and you'll be fed.'

There were three more men walking up the gangplank. 'Good morning gentlemen, my name is Bill.' I shook hands with them.

'Yes sir, I'm from stores and supplies. I need to know exactly what you need.'

'If you like to go into the galley, I will be there in just a moment.'

I glanced at the other two men.

'We are here, sir, to service the motor.'

'See that small hatch on the stern? That is the access to it.' They walked off to the stern.

One of the carpenters was going back down the gangplank and said to me, 'You would think your wife was the Admiral of the fleet!' He kept on walking.

I raised my eyebrows and walked into the galley. Les and the gentlemen were talking. Les already had a big list.

Admiral French started to stand up, but Lesley stepped forward and laughed, 'Can I help you to stand up?'

He gave a small smile.

'Colin, you do not have to say goodbyes. You'll be back,' Admiral French said, and off they went to the baulk works and the launch, which took them towards the city.

CHAPTER 42

An expensive-looking car turned up on the wharf. A well-dressed man got out and walked up the gangplank. 'I'm here to pick up Mr and Mrs Evans.' Just then Jarrett walked up the gangplank. At first I didn't recognise him in his fancy duds. Then the penny dropped. Jarrett walked up to Trevor and Margaret. 'Don't worry about your belongings. They will be taken to a hotel. Trevor, your father and mother will be arriving later. They are coming from Bairnsdale to Melbourne by train and they will be picked up and taken to the hotel. My father owns the hotel. Five others will be there also, but too many Captains. I have arranged a dinner suit for Les. Enjoy yourselves this afternoon. You have earned it.' Then they were whisked away in the black car. I put my arms around Lesley. I know it was for support. We seem to be going round in big whirlpools of which we have no control, nor could we just step off.

'No Bill, not yet, but soon.' Jacko gave that funny look and went back to what he was doing. He didn't say a word. The mechanic said he'd be back the following morning, and the carpenters had also left for the day. The man who was going to arrange the stores was walking down the gangplank. I went into the galley and sat down alongside Jarrett. He handed me a piece of paper. It said £74,067. I just stared at the figure. It didn't make any sense. I turned and looked straight at Jarrett.

'Yes Bill, that was the value of our cargo on the market, and you still have that much aboard.'

I handed the piece of paper to Lesley. She stared at it just like I had, looked at me, then looked at Jarrett. She handed the piece of paper back to Jarrett, who tore it into paper pulp, then walked over to Les's stove and put the paper into it. We watched it burn. Then he sat down again.

'Bill, so the total figure had been 18. We all sat silently for a moment. Jacko walked in and broke the mood as he was dressed in his full regalia. Ted walked in, his uniform freshly pressed.

Lesley put her arms around Les, 'You look so handsome. Tonight, you are my escort.' I'm sure he started to blush.

'We'd better get changed dear. They might think of going without us,' I said. As we walked out on the deck, I noticed the guards discreetly back out of the way.

Ted whispered to me, 'There are two down below. We haven't put the hatch covers back on as we're not hiding anything and it's not going to rain.'

We all walked down the gangplank in the dark and got into the car. I noticed that the gangplank had been stowed.

The cars didn't go to the main foyer. Instead, they pulled up at a side door and we were ushered through into a private room. This was quality, this was class, this is where Jacko's regalia belongs, the perfect Scotsman. Jarrett stepped forward, then his father, Paul, stepped forward and put his hand out to shake mine.

'I'm sorry about the journey we sent you on, but I can assure you we didn't know all of it, but you are now back with your brother,' he laughed. He shook hands with Ted like a long-lost relative. 'Thank you Ted for taking care of my son and bringing him home safely to us.' He was still shaking Ted's hand, and he threw his arms around Jacko's shoulders. Paul, Ted and Jacko hugged each other. Paul was crying, 'thank you for bringing my son home. His mother has been so lost without him. Now my family is all back together.' He stepped back, the tears were still flowing down his cheeks. He stepped forward to Les and started to shake his hand. 'From what Jarrett tells me you are an incredible man. My wife and I are so grateful to you, we can't put it into words, but she wants to know what you fed him?'

Jarrett's mother slowly walked up behind her husband. She was very humble and shy. Then she embraced each one of them. 'You took my son, my baby to sea and brought him back, a man. He can now take his rightful place with his father, and I can have his father back.' She took his arm and cuddled into him.

Jacko could not stop looking at all the fancy crystal chandeliers and the paintings. He stopped in front of one. I could see him reading the name on the bottom of the painting. '*Arthur Streeton*'. It was of the Australian desert, with the red hills in the distance, the evening sunset illuminating all the colours of the mountains, red, blues, purples, yellows and greens, in all different shades. It took Jacko back home to where he belonged.

Lesley walked up alongside Jacko and put her arm around him. 'One day we'll go back to the desert. Now, Jacko, they're serving food!'

Jacko turned and looked at the tables and the waiters, then he turned again, gazing once more at the painting. He moved closer to the painting. You would have thought he wanted to move into the painting and be part of it. Lesley waited for him. She totally understood. Her compassion and feelings for him went very deep. 'Jacko, one day you'll go home.'

He turned around and faced her. 'You promise me, Lesley, to take me home to my people?'

'Yes, Jacko.'

Lesley could see his nostrils twitching. He had smelled food.

She kept a very low profile, always standing behind me for fear somebody might recognise her.

The food and wine just kept on coming and coming. Lesley said to me, 'I do believe Jacko is full! He has just turned down more trifle!'

Jarrett did a quite long speech, but it was very interesting. He talked about the future and how people had prepared him for it, and how they'd helped him to understand the people that really made the money for the company, and thankfully talked about those who fed off the company without really putting anything back.

I loved the way he put it in words, using the sailing vessel to make his point. I saw his father and his partner talking. I knew they were happy with the man who was going to take the company into the future.

In his speech Jarrett said, 'a Captain had shown him the responsibility of commanding. How you put a man or woman where they are happiest to serve, but you let them know the fine line, so that they work as a team, not as an individual, thereby blocking the way for all concerned. This Captain taught me to treat everybody concerned with respect, then, they in turn, will treat you with respect. When you say *"Permission to come aboard sir"* you knew it was under his conditions and to not argue. 'Another gentleman aboard taught me to listen very carefully.'

Jarrett stopped for a moment, raised his eyebrows and shook his head. 'He is a Scottish, Indigenous Aboriginal. He taught me to listen to nature itself, whether you're in the city or at sea, or in the desert, and you will survive. You must always take the advice of your second-in-command. If you say, "No" then tell him why. Then he knows where to go with his command.'

It was a fantastic evening and we all thoroughly enjoyed ourselves. We got back on board at 2 am. One of the guards met me at the gangplank. He saluted me, I saluted back, he said there was nothing to report, all is well. I thanked him and he nodded. I scanned the deck expecting to see the crew at their positions, but there was nobody there, and nobody on the pumps. They had all gone and were no longer aboard, but I still had Ted, Les, Jacko, and Lesley. I turned around to Lesley, 'Where are Dominic and Phillip?'

'They left last night when you were asleep, Bill. They didn't want to wake you. They said that you would understand.'

It didn't seem right, I would like to have shaken their hands!

CHAPTER 43

At 7 am the new yardarm turned up, and the shipwrights went to work replacing it. The same day at 4 pm, the carpenters and plumbers had finished their work. I checked to see what they had done and signed the papers. A man walked up the gangplank and handed me a piece of paper. It read: *Timber arriving 7 am tomorrow, the crew at 11 am. Divers hadn't found any problems, the copper sheeting was all intact, stores and equipment were also arriving tomorrow as well as firewood.* It was signed by Admiral French PS.

Last night was a good night, enjoyed by all. My eyelids were a little heavy. I went into the galley and showed the letter to the others. I asked Lesley, 'Where is Les?'

'He is still in his bunk, asleep. He ate and drank a lot last night!'

I smiled. 'Ted, if you want to see a Scotsman when he's had too much to eat and drink, go have a look at Jacko.'

'No thank you, Bill, I will leave him alone. I've got my own problems to contend with.'

I went onto the Bridge and opened my logbook, wrote down the date and time, three days in port, crew arriving tomorrow, rest of cargo also arriving tomorrow, report from the shipwrights is good. I put down as little as possible, closed the logbook and let my mind drift. There was so much I could have put in. I thought of Lesley and how beautiful she looked last night. I had never seen her dressed up like that before, but where did she get the dress? She never went ashore. Just then, she broke my train of thought by coming in carrying a tray of coffees and food. She put them on the bench.

'Thank you Lesley. You looked absolutely beautiful last night at dinner. No other woman came anywhere near you.'

'Does that mean, Bill, that you only had eyes for me?' She smiled and sipped her coffee.

Something in me said be careful Bill! 'Well, Lesley, there were a lot of beautiful women there, but my eyes kept coming back to you. Where did you get that dress?'

'Bill, a lady always has to be prepared. It was just a little something I had tucked away.' She started to walk away.

I don't know why I said it, but, 'I do hope you had underwear to go with it.'

She turned slightly back to me, turned her head towards me and gave me a really cheeky smile 'What makes you think I was wearing underwear?' She smiled again, raised her eyebrows, and walked out of the Bridge.

Before I could sort myself out, Jarrett walked in the door with the young lady I had met at the party. 'Hello Helen, how are you?'

'Very, very happy Captain, thank you. I'm glad one of the dresses I sent down for Lesley fitted her so well.'

I couldn't stop myself, 'and she appreciated the underwear as well.'

'It was the shoes I had a problem with, Captain, but I saw they fitted her nicely.'

'Helen, to you, my name is Bill.'

Helen frowned. 'What's that noise, Bill?'

'If you pick that plate up and put it under the bench, the noise will stop.'

There were two or three snorts, and a hand came out and took the plate. Helen pulled her hand back quickly and looked startled.

Jarrett burst out laughing. 'It's just the witchy. Don't worry dear.'

'What is a witchy?'

'Just a wisp of smoke, a funny smell, a funny noise, an annoying personality and something to eat the food off of your plate.'

Just then a head popped out from under the bench. Jacko was scratching his head with both hands.

'I remember him. He had everyone laughing last night,' Helen said. 'I like him.'

Jarrett shook his head. 'Don't encourage him, dear. Bill, we have to meet Trevor's parents. They're coming up from Bairnsdale on the train, so we don't have much time. Here is the money we received for the wine. We got a good price. I broke it up into lots and turned it into cash. I will post our friend in Cape Town his portion. He handed me some envelopes. Trevor and Margaret will be working for me now. Snowy will be doing his own job on the wharf again, but will be working for me. Phillip and Dominic are also working for me. Can't waste good men. I don't know where Tommy is.'

He put out his hand and shook mine. 'If there is anyway I can do anything to help you, please call me. Do you hear me, Jacko? Just come and see me. Don't make appointments. Jacko, my home is your home. I'll put in a ship's wheel and compass on the verandah for you.'

Helen put both her hands on Jacko's face. 'And I will feed you! Jarrett, we've got to go.' They walked off and went down the gangplank.

Jacko made one of those funny little noises. 'I don't know about staying with them Bill, she's the boss already!'

Next morning I awoke early and had a good breakfast. The timber turned up at exactly 7 am. I went down the gangplank and spoke to one of the drivers. 'Good morning. How long have you been driving for?'

'For a large part of the night, we came from Walhalla in Gippsland,' the man replied.

'Well, you had all better come aboard and have some breakfast.'

'We'll take the chains off our loads and we'll be in for that breakfast. Thank you.'

All the drivers had big smiles on their faces. Another truck turned up with the firewood. The driver leaned out of the truck door. 'Are you the boss man?'

'I am,' I replied.

'Where do you want this firewood?'

'Give me a few moments. I'll see the man who can answer that question.' I went back up the gangplank and called for Les. He came down and examined the firewood. He looked straight at the driver.

'We put in an order for firewood split to the size that is clearly written on this paper, which is a copy of what you have. Now, how am I going to split those up on this sailing vessel? I only have a small firebox. Take it away and get what was ordered. If you can't, let me know now. We don't have time to waste!'

Les glanced at me and walked back on board.

'Who the hell is he?' the driver asked.

'He is the cook. You don't argue with the cook. I am the Captain of this vessel, but I'm not the Captain of his stove.'

The driver grinned. 'You made your point. I will be back.'

A man in a naval uniform walked up to me. He saluted me, I saluted him back. 'I am the Captain of the Port, sir. I once served under you on a dreadnought during the war.'

I shook his hand. 'That was a long time ago.'

'Yes, I panicked and turned the wheel the wrong way. You pushed me aside and corrected the helm, then told me to get back behind the wheel. I thought I was going to be in big trouble, but you didn't say a word.'

'Their guns were far bigger than ours. I was panicking as well and I asked for help. Ted is the only one who knows, so don't tell anybody else our little secret. I'm sorry, but I don't remember your name?'

'Captain Bartlett, sir.'

'What can I do for you?'

'We have your new cadets arriving soon and Admiral French has asked me to suggest that you and your crew put on their full regalia.'

'Yes, I will have that done. Come on board and have coffee. I'm sure there's a man here who would love to meet you.'

We walked through the galley door. Ted was going through the papers for the timber, finding out the sizes and lengths so he could load them tightly in the hull so that they would not move in a storm.

Ted looked up from his papers, a big smile came over his face and he started to laugh. In a loud voice, he said, 'Charlie.' Then he looked at the uniform. 'Captain Bartlett.' He shook his hand. 'Could we talk later? There are people here waiting for my instructions.'

CHAPTER 44

'Ted, could you put on your full regalia and any fancy bits and pieces, pomp and ceremony and all that?' Ted nodded and left.

Lesley put a plate of eggs, bacon, slices of potatoes, and onions in front of Captain Bartlett, along with a hot mug of coffee.

'Captain, I've got to change and you are going to be very busy eating all that! It's getting close to 11 am,' I said. I looked at Lesley. 'Can you put on your whites uniform?' I glanced towards Les. She nodded and didn't say a word.

I went to the Bridge. Jacko was sitting there with Cat on his lap. 'Jacko, the new crew will be arriving shortly, Lesley is coming to help clean you up!' He put Cat on the bench and stood up sharply.

'I can clean myself up, thank you!'

I didn't say a word, just went and changed into my uniform.

Right on time the naval bus arrived on the wharf. The first man off the bus surprised me, it was Mervyn Nelis! He was followed by a lady wearing a white skirt, shirt, blue jacket with brass buttons and a blue naval hat. They stood together. Then the new sailors, wearing their whites, started to file off the bus along with their kit bags. They stood in line to attention. There were ten of them. They were young and fit.

The crane kept on working, loading the timber, then Admiral French's launch turned up alongside and he came aboard. 'Good morning Bill.'

'Good morning Martin.'

'Well, Bill, we'll play the game and do an inspection.'

I nodded to Jacko—he did look good in his Scottish regalia—it was all very impressive. Ted was already on the wharf when we went down the gangplank. Mr Nelis and the lady saluted us. We returned the salute.

Mervyn shouted out, 'Attention!' and the ten cadets stood to attention. We slowly walked down between the two lines of five men. Jacko leaned over to Ted and quietly said, 'What a load of baloney!'

Ted told him to shut up, then Ted, Jacko and I went on board and stood at the top of the gangplank. Mervyn gave the orders to march in single file, go up the gangplank and line up on deck. They saluted. We returned the salute. The sixth man was having trouble stopping himself from grinning, and when Jacko winked at him a big grin came over his face. The cadets were not quite sure about Jacko's colourful regalia.

I walked up alongside Mervyn. 'I didn't expect to see you here.'

'I didn't expect to be here, sir.'

'But I'm very glad to see you Mervyn.' Then, so the cadets could hear, Mervyn shouted, 'Two lines of five.'

I shouted, 'Welcome aboard gentlemen, I am Captain Farquhar, this is Captain Coe, he is also the Bosun, if he should give you an order and you should question it, you will sit on top of the mainmast for a day! The lives of your fellow crew members depend upon you and the safety of this vessel at sea. This vessel is all you have to keep you alive. If you are aloft and your crew mate is in trouble, secure him to the mast or yardarm, do not bring him down. Continue to do your duty to this vessel and obey the Bosun's command. You will all work as a team. If I find one man who decides not to work as part of that team, he will feel my wrath.

It is my responsibility to keep this vessel afloat and keep all of you alive and well. You are the future officers of the British Navy, and you are here because you are the best of the best, but on this vessel you will start at the bottom, learning how to survive and understand your fellow man.

Captain Jacko is the helmsman. He will teach you how to read the compass and understand it. The compass and the helm are the most important things on this vessel. If you are at the helm, you never leave it until you are relieved. Never take your eye off of the compass, or the bow. There are eleven hammocks in the forecastle.' I pointed to it. 'Staff Sergeant Nelis will allocate you a hammock.' I picked up a harness. 'Each bunk has a harness in it. Any time you go aloft, you use it. If Mr Coe commands you to wear it on deck, you do so without question. Staff Sergeant Nelis take command.'

'Dismissed.' They all walked off to the forecastle.

'Very impressive. You would think we are in the Navy,' Ted said.

Admiral French walked up behind me. 'Your firewood is here, and a load of briquettes. They are compressed coal. Your stores have arrived as well. Did you see where the nurse went, Bill?'

'Yes, I did. She went into the galley. I didn't get the chance to introduce myself. It seems she wanted to stay out of the way.'

I noticed a small launch nearly alongside of us. The man aboard seemed to be very interested in what we were doing, or was it this sailing vessel? 'Ted, keep an eye on that vessel. I believe he's in restricted waters.'

The nurse went into the galley. She scanned the galley, just the lady and the cook. She thought he wouldn't be a problem.

Lesley was just about to pick up the dishes on a metal tray and still had it in her hand. She looked up at the nurse and sensed there was something wrong, but what? Lesley said to her, 'Good morning, can I get you a coffee or something to eat?'

The nurse walked over to her with a smile. Lesley didn't like that at all, her senses were all sharpened, her training was back. The nurse had her left hand slightly behind her back. She put her right hand out to shake Lesley's, who noticed the nurse was in a defensive position. Lesley still had the tray in her right hand. She started to transfer the tray into her left hand, but hesitated. The nurse started to move her left shoulder and her arm came around from her back. Lesley used the tray to protect herself. The nurse had a knife in her left hand, it struck the tray. Lesley sprung backwards, nearly falling over one of the tables. She took up the defensive position with her tray. The table was Lesley's best defence. She thought that this lady is very professional, the way she moved the knife in her right hand, holding the knife down her wrist, so that you couldn't get to her wrist, but the knife was in the downward thrust position.

In the meantime, Mervyn had decided he needed to see Lesley. He turned and walked towards the galley, leaving the crew to sort themselves out and change into their working clothes. He walked through the galley door, and for a second, he froze. The nurse spun around to face him. Mervyn gestured to Lesley to move out of the way, but his eyes remained on the knife. He had seen these before, during the war. It was a German killing knife used by special forces. The nurse moved straight at Mervyn, moving the knife in front of her own chest, ready to strike, but Mervyn was too quick for her. His right foot thrust forward and hit in her left groin, throwing her totally off balance. She staggered backwards into the kitchen. Big mistake. A frying pan struck the right on the side of her head. She staggered forward, then she felt hot needles going into the back of her right leg. Cat had launched himself at her, sinking his teeth and claws into her calf. She screamed out in pain.

Jacko heard this and raced to the galley. He went through the galley door and saw Mervyn in a defensive position and the nurse holding a knife. Cat was crouching down, snarling at her. Les had a frying pan, and Lesley was in the fighting position, with a tray. Jacko reached down to his left side to draw his sword, but his arm wasn't quite long enough to get it out of the scabbard. He looked annoyed and frustrated. He put his right hand on the scabbard, pulled it down, and the sword came out, he made a ballet gesture thrusting the sword forward, the nurse was a little confused and hesitated, but the frying pan came down once again and she was out cold.

'From now on, all soldiers will be equipped with frying pans,' Jacko laughed.

The Admiral and I raced to the door. The Admiral said, 'That woman is not the nurse.' Then he spun around, went to the baulk works, and shouted to the men on his launch. The spectator boat took off at high speed, with the Admiral's launch following quickly after it.

Two of the guards ran up the gangplank, the other two stood guarding it. The two guards on deck went into the galley with the Admiral. The impostor nurse was sitting up but was dazed.

The Admiral very angrily spoke to her. 'Get that uniform off, I don't care what you've got on underneath, but I won't have you disgracing the Navy by wearing that uniform!' Lesley helped her take the uniform off, she was wearing a petticoat underneath. Lesley was very surprised that it was silk. The Admiral started to ask questions, then he said, 'no, this is not the place to interrogate you.'

The impostor turned to Lesley. 'You have caused my family so many problems. We have been in power for the last 900 years and you want to disgrace our family with your journalists. Others have failed to dispose of you, so we have had to solve the problem for ourselves.' She raised her voice, 'You are a little nobody, what would you know.'

Jacko did one of his funny dances, but it looked strange in this big area. Then he said, 'One frying pan to bring it all tumbling down!'

One of the guards took some handcuffs out of his back pocket and put them on her wrists.

I looked at her and asked, 'How did you think you could get away with it?'

Her eyes glared at me. 'We must protect the family company at all costs.'

'So your family has used you for themselves. We know that the International money market has no boundaries, and they have sacrificed you!'

Admiral French said, 'This is a British Naval vessel. What happens on this vessel comes under English Law. I'm flying back to England tomorrow on a British aircraft, you will be flying back with me, along with your accomplice.' He turned to Mervyn, 'Could you get her something to wear, but not silk?'

The Captain of the Port handed Admiral French a document. He read it.

'Apparently, they have found the nurse. She was tied up in the barracks where your crew left from. She is a bit shaken up, but she will arrive this afternoon after having a medical.'

He turned to me and winked, then he said to the impostor, 'May I present to you, Mrs Farquhar.' He gestured to Lesley. 'Have you made a mistake and stuffed it up as well?' Then he looked at Les, 'You certainly looked after your daughter.' He turned to the guards, saying 'Get this bit of rubbish off this vessel and onto mine.' He picked up the knife and looked at it for a moment. 'A very nice heirloom. It tells us a lot.'

The Admiral's launch had returned with another man. We all shook hands, and the Admiral said, 'We will meet in the future,' but he didn't mention our destination.

The young cadets had no idea what had just happened. They were all standing in front of Ted. He gave them their orders. 'You five unload the firewood and briquettes. We will store them below. The other five, you will unload the stores. Our chef will be here to tell you what he wants, how he wants it, and when he wants the other equipment we will unload afterwards, and store below.'

One of the first five said to Ted, 'That's manual work, sir.'

Ted slowly gestured with his eyes to the top of the mainmast. The other four pushed their colleague towards the gangplank, and all said, 'Yes, sir.'

Les inspected his firewood very carefully and was even more particular about his stores. He asked Ted, 'What are those funny black things in sacks?'

'Compressed coal.'

'What exactly does that mean?'

'It is powdered coal compressed into those models. They're supposed to give a lot of heat.'

Les just scoffed. 'We'll see.'

Everything was loaded and lashed down tight. All we were waiting for was the nurse. Jacko, Ted, Mervyn, and Lesley were in the galley. 'High tide is at 8 am. We'll head out into the bay at 6 am. I want the crew up at 5 am, and we will put them into training while we are in the bay. It is a more controlled environment. When I'm satisfied, we will head out to sea, but we still have some daylight left, so we can put them into training until 9 pm. Les, can you feed them?' He nodded. 'How's the frying pan, Les?'

'It's quite all right. You didn't think I'd use my best one, did you?'

The nurse arrived. Ted and I went to the gangplank. She would have been in her 40s, well dressed and groomed.

'Permission to come aboard, sir.' She saluted us, and we returned the salute.

I put my hand out and shook hers. 'My name is Captain Farquhar, and this is Captain Coe, and you are?'

'Chris Ayres-Smith.'

'Welcome aboard Chris. Come into the galley.'

Ted clicked his fingers and pointed to the young lad who had started to argue with him. He pointed to the nurse's bags and pointed to her cabin. The young man didn't argue.

'This is my wife, Lesley.' Before I could introduce the nurse, Lesley said, 'Hello Chris, how are you?'

'A lot better now, thanks Lesley.' They were both smiling at each other, then they embraced.

'Bill, we were both in training together. I was a little bit older.'

Ted chuckled. 'Well, I wouldn't have thought.'

'Chris, sometimes he's a lovely man, sometimes! This is Les. He's our father.'

I chuckled. 'I am the Captain, but I've got no control over these two. Lesley, would you please show this lady to her quarters? Chris, when the crew aren't around I am Bill, the Bosun is Ted, and I would imagine you already know Mervyn.'

'Yes, I do. He is an old colleague. Bill, this envelope is for you.' She handed me a large envelope.

'Thank you. I've been waiting for this. If you'll excuse me, I'm going up onto the Bridge.'

I could see Ted and Mervyn with the cadets pointing to this and that. One young lad had apparently learned quickly. Facing Ted, he said, 'Excuse me, sir, we have already gone over all of this in our theoretical training.'

Ted grinned at him. 'It is one thing reading about it in a book, completely another doing it practically without even thinking, is another matter. When you are at sea, you have to carry out a command. Now, not when you've thought about it in the book. As the Captain said, our lives depend on you, so everything now will be done practically, on the spur of the moment. Can you climb the mast in the book? Can you sit on the yardarm in the book? So cadets, have you learnt from him?'

They all said 'Yes sir' and carried on with what they were doing.

I opened the envelope and took out the inside one. It was addressed to me, William Farquhar. I opened the envelope and took out the documents. One was a friendly letter.

Good morning William, it has been decided by my colleagues and I, that when you wear this medal you are higher rank than a Captain, therefore, to put protocol in the right place, you are now a Commander, you will have the papers in this envelope. PS: please don't tell Jacko, or does he already know? Fair sailing Bill, I will see you in the future.

The next papers were about the promotion. I put them aside.

On to the next document, my orders. I browsed through them.

Destination–Portsmouth, England. Vessel–Number 3 Naval Training Vessel (to use all propulsion when necessary). Crew Training Officer–Mervyn Nelis, Bosun Captain–Ted Coe. Cook–Les, Nurse–Chris Ayres-Smith, Helmsmen–Jacko Farquhar. Crew under officer training 11. There was a list of names with numbers. It said to use their number, not their name. I will read through the rest of it later. There was a listing for the cargo and stores. I picked up my logbook, opened it and jotted down as least as possible.

I went out on deck and called for Number 10 to see me. 'Good to see you, young Colin. I know that you do know we cannot give you any favours as you are a training officer.'

'Yes sir, I do.'

'How many of these cadets have been to sea as naval cadets?'

'Actually sir, none of them, only in estuaries or sheltered waters.'

'Thank you for that. Would you please go into the galley and let Cook know that we will be eating at 9 pm? He already knows this, but he just wants to see you. Your relationship with Les on this vessel is your private business. Do not let it interfere with my command.'

I nodded to Ted and Jacko, and went back on the Bridge. They followed. 'As you have probably already worked out, our crew is green. We have a lot of work to do before we can go to sea. We will leave the wharf at 10.30 pm and anchor at Mt Martha for the night. This will hopefully help them get their sea legs and give us a chance to see what we have to do to put them into shape for the sea. I don't understand the powers that be, our cargo and the value of it.'

'I do,' Ted said, 'we have a crew, the three of us, Lesley, Mervyn and young Colin, seven if you count Les. It only takes four of the crew to handle the masts, so we have a crew, an experienced crew, the rest is just a smokescreen.'

Jacko said, 'Bill, you found out the value of the cargo, but don't let it upset your thinking.' He looked straight at me. I knew he could see right through me. 'Being in command can do funny things.' He rubbed his hands together. 'Food, I can smell food.'

'Jacko, if you could get your food and come back up here.' He literally disappeared.

Ted said, 'Bill, what was the crack about command? I've been around Jacko too long now and know when he's picking up something.'

'They've made me a Commander Ted, but Jacko and Lesley don't know.'

'Well, Bill, that is your business. But do you really think Jacko doesn't know?'

I went down and visited the Captain of the Port and informed him of what we were doing.

'Captain, if you stayed until tomorrow night and left at high tide, the next day I'll have a pilot boat discreetly waiting. I know you don't need one, but you have to check that your paperwork is always correct. Watch your back!'

'Thank you Captain Bartlett.'

'I hope your voyage goes well.'

We shook hands and I left. When I got back on deck, Ted handed me an envelope. 'This came for you.'

It didn't say who it came from, it just said, *All tied up with a chicken farm, I have 3 passengers to keep me occupied on the way home.* No signature. I handed it to Lesley. She read it, nodded and put it into Les's fire.

The big motor fired a burst of smoke and she was purring away. Young Colin was the only one of the cadets who knew what was happening. They were all apprehensive, but excited. It was now all happening.

Ted ordered the gangplank in and to be stowed. I waited 15 minutes, then nodded to Ted. He ordered the bow line to be stowed, then the stern line to be stowed. He nodded to me that they were both clear of the prop.

'Take her out, Jacko.' He eased the gear stick forward and with a slight shudder we started to move forward. The city light shone on the water, the channel lights were blinking away. It certainly was a beautiful picture. We gently eased down the channel, watching the lights. Four of the cadets asked Ted whether they could go aloft, Ted said yes, and to make sure their harnesses were clipped in and secure, two others followed. Ted grinned; six cadets voluntarily climbing. Ted glanced at young Colin, who was looking at him with a grin. Ted nodded and thought seven, that is plenty when at sea. He glanced up at me with a grin. I put my thumb in the air.

I looked over at the galley roof. There was a water tank next to the chimney of Les's agar stove. 'What's that Jacko?'

'Nothing to do with me, Bill, nor is that box down there. They all belong to Lesley.'

I could just make out a small cupboard tucked in behind the galley. I went down on deck to have a closer look at the cupboard. I opened the door to see a small shower inside. I would have only just fitted in. I closed the door and went into the galley.

'Lesley, what is that cupboard doing there?'

Les discreetly moved out of the way, leaving Lesley with me.

'It is the best place to get hot water through Les's Agar. It also gives Les hot water. You said to me when we were with the plumber, tell him what you want,' she gave me a very cheeky grin, 'and I outrank you.'

I looked at her for a moment. 'Do you? I would very much appreciate it if you could put a sign up "Women only". If Jacko was to use it we wouldn't have any water left!' I always feel as if I'm playing chess and not winning.

When we got to Hovel Pile, instead of turning to starboard, down the channel, we turned to port and anchored in the deep water, well out of the shipping channel. The vessel had a gentle rock, back and forwards. Ted didn't bring the cadets down. He left them to enjoy the moment and to get their sea legs aloft.

The next morning Mervyn had them up at 5.30 am doing exercises and running up and down the deck. Daylight had just started to appear, and he had them climbing up and down the mast. Then they had a well-earned breakfast. Then back out on deck, shouting out the names of the ropes and what they did, they lowered the mainsail and stowed it again, then went through all the sails, lowering them and then stowing them. Time for lunch, and back on deck, going through the same things and shouting out the names of everything. At 3 pm, coffee, biscuits and doughnuts. Ted, Mervyn, and Jacko sat down with me and had coffee.

Mervyn commented that he was enjoying these exercises. Jacko and Ted just glared at him.

Ted said, 'I'm so glad you're enjoying it. A couple of days of this and I will have problems.'

Jacko said to Ted, 'Well, I'm younger than you, just lean on me whenever you want. I'll help you stand up, and when you want to sit down, your legs will be like jelly.'

Mervyn had the cadets back out on deck and hard at it again. He had put two of them on the pumps. 'Pump with a slow, even pump so the cylinders can fill up evenly with water.'

At 7 pm, they had their supper. Jacko had his supper, and without a word, just disappeared.

Mervyn said, 'Bill, with the paperwork that they have done onshore and the practical work today, they are ready. But Ted and I believe you should have the nurse look at number 8, he's a fighter, but the others are supporting him. He knows everything by the book and he supports the others in this area. He is a good part of the team.

I spoke to Chris, the nurse, and she examined him. 'Bill, there is something wrong. I can't put my finger on it, but I'll examine him again in the morning and think on what I observe.'

The next morning at 5.30 am Mervyn had them on deck exercising and stretching. Number 8 wasn't there. One of the cadets told Mervyn that he wasn't very well. Mervyn went into the forecastle and checked out the young man. He was lying in his hammock and had been sick. Mervyn thought it might be seasickness, but there were smears of blood on the sides of his lips and on his nose. The young lad opened his eyes. Mervyn told him that he would get the nurse and the young lad said, 'No sir, I'll be alright.' Mervyn didn't argue, he just went and fetched the nurse. She looked at him briefly.

'Sargeant, could you lift him out of the hammock and bring him up to the galley?'

Mervyn had no trouble lifting him. Chis pulled the hammock out of his way. In the galley, Chris examined him, listened to his chest with her stethoscope and then his back.

'Captain, we need to get this lad ashore. I believe the physical work yesterday and the movement of the vessel has stirred up something in his chest that has been there for quite a while.'

I turned round to Mervyn. 'Have one of the cadets signal the pilot boat to come alongside.'

We lowered the young lad down into the pilot boat, which headed off towards Frankston.

After breakfast, I had everybody lined up on deck and had Jacko ring the bell three times loudly.

'When you hear this bell ring three times, secure what you are doing and be on deck. Even if you're asleep, be on deck. You all have a logbook. You will fill it out every day, put everything in it, even if it is what you think of me or the officers on this vessel, for it will be a learning tool for you in the future. Lesley is Commander Johnson. She will teach you protocol, politics, the responsibility of your command, and why not to question your orders, just carry them out to the best of your ability. When you're with Captain Jacko, write everything he tells you down, listen to him very carefully, he is totally in-tune with nature, when he talks about the moon and its colours, the sun, the colours of the sea, the fish, dolphins, whales, migrating birds. There are many things he'll tell you that are not written down in books. He is the ancient mariner. If he says something to you that you don't understand, keep it in your mind, it is usually a warning. He is in tune with everything. He's a spooky little fella. Captain Coe, as you know, is the Bosun, just do as he says, do not argue with him. Sargeant Nelis, you already know him, will keep you fit and teach you to take care of yourself in combat. You have all done extremely well. I'm very proud to serve with you all and so are my officers. As soon as the pilot boat returns, we will head out to sea. If we were under sail, I would choose the time by the tide, but we will be using our propulsion. Now, Captain's prerogative, you may call me Captain or Bill, Mervyn is Mervyn, Lesley is Lesley, Chris is Chris, Ted is Ted, Jacko, you can call him Jacko, but with respect at all times. When we are in port, you must use our correct titles. Make seamen of them!' I shouted out, turned and walked towards the Bridge.

Mervyn shouted, 'You two go to Lesley, you three go to Jacko, you two to Ted and the rest of you come with me.'

Lunchtime came. There was no pilot boat. Mervyn changed the crew around to give them another tutor for the afternoon. Just on 3 pm the pilot boat returned. A female naval cadet climbed on board. She saluted me, and I saluted back. She handed me an envelope. 'I am a replacement, sir.' She took me by surprise, but it made complete sense.

'Have you been to sea before?'

'Yes, sir, I have. My father owns a yacht, and we have done the Sydney to Hobart race twice.'

'Welcome aboard. If you would like to go into the galley and speak to Lesley?' She picked up her kit bag and went into the galley.

The Captain of the pilot boat shouted out to me, 'We will follow you out when you are ready.' I saluted him.

'Ted, are you ready?'

He grinned at me and tapped a young man on the shoulder and instructed him to follow him. They went into the engine room. Once again, black smoke turned to blue, she was alive again. I looked at my watch, it was 4 pm. Ted and the young man came out of the engine room. The young man had a very apprehensive look on his face. He had never done anything like that before.

Ted said to him, 'We normally let her warm up a little first.' Then he pointed to two of the cadets and said, 'Follow me.' They went to the anchor winch.

'Put her into gear, Jacko.' He eased the throttle slightly forward. The anchor chain went slack and they started to wind it in. The anchor was stowed, and we were on our way again.

Ted rigged the flying jib and the outer jib. These were the two triangular sails on the bow. She gently glided up the channel towards the entrance and Queenscliff. We had an outgoing tide. When an outgoing tide meets the incoming sea, the outgoing tide wants to slide underneath the pressure of the water in the sea, creating a wave on the surface. This is commonly known as the Rip. Ted made sure there was nobody aloft and made sure everybody was aware of what was going to happen at the beginning of the channel at the heads. Jacko knew exactly what to do. Nobody needed to give him instructions. We were going to turn south west and head out to sea.

Jacko looked at the big swell and said, 'this is going to be good! With the outgoing tide pushing us we will be doing 11 or 12 kn.' He eased back on the throttle and the bow started to slide into the swell, she shook and vibrated, then rose up over the swell, spray went everywhere, then she settled down and Jacko increased the throttle. I could see the cadets looking a little startled, but they looked at each other and laughed. I nodded to Ted.

Ted started to shout out his orders. The canvas sails started to unfold and our sails were set. Jacko put the gear stick into neutral and did one of his little songs and dances. 'She's happy now, Bill, she's happy.'

'I'm going down to the galley, Jacko, to talk to Lesley.' Those little puppy eyes looked at me. 'Yes Jacko, I will arrange for food to be sent up.'

On deck, I asked Ted to have one of the cadets go onto the Bridge with Jacko and I went into the galley. I was thinking of the sleeping arrangements. Another female aboard, she can't have special treatment. She is going to be a Naval Officer just like the others.

Lesley smiled at me. 'Bill, the three of us have been arranging the sleeping quarters. Chris and this young lady will sleep in the stern, they will both have their privacy. Ted will be in the single cabin and Mervyn will be in the forecastle with the cadets.'

'Excuse me for a moment, Lesley. Young lady, if you could pick up a plate of that food and one coffee and take it to Captain Jacko on the Bridge.'

'Yes, sir.'

'Then return here. Just a moment Lesley.'

I opened the door for her and called Ted. He came into the galley. 'Ted, what do you think about sleeping in a bunk?'

'Bill, you already know the answer to that. No, no, no, for nigh on 50 years I've slept in a hammock, and I won't change. Michael made my hammock, and it is the best!' He walked back out the door.

I grinned at Lesley. 'Change of plans, Commander.'

'Well, Bill, it looks like Mervyn's the one.'

'Yes Commander,' but I thought what a predicament, three females!

The young lady walked back into the galley. 'Could you stand to attention? I am Captain Farquhar, this lady here, Chris, is the ship's nurse and this lady here, Lesley, is my wife, but she is also Commander Johnson. She was the youngest female Commander in the Navy, so if you have any problems with the younger officers on this vessel, speak to Commander Johnson. She knows by experience how to sort them out. You are an officer under training on this vessel, so you will be treated equally, except for two things: one, your sleeping arrangements and two, you will use the women's shower. Other than that, you will do everything the others do on this vessel. You will fill out your logbook every day, put everything in it, listen very carefully to Jacko. He already knows your future. One problem you will have is that the stern quarters are next to the big motor, and it is noisy. Mervyn Nelis is your sergeant, he is the best there is. Do everything he asks, settle into your cabin and return on deck in your working gear. Also we don't use the cadet's names on board, but numbers. You are number 10.'

I went back on the Bridge. Jacko had a young man at the wheel. He was standing behind him, watching. I sat down in my chair, opened my logbook and started to fill it out. Then I opened the papers that the young female cadet had brought with her. I opened a small letter first. It was addressed to me.

Captain, the young gentleman brought into our hospital has a problem in his lung. It will require surgery. If he had actually gone to sea, he wouldn't have survived, but now he has a good chance of total recovery. Yours sincerely

It was signed by a doctor. I looked at the young lad with Jacko. He looked apprehensive. I looked at my watch: 7 pm. I said to him, 'This is the most important post on this vessel. Let the wheel go and this vessel will founder and could sink. Ted and I are the only ones who can relieve you. Wait for Ted, do not leave the helm.'

Lesley came up with my tea. I handed her the letter from the hospital. 'Could you give it to Chris and ask her to read it out to the crew?'

I handed her another envelope from Admiral French.

'So Bill, you are now a Commander, but I still outrank you. I was a Commander before you,' she said.

'Were you?'

She didn't like the way I said that. She went into the cabin and rummaged around, looking through her papers, came back and looked at mine. In a loud voice, she said, 'They've made a mistake!'

'I know, dear, but it's now on the paperwork.'

'But Bill, the date is the day before mine.'

'Yes dear, so I outrank you!'

She looked at me very annoyed, then she grinned, 'No, no dear, you are my husband, but I outrank you.'

I thought about politics here, so just said, 'Yes dear.'

She left and went back into the galley.

Jacko said, 'Very, very complicated, Bill.'

'Jacko, they're very warm and cuddly on a cold night!'

The young man at the wheel just frowned at me. I wondered whether he was confused or he understood.

Ted walked in with the young lady (number 10) and told her to take the wheel. He winked at me and lightly tapped the young man on the shoulder and said 'food.' Jacko was off, leaving the Bridge to me. Straightaway her eyes went to the compass, then to the radar, then the barometer. Very impressive.

'You will find her a little more sluggish to command than your father's yacht. Just find the rhythm of the waves and bounce the bow up against them, as they are trying to push you to port. This is a very dangerous stretch of water for sailing vessels of this size.'

'The Eye of the Needle, sir.'

'You are correct.' This lady is going to be interesting, I thought.

'Dad took us sailing every school holidays and over Christmas.'

'Where are they now?'

'Somewhere in the Cook Islands.'

'What would he say if he could see you now?'

'He would just nod, and Mum would say something like, so you're in command. You have to be like your father, don't you?'

'And what would you say back to her?' I grinned.

'Well, I've already said it Mum, you married him because you loved him and I know you love me.'

'What do you want to do in the Navy after you get your ranking?'

'I want to fly jet aircraft off of an aircraft carrier.'

'That would be very exhilarating. We can show you how to do many things, but not that.' She was doing well, keeping us on course/ 'So what are we looking for?'

'The Otway lighthouse, sir.'

'Do you play chess?'

'Yes sir, I do.'

I got out the chessboard, and the game began. An hour later, I realised I was in trouble. She certainly had played a lot of chess before boarding this vessel. I sat studying the board. Move my bishop? No, if I moved to Queen, would it open for me to move?

Just then, Lesley walked in with two coffees. She glanced at the young lady. 'I didn't know whether you drank tea or coffee.'

She looked seriously at Lesley for a moment and said, 'I will try the coffee one more time.'

Lesley grinned at her and topped one of the coffees up with hot water. She put the coffees on the bench, then glanced at the chessboard. She studied it for a while, then grinned at me and raised her eyebrows. She turned to face the young lady, saying, 'This is going to be an interesting voyage. I will leave the two of you to your game,' and discreetly left the Bridge.

I thought, do the unpredictable, move to Queen. Her head moved a little sharply to one side, her eyebrows slightly lifted. I knew I was back in the game. She hadn't predicted that move, but was that Jacko in my head? I was very impressed with this young lady, the way she could keep her concentration on the compass and on the chessboard at the same time. Finally the game came to a stalemate. Neither of us had won, but we had learnt so much about each other. I thought that Admiral French must be grinning to himself. He had said to me *to make men of them*, but this young lady leaves me with a big question mark.

'sir, Cape Otway Lighthouse,' she said.

'What do you know about Cape Otway Lighthouse?' I asked her.

'Three seconds duration with 50° of darkness in the entire period. The lantern has 3 flashes every revolution, every 2 minutes and 39 seconds. Cape Otway Lighthouse is the most important lighthouse if you want to enter Port Phillip Bay.'

'Where did you first get that information from?'

'My dad.'

'How far would you say we were off the lighthouse?'

'sir, it is a clear night, no fog or cloud cover to distort the light. So, I would say 20 miles.'

'So, if you were to write in your logbook, what would you put?'

'Cape Otway Lighthouse sighted and put in the time and wind direction, course forward starboard quarter.'

'And with this being a sailing vessel, would you put in anything else?'

'sir, sails aloft, men back on deck.'

I have to stop saying men in my logbook. I have been saying crew because I've got women on board.

'If this was a naval vessel or a man-of-war, I would put everything in, even if I thought it not really necessary. Seamen are very good critics, so you need to put down everything in your logbook, because if something happens in the future, you can go back through your logbook and prove that it was reported. On a naval vessel you are God, the buck stops with you and the total responsibility is yours.'

She grinned at me. 'Dad used to say, *I'm never wrong, I am the Captain, whatever I do is right*, and Mum used to say, *Only when I'm not on board.*'

Time seemed to slide past quickly. I had been keeping my eye on the light from the Otway Lighthouse.

Ted walked onto the Bridge. 'The wind is coming from the right direction Skipper, so it's with us.'

I looked at the young lady. 'As I said, you have to put everything in the logbook, your ordinance, everything. Ted and I have been on this old sailing vessel for a long time. We know if the Otway Light is on our Stern starboard quarter, it is time to alter course. I have marked it on the chart. What is this?'

I tapped the chart with my finger. 'West South 260°, the terminology you are used to is coming about, but normally on this vessel the crew is waiting for Ted, who will give the order to the crew.'

Ted went down onto the deck and gave a few orders. The crew all went to their stations. He glanced up at me and I nodded and shouted, 'Coming about West South West 260°.'

Ted repeated his orders to one or two, but it was with patience and understanding. Everything happened like clockwork, slightly brace the yardarms, tightening some ropes, loosening others off. We were right on course. I could see that Ted was very proud of his new crew. He went into the galley and nodded at Jacko, who took a handful of biscuits and disappeared to the Bridge.

Ted shouted out, 'Number 9 to the Bridge.' The young man gave Ted a very worried look. 'Don't worry young man, Jacko is the best there is, but don't tell him I said so.'

The young cadet went straight to the Bridge. I went to my bunk, laid down, and drifted into a deep sleep. I awoke with a start. Lesley's left hand was on my shoulder. She had a cup of coffee in her right hand. 'What time is it, Lesley?'

'11.30 am.' She gently kissed me on the forehead. 'Time to get up my sleepyhead. You've had a couple of hard days, and now we're at sea you can sleep. Breakfast is on the table and here is your coffee.'

I glanced onto the Bridge. Mervyn was in command with one of the young cadets. He nodded to me and I went back into my quarters and slowly ate my breakfast.

Mervyn's head appeared in the doorway. 'Barometer is dropping, Skipper.' I nodded to him, picked up my plate and cup and went onto the Bridge.

I glanced at the barometer. 'Don't like that Mervyn. At least we will find out whether the cadets have their sea legs.' I went down on the deck and spoke with Ted. 'The barometer is dropping Ted. Have we got much water in the bilge?'

'I will take care of it, Bill.' He pointed to the young lady. 'Number 10, man the pump, number 3, man the pump.' The young lady went directly to the pump. Number 3 hesitated. Ted asked him in a very commanding manner, 'Is there something wrong, number 3?'

'No sir.' He followed number 10 to the pump.

'Ted, could you get all of them to put their logbooks on the table in the galley?'

I walked into the galley and put my arm around Lesley. 'Lesley, darling, are you having a good morning?'

She took the plate and cup from me and stared at me for a moment. With a serious look on her face she asked, 'what do you want of me Bill?'

'The cadets will bring their logbooks in here and put them on the table. Could you ask them to come in one by one, sit with you and go through their logbooks with them?'

She nudged me and grinned. 'I will have to ask Les whether I can be relieved from my duties.'

'Next time Lesley. The next time I ask you to do something for me, it will be on deck, where I am in command,' and I nudged her back.

I went over to Les. He looked at me with a cheeky grin and winked. 'You are not interfering with my crew, are you, Bill?'

'No, no Les, just my wife. The barometer is dropping quite fast Les.' He nodded, he knew what to do.

Then I spoke to Chris. 'Good Afternoon, Chris.'

'Good Afternoon, Bill.'

'Chris, the barometer is dropping, so we could have a few very sick cadets. Keep them in here as it's midships and less movement.'

She smiled at me. 'Does that mean I will not get seasick?'

'Good heavens Chris, you are an Officer in his British Navy, we don't get seasick.' I winked at her and went back out to Ted. 'Where is Jacko, Ted?'

'On top of the Bridge with a couple of the cadets. He's been pointing up at the clouds and to the horizon and explaining the movements of the sea. He's a natural teacher.'

'It will be interesting to see what they've put in their logbooks. Who's next on the Bridge with me?'

'Number 5.'

'Right, send him up.'

I walked onto the Bridge. 'Mervyn, go and have some coffee and a break, then put the cadets to work on deck doing self defence, it will take their minds off the movement of the vessel. If Ted is happy that the bilge is dry, try to work with the two on the pumps as well. I will ask Jacko to give you his crew. I don't want them up there when there's a lot of movement and nothing to tie yourself to. I shouted up to Jacko, 'Could we have your cadets back on deck please, Jacko?'

He swung himself off the roof, landing lightly on his feet. 'Bill, wind coming from the stern.' I nodded to Ted, and he came up alongside us.

'As you know, I would normally leave the sails on, but these are different circumstances. Ted, strip some sails off, whatever you think.'

Cadet number 5 was standing alongside me, waiting to relieve his colleague. I put my hand on his shoulder, letting him know I was with him. Mervyn came out of the galley and I pointed to the motor. He nodded and went off to the stern. A cloud of black smoke blew and the big motor came alive again. We had everything prepared for whatever may come. Some of our sails had been reefed, the others stowed away. The barometer was still dropping. Mervyn had most of the crew practising self-defence, just the basic movements. They had apparently been through this many times. It was interesting to see them keeping their balance on a moving deck. Good practice.

Then we felt the first shudder of the wind and the coolness that came with it. The stern lifted slightly as the swell of the first wave nestled into her. I put my hand on the young cadet's shoulder and took the wheel from him. 'Go and get yourself something to eat and drink. You have done your time at the helm and have earned your rest, but I would suggest after you've had something to eat you work with the others to keep your mind busy.' I turned to the next cadet. 'Now young lad, the game begins. Instead of the waves pushing to bow, they are now pushing the stern. They are directly behind us, so they are pushing us forward. You have to keep us on course. Look at the compass, west south west to 60°. Move the wheel to the opposite way to the compass. I know you're nervous, but take your time, think to yourself, put it together in your mind, not mine.'

This cadet was different. He needed his own time and space with no distractions. I kept one eye on the compass and one on Mervyn, who was practising his self defence. I could feel the wind increasing, the movement under my feet and the pressure on the sails. The young cadet was having trouble keeping her on course, she needed more forward pressure.

I put my hand on his shoulder. 'Reach down with your right arm, see the lever there? Push it slightly forward. Can you feel the shudder?'

'Yes, sir.'

'Good, it's now in gear and the propeller is turning. You see this little lever here? It's the accelerator. Push it straight forward. That's giving the propeller more propulsion and putting more water pressure on the rudder.'

It's been a long time since I've had propeller power in this situation. I'm learning something new every day, I thought.

I didn't say anything for 20 minutes.

'Are you finding that a bit easier?'

'Yes, sir.'

'You don't need to correct the helm so much.'

I liked the way he stood at the wheel, legs slightly apart, bracing himself for any sudden movement. He was in control. I could feel the stern rise up as the wave lifted her, then the stern slid down the wave and the bow lifted up, then dipped down as the next wave lifted to her stern. This rhythm stayed with us for the next eight hours. I watched one or two of the cadets discreetly disappear and then return to his post and continue his practice. Admiral French had chosen these cadets very carefully and wisely. They would not quit, they were the best.

Jacko and number 2 relieved us from the Bridge and we both went to the galley. The cadet stepped aside to let me in the door first. I stopped. 'I'm very proud of you. That was a difficult sea, and you kept us on course.' I would swear he grew taller all of a sudden. I walked over to Lesley. 'How did you find the log books?'

'I found them extremely good,' she replied, 'one or two small things, but nothing serious. Some of the remarks were very interesting. I'm glad Stephanie is sleeping in the stern. Her quarters are in the right place. These are young men with young men's feelings, but a little warning Bill, I'm not sleeping in the stern!' She nudged me with her elbow and walked off to get us some food.

I went up to my quarters and filled out my logbook and slept for four hours, then I relieved Jacko on the Bridge. We looked at the barometer. It was rising again, daylight was just staring to appear.

Ted had the crew on deck. One or two of them didn't look very happy, but they didn't argue with Ted. He looked up at the Bridge and nodded to me. He turned and gestured to number 2 to come up to the Bridge. 'Jacko, can you talk to the crew before breakfast about the colours of the clouds and sea, and explain to them what you see and know.'

I gestured to Ted and looked at Jacko. He knew what I wanted. Jacko was in his element pointing out this and that, telling them you can have a good idea how high the clouds are because the sun is still hiding behind the horizon, reflecting on them first, then as the sun peeps over the horizon the colours of the clouds will change. They will tell you what the weather is doing by following the clouds. He talked more and more. Everybody seemed to be totally concentrating on what he was saying. They were jotting things down on their notepads. Then Jacko asked if they had any questions. I was totally surprised at the number of them who did indeed have a question. Jacko laughed. 'I'll get Ted to answer them for you.'

Ted's voice boomed out, 'Too busy, Jacko.' He disappeared into the galley. Jacko answered their questions and added more into them, giving the cadets even more information, but he used more of his own terminology, so that each one became a story in itself.

Finally, Les came out of the galley, put his hands on his hips and shouted, 'Get in here now, all of you, for your breakfast.'

Jacko quickly walked past him. Les scowled at Jacko. 'Good God, you can talk and talk.' He gave him a little nudge on his shoulder.

Jacko said, 'Well Les, I wasn't hungry!'

'That will be the day, you funny little man,' Les shouted.

After breakfast, we had the cadets working with their sextons, taking the quadrants and jotting them down on their pads and comparing their results with each other. In the afternoon they spent some time with Lesley on the politics, protocols and responsibility of command within His Majesty's Navy, the unwritten laws of the sea and a deep understanding of command between two Captains. You do not question the Captain's command. His orders come from higher up the chain of command and he must take into consideration the repercussions of his orders.

After all of that, coffee and biscuits came out, then they were back out with Mervyn practicing self defence until darkness fell. Then they had a short break before going back out with Jacko to study the stars.

'All of you, take out your small compass and your notebooks. Lay flat on your back, look up at a star directly above you, mark it in your mind. In the next two hours it will move its position, so mark it in the centre of your notepad. Write down the ship's course, using due north. You all should know north and magnetic north. Now you can plot the star's course. Look at your watch every ten minutes, and plot that course. You all know longitude and latitude. You know the direction of the stars as they revolve around the earth. If you did not have a compass in the desert, you'd walk around in circles; at sea you would sail around in circles, but if you have studied the stars, they will tell you whether you are travelling longitude or latitude; they will tell you where you are.' Jacko worked with the cadets practically. He did not tell them how to use calculations, but to use nature itself, so they could visualise in their minds, not on paper. They all listened to Jacko, trying not to miss anything he told them.

Finally, Les peered out of the galley door. He didn't have to say anything. Supper was being served.

Jacko said, 'Tomorrow night we will talk with the migrating birds, the whales, dolphins, penguins and fish. You are dismissed.' Jacko's mind was back in the desert, teaching the young ones to survive.

The days were sliding past quickly. The cadets talked to each other, helping their colleagues understand, or put into perspective, what they had learnt. I don't think they realised that we had become the students

DAISY MAY – THE SEQUEL

as well. Their different views and ideas, talking to them on the Bridge when we were alone, being able to talk deeper and with more understanding. They were the future; we were the past!

Very quickly, we were headed into the Indian Ocean towards Madagascar. The cadets all had a nice suntan on their bodies, but number 10, Stephanie, had been very discreet.

Lesley and I had taken it in turns to check the logbooks. First thing, early one morning before the sun had started to rise, Ted had the cadets scrubbing the decks.

Lesley walked up behind me. 'Bill, I was reading Stephanie's logbook. It is very good, but she had mentioned how good the boys were looking with their suntan, exercises and good food. I will have to look more carefully, Bill, I've been missing something.'

She walked away from me, wiggling her backside. I thought this is why sea Captains don't like women aboard. It makes life very complicated.

We had altered the way we were working with the crew so they didn't get bored or complacent. Self defence first thing in the morning, they were all standing on deck, their hands behind their backs, legs slightly astride. Mervyn's voice boomed out. 'You have all been studying your self defence and movements to perfection, but now your training begins.'

Lesley was standing there watching them.

'Number 6, step forward. Lesley Farquhar is a fugitive, apprehend her!'

Lesley lifted her eyebrows. Number 6 stepped forward without hesitation and started to apprehend Lesley. To his total surprise, in a second, he was flat on his back and Lesley had his hand twisted backwards and her foot on his shoulder. Mervyn walked up and looked down at him.

'What went wrong, number 6? You are bigger and taller than this lady.' Lesley still had a hold of him. 'This lady is about to dislocate your shoulder and break your hand. What are you going to do about it?'

Frustration got the better of the cadet and he shouted, 'I can't do anything!'

Mervyn nodded to Lesley, and she let go.

'Number 7, step forward. Mr Coe is a fugitive, apprehend him.' Number 7 did the same thing, but we noticed with a bit of caution. He moved forward to Ted and Ted spun around on his left leg, thrusting his right leg forward, hitting the young cadet in the chest. He went backwards and Mervyn caught him.

'Number 4, step forward. You see that funny little man with the white beard? He has been stealing biscuits, apprehend him.'

This cadet was a bit more cautious. He turned to Jacko and grinned. 'Excuse me, sir, I have been told you have been stealing biscuits and I have to apprehend you.'

Before the cadet could blink, Jacko was climbing the mast like a goanna seeking refuge. Mervyn burst out laughing, and so did the others.

'This exercise was not meant to embarrass you, but to teach you to be prepared for the unpredictable. Your opponent must stop you and will do any movement they can to block you. Because all of you are well and healthy, you do not require the nurse, so Lesley Farquhar will be working with you as well. Your self defence training begins, but first you will all climb the rigging and apprehend Jacko.'

Lesley put her head to one side and thought, *this will be interesting and entertaining*.

They all took off up the main mast. Jacko climbed to the very top, wrapped his legs around the mast just past the main royal stay, and sat on the top. He had a very good view of the ship, slightly rolling backwards and forwards, and from one side to the other.

The young cadets realised they couldn't get to him and there was no way to apprehend him.

'Back on deck,' Mervyn shouted, then in a louder voice he shouted out, 'food, food!'

Before the cadets realised what had happened, Jacko had slid down the rigging and was on the deck before them. He did one of his funny little dances, went past Lesley and into the galley. Lesley raised her eyebrows and grinned at the confused cadets.

Mervyn said to them, 'That is what a goanna would do in the desert to escape.' He then split them into two groups, Lesley had one, Mervyn the other, and they went to work.

I took one cadet with me to the Bridge. He handled the compass really well, and it only took him half an hour or so to work out the movement of the vessel. 'You've been around sailing vessels before young man?' I asked.

'Yes, sir. My father and mother have a launch in Sydney Harbour.'

I thought that sounded a bit strange, the way he said it, not we had a launch, but his parents do. 'If my parents are not working, they are on the launch where they can be alone together. Their careers are very demanding and they often spend time apart, but they are good parents, we didn't need anything. We've both been given good educations, although we've spent most of our lives in boarding schools.'

'You have a brother?'

'Yes, sir. I also had a sister, but she died very young.'

'So what do you want to do in the Navy?'

'Well, I didn't actually know, until my father put an automatic pilot in the launch. When I was on leave, he showed it to me and we talked about the future in navigation. He talked about putting satellites into space, and bouncing radio waves off them. They bounce back to earth or back to another satellite, going further around the globe, giving you information as to where you are. It fascinates me, but talking to Jacko on the Bridge and his way of thinking and explaining navigation, migrating birds, fish, whales, dolphins and many other species that migrate and return to the same place, in the same month and day, to breed or feed, how do they do it? The word navigation is fascinating to me. If Jacko can do it to the laws of nature, and we have to put a mechanical device in space, are we missing something that Jacko is trying to tell us? If there are other human beings around the world who can do the same, ancient seamen navigated all around the world centuries ago. I can leave this vessel, go higher up in the Navy, study navigation, but I will not learn what Jacko can teach me in the Navy. I need to be with the ancient seamen and the world of technology, put it all together Captain. It fascinates me and I know it is going to take me into the future, where I want to be.'

'Do you play chess?'

'No sir, but I've studied the moves on the chessboard.'

'Play chess with Jacko, study his moves, then you'll understand the ways of the desert where he comes from.'

Jacko relieved us of our watch at the helm, he was with number 10. Jacko gave me that funny look with his eyes that I knew it so well. 'What's wrong Jacko?'

'Can I spend some time at the helm?'

I put my hand on his shoulder. 'Yes Jacko, take the wheel and play chess with Stephanie. Teach her all you know and be in the desert with her.'

I gestured to my colleague, and we went down to the galley. Lesley spent the afternoon going through the do's and don'ts of command. 'Never think you know more than the officer in command of you, only suggest. Have your figures and paperwork checked and rechecked before you suggest anything to your commanding officer, because he will hand that suggestion onto a higher command, so do not be wrong, and don't back down if he questions you, because you will know you have done everything correctly, haven't you? Do not condemn a junior officer, he will be trying to do his job to the best of his ability. If you feel he could be doing a better job, in a different position, suggest it to your commanding officer. So the team can function as one, never put your personal feelings first. The responsibility of your command comes first.'

I'd finished my lunch, had my coffee and thought, *I must remember all of that*. I smiled, and went back to the Bridge to fill out my logbook, or was it to watch a chess game? I had one eye on their game and the other on my logbook, weather, compass, the barometer, and a few comments on the crew. I saw Stephanie's head go back, as if she was surprised. So Jacko has made a move which she hadn't been prepared for, he is back in the desert. I wrote down in my logbook, number 10 female, the only female in the training course, when she is in her self defence demonstrations, it is like she is holding herself back, but why? Is it not her particular abilities? I know the young men are very fit, they don't wear their singlets on deck, just their shorts, is that distracting her? The whole crew treat her with the upmost respect. Is there something we don't know about number 10, and they do.

Just then Jacko's head shot up. 'Put the Union Jack on her mast and any other naval flags we've got.' Then his head went back down to the chess game and the compass. Here we go again. Jacko's given me a warning, but what? Another problem. I went back on deck to talk to Ted. I was annoyed, because it's something I should have known myself.

'Ted, do we have naval flags aboard?'

'Yes Bill, in a small box below.'

'Jacko wants to put them aloft.'

Ted stared at me for a moment. 'What is that spooky little fellow up to now?'

'Ted, you know if I asked him, he couldn't tell me. Could you bring up the box, go through them, and put the Union Jack up. Ted, when Stephanie, number 10 is doing her self defence, what do you see?'

'Bill, whoever her opponent is, she is ready for him. She is on guard and her opponent knows it and hesitates.'

'Ted, this is not a British Man of War, but a training vessel. Are the cadets properly dressed?'

Ted thought for a moment. 'It is always said you don't have one woman aboard, especially young and attractive, and we do have one young lady aboard, who is very attractive and the right age. We have nine young men

357

with very healthy minds and bodies. That would put her on guard working at close contact.'

I sighed. 'Changing the subject Ted, we are entering dangerous waters, we are going to pass the Mauritius Islands, which are just a few nautical miles from Madagascar, and you know that as well as I do, the wind from our port side is pushing us to starboard, and the current is coming directly into our bow. I want to alter course 10° to port, how will that effect the yardarms?'

He nudged me and grinned, 'I would suggest sir, leaving them as they are. Wait and see.'

I nudged him back, grinning, 'You use words that confuse me,' and walked off to the galley.

'Lesley I wonder if you could do something for me,' I asked.

Her eyes twinkled, but she kept her face serious. 'Could you read through number 10's logbook and see if there's anything disturbing her in her self defence with the rest of the crew?'

I went to kiss her on the forehead but noticed there were eyes watching us. I thought better of it and went out on deck.

I walked up to Mervyn, who was in conversation with some of the cadets. 'You are all doing very well with your self defence, but you are being trained as officers in command, you allocate your officers and your crew to carry out certain tasks. If you find yourself in a dangerous situation, you have to make quick decisions, you have to know your men, who is best at what and who you can allocate to do a certain task. You work through your officers, which officer, who to put with him to achieve the task before you. You have been working with nine other colleagues. Use their number not their names. Create an incident in your mind that may occur aboard this vessel. Choose your officer and three of your colleagues to solve the problem. Write all of this down in your logbook.'

Mervyn turned around and looked at me. 'Morning, Skipper.' I gestured to the baulk works where we couldn't be heard.

'Mervyn, number 10, we have noticed she holds herself back during her self defence, what are your opinions?'

'Bill, she interests me. I would like to create an incident where she has to protect her life and see what happens. It would be very interesting.'

'So Mervyn, you're telling me not to be concerned.'

'Yes, Skipper.'

Just then I felt a tremble on the deck. I stretched my toes out trying to feel more. I looked up at Jacko, he gave me a small nod. I glanced at Ted, his eyes told me he'd felt it as well.

I put my hand up to Jacko and gestured for him to ring the bell three times, which he did, and everybody was running on deck. I was impressed how quickly they had assembled on deck.

'Stand at ease. We have a bit of a problem. The barometer is slightly dropping, the wind is coming from our port side midships, there is a current pushing us from our port side, we have another current pushing from our starboard side. Port side is warm, starboard side is cold. We are approaching Madagascar on our starboard side, and are doing approximately 6-1/2 knots, but the tide and the wind are pushing us to starboard. We have islands on our port side, we cannot tack, we have no room. How would you suggest we solve this problem? Talk amongst yourselves for a few moments.' I knew that number 10 and Jacko were listening from the Bridge, but still playing their game of chess. Mervyn was leaning on the baulk works with a slight grin on his face.

Ted walked up alongside me. 'This is going to be interesting, Skipper.'

We waited for about ten minutes, then number 5 stepped forward, He saluted me and I saluted back. 'Permission to make a suggestion, sir?'

'You have my permission.'

'Captain, sir, we would suggest stowing our upper sails, leaving on the flying jib, outer jib in the jib for sail mainsail spinnaker.'

'Thank you number 5, enter into your logbooks the reason why you have stowed so many sails. Number 6, what else would you suggest?'

'sir, Captain Jacko has talked about the colour and texture of the clouds. It appears that we have grey clouds on the horizon, not necessarily strong winds. Prepare for collecting rainwater and doing our washing.'

'Number 2, your suggestions.'

'Yes, sir. Check our rigging to make sure they are not tightening up too much with the damp weather and prepare to slacken off.'

'Number 1, your suggestions.'

'Yes, sir. If we have good rain, clean all the salt from the windows and anything else on the vessel which needs cleaning, including the deck.'

'Number 7.'

'sir, Captain Ted, the Bosun is resting.'

'Number 7 you are the acting Bosun. Put your crew to work.'

He looked slightly shocked, but didn't hesitate and started to shout out his orders. I stood with my legs slightly apart, my hands behind my back, trying to keep a stern face. I really wanted to grin. I wanted very much to laugh out loud, because I was so proud of them. It just happened, like clockwork. I heard the motor come to life and I could smell the smoke. I heard number 7 shout out 'number 10 engage forward motion.' I could feel the change in power under my feet as the vessel responded to the new source of power.

Ted whispered to me, 'Bill, does this mean my life becomes easier? They certainly know what they are doing.'

Lesley had her arms behind her back in the position of command, looking very satisfied. I turned to Ted and said, 'Coffee Ted? I don't think we're needed here.'

As we walked past the young man in command I said, 'I would suggest, sir, that you check to see if the sea cock is open for the big motor to cool.'

The rain squall started and everybody went to work, washing, cleaning, bathing, filling our water tanks, slackening off ropes, scrubbing decks well into the night. Jacko and I were on the Bridge watching. We had never seen a crew so enthusiastic in their work.

'Jacko, how's the crew doing at the helm?'

'They be doing good Skipper. You could leave them at the helm at any time, but a bit of trouble with one.'

I grinned, 'That would be number 10?'

'Yes Bill, she doesn't like it when I beat her at chess. She keeps her cool, but I know it's coming. She's going to beat me. I learnt so many things in the desert, but she is putting it all together and will know more than me!'

'Jacko could I be here when she does.'

'You, my brother, should be on my side.'

I grinned at him.

'Bill, there is land on our starboard side, the birds are heading home to roost, but we have birds in the rigging, the rainstorm must have worn them out.'

'It's a good place to rest, Jacko. I expect to see the lighthouse on our port side just on dawn, so you and I will stay here. We should see, or should I say, we will see two flashes every 10 seconds, repeated white flashes every 10 seconds.'

I sat down and started to fill in my logbook again. I enjoyed writing down the development of the crew and wrote something on every one of the cadets. I couldn't help mentioning number 10's ability to keep cool whilst playing chess with Jacko.

Just then Lesley walked in with coffee and food and put it on the bench. Then she rubbed her fingers through Jacko's hair. 'It's very interesting, Jacko, reading the comments of the crew in their logbooks. They don't forget anything you say or explain to them. I wish you'd been around when I was doing my training, you would have made it so much easier and more fun for me. Enjoy your supper. There is a little more cheese on your plate!' She kissed him on the forehead. 'I'm going to turn in now Bill, I have had a very interesting day and I'm very proud of all of them.' She went through to our quarters.

Jacko reached out with his foot and nudged my leg. I opened my eyes and thought to myself, I wasn't asleep, but only I know the truth.

The light was faint on the horizon. We both watched it until we could make out the flashes. I let out a deep sigh, right light, right place, Port Louis.

'Take the helm, Bill.' I didn't argue with him. I knew he needed to relieve himself. Even Jacko has nerves looking for something in the dark and talking to the witchy. He came back with two cups of coffee and one cup of tea, and his mouth chock-a-block full. He handed me the tea, and I took it into Lesley. I gently touched her shoulder, she pulled the blanket back over her head and said, 'If you are not tall, dark and handsome and passionate, go away!'

'I am your genie, I will give you whatever you command.' There was a wiggle under the blankets.

'I want another hours' sleep. A hand reached out for the tea and took it. I thought it wise to back off and go back onto the Bridge before I wore a pillow.

Back on deck, Ted was sipping a cup of coffee. 'You been up all night Ted?'

'Yes Bill, I want the boys to see the lighthouses.'

'I'll go and get them up.'

I left Ted drinking his coffee. I walked up to the forecastle and shouted out, 'All hands on deck, jump to it.' I turned, went back to Ted and winked at him, then went to the stern. The big motor was going boom, boom, boom, to a gentle rhythm. I banged on the top of the hatch, 'All hands on deck, jump to it!' and walked back to Ted. Daybreak was just starting. I could just see the red glow on the horizon along with the black outline of the islands to the bow. Everybody turned and looked forward to white flashes every six seconds. I thought, *why were you worrying, here they are, The Mascarene Islands, The Saint Denis Lighthouse, longitude 55°, latitude L20°.*

'Number 10 to the Bridge, number 5 to breakfast, then to the Bridge.' I went back up onto the Bridge, sat down, opened my logbook, picked up my pen and glanced up as number 10 was relieving Jacko. I looked up, checking the lighthouse, I wanted to be sure I was on the right course and filled in my logbook. 'Well number 10 how's the chess game? I saw the flinch of annoyance in her eyes. Are you winning?'

She didn't speak for a moment. 'No sir.'

'But you are winning, you are learning the ways of the desert and he knows it. You are now getting into his mind, and he has got into yours, human nature in us white folk has become predictable. Jacko doesn't play that game, he always thinks well ahead, has always got his eye on the horizon. You have learnt a lot by playing chess with him. Now he's worried that you may win. Remember when you first came aboard we had a little exercise. Lesley said you were predictable, that's how you'd been programmed. Then we said apprehend Ted, he then had a weapon, we then said apprehend Jacko. When you went to do that he shot straight up the mast like a goanna would, to protect himself. You all chased him up the mast. He went to the very top, where you couldn't get to him, then he slipped down the rigging to the end of the yardarm, then down the next sail and the next sail, and he was back on deck before you could blink! Leaving you all stranded up the mast. That's how he thinks.'

Number 5 walked onto the Bridge with a plate of bacon and eggs and a sticky bun, he put it down on the bench for number 10. I took the wheel.

'Number 5, I want you to get your sexton. Better still, take mine and take our bearings. Do not discuss it with anybody, and return here.'

He didn't hesitate. He took a pen and paper and went out on deck and started to take the bearings. I saw Ted and Jacko looking at the sky.

I put my head out of the Bridge and looked up to see what they were looking at. There was an aircraft flying very high above us. I looked at my watch and jotted down, *aircraft flying high above* and the time.

Ted walked onto the Bridge, he looked at number 10. 'I would eat that very quickly if I was you, Jacko is on deck! Skipper, I saw that aircraft yesterday about the same time. I recorded that on a piece of paper as well.'

'Ted, have you got the flags on deck?'

'Yes, Skipper.'

'Pick one of the cadets and discuss with him which flags we should be flying and where, stop the motor and put all our sails on, we have a new course coming up shortly. Number 5 return to the Bridge.'

He saluted me and I returned the salute, which is the correct thing to do to a Captain on the Bridge.

'sir, we are very close to the Tropic of Capricorn.'

'So number 5, here are the charts. You have your bearings, plot a course from here to Port Elizabeth, but I want to stay 20 nautical miles from it. If you doubt your figures, remember the safety of this vessel and the lives of your crew totally depend on you getting it right. It doesn't matter if you check them ten times, so long as you are satisfied in your mind that you are right to go ahead.'

I picked up the dirty dishes. 'If you would both excuse me, I'll be back.' I went into the galley and gave Lesley the dishes. She smiled at me.

'I do love you Bill when you make me feel important. Do you have any more dishes for me?'

'Lesley, coffee and tea and to sit with you for a few minutes would be nice.'

We sat together for a few moments. 'Lesley, I remember asking myself what happens when we get back to England. Now I'm asking myself the same question again. How much more can Les take? The years are catching up with him and it worries me. Jacko longs for the desert again, and

I know Ted is tired and his body is becoming weary. Asking them to go back to sea again, somehow I don't believe it will be right.'

'Bill, are you also looking at yourself?'

'I look at Jacko, Lesley, and my mind goes back to the Diamantina River. I know mum would want me to take Jacko back, but what would happen to *Daisy May*. I don't have any control over it. She now belongs to the British Navy, and no matter what paperwork I have from Winston Churchill, she is still a British Naval vessel.'

Lesley cuddled into my arms. 'Whatever happens Bill, all three of us will be together. Bill have you noticed Cat is spending more time with Les. Whenever he has a chance, he sits on Les's lap.'

'Lesley, Cat is no fool, he knows who feeds him.' I put my arm around her and cuddled her into me. 'Yes Lesley, the three of us always. I must return to the Bridge. Thank you for the coffee.'

'Any time Bill.'

I got up and returned to the Bridge. 'Number 5, do you have a course?'

'Yes sir, south west 240° puts us 20 nautical miles from Port Elizabeth, which is just down from East London.'

'Number 5, where will the wind be hitting our sails.'

'From our stern, sir.'

'Inform Captain Coe we are going to change course to south west 240°.'

He disappeared through the door to the deck. I had time to check his course. I couldn't argue with it, he was right. He returned, still looking serious, but content with himself.

'Number 5, what is your next duty?'

He hesitated slightly. 'Give the helmsmen the new course.' I nodded.

He said, 'Helmsmen, I have the Captain's permission for us to alter course to south west 240°.' He then stepped to the door and nodded to Ted.

'Your next duty?'

'Check the barometer, time and put this in my logbook, and our sails aloft, and the condition of the sea.'

'What else could you think of to put in your logbook? Just take it easy and think, don't let me panic you. You could mention that we have had the motor re-fuelled, and that the crew is doing well, we have replaced the water and scrubbed down the decks and are about to raise our flags. Two coffees and one cup of tea please number 5, and could you ask Ted to send the cadet who is looking after the flags to come to the Bridge. Thank you number 5.' He started to disappear. 'Stop number 5.' He appeared in the doorway again. I smiled at him. 'Is there something you forgot?'

'sir, yes sir. He stood to attention and saluted me.' I saluted him, turned and looked at the radar. I could just see the edge of the islands, but I could see Madagascar. We would be 20 nautical miles from the Cape of Santa Maria, which is the tip of Madagascar.

Number 10 said, 'you don't trust that do you, sir?'

She startled me. I wanted her to be observant, but she had struck a sore point in me. 'It's not that I don't trust. In 40 years I have had to use all the knowledge the previous Captain had given me. Captain Walter Wright and Jacko, and this pair of eyes. I am weary of trusting them. When you are a Captain, you will have everything to aid you, but I hope you will use the knowledge you have experienced on this sailing vessel. Put the future knowledge with the knowledge obtained aboard this vessel, and you will be one hell of a Captain.'

'I beg your pardon, Naval Pilot,' she grinned.

Number 7 appeared at the doorway. 'Permission to enter the Bridge, sir.' I grinned and thought, *I have started something now!*

'You have my permission.'

'Captain, sir.' He saluted, I returned the salute.

'At ease number 7, at ease. You have chosen the flags which will go aloft?'

'Yes sir.'

'Your suggestions number 7?'

'The Union Jack first sir, the White Ensign below that, and the Union Jack on the stern.'

'Number 7, why the Union Jack first?'

'Because we have high-ranking officers on board, sir.'

'That is correct number 7. We have two Commanders aboard, one with a particular medal, we have two Captains aboard and a high-ranking staff training officer. In our training manuals it suggests protocol. Number 7 inform Captain Coe of your decision and carry out his orders.'

'Yes, sir.'

'Was there a flag in the box regarding this being a training vessel?'

'No sir.'

'Thank you number 7, return to your duties.'

He stood to attention and saluted me and I returned the salute. He took 3 paces backwards, turned and left. I thought somebody had put a lot of training in protocol into these cadets.

Number 5 had been waiting outside the door with coffee and tea. He requested permission to enter and put them on the bench. I thought, *please don't salute me.*

'Thank you for the coffee number 5.' I sat down in my chair and relaxed. 'Number 5 sit down in the other chair. Where do you come from lad?'

'England, sir, but we've been living in Australia for quite a while. I have been attending boarding school and university in Australia. After this cruise I would like to return to Australia.'

'Why would you want to return to Australia?'

'There is something about Australia, sir. When I think about it I have a warm feeling inside, the weather is better, there's very little class distinction with the people, you can do whatever you want, if you put the work in.'

'So how did you get a position aboard this sailing vessel?'

'I told my father that I wanted to spend some time on a sailing vessel and he agreed with me, so I filled out a request, and now I'm here. I believe it's the best thing that's happened to me. We have all become friends, companions, we will always be friends, no matter what happens in life, we all will be part of each other as a team.'

'Could you put that in your logbook?'

'Yes, sir.'

'I'm going to shut my eyes for a few minutes, please wake me if you have any problems.'

I opened my eyes, and it was darkness all around. I wondered how long had I been asleep. Lesley was sitting in the other chair and Mervyn was at the helm. I knew that I'd gone into a deep sleep, which I so desperately needed. I had no worries with Mervyn at the helm and Lesley by my side. I had a sense of peace within me. I wanted to close my eyes again, but what I wanted, I knew I couldn't have. I am the Captain.

'What's Jacko up to Mervyn?' I asked.

They both turned their heads towards me. Lesley chuckled, 'you should wake up and see Bill.'

I got up off my chair and looked out of the window. Jacko was on deck and he had drawn a big circle with chalk. The crew were all sitting around it. He had candles on plates around the circle and he had drawn lines from one to the other. 'What is he up to Mervyn?'

Mervyn gave a small chuckle. 'He has drawn a circle, inside that is another smaller circle, that is the earth. He is using candles as the major stars that move around the galaxy. He keeps moving them to represent the galaxies moving in their orbits around the globe. Jacko would point to this star, that star, and point up in the air to other stars. Even Chris the nurse was there listening to what Jacko had to say.' Jacko was a natural born teacher and entertainer.

'I'm going to get something to eat and a coffee,' I said.

'Could you get me some tea as well please, Bill,' Lesley said.

Mervyn wasn't going to miss out. 'Coffee for me Bill, and some sticky buns.'

I gestured to them with a slight bow. 'Is there anything else madam or sir would require?'

Mervyn grinned, 'I think that will be all, thank you waiter,' and with that I left the Bridge.

In the galley I found Les asleep in the chair with Cat on his lap. Cat opened one of his eyes, then closed it. I quietly got what I needed and went back to the Bridge. Lesley drank her tea and then turned in for the night. Mervyn and I talked, trying to sort out the small problems which might come up in the future. Jacko's group then broke up, and they all retired for the night. 'Sleep Mervyn.'

'Yes, Skipper. The crew are always starving for information. Youth is a wonderful thing when you have it. Where did mine go? See you in the morning, Skipper.'

I nodded, and he left. Time to myself to think. I watched the horizon and the new dawn slowly crept in over the skyline on the horizon. I watched as the pink colour slowly crept in, but the sea was still black. This is how I would start painting a canvas, two strokes of the brush with colour, and others of a faint blue. I would put in another colour of green for the sea, then a little bit of yellow on the horizon, also a bit of red as the sun started to glow, then I'd mix more colours on my palette to give the sea more colours. How many more? I could use every colour to bring this sea to life. I could put some white on to represent whitecaps on the waves, to make them come to life. I could then make the sun a bit bigger. What colours would I need then? It's endless, the whole beauty of a sunrise at sea. Could I really leave all this? How much would I miss it?

Jacko's voice startled me. 'The colours in the desert are the same, Bill.'

I had to accept he was in my head again.

'Yes, Jacko, you're right. Wherever you are on the globe, the beauty of it is always the same.'

Just then number 10 walked up to the Bridge. 'Permission to enter, sir.'

I kept staring at the horizon, not looking round. 'You have my permission,' and I made a brief salute without taking my eyes off the sea. I said to Jacko, 'two cups of coffee and two cups of tea.' He started to walk out of the door and gave one of those funny little dances of his.

'I'll wash your paintbrushes out for you as well Bill,' he said.

I hunched my shoulders. Nothing is private from him.

'Captain, how long will he be?'

The question puzzled me. I turned around and looked at her. Well he has gone for coffee, but oh my god, Les is cooking breakfast, so he will be quite a while. We all make mistakes Stephanie, and I just did a big one sending Jacko for coffee and tea, which will be cold by the time he gets here.

If the wind doesn't increase and the whitecaps stay as they are, it should be a good day, but we have to be careful of the currents coming down the African coast. We have to make sure they don't push us into the roaring forties. Keep your eye out for little waterspouts, there could be some whales around and we will see porpoises or dolphins. The closer we get to North London, there will be plenty of seabirds.'

I stepped aside so number 10 could take the helm. I glanced at the horizon for just a bit longer, taking in its beauty. I said to number 10, 'I'll be back in just a minute,' and went down to talk to Ted.

I glanced at him. 'Yes Bill, everything is hunky-dory, they certainly gave us the best canvas, we haven't had any problems with the sails. Our crew is certainly doing a good job. I love watching Mervyn in his training sessions. They certainly are making him sharpen up when they believe they've got one thing right. They're starved for the next challenge. Bill, that aircraft is back; look up there. Jacko saw it first and he just stares at it.'

'Ted could you send up number 2 in about 2 hours, ask him to bring his sexton with him and a notepad, and keep an eye on Jacko, he knows something.'

I went back onto the Bridge. I felt there was something wrong, but what? Whose aircraft are they? Jacko suggesting we put our flags aloft, and the way he's been staring at the aircraft…

'Stephanie.'

'Yes, Skipper.'

'If you felt there was something wrong while you were standing on this Bridge, what would you think it is.'

'Well, Skipper, if you look on the radar, there are three dots, one is bigger than the others.'

I stared at them. There weren't any small islands in the vicinity, and they are not ships. Just then, Jacko walked onto the Bridge.

'Big problem Bill, big problem coming. Loud noise, people who are no good are coming for Lesley.'

Stephanie couldn't contain herself. 'What people?'

Stephanie's voice brought my thoughts. Back to the three dots. Jacko doesn't know that Stephanie has warned us. He turned around and started to leave the Bridge. He spoke the same three words in his own language.

Stephanie was staring at me. 'Stephanie, as you know, one word means many things in his language, bad water, bad wind, bad rain, bad fruit, anything that isn't good.'

We were approaching the three dots on the radar, on our port side. I rang the bell three times. The crew were on deck immediately. I got my telescope out and focused it on the horizon. Jacko was standing along-side me. 'Three small boats,' he said.

I picked them out in my lens. Pirates! One large boat, a mother boat and two smaller boats. They would have been capable of high speeds. I shouted down to Ted and Mervyn. 'Be prepared for pirates trying to board port side.'

Ted started the motor. 'Jacko relieve number 10 from the helm. You know how to deal with little fishing boats. Number 10 report to Mervyn.'

I remembered Jacko's words. *Not really nice people looking for Lesley.* I felt a shiver of panic. I leaned out of the Bridge and shouted to Lesley and Les to get back into the galley where they would be safe. Chris was to go with them. They hesitated for a moment and then they were gone. I put two fingers up to Mervyn. He knew what I wanted and told the cadets to protect the women. They went into the galley.

We were starting to approach the pirates. Then Jacko pointed to the horizon. There were three slightly horizontal dots on the horizon, one slightly above the other, they were getting bigger and dropping down closer to the sea. I could hear a roaring sound that was uncomfortable to my ears. One was nearly touching the sea, the other was slightly above that one but just a little higher, the third one was behind the second one, but a little higher. We all put our hands over our ears trying to protect them from the sound, but it was still painful. The three jets passed over the small boats, terrifying the crew. Some of them jumped overboard, terrified as the jets passed so low over them. In a matter of seconds they had passed us and were heading back up into the sky. We were gliding past the pirates. They were in as much shock as we were. Then Jacko pointed to the horizon, and the planes were coming back again, at the same level to the sea. We were looking towards the stern when the jets passed over them again, in formation, with that deafening high-pitched roar, then they went back high into the sky.

We all just stood staring towards the stern. What just happened? How would I explain it? We are definitely being watched. Jacko had warned us with the flags. Before Madagascar we were just another sailing vessel, after Madagascar we were a British Naval vessel with high-ranking officers on board. I put my hands on Jacko's shoulder and slightly squeezed them. 'Coffee Jacko, doughnuts and biscuits?' He nodded. I knew the only thing that would calm him down was food!

I walked alongside Ted, 'I wonder what they do for kicks on land? Could you stop the motor please, Ted?'

'How is Jacko?'

'I'm going to get him some food.'

Ted grinned, 'that will do the trick.'

'Could you give me number 2, keep the other cadets busy Ted. It's the best way.'

I spoke to number 10. 'Go back onto the Bridge and play chess with Jacko to keep his mind busy. But remember, his trauma would be greater than yours at the moment.'

I put my hand out and made it quiver, winked at her and pointed to myself. She smiled and went straight to the Bridge.

Mervyn walked up to me and smiled a very cheeky smile. 'You trained ten cadets to be the best. An incident happens where you can put them to work and three naval jets spoil all the work I've done. I'm going to write to somebody. It certainly isn't British Cricket.'

'Mervyn, put them back to work, keep them busy.' I smiled at him. 'You worry me, Mervyn. I'm trying to stay out of trouble and you would love trouble!'

I went into the galley, stared at Lesley for a moment and thought, *I don't ever want to lose you.*

She smiled at me and said, 'Well, that broke the boredom, didn't it Bill?'

'Lesley, could you please give me three plates of food? Fill one of them up for Jacko to keep his mind off the problems.' I looked at the two young cadets, who'd been ordered to the galley, with their faces full of sticky buns. 'Thank you cadets for carrying out the order straightaway to protect the ladies. I know you would have preferred to stay out on deck where everything was happening. Get yourself some more sticky buns and return on deck.'

I glanced at Les, he had a frying pan in his hand and was shaking it in the air, smiling at me. I put my thumb in the air and smiled back. Lesley gave me the plates of food. She had three mugs in one hand and a large plate of food in the other. We both went back to the Bridge. Lesley put the plate of food down in front of Jacko, then put her arms around his back and put her head on his shoulder and whispered something in this ear. He leaned his head over to her, but his eyes were on the food. Lesley glanced at me and went back into the galley.

'Number 2, take our bearings with your sexton, write them down in your notebook and return to the Bridge.' Jacko glanced at me and then at the sea. Seabirds were feeding on the surface of the sea. I glanced at the radar and could just make out land on our starboard side, East London. If it was dark, you would see the lighthouse.

Jacko said to number 10, 'Look over there. There are killer whales feeding.' There was a pod of about six. Number 10 was fascinated, watching them surface and then dive into the water again, hardly making a ripple.

Number 2 returned to the Bridge. I asked him to go back out on deck and take notice of what's on our port side and our starboard side. As he walked past number 10, she grinned at him. I could see him take note of the grin. He knew to sharpen up.

'Stephanie, number 10, I would appreciate it if you didn't talk to him while he's being trained.' I smiled at her and she gave me that little girl's smile back.

Jacko moved his chess piece in front of the Queen. Why? Then Stephanie made three moves and said, 'Checkmate.'

Jacko was staring at the chessboard. She reached forward and took one of his sausages, then broke it into two pieces, giving me one piece and put her thump up in the air. I burst out laughing. I had never seen a look like that on Jacko's face. She had beaten him at his own game. I was disappointed Ted wasn't there to witness it. I couldn't wait to tell him.

'Number 10 go down on deck and ask Captain Coe if he would think of staying 20 nautical miles from Port Elizabeth or 30 nautical miles. When he tells you, ask him why, but remember he is a superior officer.'

Ted was sitting on the hatch covers with three of the cadets. They were going over their rope splicing. 'Excuse me, sir.' Number 10 saluted him. Ted stood up and saluted her back. I was watching them when number 2 came back onto the Bridge.

'Just go over your figures number 2, I'll be with you shortly.'

Number 2 dropped his salute. 'Sir, the Captain has asked me to ask you would you stay 20 or 30 nautical miles from Port Elizabeth?'

Ted didn't move his head, but his eyes went up to the Bridge. 'I would suggest to the Captain, 30 nautical miles.'

'sir, the Captain has asked me to ask your opinion why?'

Ted thought for a minute, *thank you Bill!* 'Well number 10, we've had a good wind from the stern for the last couple of days. Once we pass East London the winds and currents will change. Cool and warm currents will be trying to mix. If we have a wind from our port side and the currents and tide are playing games with us, 20 nautical miles from this could be very dangerous. There are rocks, small islands, and pirates. There have been thousands of sailing vessels wrecked along this coast. If we wanted to tack, we would be entering dangerous waters. Giving our-selves an additional 10 nautical miles means that the roaring forties will not interfere with this. I know we have a motor, but I like to keep an ace up my sleeve. Do you have any more questions number 10?'

'No, sir, I don't. I know the roaring forties would take us back to Australia. Thank you Captain Coe.'

'Number 10, return to the Bridge.'

She returned to the Bridge, where I asked her, 'Well number 10, what did you think of what you've just done? You have obtained the knowledge of another person to help you make your decision.'

'That is correct,' she said.

'If, in life you don't make mistakes, there is something wrong, but when you've got the responsibility of command and your crew's lives, your fellow officers will give you food for thought. Not only your officers, your fellow crew members as well. Each one of them has special skills you do not have. Number 10 could you return the dishes to the galley and fetch two coffees and one cup of tea? Number 2, do you have your bearings?'

'Yes, sir. I want to be 30 nautical miles south of Port Elizabeth, then a course 30 nautical miles south of Cape Agulhas.'

'Number 2, if we are too far out to sea we would not see the light from the lighthouses. How else would we see them?'

'Because of the curvature of the earth, we may see them on the clouds or mist.'

'Where did you learn that?' I asked.

'From Jacko.'

Jacko was rubbing his fingers up and down his shirt. Number 10 returned from the galley, 'Number 10 take the helm and show Jacko how to play chess.'

'Yes sir,' she grinned.

'Number 2, you have your figures?'

'Yes sir.' He handed them to me.

I studied them. 'Are you 100% sure you're right? This is a very rugged coastline. I suggest you go over your figures again.'

I certainly enjoyed my coffee. Once again, I was enjoying the beauty of the sun, sea and the birds.

'sir.'

Number 2 broke my thoughts. 'So you are right, number 2?'

'I believe so, sir.'

'As the Captain, I would prefer Yes sir. Our course?'

'West sir. Due West.'

'Enter that in your logbook number 2 and show me the reflection of the lighthouse. It will be dark shortly, and Jacko may help you. I'm going to get something to eat.'

I sat down in the galley quietly eating my supper and sipping my coffee. What has happened aboard this vessel? *Daisy May* might have changed her name, but she is still the same. Ted, Jacko and Les are still part of her. Cat is part of her, but everything else has changed. We are in the past. We can't change, but everybody else with the exception of Lesley are in the future. What will happen when we reach England? I know we have to accept and not argue or protest.

'Chris here, sir.' She walked up alongside me. 'May I sit down, sir?'

'Yes certainly Chris. We haven't had much of a chance to talk have we, but you call me Bill.'

'Your brother fascinates me. When you're talking to him, it's like he takes you through a door into a different world. He becomes, like, you talking to somebody in another dimension, and his conversations fascinate me. But you too, are caught between the two, aren't you?'

'Yes, we were brought up in the desert as brothers. Mum loved him. He is so special and precious to both of us.'

'But Bill, I have another thing to discuss—the crew. Stephanie, number 10 and I share the same quarters. She tells me the crew don't sleep very much, they go over everything they have learnt during the day and discuss it so that each individual cadet understands perfectly. Stephanie would like to join in, but she can't because her quarters are in the stern. Their training has been intense, but they have enjoyed every bit of it, especially that with Jacko. I'm concerned they not sleeping soundly, they are too wound up with their thoughts.'

'Thank you Chris, I was thinking of giving them time to themselves when we got into the naval dockyard at Queenstown. Could you leave it with me, and I'll give it some thought.' I looked at my watch, still enough time for another cup of coffee. 'Would you like a coffee, Chris?'

'I would prefer tea, Bill.'

I got two cups and a plate of biscuits and brought them back. I sat down next to Chris. 'Where do you come from, Chris?'

'Originally from England. I married, divorced, met a government official, married him. I should have married him first. He passed away.'

'So you are a trained nurse by profession?'

She hesitated, 'Yes, but in the Navy you train as other things as well. Operating in the theatre, studying the heart and other parts of the body, psychology, trauma, how the brain works.'

'That's a wide range, Chris. What happens when we get to England?'

'The Navy is my life Bill, they will give me another assignment. I might even get another cruise. I will ask Les to give me another degree in dirty dishes and pots and pans on a sailing ship!'

Les walked over holding a frying pan. 'Are you interfering with my crew again?'

'No Les, I'm just leaving.' I got up, backed away from him and discreetly disappeared through the door.

Darkness was nearly upon us. Number 2 was standing next to the baulk works with several of the crew. They were looking over to the starboard towards land. Jacko had joined us.

'Number 2.' He spun around and faced me. 'When I asked you this morning to go out and look towards our port then over to our stern, what were your observations? Turn around and look again.'

'There are large white killer whales, birds feeding by diving into the sea, small flashes of fish are in the water, on the starboard side you could just see the clouds above the land.'

'Could you see the land without a telescope?'

'sir, what makes you think there was land? Captain Jacko showed us the difference between cloud over land and clouds at sea, and the difference between mist and fog.'

'So what are you looking for now?'

'A reflection of light on the clouds. Where we lived, there was an escarpment. When it was dark, a car would go up it, and their lights would reflect on the clouds. My sister and I used to watch them from the verandah.'

Three of the crew shouted, 'There it is!'

'Count the flashes and the distance between them and put them in your logbook. After supper you're with Jacko for one hour.'

I went back to the Bridge. Number 6 was standing at the wheel, his eyes fixed on the compass. The sea was pushing us from the stern, and it was not making it easy for us. 'Wake me, Mervyn, at the end of your watch.' I turned in to sleep for about four hours.

Mervyn woke me. It was time for my watch.

One of Lesley's eyes opened.

'Are you going to take this watch with me, Lesley?'

There was a grunt, and she rolled over pulling the blanket with her. So, I guess not!

Jacko walked in with three coffees and his plate of food. He put them on the bench and nudged Mervyn away from the wheel. Then he stared at Chris.

'I couldn't sleep Jacko, so I kept company with Mervyn. Is that all right?' she said.

'As long as you don't want to take my place at the helm,' Jacko replied.

As Chris slowly walked out of the Bridge, she winked at me and gave Jacko a cheeky grin. 'That would look good on my resume. I may talk to you later, Jacko.' She went off to her quarters.

Jacko and I didn't say much during our watch, but we enjoyed watching the daylight creeping in and the movement of the birds feeding on the whitebait.

Mervyn had the crew on deck exercising. Ted had sent number 7 to the Bridge.

'Permission to enter the Bridge, sir.' He saluted, I returned the salute.

'Take the helm number 7. There's one person missing.'

'He's asleep,' Jacko said.

Here we go again. I went down on to the deck. 'Mervyn we're one missing. I've got number 7 on the Bridge, where is the other one?'

We both went into the forecastle, and there he was sound asleep in his hammock. I went and got the nurse, who examined him.

'He is in a deep sleep, just leave him, he's exhausted.'

I stared at Chris for a moment and said, 'Follow me.'

I stood in front of the crew. 'Attention!' Mervyn said, and they all carried out his order.

'You have been a marvellous crew. You've studied, you've listened, you have performed, you do not question, you just do it. I'm extremely proud of all of you. Each one of you can be left at the helm knowing this vessel is in safe hands. You will all have two days rest. The only duties you have is when the sails need to be changed under Captain Coe's instructions. You are dismissed!'

They all just stood there, looking totally lost and confused.

'You have earned a rest, go lie in the sun, sleep in your hammock, but rest.'

They all slowly went into the galley. I went back to the Bridge. Mervyn followed me. 'Number 7.'

'Yes, sir.'

'You heard what I said?'

'Yes, sir.'

'Join your comrades and rest.' He saluted and left.

'We've been pushing them hard,' I said to Jacko, 'but they have been pushing themselves harder. At 4 pm tomorrow we will tack West 310° for Cape Town. The swell is down, the wind has dropped and is coming from the stern. We know that the cold waters flowing down from the Atlantic Ocean are unpredictable at the Cape.'

I was waiting for Jacko to make some sort of comment to warn me, but he hadn't said anything.

The crew slowly came out of the galley. They were well fed and started to lay down on the hatch covers. During the day I found them all in a group talking together, but number 10 wasn't there. In the afternoon I went down to get Jacko and myself a coffee. I asked Chris if number 10 was alright.

She hesitated. 'Yes, Captain, but it's her time of the month.'

I nodded. Nothing more to be said. Chris went back to what she was doing with Lesley. I sat down for a moment, sipping my coffee with time to myself to think. I noticed one of the cadet's hair had grown and he had a long beard. It needed trimming. Lesley walked up to me and gave me a cheeky grin. '

Do you mind if a young lady sits down with you, sir?'

'You're a bit forward young lady, but please do Lesley.'

'I would like a couple of days with just you and me, with nobody else to give us any problems.'

She leaned into my shoulder. 'Yes, Bill. In three days we will be in False Bay Naval Harbour, Simon's Town.'

'I noticed one of the cadet's hair and beard needing trimming. Could you maybe arrange for their hair and beards to be trimmed tomorrow afternoon? If you need Jacko, he's yours. Jacko, Mervyn, Ted and I are not exempt, and could you have the cadets make sure their uniforms are perfect? All gleaming white, and the officer's uniforms are to be the same.'

'Yes Bill, but I will be doing your hair and beard. Be on deck in 15 minutes!'

I shouted out, 'Oh no, what have I just done.'

'Bill you gave me the work. I want some fun.'

'Yes Lesley, that's what I'm afraid of.'

I picked up Jacko's coffee and doughnuts and went back to the Bridge. I put them down in front of him, he did one of his little chants. 'Do you want me to sharpen the scissors, Bill?'

'I would just want one thing, to be private. Jacko always knows what is in my mind.'

'Jacko, at 5pm we alter course to West 330°. I don't like the humidity in the air. I would expect thunderstorms and rain about midnight. I would like to have been in False Bay by then, but we won't make it in time. This course takes us straight into the bay. We will pass our destination and alter course again to South to 20, that should take us straight into the harbour. I would like to leave all sails on her for as long as we can. Yes Jacko, it's my pride, because I'm so proud of our crew, and I want them all to experience it. I don't believe it will ever happen again.'

Jacko's head dropped down slightly.

'Yes, I know Jacko, how you feel.'

He started to eat his doughnuts, then he chuckled to himself. 'Lesley is waiting for you, Bill!'

'Shut up Jacko. Your turn is coming!' I tried to reach out for one of his doughnuts, but he was quicker than me. I went down on the deck and sat down on the bench. I hope this is a warning for the crew. I listened to the scissors go clip, clip, clip. I didn't say a word. I just watched Jacko on the Bridge with that silly grin on this face. When Lesley had finished, I went to relieve Jacko at the helm.

I nodded to Ted, and we altered course to West 330°. Ted had the yardarms ready and everything was tightened up and in order. We could see the clouds on the horizon—cold air, big fluffy white clouds. The wind was still with us, starboard stern quarter. I wanted to rub my back on the door posts. Loose bits of hair were inside my shirt and driving me crazy.

I saw Lesley come out of the galley looking angry. She walked towards the stern then went round the back of the Bridge to the starboard side to where the ladies shower was. She put both hands on her hips and in a very loud voice said, 'Haven't you anything better to do number 7?' There was no reply. Lesley's voice boomed out again, 'then find it!'

He said, 'Yes ma'am.' Then he went into the forecastle. I saw Chris coming out of the galley and she walked around to where Lesley had just been, then she returned to the galley. Is this secret women's business? Where is Jacko when you need him? I cannot leave the helm, there is no-one to relieve me. I watched the lightening on the horizon and heard the thunder. One or two of the cadets came out to watch nature's spectacular show. Darkness was with us again. The lightening looked even better, it was apparently travelling in a different direction to us and as a consequence, we wouldn't be getting any rain.

Cape Agulhas on the starboard side. I could just see the lighthouse. Jacko relieved me at midnight, and Ted walked in as well.

'What were the women doing, Ted?'

'What do you mean, Bill?'

'I don't know, that's why I'm asking you.'

'I don't know what the women were doing Bill. I stay out of their way.' Jacko stood at the helm looking so innocent.

'I'm going to get coffee and something to eat.' I tapped the chart with my finger. 'We are here early morning, you should see Danger Point Lighthouse port side.'

I sat down at the bench and Lesley brought me a coffee. 'Lesley we should be in port about 4 pm tomorrow, we will have all the crew and officers in uniform. I would suggest 2 pm. I don't want the crew leaving the dockyard. If you could ask Colin to phone his mother to meet him at the dockyard gates, I will arrange a pass for his mother and sister. But Jacko will be a problem. If Mr McGregor knows he's in port, who knows what will happen.'

I ate my meal and waited for Lesley to say something, but she didn't. I remembered what Ted said, *stay away from the women* and Jacko not saying a word. *Take their advice Bill.* I didn't ask. Lesley looked at me seriously. 'Could you and I go somewhere, just the two of us and sit quietly together.'

'Yes Lesley, I would like that.'

Les sat down beside us. 'Bill, would we see the children?'

I looked at him. He never asks me for anything. 'Yes Les, I know Jacko wants to see them also.' I glanced at Lesley, 'So do you.'

'Yes Bill, and so does Ted.'

'I will arrange it. I must close my eyes for a moment.'

I kissed her forehead, got up and put both my hands on Les's shoulders, I gently squeezed them. I noticed Cat was sitting by his feet. It wasn't time for his food.

I felt a hand on my shoulder and opened my eyes. Lesley was there with coffee and my breakfast. I sat up and put the pillow behind me. 'Who is at the helm?'

'Mervyn, Jacko and Chris are cutting hair. The rest of the crew are cleaning themselves up and attending to their uniforms using plenty of spit and polish.'

I looked at the clock on the wall, 9 am

'Yes Bill, we are inside the bay and the weather is moderately calm. Ted has all the canvas aloft.'

I grinned at Lesley, 'And who is going to cut Jacko's hair?'

'Les has already cut it and shaved his beard and the back of his neck, and the crew all have samples of his hair. Stephanie has plaited it down both sides of his beard.'

'This I've got to see. Did he give Stephanie any trouble?'

'No Bill, but Ted did.'

I got up and Lesley pointed to my uniform. I put it on. She pointed to my socks. 'You only put socks on when your feet are cold!'

Lesley said, 'Stop grumbling and put your boots on.'

I shook my head. Lesley stood looking at me, then she started fiddling with my collar and tie, straightening my shoulders. 'I should have pressed that a little bit more Bill.'

I sighed, 'So this is married life?'

'Yes Bill, gives us something to do. You are my man, and I want you to look your very best.' She kissed me on the end of my nose. I went to the Bridge.

'Mervyn,' I winked at Lesley, 'I would suggest that you put your uniform on and present yourself to my wife so she can straighten you up and have you looking your very best.' I winked at him.

'Bill, I haven't had a woman fussing over me for a long time, and twice in one day. My hair and my uniform. I will put that in my log-book.' He turned and walked out of the Bridge, then he stuck his head back in the door. 'Permission to leave the Bridge, ma'am.'

'You have my permission, Mr Nelis.'

I stood at the helm watching the small craft. People on them taking photos and waving. All the crew had their uniforms on, even Jacko. I had a great sense of pride within me, but shook my head when I felt the tears trickle down my cheeks. If this is how it's going to end, I certainly would be satisfied.

CHAPTER 45

I noticed a beautiful, extremely well kept white schooner nearby. It had wooden handrails on the stern of the cockpit, all very well varnished. I would have said it was in a walnut stain, by the way the bow carved up and married with the bow spread. I don't know why the sails looked familiar, the way they curved to catch the wind, absolutely perfect.

Then I heard Jacko shout out, 'Michael, Mickey, Mickey.' A man at the helm waved, then put his thumb in the air. Is it Michael? He had two women with him. That could be Michael. He had black hair, going grey and a grey beard. Yes, it is Michael!

Les was now standing on the starboard side. Ted had joined him and Lesley was there too. I waved my arm out of the Bridge, then blew the fog horn. I wanted to turn into the wind to stop her, but I couldn't. There were too many small vessels. I saw a lady talking to Michael, pulling at his sleeve, pointing at us. She seemed to be very excited. She went below and returned with two flags, waving them in the air. Lesley waved her arms. She came up onto the Bridge.

'Bill, it's Michael and Jackie Evans. Jackie wants to come aboard.'

'Let Michael know I'm turning into the wind, but still keeping headway.'

Lesley went down on deck and was signing with semaphore using her arms. Jackie did the same back. Michael put his thumbs in the air. I glanced up, looking at the yardarms. They had been braced closer to the starboard side. Michael's' mainmast would be very close to them if he came alongside. Ted had the hatch open and lowered the ladder down. Michael, being a professional seaman, had noticed the yardarms. He had Jackie standing on the port side, just in front of his mainmast, easing his schooner into our starboard side at a slight angle. He was aware of his bowsprit on our hull and watching his mast, wave movement and sails, which were blocking his vision.

Jackie put both her hands out and grabbed the ropes on both sides of the ladder, then stepped off the schooner. Both her feet were on the ladder. Michael eased his schooner away from us, wiping his forehead with his hand. I gestured back, wiping my forehead with my hand as well. I watched Jackie and Lesley embracing each other, laughing. Jackie turned around and waved to Michael. He waved back. Jacko was bouncing up and down like a schoolboy with a new puppy. Jackie put her arms around him and cuddled him with so much love and affection, then she pushed him back, but still holding him with her hands.

'What have they done to you, Jacko?' She was looking at his beard with the plaits on both sides and his Scottish uniform.

'I am an Aborigine in a Scottish clan and I am a sea Captain and keeper of my people, but I am also a Freemason from the Diamantina River in the Channel Country of Australia.'

She just stared at him. I could see the tears in her eyes and she cuddled him with so much love and affection.

Damn, that's twice today, I've got tears in my eyes. *You're getting soft, Bill*, I chuckled to myself. I noticed that both Ted and Les had tears of joy also.

I couldn't see Mervyn. Jacko took Jackie's hand and led her to the Bridge. Jackie and I just looked at each other. 'Jackie, you and I have never met as friends.' I put my hand out and Jackie shook it. 'What are you doing with Michael on a two mastered schooner?'

'It is a long story, Bill, and I think Lesley should be here as well.' I stared at her again. She has been part of this frustrating circle I've been in, with no answers.

'Jacko, could you ask Lesley to come up to the Bridge and I think Jackie would like a cup of tea.'

I looked at the compass, then my watch 2 pm. The barometer was looking good.

'You are looking well, Jackie,' I said.

'Yes Bill, I've never been healthier and relaxed.'

Jacko and Lesley walked onto the Bridge. Cat was following them. He jumped up onto the bench and sat on Colin's blanket.

Jackie put her hand out and took Lesley's, squeezing it. 'First thing, Bill, is it possible for me to return to England with you? If that's your destination?'

I bit my lip as I thought. 'Yes, certainly. Lesley, you have a spare uniform, don't you?'

'Yes Bill, I do.'

'Could you give it to Jackie while we're in port? Jackie, you are an assistant nurse. You do not wear any braids or medals and stay discreetly out of the way. If you would go with Lesley and put that uniform on to stop any loose chit chat. Drink your tea first. Jacko, go and fetch Mervyn and Ted.'

He returned with both of them. 'Jacko, go down and talk to Les and Chris discreetly and tell them what's just happened here, and return. I have informed Ted and Mervyn. Mervyn my friend.'

'I know Bill. I will sleep in the forecastle and Jackie can have my cabin,' Mervyn said.

'You are a true gentleman, Mervyn.'

That's that problem solved. Jacko returned and Jackie came out of our quarters, dressed in a naval uniform.

'Jackie, you said you had a lot to explain?'

Ted broke in, 'Bill, I've got work to do. We'll be in the harbour this evening, and Mervyn said I have to get the crew in shape. Please excuse me.'

'Jackie, I'm listening,' I said.

'Somebody in the department faked Lesley's death and Lesley's sister was informed of her death. She and her husband flew back to England from Melbourne, Australia. Nobody realised your sister Peggy, or Margaret, is married to Ted Jones, who was a high-ranking police officer in London. He was one of the best with extremely high principles, and who would not bend, either for politics or politicians, so he was tactfully transferred to Australia. He is very well respected by his colleagues in England and he is a Cockney. Your apartment was bugged. He soon sorted that out and returned the bugs to me. They had faked your death by putting a corpse on the footpath below your apartment, saying that you had committed suicide. When your sister contacted your solicitor, Mr Fredericks, he punched holes in the death certificate. Mr Fredericks is a highly respected solicitor for his honesty and he will not bend the rules. Ted Jones and his colleagues in the police force found another Lesley Johnson, who had died, and they had used her death certificate.'

'You were a high-ranking officer in the British Navy and still very much alive and on special assignment. Peggy and Ted returned to Australia. I know that you have journals, Lesley, containing a lot of very important information on high-ranking people in British and German society, which they do not want exposed to the general public. They will go to any length to obtain and destroy them. We subsequently went to Dartmouth and spoke to a solicitor there. That's where I met Michael and he showed me the way out of the department. I have retired along with my colleague. I cannot mention her name because she knows too much as well. I need to return home to England, to my house in the Cotswold's. The three of us have sailed everywhere through Europe, the Mediterranean, islands of Greece and so many other places.'

Lesley and Jackie went down to the galley where they could talk more in private.

I looked at my watch. 'Jacko, South 20°.'

We were heading straight towards the entrance of the Port. I waved to Ted to come up onto the Bridge. 'Jacko, could you take your sword off please and lay it on the bench? I don't want you tripping over it. Ted, I'm going to take her in as close as I can to the port.' I winked at him. 'I would suggest all hands on deck dressed properly. Lesley, Chris and Jackie on the whipline, Mervyn and the rest of the crew to stow sails when you give the order, then Chris and Jackie on either side of the stern, both wearing their white uniforms. One man on the bow, one man on each end of the mainsail yardarms, the rest lined up across the deck.'

As I was talking to Ted, I saw a launch flying a naval flag coming towards us at high speed. 'What do you think, Jacko?'

'It is a pilot boat. Bill,'

'Lower the ladder, Ted.' The launch did a wide sweep and came alongside our starboard side. I saw an officer take the ladder and climb aboard. He looked fit, and he was tall, but climbing the ladder, he was very clumsy. Ted and Mervyn helped him aboard. A lady followed him up the ladder and the launch moved away from our side. Jacko, Mervyn, Ted and Lesley were there to meet him.

He looked at Ted, and seeing that he was a Captain asked, 'Permission to come aboard, sir.'

'You have the Captain's permission.' I could see in his eyes he was questioning himself. *You have the Captain's permission.* Then he looked at

Lesley and saw that she was a Commander, he saluted her, she returned the salute.

Lesley smiled, 'Welcome aboard, Captain.'

Then he looked at Mervyn and could see that he was also a high-ranking officer, a staff sergeant.

What am I doing on the Bridge? I should be down there. Jacko should be at the helm. Does he know what is going on? What is he up to? I had asked him to take his sword off. I took the helm while he did it, then I asked him, 'What do you think about that?' Then, whilst I was talking to the others, Jacko slipped out of the Bridge. The Captain who had just come aboard introduced himself as Captain Tiny Harrison, Captain of the Port.

Jacko stepped forward and Captain Harrison shouted out, 'Jacko!' and started shaking his hand. I couldn't see his hand grip as he had put his other hand over the top of it, then he put his arms around Jacko and embraced him, but Jacko's head only came up to Captain Harrison's chin. Jacko stood back and gave the sign of Fidelity and said to Captain Harrison, 'I am now a fully fledged Freemason.'

Captain Harrison shook Jacko's hand again, then appeared to wipe his big nose with his hand. I could see he was feeling very emotional. 'We have a lodge meeting tonight. McGregor is going to love this.' Captain Harrison shook himself, he looked at the beautiful blonde lady standing by the baulk works. He said, 'Excuse me, this is my secretary and dear friend Joyce.'

She took no notice of the others but went straight to Jacko and gently put her arms around his neck and kissed him on the end of his nose. 'How are you, Jacko? Getting a little tired listening to my people and the desert.' She cuddled him with so much tenderness. 'Are you going to entertain us tonight in the South?'

Jacko's face lit up. 'Yes, yes, come to the Bridge and meet the Captain.'

He turned to Lesley. 'Would you please get Joyce a cup of tea?'

Lesley winked at Joyce. 'Certainly sir, straight away. Joyce, when they get to be an Aboriginal Scotsman and a Captain, they can be a pain!'

Joyce smiled back at Lesley, then they went to the Bridge.

Captain Harrison looked at Bill, then to his uniform and saluted, 'Permission to come onto the Bridge, sir.'

I saluted him back, looked at Jacko with a scowl that you would use for a naughty child. I had noticed him walk up the deck with a limp, but because he was such a tall man, it was really a waddle.

'Captain Tiny Harrison sir, I would suggest you call me Bill.'

'Then I am Tiny. It is a nickname they gave me a long time ago, and it stuck. I would like to present my colleague, Joyce.'

I shook her hand. 'Welcome aboard Joyce.'

'Bill, I wasn't informed you would be entering my port, and when I saw the flags,' he raised his eyebrows, 'well, I'm here.'

'Tiny, I see you have a bad leg. Please sit down.' He sat down in the chair and grinned at me.

'Yes, I did have a bad leg, but I don't anymore, just this artificial leg. Climbing aboard on a rope ladder made it a little sore.'

Joyce said with a bit of anger in her voice, 'He is his own worst enemy. He will not give in.'

I looked at my watch, then to the Port.

Lesley walked in with tea and biscuits and put them on the bench. She turned to face Jacko. 'Would there be anything else, sir?'

'Are the biscuits for me?'

'No, sir.'

'Go down onto the deck with Lesley and prepare yourself. You don't have time to go into the galley,' I said to Jacko as I took the wheel.

Tiny grinned at me. 'He gives you trouble, Bill.'

'Not exactly trouble. He is my brother, so if I talk to him the same way our mum used to do, he isn't any trouble. What annoys me is he knows everything before me. The minute he saw your launch, he knew you were on it.'

'So Bill, you are a naval training vessel?'

'Yes we are, and our cargo is timber for the Portsmouth dockyards in England.' I looked at my watch and the compass, 'Excuse me.'

I nodded to Ted.

Tiny said, 'This I've got to see,' and stepped out of the Bridge.

We heard the big motor start and a burst of black smoke, then blue, and the sound of that gentle rhythm. Fortunately there weren't any hiccups. Everything went like clockwork as the sails were stripped off the masts. I put her into gear and eased the accelerator forward. She was easing steadily forward. We had put on a good show for the spectators in their boats.

Tiny walked in and sat down. 'What stores do you want, Bill?'

'We will need diesel. Les, the cook, will give you a list of what he requires. He will require firewood for his stove, but he will give you the size.'

Tiny glanced at Joyce, who was writing this all down on a notepad.

'One of my crew comes from Cape Town. His mother and sister will be coming aboard to see him. I don't want any of my crew leaving the harbour. An old member of my crew might also visit us.'

'How long will you be staying?' he asked.

'Two nights, leaving early morning with the tide.'

We tied up at our berth. Jacko had turned her around, so that she was facing out to the sea, the starboard side up against the wharf.

Tiny shook my hand. 'I will see you in the morning, Bill. Can I take Jacko with me and return him in the morning?'

'Yes, you may. When he leaves, I'll have my back turned, so that I don't see. When you pick up the list from Les, let him know you're taking Jacko. He feels responsible for him,'

Jacko put his sword back on. 'Jacko, I know what would Mum say.'

He grinned at me and said 'behave yourself!' Just then Jacko said to me, 'we are going to have fun tomorrow Bill.' Then he was off. I thought, *what does he know now that I don't?*

CHAPTER 46

Just on daybreak, Ted woke me. 'Fuel truck, Bill.' Lesley was already in the galley. I dressed and went down on deck. The driver of the truck had already found the food. He would have smelled it as soon as he got out of his truck.

I walked up to him, put my hand out and said, 'I am Bill.' he shook my hand and replied in a gravelly voice, 'I am Roscoe.'

'Pleased to meet you, Roscoe.'

He grinned at me, looking at my uniform. 'Every officer I have ever met is a toffee nose, but you are a fair dinkum, true blue Aussie.'

'So you're Australian, Roscoe?'

'I am.'

'What did you do in Australia?'

'I drove heavy haulage trucks all over Australia.'

I frowned at him. 'And what brings you to Cape Town?'

'My missus. She wants to spend some time with her parents. Her mum isn't in good health. That's why I retired. Six months here, then we return home to the grandchildren.'

'Ted will look after you, Roscoe. Just a thought Roscoe. You wouldn't know a Paul Smith by any chance, would you?'

'Yes, I do. He works for the Department of Supply. He was a good truckie in his day.'

I tapped him on his shoulder and went to have my breakfast with Lesley and Jackie Evans.

Number 10 was just leaving the galley. I said to her, 'Stephanie, you didn't have anything to do with those three jet aircraft, did you?'

'No, Captain, but I fell in love with them. One day I'm going to fly one!'

Jackie told her, 'Dream high, work hard, keeping asking for transfers to the right places and you will fly one.'

Just then a Naval Officer walked in. He looked around the galley. He spotted me and had a very arrogant grin on his face. To me, he had the little man syndrome. I stood up, so that I was looking down at him and saluted him. 'What is your business aboard this vessel?'

'You have training seamen aboard this vessel?'

'No, I do not! I have training officers aboard this vessel.'

I could see Mervyn Nelis and some of the other officers listening.

'I am the training officer of this port. I would like to challenge your training crew to a self defence demonstration with my crew, under the grounds of training.'

'I would give my training officer permission to do that if that's what he wants.' Mervyn got up and walked over. 'I would like to present to you Mervyn Nelis, Staff Sergeant Special Forces.'

With a grin in his eyes Mervyn said, ' My cadets haven't done that much training because of the movement of this vessel, their training duties and their duties aboard this vessel, but I think they would enjoy a bit more self defence training. So, if you would sign a document saying that neither party will hold any animosity or claim to the opposite party under naval training.'

'Yes, certainly, my people are very good. In fact, I'll put a fiver on them.'

I asked him, 'Where would this take place?'

'In our gym.'

'Then you can bet a fiver with Mervyn.'

Mervyn looked a little worried and just shuffled his feet.

'I don't know, but I suppose I should have faith in my crew and to prove it to them that I have complete faith in them. Would you say £10?'

The other training officer said yes, and they shook hands.

Mervyn suggested a time of 12.30.

'How many of my crew do you want?', he asked.

'How many have you?'

'10.'

'I have 10 also. See you at 12.30.' He saluted, turned, and left.

I grinned at Mervyn. 'That was a very cheeky move £10.'

'Skipper, the game is getting serious.'

'Well, as long as nobody bets on anything on this vessel.'

The training officer walked into Tiny's office. Tiny had his head bent forward over his desk. He always had a cushion on his chair because his legs were long and it protected his false leg. He didn't look up. 'What do you want?'

'I've arranged for a training exhibition between the *Mary Moore* crew and our crew at 12.30 pm, to give our crew more training in self-defence. I made a bet of £10.' He had a big grin all over his face.

Tiny slowly looked up at him. 'You stupid, arrogant self-centred fool. It is an officers' training vessel, hand picked because they are the very best. Mervyn Nelis is a high ranking British Staff training officer, didn't you look at the braids on his uniform? He doesn't work for just one force, he works for them all. When there is trouble there are two Commanders high-ranking, didn't you notice their braids? There are two Captains aboard. Why they did not inform us they were coming into our port? Something big is going on. It's not up to us to interfere or ask questions. What else have you done?'

'Well, I signed a document saying no responsibility, no blame.'

'When is this happening?'

'12.30 pm.'

'What the fuck am I going to do with you? Get out of my office and get a doctor and nurse to attend the fight. We might have more training to keel haul an officer, that will go down nicely in the log, won't it? Now get out!'

I was standing on the deck talking to Ted when I noticed a lady with a girl and a young man in a navy uniform walking down the jetty. There was another man as well. At once, I knew who he was. Ted glanced up at the jetty, then headed for the gangplank. I walked over to young Colin and nodded to Mervyn. 'Your mother and sister are here.'

He stared at me for just a moment, then I saw the tears flowing. He turned and walked towards the gangplank. His mother and sister walked up the gangplank and they all embraced each other. I didn't think they would let each other go. I looked up. Michael was standing at the top of the gangplank. There were tears in my eyes. Ted walked up to him, put his arms out, and shook him. I said to young Colin, 'take your mother and sister into the galley where it's private.'

I walked up to Michael. We both stood staring at each other. I put my hand out and shook his. 'You look good, Michael, but I think you had better go and see Les first.' I tapped him on his back. 'It's good to see you, Michael.' I could see the emotion in him. His lips were quivering. His emotions had caught up with him and he couldn't talk. Ted took him to Les.

Roscoe was topping up the diesel tank and the 44 gallon drums. The crew were unloading the firewood and storing it below. Roscoe said, 'All the vessels now use oil for their stoves.'

'Don't mention that to Les, he will chew your ears off. You can't cook good food with oil. He tried compressed coal dust. They called them briquettes. They are still below.'

Suddenly, we heard a noise coming from the other end of the jetty. Roscoe said it was Bagpipes. We could see men in full Scottish Regalia with their kilts swaying backwards and forwards as they marched down the jetty. A Scotsman was in the front waving his staff around. They all looked magnificent. The sound of the bagpipes and drums keeping a rhythm made the hairs on the back of my neck stand up. Because we were watching them at an angle, I could see Jacko holding two children's hands on either side of him, with the squad of 10 Scotsmen marching behind them. Because Roscoe's attention had been on the Scotsman, he shouted out, 'Idiot.' He had nearly overflowed the drum of diesel.

'Excuse me, Roscoe.' He laughed.

'They will have a plum in your mouth yet.' I grinned and went to the gangplank. Everybody had turned up on deck, but Michael had climbed up onto the first yardarm of the main mast, which puzzled me, but there was too much going on to worry about it.

The Scotsman and his staff with the silver knob walked up to the gangplank and stood in front of me. 'Permission to come aboard, sir.'

I put my hand out and shook his. I was trying not to laugh. 'You certainly have my permission, Mr McGregor.'

'Thank you, William.' He turned and walked onto the deck. The bagpipers followed him in rows of two, then a younger gentleman in a Scottish uniform, carrying a violin case, walked forward.

'Permission to come aboard, sir.'

I looked down at him, put my hand out and shook his hand. 'You have my permission, Mr McGregor, and I'm certainly looking forward to hearing you play your violin.'

'It will be my pleasure, Uncle Bill.'

Then he walked up to Lesley and Les. His eyes were looking around the deck. 'Where is Margaret?'

Lesley told him that she is in Australia with her husband Trevor. He turned around and looked straight at his sister as she was coming aboard. He walked back to her. 'Daisy, Margaret isn't here. She is in Australia with Trevor.'

Her facial features changed. She looked so sad, then she turned and walked up to me, put her hands on her hips, stamped her foot and said, in a very commanding tone of voice, 'Where is Totty?'

I shouted out, 'Captain Coe to the gangplank.'

Ted stepped forward. Daisy did a little curtsy to me. 'Thank you Uncle Bill.' She went straight up to Ted, shouting out, 'Totty, Totty!'

Ted went down on one knee, caught her, and put his arms around her and cuddled her. She cuddled him back.

'Totty, I've got so much to tell you,' and she didn't stop talking. I could see Ted's emotions, too. He's never had a friend like Daisy, who loves him for who he is. She trusted him so deeply.

A voice yelled out, 'What are you doing down there, drongo?' I would swear that Jacko flew up to Michael. Talk about squawking cockatoos. They were the best. Michael knew that on the yardarm he could have Jacko all to himself. They just kept laughing and talking.

The bagpipes started to play and Robbie McGregor took his violin out of the case, ready to play. Captain Harrison stood behind me. 'Bill, I thought you wanted to come into the harbour quietly and leave quietly?'

'So did I, Tiny.'

'Bill, for politics and the unpredictable, could you stay aboard while the cadets are exercising in the gym? Your stores have already arrived and are ready to be unloaded. Two of my cadets will unload them for you. I have arranged showers and baths for you and your crew at 6 pm, in two shifts.'

Just then, the bagpipes stopped playing and Robbie stepped forward with Daisy. She curtsied like a ballerina and Robbie started to play his violin. He was extraordinary and Daisy had obviously had ballet lessons. We all watched and listened, spellbound, for at least an hour. Then they both took a bow.

I saw the crew trotting off behind Mervyn to go to the gym. Tiny followed them.

Everybody else clapped loudly. Jacko turned up on deck and gave Daisy a little gesture. He waved his hand for Robbie to start playing again. As Daisy and Jacko started to dance, everybody found it most amusing, either smiling or laughing.

CHAPTER 47

Mervyn and his squad were lined up in the gym. Mervyn was very impressed with the highly polished timber floor. Their opponents were lined up in front of them.

Tiny shouted out, 'Let the games begin!'

Mervyn nodded to number 10. She stepped forward and her opponent stepped forward. He was quite a heavy lad, about 6 ft tall. He wanted to make an impression and came towards Stephanie like a steam train bouncing up and down as he ran towards her. Stephanie, like a ballerina, stepped to one side as the young lad went forward with his right foot and started to put his weight on it. Stephanie kicked it and he lost his balance. He was moving too fast. He hit the floor with a loud thud and slid along the floor for at least 10 ft. He just lay there, stunned.

Stephanie looked at the next man. Put her hand up with the palm of it facing herself and gestured with her fingers to the next opponent. He took more time and made the classic move with his right hand, but, before he could even blink Stephanie had gripped it and twisted it, thrust her hip to one side of him, and he too was flat on his back on the floor. She twisted his arm and put one foot on his shoulder, bent his hand backwards. The young lad froze on the floor knowing he was in deep trouble. Stephanie glanced at Mervyn. She could see the glint in his eyes.

'Stand at ease, Number 10.'

She took her foot off the lad's shoulder, still holding his hand, just in case he retaliated. She slowly let it go and returned to her place. Not turning her back on him, she gestured to the next young man. Mervyn didn't stop her. He wanted to see what she could do. He was already fascinated by her performance.

The next young man took a boxer's stand, putting his hands up ready, but not actually clenching his fists. He felt he was ready for whatever she might do. He gave her a warning punch, but as he was pulling his punch back, Stephanie's fist came out like lightning and hit him in straight on the jaw. He staggered back and before he could recover, Stephanie had hit him twice more. The young man slowly sank to his knees. He looked up at Stephanie. She nodded, letting him know not to stand up. He grinned and nodded. Stephanie stepped forward and helped him stand up.

Stephanie went back to her position. Mervyn called another number. The two young men stood facing each other; summing each other up. Mervyn noticed his man faced an opponent who appeared to be a bit timid and shy. He was about 5 foot 4 inches and frightened out of his life because of what he had just witnessed, but he stepped out, moving his right foot forward and thrusting his right arm out. Mervyn watched his man shaking his head. 'No, no, put your arm down. You have practised 10 movements in self-defence very well, but you now have to learn. If you had ten movements, you know the ten movements, but you have to learn six + four also make ten. You have to learn to put these together and make them work. If you are making a cake, you have ten ingredients, but you must put those ingredients together in the right way to make the cake. Do you understand?'

The young man thought for a moment. 'Yes sir, I do.'

'Well, stand back. Put in the ingredients to make the cake.'

The young man did this and Mervyn's man let him throw him. He stood back up.

'Now make another move towards me, mixing the cake!'

His opponent did the same thing again in a different mix. Mervyn saw this man let him do it. He stood up again. *We have a training officer who puts everything in a practical way. With our officer, we have the best,* he thought. 'Thank you for working with me.'

I don't think Mervyn had ever felt so proud of his cadets before. They acted as professionals, not mere amateurs. Finally, they had finished. The doctor walked up to the young man who had been punched in the mouth. 'Are you alright?'

'Yes, Doctor, but I don't need you. I think I need a dentist.'

Mervyn walked up to their training officer and put out his hand. Tiny stepped forward with a grin.

'We have this tin here.' He held up his hand with the tin in it and shook it so that you could hear the change rattling. 'We, the humble people of this naval base, try to do the right thing to support others. The local scouts need help, so a small donation would be so helpful for them.' He held the tin high.

'Would £10 be enough?'

Tiny looked at Mervyn with a frown. 'They would be so grateful, Mervyn.'

The other officer said, 'I don't have £10.' Tiny looked at him angrily. You would have thought he had been a policeman.

'I will talk to the Paymaster. I think he would be quite willing to take it out in instalments. You and your cadets had a good day's training.' He nodded to Mervyn and saluted. Mervyn Saluted back.

He turned to his cadets and said, 'Stand to order, attention.' They all saluted their opponents, who saluted back.

Mervyn turned and walked towards the door, looking at the floor. He thought a heavy man slides on that well! They all filed back to the *Mary Moore* in single file.

CHAPTER 48

Daisy said to Ted, 'Could we stay on board tonight? Robbie will play his violin.'

Ted glanced at me, and I nodded discreetly. Ted looked at Daisy. 'If Mr McGregor says it's alright, yes.'

Mr McGregor smiled at her. 'I will be here at daylight tomorrow morning. When you're 21, I'm quite sure Ted will marry you, but he would sign his name Totty. We will see you in the morning.'

Mr McGregor and the pipers filed down the gangplank and took up their positions. The drums started the beat, the bagpipes started to play. They marched down the jetty.

I turned to Ted. 'Nobody would believe you, would they Ted?'

'No Bill, they would just be our memories. Excuse me Bill, a little girl wants to talk to me.'

I nodded to him and turned to Mervyn, who had just returned. 'So you won your £10?'

'Yes Bill, but you know Tiny? Tiny won with a tin for donations for the scouts.'

'Mervyn, when he stepped aboard, I knew not to underestimate him. Ted, Jacko, how would you like a good hot bath and a good port?'

They didn't argue, just went and got their gear. The five of us walked down the jetty, dreaming of that hot bath. Les was walking in front of us. I thought he was going to break into a run at any moment.

We had returned from our baths and were sitting in the galley, the women having gone for their baths. We were talking about Michael and how good it was to see him again. Jacko burst out laughing. 'Boiled Lobsters coming down the jetty!' The women were returning.

Robbie told us how he was part of an orchestra and was taking violin lessons. Daisy said, 'and I am a ballerina, practising with other girls.'

Robbie started to play his violin again. We all sat there listening. It will be a memory we would never forget.

Just before daybreak, Lesley and I got up, dressed in our normal clothes, and went down to the galley. Les already had hot water on his stove. He smiled at Lesley. 'That's a nice hot lobster Bill, that you've got with you.'

Lesley looked at him, a little startled. Les doesn't normally make jokes. She put her hands on her hips, 'What's this about boiled lobsters?' He smiled at Lesley, 'Jacko said you all looked like boiled lobsters!'

'Did he now? I'll sort him out!'

I turned around so that she wouldn't see me grinning, but it didn't work. She slapped me on the backside.

I heard the gangplank being lowered and walked outside. Ted was there with two of the crew. Mr and Mrs McGregor and Tiny were waiting on the Jetty.

Ted said, 'Welcome aboard,' and we all went into the galley.

Tiny handed me an envelope. I looked at him. 'You have another cadet joining you. He is on his way from the airport. It comes through to me as top secret. I don't know anything more,' he said.

Tiny's nostrils were twitching. He could smell breakfast cooking, bacon, eggs, onions, mushrooms and tomatoes. He grinned and sat down. Les put a plate in front of him, saying 'Big man, big meal.'

I thought that Jacko must also be smelling this, and before I could finish my thoughts, Jacko walked through the door with the two children. Jacko looked at Tiny's plate, Tiny laughed, 'Les said you wouldn't be hungry this morning, so I could have your breakfast as well.'

Lesley said, 'Jacko, I agree with that, boiled lobster!' and went back to preparing the children's breakfast.

Eventually, everybody was saying goodbye. Daisy was cuddling Ted. She said, 'Thank you Totty for coming back to see us.' She kissed him on the nose 'goodbye Totty.' She went back and took Mrs McGregor's hand and lent against her side, with tears in her eyes.

Robbie was shaking everybody's hand. When he got to Jacko, he said, 'Thank you for bringing us home Jacko. They say you are the keeper of your people. Daisy and I will always be a part of you.' He lent against Jacko the same way you would lean against a big tree in the Australian desert. Before I could wipe the tears from my eyes, they were all gone.

I shook myself and said to Ted, 'Prepare her for departure.' But I knew I had to wait for another. Who is it? Then I noticed a young man walking down the jetty. The crew had noticed him as well and were crowding around the gangplank. Number 7 had walked down the gangplank onto the jetty and said something to him and picked up his rucksack. They both walked up the gangplank. He stood before me, 'Permission to come aboard sir,' and handed me an envelope. This was the young lad who had been put into hospital in Frankston, Australia.

'You certainly have my permission, young man. You will explain to the rest of the crew why you have been absent. When you have done that, get yourself some breakfast. We are all very happy you're back on board. Captain Coe, take us to sea.'

I heard the big motor start as I was standing on the Bridge, and Ted's shouting, 'Cast off stern,' Ted nodded to me, the stern line was clear, Jacko put her gear lever to the stern and turned the wheel hard to port, we moved away from the jetty, I nodded to Ted, and Jacko eased her into neutral.

Ted shouted out, 'Let the power line go!' I watched the crew bringing in the bow line, and waited for Ted to nod, but he just turned and grinned.

'Jacko, take her out to sea.'

We headed out of the harbour. Jacko slowly turned her out into the bay. I nodded and he turned the vessel due South. I nodded to Ted, and he shouted out his orders. Everybody was assisting in putting her full sails on her. Jacko put her into neutral. The big motor shut down and all was silent. I leaned out of the Bridge. 'Ted, could you send up number 7? I winked at him, and number 11.'

I went back onto the Bridge and opened the letter number 11 had given me. I took out the papers and browsed through them, a medical report, which I didn't understand, but it did say fit for normal duties. I will give this to the nurse. There was a sealed envelope addressed to me. I opened it. It was from Admiral French.

Number 11 is highly intelligent. We will be training him in the intelligence department. I leave everything up to your discretion. You have the very best to give him what we will be requiring for him for the future. We do not want him to feel he is getting more attention than the others.

I sat thinking about what I had just read when Jackie Evans turned up.

'Number 7 and number 11 are at the Bridge door.' 'Permission to enter Bridge, sir.'

I acknowledged their salute. 'Number 11, take this down to nurse Chris, ask her to read it and then return it to me. Number 7, you have qualities I admire. Sergeant Nelis has referred to your tactful way of working with your opponent yesterday using your ability to take command of the situation with your opponent. I want you to take number 11 under your wing. He has a lot to learn. The foundation of your learning has been done. In my opinion, it is up to you to choose your own destiny.'

Number 11 returned. 'Number 7 return to your duties.' We both saluted. I thought of Roscoe's words: *They'll put a plum in your mouth yet.* 'Number 11, you have missed out on a lot of training, so you will have to catch up. If you do not want to learn about rigging the sails or climbing up the mast, it is up to you. I will not enforce it upon you. I want you to ask questions. This course covers practical and theory. You will work with Number 7, take your sexton, compass and notepad, take our bearings, then plot a course past Cape Town. I want to be 30 nautical miles from Cape Town in the Atlantic Ocean.'

He saluted and was gone. It surprised me how quickly he returned.

He said, 'Excuse me, sir,' and went straight to the chart. His pencil worked very quickly on his notepad, then he went to the chart and did the rest of his calculations. 'West 20° sir.'

'I have said this to the others, this vessel's survival, the crews' lives depend on you, make a mistake and all is lost. How many times did you check your figures?'

He looked at me a little confused, 'Once sir.'

I didn't want to insult his intelligence. His figures were correct. 'Your figures are right, but in the future, you may be responsible for a battleship, an aircraft carrier or an aircraft. It is the policy of all Captains to check their figures at least three times. That is the normal practice. Could you give the helmsman your command and alter course?'

He shouted out, 'Helmsman, alter course.'

'I said to him, have you forgotten something?'

He looked at me, puzzled.

'Number 11, we are under sail.'

'Yes sir, I understand.' He went to the door of the Bridge. 'Captain Coe, we are altering course 320W.'

Ted answered him back, 'West 320, sir.'

Jacko looked at me and raised his eyebrows.

'Number 11, take the helm. Jacko, have a break.'

Jacko disappeared to you know where. 'Now, Number 11, watch how your Bosun is preparing everybody to alter course. He has his crew ready to brace the yardarms.'

Ted nodded to us, and I said to Number 11, 'shout out west 320°.' He did this, then altered course on the compass. The yardarms were braced to catch the wind, and all was in order.

'Number 11, have you been aboard vessels before?'

'Yes and no, sir. My father had a fishing boat on which we spent many good days, but I've never actually been to sea. I have studied everything I could on commanding a ship, the stars, wave patterns, currents and tides on entering and leaving a port, channel markers, currents around the world, seabirds, dolphins, and whales and where you would find them. The type of winds in different parts of the world, cyclones or hurricanes.'

I thought, *the Navy's not going to tell him where he's going! He's going to tell them!*

'Why are you aboard this vessel? Your mind is full of information. In theory, it will serve you well in the Navy, but I need you to spend time with Jacko and Commander Johnson. Your mind works extremely fast. It's like a sponge thirsty for knowledge, but remember this, other people's minds don't work as fast as yours. When you're working with them, gauge their level and slow down to it. Don't get frustrated with them. Never, ever, lose your temper. If you lose your temper, you have lost control of yourself and you can do so much damage mentally to others. Play chess with Jacko. He will teach you how to control yourself.'

'How did you know, sir, about my temper?'

'Son, I'm an old sea Captain. I have been given a crew. If I didn't like one of them, I couldn't say leave the vessel and get another, I am at sea. This is my crew for 95 days. You have to understand each member of your crew, and put them where they will best serve the vessel, put them in the wrong place, they will be useless, put them in the right place, they will be brilliant. You can be stern on commanding, but don't lose your temper. If you find your compass is not on course, you cannot blame the compass, it is you who have lost your control and concentration on the compass. Every individual under your command is the compass. Do you play chess?'

'No sir, but I know the moves.'

I got the chessboard out and we started to play. This cadet was a quick learner. I grinned. This should sharpen Jacko up. I had won the game, but I don't think I would so well the next time. Jacko returned to the Bridge.

'Jacko, take the helm, play chess with Number 11. He has a lot to catch up on. Debate the stars, debate, debate everything you think he should know in a practical sense. Then Number 11, you and I will talk about Jacko, but don't ever forget, Jacko and I are brothers!'

He looked at me very seriously, searching in his mind for an answer.

I went back down to the galley. I wanted to spend some time with Lesley. Mervyn was on deck discussing command of their troops under pressure and how to handle yourself and keep control.

'Now, take half an hour, discuss it amongst yourselves,' he nodded to Number 10 and walked over to the baulk works. She followed him. 'Where did you learn to box, Stephanie?'

'My dad was a boxer. He had his own gym.'

'The way you punched, I've seen it before. Who is your father?' She stared at me for a moment.

'My father is Lionel Melvin,'

Mervyn smiled, 'your father fought under the name of Billy Miles.'

'Yes, he did, and he fought Sands and won.'

'Yes, he did. Stephanie, I knew he was going to America to fight, but he didn't go. Why?'

'My mother was pregnant with me. He wouldn't leave her or take her to a strange place. She needed her mum and her friends around her.'

'Your father was extremely high in principles and ethics.'

'Yes, he was. Did you know my father?'

'Yes, I did. He was a good friend to my wife and myself, but that was in a different time and place. How are they now?'

'Dad has a lot of trouble with his knees. Mum is doing alright.'

'They must've been doing a fair bit of self defence in your father's gym.'

'Yes, I used to enjoy working out with them both.'

'If you would excuse me, Stephanie, I need a nice cup of tea.'

CHAPTER 49

I handed Lesley the letter from Admiral French. She read it. 'Yes Lesley, he thinks extremely fast and is quick. I want to see him play chess with Jacko and see who gets into whose mind!'

Lesley handed me a logbook, 'Read this, Bill.'

I started to read it,

We hadn't seen Stephanie, she didn't come to breakfast, she hasn't come to exercises or lunch, we were all worried, what's wrong? I had been made spokesman to find out, later in the afternoon, 3 pm I was informed that Stephanie was coming out of the stern hatch with a towel over her shoulder, by the time I got there, she had gone into the ladies shower, so I thought I would wait, but apparently I had set myself up. Commander Johnson suddenly appeared looking very angry and told me to find something better to do.

I handed Lesley the logbook back. That was the day Stephanie needed time to herself.

'Lesley, I wondered what all the commotion was about that day. You didn't say anything, so I thought it wasn't any of my business. This young cadet is starting to impress me. Mervyn told me about what he did in the self-defence practice in the gym.'

Lesley smiled, 'Yes, he told me he was very proud of him and he also told me about the £10. The Scouts have done well.' I nodded to Chris, and she came over.

'What do you think, Chris about the medical report? I don't understand the doctor's wording.'

'Well Bill, he is perfectly alright, but my thoughts are no physical exercises such as self-defence, the wounds still wouldn't be 100% healed, wrong knock and the wrong time could be trouble.'

'Thank you Chris, I will enter that into the logbook. Chris, your boss is looking at us and I have two of his crew.' She smiled at me and picked up the plates and went back into the kitchen. I nodded to Jackie, 'How is your cabin Jackie?'

'Very comfortable, thank you, Bill. A little more room than I've had before. I didn't realise how much I had missed hot water.'

I handed her the letter from Admiral French. She raised her eyebrows and smiled. 'Admiral French, well I never.' She read it, looking very serious.

'So, can both of you work with him? He is very quick thinking and on the ball.'

Jackie handed me the letter back. 'Yes, Bill.' Lesley nodded.

I said to the ladies, 'Give him one extra hand in the galley and he is still scowling at me.'

Jackie laughed, 'Bill, we are his harem, and he doesn't want to share.'

CHAPTER 50

I didn't sleep very well for the next three nights. The seas here are very unpredictable, with cold and warm currents, but apart from a few white-caps on the waves, we were doing well.

Ted had braced the yardarms twice, and we still managed to main-tain the same course. I asked Ted to give me Number 3. We saluted each other. 'Number 3, take our bearings and chart our course.'

'Excuse me, sir.'

'Yes.'

'Do I have to play chess with Jacko?'

I grinned at Jacko. 'No, that is purely up to you. I've been going over your logbook, the only weakness I can find, and I didn't say any-thing was wrong, just a little weakness with your star calculations. If you are on a battleship, you would have all the technology there to help you, and you would be 100% correct, but if you found yourself in a life-boat without a compass and writing pad, it would be very different. So, work with Jacko tonight on top of the Bridge. Just you and Jacko. How Captain Bligh navigated himself in a lifeboat through some of the most dangerous waters was by navigating with the stars. But while you're on this Bridge in the daylight, talk whatever you wish, but keep us on course.'

The young cadet disappeared with his sexton and notepad. He came back, studied his chart and his figures. I noticed he'd done it more than four times.

'Sir, if we travelled due north, we would eventually reach land approximately at Sette Atama off Gabon. If we headed west 325°, we would miss land altogether and miss Cape Verde and the islands.'

'Then alter course at latitude 15. What would be your suggestion, Number 3?'

'Course west 325° sir.'

'Why?'

'This is a direct course and the trade winds would be with us at this time of the year, and the small squalls of rain would be good for our rigging. Before latitude 15 we would pass the equator.'

'What is your opinion, Jacko?'

'I think he's put it together well. Number 3, inform the Bosun we are about to alter course.'

Number 3 stepped out of the Bridge and shouted out, 'sir, Captain Coe, we are about to alter course west 325°.'

We waited for Ted to give us the nod. He turned around and nodded to us, and shouted out, 'West 325°' and Jacko altered course.

The next morning after breakfast, the crew were assembled on deck. 'Number 7, step forward.' He did so. 'For the next two days, that is today, tonight and the next day you are the Captain of this vessel. Number 4 step forward, you are the Bosun. Captain Coe.'

'Yes, sir.'

'Find yourself a comfortable seat and take notes. Number 11, today you're with Jackie Evans. Number 7, take command.'

I turned and went into the galley. Mervyn was at the helm. Number 7 turned to number 10, she stepped forward and saluted. He saluted back, 'Take the helm.' She didn't argue. 'Number 2 to the Bridge.' He saluted and joined her on the Bridge. 'Number 3, the windows in the Bridge need cleaning, inside and out, then do the galley, I feel the deck needs a wash and scrub. To your duties.' They didn't argue, just went off and did them.

Mervyn came down from the Bridge. Number 7 said to him, 'I suggest you rest sir and take back your squad after lunch.'

'May I suggest to you Number 7.'

'Yes, sir?'

'I am not, sir, you are. You discussed the work with your Bosun. He allocates the work. I will be back on deck after lunch, sir.' Mervyn saluted and number 10, looking surprised, saluted back.

Mervyn passed Ted. 'How are you Ted? Fancy a game of golf?'

Ted replied, 'Jolly good old chap, perhaps we could have a spot of lunch afterwards.'

To which Mervyn replied, 'Right O, old chap, meet you on the course.'

Number 7, the Captain, stood on the deck, his hands behind his back, watching his crew scrubbing the deck. Ted could not contain himself. 'Excuse me, sir.'

The cadet turned around and walked over to Ted. 'Yes, Captain Coe.'

'Why does this vessel have a Bosun, and what are his duties? And what are your duties? Don't answer me straight away. Think about it.'

'Yes Captain, sir.' He got up and went into the galley. Number 7, the Captain, went up onto the Bridge. 'Number 2, could you take our bearings please?'

He grinned at the Captain and saluted him. After he left, Number 7 said to Stephanie, 'I'm doing something wrong Stephanie, what is it?'

She frowned at him. 'Being Captain has gone a little bit to your head, the army has a sergeant, this vessel has a Bosun, the commanding officer talks to the sergeant or to the Bosun, the sergeant then tells his troops what to do, the Bosun tells his crew what to do, you are not the Bosun, you are the Captain, the officer. Does that make sense, sir?'

'Yes Stephanie, it does.'

Stephanie said, 'We are in the British Navy. Everything has its political chain of command. Dad taught me that.'

The young cadet returned with his bearings and wrote them down. Number 7 thought for a minute, remembering what the Captain had said to him. Check everything, the responsibility is the Captain's. If he gets it wrong, the vessel sinks. He checked his bearings and figures. They were correct, but he did check them three times and entered them in his logbook.

Number 7, the Captain, went down onto the deck. Number 2, his Bosun had a bucket of water in his hand. Number 7 instructed him, 'Bosun, put the bucket down. We have enough crew to keep busy. You are the Bosun, you tell the crew what to do, you don't do it. We will inspect the deck and the windows. What do you think about that corner. Could it be cleaned?'

'Yes, sir.'

'Take a note. I like the way the ropes are curled up nice and neat. Good job.' They both inspected the windows. They were done to the Captain's satisfaction. 'You can be very proud of your crew Number 2, the Bosun,' He put his hand on the Bosun's shoulder and gestured to the galley, where they sat talking about their separate responsibilities and how to keep the crew busy when they were not doing their training courses.

The day slid past and the new Captain checked that the navigation lights were working. He asked the Bosun whether the oil had been checked in them, he did so and was satisfied. He walked up to me. 'Sir, if you and Captain Jacko could take the first watch at the helm, myself and number 5 will take the midnight watch.'

I was a little surprised at first. 'Yes, Captain.'

Jacko saluted him, 'Yes, sir.'

We were relieved at midnight. At 4.30 am there was a knock at the door. I sat up in my bunk, too late. I hit my head on the ceiling. Why do I keep doing this? 'Yes, what is it?'

'Captain, we have another vessel approaching us and it disturbs me.'

I slid down off my bunk and went onto the Bridge. I could see the navigation lights of an approaching vessel, green and red navigation lights. We should see only the green. The young Captain pointed to the radar, 'we are on a collision course sir, they must have radar and they should see us with all our sails on and the early morning light behind us, and, we have the right of way, being a sail vessel.'

'Number 7, you are the Captain of this vessel. You have to make the decision, but I'd like to know why.'

'sir, if that vessel has automatic pilot and whoever is on the Bridge is not paying attention, they would not know we are here. I would alter course 5° to port.' I raised my eyebrows at him. He shouted out, 'helmsman 5° to port.' The red light started to fade and we could only see the green. I didn't realise Jacko had come onto the Bridge and was standing behind me.

He whispered to me, 'All is well that ends well.' He had been watching this all the time, ready to take over if necessary. He got my telescope out and targeted it on the other vessel's Bridge. The faint light of the early morning was just starting to dawn. Jacko kept looking as the vessel was passing us. There wasn't anybody on the Bridge. Jacko looked at me with a slight grin. He put his hand up in the air, found the chain and pulled the fog horn three times. As the vessel had nearly passed us, a man appeared on the wing of the Bridge.

The young Captain shouted out, 'Helmsman, return to our normal course.'

All of our crew had turned up on deck, looking at the stern of the other vessel. Lesley came up alongside of me, 'What's wrong, Bill?'

'I don't know dear, you will have to ask the Captain.' She looked straight at Jacko.

'You made that noise, didn't you? I will see you later.' She went back into the cabin and slid the door closed, opened it again, put her head out and said to Jacko, 'She who laughs last, laughs best,' and quickly closed the door.'

The young Captain just laughed, 'No blame, no shame. I didn't give the order.'

I put my hand on Jacko's shoulder, 'I never gave an order either, Jacko.' I turned and went back to bed until 6.30 am.

We still had all our canvas aloft. The barometer was dropping slightly. I could see the young Captain talking to the Bosun on deck. They were both looking up at the sails. Ted was sitting, watching them. The young Captain put his hands behind his back. The Bosun shouted out his orders. The crew went to work, bracing yardarms a little further to catch the wind better. Ted had a smile on his face. The young Captain made a small gesture to his Bosun and returned to the Bridge.

We repeated this exercise of a new Captain and Bosun every two days. There were strong winds and calm days.

The day that Number 10 took her turn as Captain, we were punching into a big swell, twice we had to tack. Number 10 handled it well. We didn't criticise them if they made small mistakes. They just need time and more experience.

The vessels they would eventually be taking command of would be totally different from this one. This old bark sailing clipper is the best foundation of a career. There was no easy way out, you had to do it the hard way. If they found themselves stranded at sea without a compass or sexton, they could still find their way to navigate to home.

When the seas were rough and the vessel was yawing, Chris, the nurse, would pack number 11 tightly into a seat where he could not be knocked around. She said to me, 'I know the doctor said he was fit for duties, but he didn't expect him to be at sea in a sailing vessel when the seas were rough.'

It was Mervyn Nelis who was having trouble. He had trained them well, but sometimes too well. When he was lying flat on his stomach or when he was lying down looking up at his opponent, he wondered what was happening. I was also worried about Jacko. At one point I'd taken him off the wheel, but he was enjoying teaching. We wouldn't know what he was going to do next. He had a long-term plan to teach them, and to show them all of his experiences at sea. They were becoming as one with the sea, its movements, its twists and turns, to understand the wind. It is nature, it is alive, breathing and living according to nature's laws, not man's laws. The wind has been part of nature since time began. Jacko showed them how the different clouds had their own identity. Respect them and they will show you what is coming, what nature has in store for you. Ignore them and you're lost in the desert. Watch migrating birds in the desert, they will show you where the water is, at sea, they will show you where land is.

We had reached the point of the Atlantic Ocean and the English channel, longitude 7, latitude 48, just on daybreak. Jacko and I were on the Bridge watching a vessel coming towards us at high speed, pushing spray high up in the air.

Jacko said, 'They are flying the Union Jack on the stern. Big Boss Cocky on board.'

I went down on deck and spoke to number 5. 'Excuse me, sir, there is a small craft coming towards us with a Union Jack flying on its stern.' There might be an admiral on board.'

He stared at me. 'You are the Captain.'

I thought for a moment that I might be pushing the cadets too far.

'I would suggest, sir, that the ladder be lowered, and he is piped aboard. I know I'm leaving it in good hands. Think about it, take your time. You are the Captain aboard this vessel.'

I enjoyed watching him. He walked straight to his Bosun, talked to him for a moment, and walked to the baulk works. Two of the crew were lowering the ladder. Others had gone to the forecastle to get their whistles. Jacko turned into the wind and she slowly came to a stop.

The launch pulled up alongside of us. The sea was moderate, with little movement between the two vessels. A seaman came aboard first. He had a harness with him which he lowered down to the other vessel. The harness was put around a lady. She started to climb the ladder with the harness helping her.

Number 5 stepped forward. 'Welcome aboard, ma'am. I am Martin French, training Captain'. He saluted her. She returned the salute. Number 5 stepped back to let the next person aboard. Then the Admiral came aboard. Number 5, acting Captain, for a moment, didn't look himself, however he soon got his composure back. He saluted the Admiral. 'Martin French, sir, acting Captain.' The crew gave the salute with their whistles, the rest of the crew all lined up, ready for inspection.

I went down on the deck and faced the lady. 'We meet again, Mrs Henderson.'

'Took your time, William, didn't you?' She smiled at me. 'Cup of tea William?' She nodded to Lesley, then looked at Jackie. 'I underestimated you Jackie, I didn't think you would get on board. It's good to see you both.'

'Yes ma'am,' and the ladies went to the galley.'

Admiral French inspected the crew with the acting Captain, then he said to Number 5, 'You have a very fit crew Captain, I think we need to talk.'

'If you will excuse me for a moment, sir.' He turned to his Bosun. 'You may dismiss the crew.'

The Bosun saluted him, he saluted back, as the Admiral and Number 5 walked away, the Bosun shouted out, 'Dismissed, return to your duties.'

I watched Admiral French and Number 5 walk away to one side. I could see the pride and emotion in the Admiral's face as he looked at his son.

I heard him say, 'I'm so proud of you, I put you with a vessel with a Captain who came up the hard way, at sea. I'm so proud of you. Your mother is waiting for you in England. I cannot be your father on this vessel, but in England, I can be.'

'Dad, the experiences I've had aboard this vessel will stay with me for the rest of my life. It is the very best training you have given me, but there are two parts to this training. One is with Commander Farquhar and this vessel, the other is with Captain Jacko and Commander Johnson. If you would excuse me, sir we have a new course to plot.' He saluted his father, who returned the salute. He took three paces backwards, turned and walked over to me. I could see the tears in his eyes. He saluted me. I saluted back.

'We have a new course to plot, but I have not as yet been given the destination. If you'd like to go to the forecastle, compose yourself, then return to the Bridge, where I will be.'

Admiral French walked over to Ted. I could see by the look on Ted's face they were having a very serious conversation. Ted kept nodding his head, then he smiled at the Admiral and shook his hands.

The Admiral turned and saw me looking at him. I nodded towards the Bridge, then everybody within earshot was startled. It was a woman's voice, laughing and shouting. She was clapping her hands. Ted yelled out, 'She has beaten him again! That's pushed the cocky little cocky off his perch.'

The Admiral and I walked onto the Bridge. I acted surprised. 'Is there something wrong, Jacko? You don't look happy.'

'Bill, you've been playing chess with her, and you have played in the desert. Now Bill, you will not win either.'

The Admiral looked down at the chessboard, then burst out laughing. He put his hand on Jacko's shoulder. 'I think the witchy would be laughing too, Jacko.'

The acting Captain walked onto the Bridge. 'Is there something wrong, Number 10?'

'Nothing wrong sir, everything is right.'

He looked at the chessboard. A big grin came all over his face. 'Sir, do we have a destination?'

The Admiral replied, 'Yes, Portsmouth.'

'Thank you, sir. Number 10, take our bearings, plot a course to Portsmouth.'

Number 10 picked up her sexton and notepad and went down on the deck. I looked at the Captain, then the acting Captain, and discreetly walked out of the Bridge and left them together.

I walked up behind Ted, 'Portsmouth North 78°.'

Ted replied, 'The wind is coming from our port side.'

'So then it should be coming right up to our stern, and we will be running into the tide. There will be a few whitecaps.' I tapped Ted on the shoulder and went back to the Bridge. Number 10 followed me in and went to the chart and did her calculations. She checked them three times more.

'sir, North 78° longitude, one latitude 15°.'

The Captain stepped outside the Bridge and nodded to his Bosun 'North 78°,' and came back to the Bridge. He glanced at the deck, making sure everything was in order as the helmsman swung the vessel north and lined his compass up to 78°. The yardarms were braced to pick up the wind directly from her stern. We were on course and everything was tidied up on deck.

Admiral French raised his eyebrows to me. 'Captain, sir, could I ask your navigator a question?'

The Captain looked at the Admiral, 'Certainly sir.'

'Number 10, why did you check your figures three times?'

She saluted the Admiral. 'Sir, if you have made a mistake, because we are only human, our vessel and its crew are lost. We have been told to check our figures three times, even more if we have any doubts, to make sure we are 100% correct.'

I looked at Number 10. 'Could you tell Admiral French what you want to do in the Navy, in the future?'

'Yes, sir. I would like to fly aircraft from an aircraft carrier.'

Admiral French studied her for a moment. 'Would you check your co-ordinations three times?'

'I would be taking my orders from a Flight Commander and I would not question them, but if I was a flight Commander, I would be pre-pared for the unpredictable and take evasive action, according to my training. The minute I left the briefing room I would have my figures in my mind, sir, at 300 miles an hour, it must be instant and no mistakes.'

The Admiral nodded and looked at Jacko. 'When you play chess with her, I would certainly like to watch. William, could you have Jacko, Ted and Les come to the galley?'

I glanced at the Captain. He nodded and turned to Number 10. 'Number 10, take the helm.' The cadet looked at me, 'I'm disappointed sir, I thought I was going to watch a chess game.' He winked at Number 10.

Jacko said, 'You lose one, or maybe two games and everybody thinks it's funny, ha ha ha.'

We all sat at the bench in the galley. Les was wiping his hands on his apron. He sat down. Cat jumped up on his lap and sat there look up at Les. He knew he was part of the meeting.

'To you all, I am Vera Haddy. That is my married name. I don't really like what I'm about to say, but Winston Churchill had a contract with you all regarding his vessel and its cargo. It's a binding contract, so will be honoured. The British Royal Navy will buy your share of this vessel. It will remain a training vessel for the British Navy.'

She glanced up at the Admiral, he continued, 'Ted is going to remain with her for as long as he wishes. Les, you have told the ladies that you and your twin brother have a bakery and cake shop.'

'Yes, we do. The last time we were in England we bought it.'

The Admiral continued, 'Bill, Lesley, and you, Jacko, do you want to go back to the Johnson property on the Diamantina River?'

Before we had a chance to say anything, Jacko was standing on his seat. 'Yes, we do.' He sat down.

'I think the decision has been made.' Lesley pressed into me.

Vera spoke again. 'The Australian Government has been concerned for the indigenous people of the Diamantina River. The Johnson property covers many thousands of acres. Jacko and you would be the custodians of this property. Any profits made from livestock would be yours to do with, as the three of you wish. They will repair the homestead, sheds and cattle yards, employing the local indigenous people.' She looked at Admiral French. 'When we get into Portsmouth, I would like you all to have your belongings together that you would need for four days. You will be provided with suitcases. There will be cars waiting for you to take you to Buckingham Palace. Ted, we will need you to supervise the unloading of the cargo with Mervyn Nelis, so you and Mervyn will also be going to Buckingham Palace three days after the unloading. Jacko, you will be in full Scottish Regalia. Oh, I nearly forgot, you will be going to your hotel rooms first, to refresh yourselves.'

Lesley said to Jacko, 'Don't worry Jacko, I'll scrub your back for you.'

Ted said in a low voice, 'I'll give you a wire brush!'

Admiral French stood up. 'When you first came to Dartmouth, what was your cargo?'

I thought that was a loaded question. 'Wool bales.'

427

'You had nothing else but wool bales? You didn't see anything else?'

'No, we didn't.'

'What is your cargo now?'

'Timber.' I paused. 'Timber crates.'

'Did you see inside those crates?'

'No.'

'So, if anybody said to you, do you have uranium, you would say you had wool bales. If somebody said to you did you have gold, you wouldn't know?'

'Admiral, that is correct.'

'I know I'm offending you, Bill, but this is for the sake of politics. If the general public was to find out what your real cargo was, it would be a nightmare for any government. Everybody would like their little piece. We can do more with it as collateral and use it as a generator with the little gold England has.'

I thought, *politics, nicely tucked away on the Diamantina River, see nothing, hear nothing, speak nothing, it certainly doesn't sit well with my principles.*

Vera said, 'Lesley, could we have a nice cup of tea together as friends, like we used to do?'

The last four words puzzled Lesley. 'Yes, Vera.'

Les picked up Cat and went to the galley to make tea and take some biscuits out of the oven.

Vera sniffed the smell of biscuits. She smiled at Lesley. 'Would Les think of marriage? No, that wouldn't work. I am already married.'

Les brought in the tea and biscuits. There wasn't anyone else in the galley.

Vera said, 'Politics has many corners in a big room. Your journals. What do you want to do with them?'

'Put them in the National Archives.'

'Lesley, I'll arrange that. Leave it to me. Speak to nobody else Lesley. When this is over, I'm retiring to my little house in the Cotswolds. My granddaughter is living in it at the moment with her husband and children,' she sighed, 'but there's plenty of room for me.' Vera smiled at Les. 'Sit down, Les, and have tea with us.' He sat down with his tea and biscuits, Cat jumped up on his lap. 'What's going to happen to Cat?' Vera asked.

Cat's head swung around and looked straight at Les. 'He is staying with me. He's my best friend and we belong to each other.'

Cat's head turned around and looked straight at Vera.

She shook her head. 'Cat and Jacko, I wish we knew what they know.'

CHAPTER 51

Admiral French approached Mervyn. 'Could we have a word please, Mervyn?' He took an envelope out of his inside pocket and handed it to Mervyn, who opened the letter and gave the Admiral a suspicious look. He started to read the letter. There were fancy names and titles on the letterhead.

> *Sergeant Nelis, we offer you a new commission. You would not be going back into a war zone. We need your expertise to teach others how to command, to be an adviser for high command. We lack people of your experience and expertise. You would be travelling abroad as an adviser to command, you will be given a higher status, a house, your own car and chauffeur, and two secretaries. You will have an expense account and your salary will be paid on the first of every month for your contribution to the services. This office you are entitled to.*

The letter was signed by both Admiral French and the Prime Minister.

Mervyn looked at the Admiral. 'You make it very hard to refuse. Yes, but I will need three weeks in Australia.'

The Admiral handed him a pen and Mervyn signed the form.

'Mervyn, you car will be waiting on the wharf for you, anytime you require it.'

He took a step back and saluted. Mervyn, with a little hesitation, saluted him back.

The Admiral grinned. 'Could you have all the cadets' logbooks in the galley please and join me there with Lesley?'

Lesley, Mervyn and the Admiral slowly went through the logbooks, discussing each one. The Admiral wrote down everything in his own journal.

They stopped so that the crew could have their supper, but continued on afterwards. They finished at 11 pm. The Admiral then got some official documents from his briefcase, put his name and number on the documents according to the information he had in the individual's logbook and on the advice of Mervyn and Lesley. By 3.30 am, he had finished.

Les brought him breakfast, coffee, and a glass of liquid. He grinned at the Admiral. 'I keep this for special occasions, for very weary and tired people.'

Lesley walked into the galley with Jackie ready to assist Les with breakfast.

We hadn't assigned another Captain or Bosun, their training had been completed.

After they had finished their breakfast, the Admiral addressed them all. 'Put your uniforms on and wait for your number to be called. Commander Johnson, could you please also put on your uniform and return here? Also ask the Captain to return here with his uniform on.

Mervyn has relieved the Captain on the Bridge while he got changed. He wanted to be with Jacko at the helm for one last time.

Jacko did one of his funny little dances and said to Mervyn, 'So you are now Big Boss Cocky, Big Boss Cocky.'

'Jacko, shut up. I don't want anybody to know yet. I still have to get used to my command. Jacko, you could have let me know earlier.'

'Not my business Mervyn, I teach you everything I know about the desert, we have played chess like we were in the desert, you must now look over the horizon and watch your back, fly high, see everything around you. We will all miss you, but we will always be with you. Call us in your mind and we will be there.'

Just then, Lesley and I came out of our quarters. The three of us went down to the galley.

The Admiral gestured to Jackie, could you ask Number 1 to come in please?'

Number 1 came in, stamped his right foot, saluted and stood to attention.

'At ease Number 1. I have suggested to the board that you would make an excellent Captain First Class, that you be given your own command. Here are your papers and your logbook, where you are to report to and the time is on your papers.'

The Admiral stepped forward and put out his hand. Number 1 shook it, then he shook all our hands. He saluted, turned and left.

Jackie called Number 2. We eventually got to Number 10. She entered, saluted and stood to attention. 'Number 10, I have suggested to the board that you be made a Captain. From here you will go to the Academy to do your training to become a pilot.'

The tears started to flow from Stephanie's eyes. She looked at each one of us. 'Number 10, Stephanie, here is your logbook and your papers. Where you are to report to and the times is on your papers.'

Number 10 took a little time to compose herself. 'Thank you so much.'

'No, don't thank me, thank yourself for the work you put in. Commander Lesley Johnson is extremely proud of you. She knows what you've been through and the work you put in.' He put out his hand to shake hers. We all shook her hand. She stood to attention, saluted, turned, and left.

Number 11 was next. He entered, saluted and stood to attention.

'At ease Number 11. You are assigned to Mervyn Nelis to be his personal secretary. If he travels overseas, you go with him. It will all be explained to you in the future. You will also be given your own secretary. You will stay with Mervyn Nelis here, for the next four days. Do you have any questions?'

'No, sir.'

'Mervyn Nelis is your Commander. Your rank will be given to you later.'

Number 11 saluted and went back through the door.

'Bill, Number 7 has the ability to command. He's been mentioned in every logbook. He was apparently their spokesman. He sorts out the situations very quickly, very practically.'

'He doesn't know it, but he's been assigned to an aircraft carrier. I hope one day he's in command.'

Lesley and I went back to the Bridge where we could be alone. Jacko didn't look happy. Lesley asked him, 'What's wrong, Jacko?'

'How are we going home?'

'I don't know, Jacko.'

'I don't like it, don't like it at all, no, no.'

He stamped his foot on the floor and handed the wheel over to me, and headed for the galley.

'Lesley, it never stops. He lets you know something is wrong, but never tells you what.'

'So Bill, when we reach Plymouth, we will be picked up in a car and taken to Buckingham Palace. I did hear right, didn't I?'

'Yes Lesley, why?'

'I just want to see my friend Marcia and go home with you.'

'Yes Lesley. I just want to walk away and let it go, too. My body is tired and weary, my mind just needs time to rest. I just want to lie in the billabong on the Diamantina river and relax.'

I could see the Admiral talking on a handheld radio at the bow, then he looked up at the main yardarm. Jacko was at the centre. Five of the crew were on one side and six on the other side. They were all looking towards the bow. Ted came onto the Bridge, 'We've got a mob of cockatoos on the main yardarm.'

'Leave them alone Ted, it's Jacko's moment.'

I wanted to be with them, but my place is at the helm. 'Ted, when they come down from the yardarm, which won't be too long as it's getting colder and the breezes are picking up, ask them to be fully dressed in their white uniforms and have all their gear packed in their rucksacks.' I paused for a moment. 'Ted, it will never happen again. Strip her of all her sails at 8 am and start the motor. Please don't look at me like that Ted, something in me is breaking and I have to be in control and so do you.'

He nodded and walked out.

Vera asked Jackie, 'Where are you going after tomorrow, Jackie?'

'To my house in the Cotswolds. My granddaughter has been looking after it for me. It's my time to sit down in a chair and rest.'

Vera put a hand on Jackie's arm. 'Yes Jackie, I'm going to my house in the Lake District. I've also had enough. Our time is finished, like this beautiful sailing vessel, our time has come, we've done our part and now we must step aside. Now I can spend some time with my husband.'

CHAPTER 52

At 8 am we were rounding the Isle of Wright. Ted was shouting his orders. Sails were being stripped off and stowed, the big motor was turning over. Jacko was dressed in his full uniform in the galley and Stephanie was doing little plaits on his beard, she had also made little green bows for his plaits. She trimmed his hair and shaved around his beard. She knelt down in front of him, looking into his eyes. 'Thank you, Jacko, for showing me your world and teaching me everything you could for my future. One day I would like to walk with you in the desert where you are free.' She gently kissed him on the lips. 'I will never forget you.' Jacko had trouble controlling his tears and emotions. He stood up and put his arms around her and said something in his language from the Channel country. He looked at Les with a sad look on this face, turned and went back to the Bridge, back to the helm where he felt safe and in control.

Stephanie turned to Lesley. 'What did he say?'

'Stephanie, in his native language and in mine, one word can mean many things. He said you are the cool breeze in the desert, you are the fresh water in the desert, you are sweet nectar, you smell of the spring rains and the blossoming flowers, you are the moon and the sun. It can also mean a lot more than that. If he could put it into poetry for you, he would.'

Stephanie put her hand to her mouth. Her eyes were swollen with tears. She turned and left the galley where she could be alone.

Vera took out a handkerchief from her pocket and dabbed her eyes. 'Why do I keep blubbering on this vessel?'

Les brought her a cup of tea. 'Vera, this vessel has given you something back that you have had locked away for a very long time.'

I was standing at the helm. Cat was on the bench looking out of the window. Lesley was standing alongside me, and we were watching the golden rays of the sun on our masts and rigging. I could see Cat slowly moving his head backwards and forwards as if he didn't want to forget this day.

Jacko came onto the Bridge and leaned up against Lesley. She put her arm around him. She knew he was emotionally upset. What was now going to happen, for the future had come, something had triggered his self-control. Cat was looking at him, he was looking at Cat. They stared into each other's eyes. I knew that they were talking together in each other's minds. This continued for about five minutes, then Jacko walked over to Les and put his arms around him and held him. He then picked Cat up in his arms. Jacko gently moved me out of the way and took the helm. I sat down at my small desk tidying up the paperwork, making sure I had signed all the papers Admiral French had given me. I stood staring at the last one. Once I signed this piece of paper I was no longer the Captain of *Daisy May*. A voice deep down inside me *Bill, we know the time has come. Her time is finished, she is part of the past.* I signed my name.

I am no longer the Captain of *Daisy May*. My time has come to step aside.

Lesley's head came around the corner of the door. 'Bill, there is a small boat approaching. It appears to be a pilot boat.'

I closed the folder and said to myself, *I was once the Captain of the Three Mastered Schooner. I have lived it, I have been alive, it will never come again.*

I went to the Bridge and looked at the approaching boat. I went down on deck and nodded to Ted. No more shouting orders, no sir, yes sir. Ted had the ladder lowered, ready for the pilot. He climbed aboard and I met him as he entered and stood on deck. He looked nervous, but in control. He saluted me. I didn't want to salute him back. I just wanted to shake his hand as a friend would, but I'm wearing this uniform, so I saluted him back. 'Captain Farquhar.'

'Captain Jordan, sir, your pilot.' He glanced up at the flag on the mast, the Union Jack.

'Come to the Bridge young man.' He followed me as we entered the Bridge. 'Jacko, this is Jordan, our pilot. Jordan, this is my paperwork.'

'sir, I have been told not to worry about paperwork, just to stand on the Bridge and answer any questions you have.'

Jacko looked out the door and under the bench, and all around the Bridge. 'I am here, is everybody else?'

'Jacko keep it to yourself. This man is confused enough already, don't make it worse.'

The young man was staring at Jacko, totally confused. Lesley said, 'yes he is confusing, he is the only Aboriginal Scotsman in the British Navy. Very, very rare. He is also a Captain in his Majesty's Navy. They want to keep it quiet because he can see over the horizon, so everybody would be fighting over him. Come down to the galley and we will see what we've got in store for you. Follow me. We will be back shortly.' As they walked away, the young man nearly tripped over looking back at Jacko, they walked into the galley. Lesley said to him, 'Don't salute everybody, you're officially not here. Take a seat next to this gentleman. Just put it down in your mind as part of your training.'

Les brought him tea, biscuits, doughnuts and slices of bacon with onion.

Lesley put her hands on Mervyn's shoulders, 'Could we talk?' She gestured to the door. They stood next to the mainmast. 'Mervyn, Vera is arranging for my journals to be put into the National Archives. If you give me yours, I can put them with mine. They will be safe for 30 years.'

'Lesley, wait here, I will get them.' He returned with a very large envelope, which he gave to Lesley. 'My journals are in here.'

'Thank you Mervyn.' She went back to the Bridge.

The Admiral said to the young man, 'I know who you are, and I know all about you. I also know what you want to do in the forces. You have studied hard, your marks are extraordinary.'

Mervyn walked into the galley. The Admiral beckoned him. 'Mervyn, could you bring in your secretary please.' Mervyn turned and left. 'Now young man, I am transferring you to special forces, you will be Mervyn Nelis's PA's secretary. Everything from now on is top secret. You are not here.'

Mervyn walked into the galley with Number 11. They sat down and the Admiral said, 'Number 11, this gentleman is your secretary.'

The Admiral looked at Mervyn. 'My job has now been done, Mervyn Nelis. I look forward to working with you and for you in the future. I have no more jurisdiction over you.' He stood and saluted Mervyn. Mervyn stood up and saluted him back.

'Admiral, when we are in private we just shake hands.' He put his hand out and shook the Admiral's.

The bell rang three times. A voice boomed out, 'All hands to their stations.' Lesley and Jackie stayed in the galley, helping Les.

The pilot was on the Bridge with Jacko and myself. The crew were lined up on deck with Mervyn Nelis. The nurse, Chris, was standing by the mainmast, all in white. We were entering Portsmouth. The high ground on our starboard side looked so green and lush. The harbour looked very confusing with all the naval vessels, in different sizes, air-craft carriers, submarines, they all had their own special berths. The pilot kept talking to Jacko, 'You see that wharf crane over there to your port side, that is our berth.'

'Do you want her bow facing back out to sea?' Jacko asked him.

'I will take your advice, Jacko.'

We could see a bus on the wharf, three cars and people waiting. Jacko brought her in beautifully. She had just kissed the wharf and stopped, and we were tied up. Ted was bracing the yardarms ready for her to be unloaded. He came up onto the Bridge. We all just stood there, silently. Then Ted, in a low voice, said, 'What am I going to do without you Jacko, you're funny, frustrating, unpredictable. What am I going to do when you're not there backing me up in a storm, or a gale when the ice is on here, or when the sails have to be reefed in a sudden storm? When I knew you were at the helm, I didn't worry. When you told me to go and sleep and you'd just take over.'

'Ted, just call me in your mind and I'll be with you. Ted, you must understand I have to go back to the desert, to my people.'

Ted put his arms around Jacko's back and gently tapped his head on Jacko's shoulder.

He slowly turned around to me and looked at me with a lost look on his face. 'Bill, we have been together for a long time. I have been very proud to be your Bosun.' He put his hand out and I shook it.

'Ted, I don't have the words to express what I want to. Take care of yourself Ted, you have been the best Captain Coe.' We embraced each other. 'Fair winds to you and calm seas.' Ted turned and walked down to the deck.

I went down to the deck. Lesley was there with Admiral French. We slowly went down through the crew as they stood to attention, and we shook their hands. I addressed them, 'I and my officers are extremely proud to have served in his Majesty's Navy with you all, walk with pride in yourself, you are all the best.' I saluted them. They all saluted back. Number 7 shouted out, 'Three Cheers for the Captain and his Officers.' They cheered three times.

Mervyn stepped forward. 'You are all dismissed. Pick up your gear and board the bus.'

In a matter of minutes, they were gone. I looked at my watch: 10.30 am.

The crew were already taking the hatch covers off her ready to unload her cargo. Lesley and I went into the galley. There was a cat box on the bench. I noticed that Cat was sitting in it. Les's belongings were alongside it as well. Jackie wasn't there. 'Vera, where is Jackie?'

She looked at me very seriously, 'Who is Jackie? I don't remember seeing a Jackie on board, did you, Admiral?'

He gave me a sly look. 'No, I don't.'

Lesley whispered to me, 'She slipped away early this morning. She was never aboard.'

I thought, *I never entered her in my logbook.* I felt disappointed. I never got to say goodbye. I went to Chris and put my arms around her and gently cuddled her. 'Goodbye Chris Ayres-Smith, thank you for your friendship and help on this voyage.' I stood back. 'Where do you go from here?'

She bent her head slightly, getting her composure together. 'To Dartmouth Naval Hospital and await my orders.'

'Thank you, Chris.'

I walked over to Les and threw my arms around him. 'You have been our father, you have taken care of us. When we have had problems, you have listened to us with compassion and understanding. You've treated our bruises and sores. You have let me know when one of my crew is not well, and not to send him aloft. You have looked after my brother with tender, loving care and been his father as well.' I felt the tears starting, 'What can I say to you, Les?'

'Bill, a part of me is being torn apart. I am losing my two sons, but we must accept it and walk away, or it will destroy us. Bill, I have enough good memories to take me through the rest of my life. *Daisy May*, Colin, Ted, Jacko and yourself. Now let me go. Jacko and I have said our good-byes in our own way.'

Two of the cadets walked into the galley. The Admiral pointed to Les's belongings. One of them picked up the Cat. Les said, 'No, I carry Cat,' and they all left, but once on the deck, Les looked up to the top of the mainmast where Jacko was sitting and nodded to him. He stood there for a moment looking up, then turned and walked down the gang-plank to a waiting car. Jacko watched the car until it went into the distance, then he climbed down to the deck.

Lesley picked up her bag, and the cadets picked up the rest and took them down to a waiting car. Mervyn, Lesley, and I stood on the deck. I faced Mervyn and saluted him. 'We have said everything that needs to be said. I was once a Captain, but you have been my friend.' He returned my salute, and we parted as officers in his Majesty's Navy.

Lesley threw her arms around him and pressed her head into his shoulder. He picked her up like a child and carried her down to the waiting car and gently put her down as he had done a long time ago when they were escaping from the Germans. Lesley ran her hand over his hair and kissed him gently on the lips, turned and got into the car, wiping the tears away with her hands. Mrs Henderson put a hand on Lesley because she knew she was there when they rescued her and Jacko.

CHAPTER 53

They were on their way to London. Jacko was fascinated by the countryside, the light green of the trees and the grass. England is so different from Australia. Eventually, they turned up at the hotel. I remembered it well. I had stayed there with Mervyn at the beginning of the war. The porters took our bags to our rooms. Lesley and I had one, and Jacko had the other. There was an adjoining door between the two rooms. Light refreshments were brought up to the rooms.

We freshened up ready for what was in store for us. Jacko knocked on the adjoining door. Lesley opened it, Jacko's eyes went straight to the plates, looking for leftover food. He looked disappointed. There was a knock on the main door and Mrs Henderson walked in. 'Are you all ready. The car is waiting.'

Lesley looked at me with a worried look on her face. 'Where do I put Mervyn's journals?'

'Give them to me.' I pulled out the top drawer and put them on the plywood base and slid the draw back.

Mrs Henderson laughed, 'dirty washing Bill?'

We went down to the waiting car. The chauffeur opened the door for us. We recognised the man, he said to us, 'Could you please get in the car,' and in a whisper he said, 'Shut up, Jacko.'

We all got into the car. The chauffeur closed the doors and got into the driving seat and drove off. 'I am your driver, William, while you are in England.'

I grinned and Jacko said, 'how is your shoulder?'

'A little stiff at times, but generally doing well.'

'I thought you were going to retire.'

He laughed, 'What is retirement Bill, doing something you like doing, like driving a Rolls Royce around London and getting paid for it! Don't worry about the police car behind us, it is with us.'

Lesley said to him, 'You're not just the chauffeur, are you?'

'No, I am here to see nobody interferes with you, and I'm armed. When you have no need of this car any more, I will be assigned to somebody else in the same capacity.'

We drove through the gates to Buckingham Palace and through to a courtyard. We got out and Lesley took Jacko's arm. He was still feeling the leather seats in the Rolls Royce. Mrs Henderson followed us inside the Palace. It took our breath away, the beautiful big paintings, the columns and artefacts. We went up a grand stairway and were ushered into a beautifully furnished room with paintings of past Kings and Queens, statesmen of the realm.

Refreshments were being served. There were other people in the room also, Naval Officers, Army Commanders, some in dinner suits, ladies beautifully dressed, but I couldn't see Mrs Henderson. Jacko was way out of his depth. Lesley held his hand for support.

About an hour passed and Admiral French seemed to turn up from nowhere. I could see some of the other guests discreetly looking at him. He said to Jacko, 'don't worry about them Jacko, they're only trying to climb the greasy ladder in society. After the ceremonies are over, the Queen would like to have tea with you, your reputation fascinates her, just hold on a little longer.'

I asked the Admiral, 'Where did you place Colin Garland?'

'According to Mervyn, he showed a great interest in submarines. We need dedicated officers in that field.'

'Thank you. His father was one of my original crew, the best. And your son, Admiral?'

'He wanted to be on a frigate protecting other vessels, so that's where he is. I cannot help him anymore.'

Just then, Mrs Henderson appeared. She gave Lesley a document, Lesley read it and passed it on to me. It said, *By orders of the Crown, Commander Lesley Johnson's journals are to be handed over to the National Archives offices and sealed for 30 years.*

The signature on the paper, nobody could argue with. Mrs Henderson bowed her head to us.

'Commander Lesley Johnson, Commander William Farquhar and Captain Jacko Farquhar, his Majesty will see you now.'

Everybody in the room was looking at us as she ushered us out of the room. Admiral French followed. As we walked across the hall to another set of double doors, they seemed to open automatically. We walked into the room, Jacko and I stood together, Lesley stood slightly apart from us. A man standing at a desk had his back to us. He turned and walked over to Lesley. She bowed her head.

The King said, 'I am so pleased to meet you. I have read a lot about your achievements during critical times. Mrs Henderson and Winston Churchill have spoken to me quite often of your achievements in shortening the war. I will now award you with the Victoria Cross for your dedication and your personal sacrifice to the Realm.' He put out his hand to one of his aides, who placed the medal in his hand. The King put the red ribbon over Lesley's neck so that the medal hung down on her chest. 'I will now install the Order of the Garter upon you.' He put his right hand out to one side, an aide placed a sword in it. Mrs Henderson asked Lesley to kneel on one knee. Lesley did as she was asked. The sword was placed first on one shoulder, then the other, then he said, 'Rise, Knight of the Garter.' He handed the sword back and took Lesley's hand to help her stand.

'Lesley, you are a remarkable woman, the Queen and I would like to have tea with you afterwards.' He lent down towards her and whispered into her ear, 'who are these vagabonds you have with you?' Lesley smiled, everybody said he had a way of relaxing you.

Lesley put her hand out to me. 'Your Majesty, may I present my husband, Commander William Farquhar?'

The King stepped in front of me. I bowed my head and he put his hand out and shook mine with a Masonic handshake. He gave a little chuckle, 'The last man to replenish the Treasury was a Pirate, but you are an outstanding Naval Officer, you and your crew have replenished the Treasury, you have been a Captain of a Dreadnought during the war and have an outstanding record. You have taken a sailing vessel where few people could take one, and you have rescued one of our most important Officers.'

'Excuse me, sir, I could not have done it on my own. My brother and my Bosun Ted Coe were with me the whole time.'

'Yes, they have told me. You are a man of extremely high principles. I now award you the Victoria Cross.' He put his hand out, and an aide placed the medal in it. 'Wear this and your other medals with pride.' He reached out and touched my Australian clip. 'But I think you wear this with even more pride.' He tapped it with his finger.

He nodded to me and stepped in front of Jacko. A bagpipe started to play, but very softly. 'You are Captain Jacko Farquhar, born in the desert, which they call the Channel Country. You are Commander Lesley Johnson's uncle and you are Commander William Farquhar's brother.

You are a full blood Aborigine. The Scottish people had so much pride in you that they made you one of their own. They installed one of the highest honours you could have, not only as a Freemason, but a Knights Templar as well. You have stood by your brother at the helm for 40 years, you saved our forces from Dunkirk, you played a major part in rescuing Commander Lesley Johnson, then you assisted your brother to replenish the British Treasury, I now install upon you The Victoria Cross.' He reached out to his aide and placed the ribbon, with difficulty, over Jacko's head. He did so gently and smoothed out the ribbon. His Majesty, the King gently placed the medal on his chest. 'I must say, Captain Jacko, it sits well with your Scottish Regalia. You are the first Aboriginal Scotsman, Captain and Freemason I have ever met, but they tell me you are also the Keeper of your people. So am I, the King, the keeper of your people. We both have the same status. Your name will be put down in the ledger as a visiting King for history to record.'

He put his arm around Jacko's shoulder. 'Now come into the drawing room and we will have tea with the Queen.'

Jacko put his free hand behind his back and waved it to us to follow. I thought *you cheeky little sod*. We had a wonderful tea and got back to our hotel at 1 am. I awoke at 7.30 am, but I had slept soundly. Lesley was still asleep, lying on her back with her mouth wide open. I wanted to put my finger in her mouth, but I didn't want to lose it. *Not a good idea, Bill.* I opened the adjoining door to check on Jacko. He had put the blankets on the floor and was asleep on top of them. For him, the bed was too soft.

I picked up the phone. To my surprise, a voice answered straight away. 'Yes sir, how may I help you?'

'Yes, good morning.'

'Good morning sir.'

'Could I have two coffees, one cup of tea, three bacon and eggs?'

'Captain Farquhar, I assume the coffee would be in mugs?' He surprised me. 'Yes sir. I remember meeting you at the beginning of the war.'

'Make that three mugs of coffee.'

There was silence on the phone. 'Yes, I understand.'

'Just tell your superiors that a Knight of the Garter has requested it,' and hung up.

I went back to Lesley, who was sitting up in bed. 'Put a dressing gown on. You are about to receive your first visitor now that you are a Lady of Society.'

Lesley frowned at me and went into the bathroom, brushed her hair and put on her dressing gown. She came back into the bedroom and sat down at the table with me. She put her medal on the table and sat staring at it. 'All those people died, I can still see their faces, and the King gives me a medal and a fancy title,' she said. 'It doesn't sit right with me Bill. I know now why people put their medals in a cupboard and never get them out.'

Just then, there was a knock at the door. I got up and opened it. There was a well-dressed man there with waiters standing behind him. 'Good morning sir, I am the manager, sir.'

It didn't sit easy with this man. In my mind, he was too smooth. I stepped aside so the waiters could come in. They put the plates and dishes on the table and the coffees, three coffees, one cup and a teapot, along with milk and sugar. I recognised the waiter and put my hand on his shoulder and said to him, 'Sit down, it's good to see you again.'

The manager started to sit down, and was looking at Lesley's medal. I quickly said to him, 'There are only four chairs. Thank you for our breakfast. I will call you if there is anything else we need.' He raised his eyebrows, stood back, and looked highly offended. I ushered him out of the door and politely closed it behind him.

The waiter started to laugh. 'That has made my day. I'm taking up another position at another hotel next week. He makes everybody's life a nightmare, trying to highlight himself amongst the guests.'

'I'm trying to remember your name, sorry.'

'Fred, sir.'

'I am Bill, this is my wife, Lesley.'

He took the lids off the plates of bacon and eggs.

Lesley put her finger in the air and said, 'One.' She put two fingers up, 'Two.' Then she put three fingers up, saying 'three,' then she said, 'four.'

Jacko's head appeared around the connecting door. He was sniffing the air. 'Fred, this is Jacko, Lesley's little puppy dog.'

Fred just stared at him. 'Yes Bill, I saw him yesterday. We are all confused.'

Lesley said, 'Come and have some breakfast, Jacko, we've got a busy day ahead of us.'

As Jacko was stuffing food into his mouth, he said to Lesley, 'The medals we got, what do they mean?'

'Well, the Victoria Cross is the highest and most prestigious award of the British Honours system. It is awarded for the most conspicuous bravery or some daring or pre-eminent Act of Valour or Self Sacrifice or extreme devotion to duty in the presence of the enemy.'

Jacko put his head slightly to one side, his fork full of bacon and eggs. 'All very interesting,' and he stuffed the fork into his mouth.'

'So Fred, what did you do during the war?'

'I ended up flying Lancaster bombers. The second raid I did, we got shot up, but managed to get back to England. I landed her in a field. When we touched the ground, we hit the land quite hard and a pedal shot up and broke my ankle, but we landed safely. I couldn't fly again and was posted to a desk job. Somebody was looking after me.'

We finished our breakfast. Lesley picked up the phone and gave the receptionist Marcia's phone number and asked if she could ring it.

'Yes, I will put your call through straight away.'

Then Lesley said to Jacko, 'Follow me.' She marched him into his bathroom, put the plug into the bath, turned on both taps and told Jacko, 'you can adjust the hot water to what you want and become a boiled lobster!' She left him to it and shouted out 'clean underpants.'

CHAPTER 54

The phone rang. I picked it up and said, 'Yes.' Just as Lesley had shouted out clean underpants.

The voice at the other end said, 'I beg your pardon?'

I handed the phone to Lesley. 'Marcia, Marcia, it's Lesley, we're in London. Yes, we will be leaving in about 20 minutes. Yes, there will be three of us for dinner,' and she hung up.

I looked out of the window. I could see our car waiting. Lesley got Mervyn's journals, and we left with the medals in our pockets. Lesley had made sure she also had her journals with her.

The car pulled up outside Marcia's house. She was waiting outside the front door, and looked very surprised at seeing a Rolls Royce. Marcia and Lesley embraced each other, laughing with tears in their eyes.

'Marcia, this is my husband, Bill,' I shook hands with her, 'and this is Jacko. He is my uncle.'

Marcia cuddled Jacko. 'I remember Lesley talking about you.'

Then Lesley said, 'Marcia, is there food for one more?'

'Yes.'

Lesley said to the driver, 'You're with us.'

He looked surprised, and she said 'you are one of us, so don't argue, I'm quite sure your colleagues in the Police car will look after the Rolls.'

He turned to the Police car, put both hands up in the air, shrugged his shoulders and followed us into the house.

We went into the front parlour. Mr Fredericks put his arms around Lesley and cuddled her. 'You have been a lot of trouble, Lesley. I, your sister Peggy and her husband Ted, have been trying to sort out the wicked web of deceit and lies. Ted Jones was no fool. He and his colleagues sorted most of it out.'

'Mr Fredericks, I haven't heard from my sister for a long time.'

'I have mail for you.' He came back with a bundle of letters and handed them to Lesley. Some were from her flat. 'I have paid the bills. I wish my electric bill was as low as yours.'

Marcia took Lesley's hand. 'She is mine dear.' They both went into the kitchen, chattering away together.

Mr Fredericks took me aside. 'Bill, I was informed that Lesley had died, that she had taken her own life, so I informed Peggy in Australia. She flew to England with her husband Ted, who had been a high-ranking police officer in London, and being a Cockney, he understood London well. He was very highly respected, therefore he had many contacts with his colleagues in London. Lesley's apartment was bugged. Ted, being the professional, sorted that out very quickly. Lesley's death certificate didn't make any sense, his colleagues sorted out that she was still an officer in his Majesty's Navy on assignment. There were those in government wanting to hide her because she had journals all about the German people and high-ranking people and their involvement in both sides of the war. It was a very dangerous situation for the individuals. They wanted to destroy them and keep their dirty secrets safe.'

Peggy and Ted returned to Australia. I heard from my own people in court that they were looking for a lady named Jackie Evans. My professional instincts tell me you know all about it.

'Yes, we do. She is a good friend of ours.'

Jacko's voice broke in, 'and she can cook good tucker. Spaghetti Bolognese with a pinch of garlic, very good tucker.'

Mr Fredericks laughed. 'Not as good as Marcia's.' He pointed to his stomach.

I said, 'Yes, Lesley tells me we've got to go to the apartment after this.'

Mr Fredericks looked at me seriously. 'We have got what she wants.' He left the room and came back quickly with an envelope, on which was written *I knew you'd find it, little sister.* 'I didn't have a clue as to what was in the envelope.'

I put it into my top pocket and said, 'Thank you.' I could see Jacko's nostrils twitching, then Marcia walked in with food.

'Dinner is served.'

I put my hand on Jacko's shoulder. 'Slowly Jacko.'

We walked into the dining room, where Jacko's eyes got even bigger. The table was laden with food, hot roasted pork, chicken, with steam rising up from it. Baked potatoes, cabbage, peas, turnips, and parsnips.

Marcia loaded Jacko's plate up with everything and a freshly buttered roll. Mr Fredericks was opening the wine. I could see Lesley had a slightly worried look on her face, so I handed her the envelope. She read what was on the outside of it and touched the cut corner and smiled back at me.

'Jacko said to me that the envelope smelled of pepper.' She started to laugh. She put the envelope into her pocket and started to enjoy her meal.

I would swear I could see Jacko's stomach getting bigger. The conversation was very light-hearted, and I was enjoying myself. I remembered saying something and everybody laughed. Jacko said to me, 'You haven't told one of your jokes for years.'

Marcia and Jacko picked up the dishes and took them to the kitchen. I could faintly hear Jacko talking and Marcia laughing out loud and then

Jacko returned carrying a tray of bowls—fruit, ice-cream and topping. Marcia placed a bowl in front of each one of us, but when she got to Jacko, there weren't any bowls left. He held the tray to one side, put his shoulders back, and returned to the kitchen. He came back carrying a huge bowl.

Mr Fredericks asked him, 'Where are you going to put it all?'

Lesley and I just grinned. I lent over to Lesley, 'I bet he licks the bowl.' She grinned.

We finished our sweets and Mr Fredericks waited for Jacko to finish his, then he said, 'Coffee in the lounge.'

Lesley sat down next to me and took out the envelope. She took a key out of it and handed it to me. 'This is the key to a bank deposit box where all my journals are.'

She looked at Jacko sitting in a comfortable armchair and dozing off to sleep. 'Bill, if you stay here with Jacko, Mr Fredericks and I will go to the bank, then on to the National Archives office. Having my solicitor with me will make it more official if someone else has to sign. His signature will be the right one.'

I looked at my watch. 'You don't have much time.'

'Then we will leave now.'

Mr Fredericks nodded, got up and went to the cupboard to get his coat. He walked to the front door. Our driver followed him. Lesley picked up her jacket and bag and they were gone. I watched the Rolls Royce drive off and the police car follow them. I felt concerned.

One of Jacko's eyes opened. 'They will be all right, Bill. Lesley is a big Cocky.'

Marcia and I talked about their friendship. I talked about the Diamantina River and where it is in Australia. I drew a diagram on a piece of paper and explained to her why it's called the Channel country. 'Both of you should come to Australia and spend some time with us and Jacko's people. You will find it is so different; it has a special, magical beauty of its own. The land is as old as time itself.'

Marcia excused her self saying, 'I really must do the dishes and clean up.'

'I will help you.'

We talked more while we were doing the dishes.

Lesley and Mr Fredericks arrived at the bank. He chuckled, 'Your brother-in-law is a cockney. He calls the bank the old lady.'

The driver didn't go to the front, but went to the back gates and handed his card to the gatekeeper, who glanced at Lesley when he opened the gates and bowed his head as they drove through. The police car followed. Mr Fredericks and Lesley were ushered through a back door and into a well-furnished room where a well dressed gentle men said, 'How can I help you, madam?'

Lesley handed him the bank deposit key. He bowed his head and left. He soon returned with the safety deposit box. She took everything out of the safety box and put her journals, along with Mervyn's, in another secure box. Everything else went into her bag, with the exception of the gloves that Michael had made for her. 'I will wear them,' she said to the gentleman. 'I will no longer be requiring this deposit box.' She signed the discharge form.

'Could you put your password on the bottom madam?'

She wrote *little sister.*

'Thank you madam.' They returned to the car.

The driver said, 'I have informed the Police where we are going. They will be waiting for you.'

Once again, they drove through the double gates and security checked their papers.

CHAPTER 55

Once they arrived at the National Archives Office, a lady and gentleman welcomed them and ushered them into an office. The gentleman ushered Lesley to a chair at a very long table, which was obviously used as a meeting room. It looked very impressive. He handed her a beautiful pen and sat down opposite. Mr Fredericks sat on Lesley's right side. The gentleman said, 'My name is Wally Simpson.'

'It is very nice to meet you Wally, I am Commander Lesley Johnson. Mr Fredericks said you already know me.'

She handed him her papers. He read the first one, looked at Lesley, then looked at Mr Fredericks.

Mr Fredericks said, 'Yes, by orders of the King.'

Wally read the next paper. It gave Lesley's title. Lesley put the package on the table, which contained the journals.

Wally looked at them. 'Excuse me, please, for just a moment.'

He went through a door into another office. They could hear a typewriter clicking away. Twenty minutes passed before he returned and handed Lesley the paperwork.

She read through it, then handed it to Mr Fredericks, who scrutinised it thoroughly. 'Wally, this is wrong. There isn't a date.'

Wally replied, 'Yes there is. It's on the top of the paper.'

'Wally, that only tells me when this piece of paper was printed, it should say on this day, Thursday, Friday or whatever, then for example 22nd February and the year you have received the documents, and who from? Put her full title and By Order of the Crown. There is a number on the top of the paper. These documents are not for the public and are only to be read with permission from the Crown in thirty years. State the date and the year, and the number you place with the documents and who their from. State her full title. Don't play politics with me, Wally. Do it right, keep it on the square.'

'Mr Fredericks, I don't normally do this, sir Malcolm does, but he is indisposed.'

'I quite understand that, but if you alter documents to suit others, they must be done correctly.'

Wally went back into the other office. They could hear his secretary typing. Mr Fredericks said, 'The gentleman he just spoke about is one of those who couldn't make up his mind which side he was on during the war, so your documents could be quite damaging. I should be totally honest with you Lesley, when your sister Peggy and Ted came back to England there were too many loose ends, I wanted to know the truth, and I wanted to find out about those who wanted to end your life, The Germans, the Aristocrat's daughter, and one or two others, and the other one who bought the chicken farm in Australia with Government funds, for those who wanted to provide them information. They are now in prison under the securities Act for Treason. You can thank Admiral French for that. They named it the "Frying Pan".'

Just then, Wally returned and handed Mr Fredericks the paperwork. He read it very carefully, scrutinising every line and every word. He nodded to Wally, wrapped the package with paper and put a seal on it. It had its number and the information on it.

Mr Fredericks put his hand up to Wally, who put a pen in his hand. Mr Fredericks handed it to Lesley. 'Sign here, here and here.'

Mr Fredericks also signed in three places as a witness, but he then printed his full name and qualifications.

Wally picked up the parcel and placed it on a tray. He put it into a chute on the wall and it disappeared.

He turned to Mr Fredericks. 'Now, nobody can touch it.'

Mr Fredericks said to Wally, 'I will see you on Thursday. This is the fourth Thursday of the month. Will your wife be in the South?'

'Yes.'

'Good, I will let Marcia know.'

CHAPTER 56

Mr Fredericks rang his wife and said, 'we're on our way home dear. Yes, the driver will be staying for a meal.' The police car followed them back, but left when they arrived at Mr Fredericks's house.

Once again, we were sitting around the table with more food. Jacko was like a little boy. He couldn't wait. Lesley was having trouble controlling him. Fresh sausages with onions, mashed potatoes, peas, carrots and a few other vegetables. For sweets we had vanilla slice with whipped cream, ice-cream and strawberries marinated in a little wine, chocolates with nuts and other tasty little things.

We all went to sit in the lounge room. Lesley said to Mr Fredericks, 'I don't really need my flat anymore, I will give you Mervyn Nelis's secretary's phone number, if you could ask him to arrange for Les, one of Bill's crew to take over the flat and I will pay all expenses. If Les protests, don't argue with him, let him pay the rates and electricity. He has a very big sense of pride. As you know, the flat is fully furnished, it is now all his. I will have to return to England once a year to attend a special function on the night of the Garter, then Marcia, you and I can be together once a year and you will both be my guests at Buckingham Palace.'

We talked until one in the morning. Then the women said their good-byes, tears in their eyes, cuddling each other. I shook Mr Fredericks's hand and thanked him. Jacko did the same, then he cuddled Marcia. Our chauffeur thanked both of them and said goodbye. We returned to our hotel.

CHAPTER 57

In the morning, I was awake at 7 am. I couldn't sleep any more. I peeped into Jacko's room. There he was flat on this back on the floor, arms and legs spread out, snoring peacefully. I thought *food makes him sleep very well. Any more and he would have burst!*

I went out on the verandah, looking at the city of London. The last time I saw it, life was in turmoil. Now everything is slowly being put back into place. I thought of the lady who had offered me a cup of tea. *We gave them buggers what for, didn't me?* The men were filling in bomb craters. Did it all really happen? Yes, it did, but Lesley, Jacko and I are going home. We can leave it all behind. It is now just history. Will those in the future understand? The biggest problem that I have now is Jacko. How am I going to get him on an aircraft back to Australia? I went back inside.

We all had breakfast and packed our belongings. Our chauffeur took us to Croydon airport. There was a naval aircraft there waiting for us. I looked at Jacko; he was starting to panic. Lesley held his hand and said, 'They serve food on board the plane and I have arranged for you to have ice-cream, lots of ice-cream and cream and yummy cakes.'

He didn't really want to go with Lesley, but he slowly followed her up the steps into the aircraft. It was comfortably furnished as First Class. We were strapped in and soon, without any hesitation, we were heading down the runway. Jacko's eyes were as big as saucers, he was clenching Lesley's hand. 'I don't like this Lesley, not good, you stay with me until we get home.'

'Yes Jacko, we won't leave you.'

The seat-belt warning light went out. We left ours on to give Jacko a feeling of security.

A steward walked up to our seats. 'Excuse me ma'am, the food that you ordered is ready now.'

'Coffee for the gentleman, tea for me and food for this gentleman.'

I could see the twinkle in Jacko's eyes.

'Could you make the coffee strong, please?'

Soon Jacko had finished his cake, ice-cream and cream, and sat back in his chair and closed his eyes.

Lesley laid the seat back for him and did the same to her own seat. She held onto Jacko's hand and closed her eyes. I could see that the last couple of days had caught up with them. They were both soon in a deep sleep. I watched the clouds out of the window. My thoughts drifted back to *Daisy May*.

CHAPTER 58

Mervyn and Ted stood with their hands behind their backs watching *Daisy May* being unloaded. Men with clipboards were writing everything down. A flag had been raised on the mast, indicating that there were explosives on board. Signs had also been placed on the wharf, warning of explosives. Security had been stepped up. A man was blowing a whistle at the crane operator who was loading the trucks. By 4 pm, they had finished. Tray trucks with canopies on their sides had arrived and the drivers and crew were rolling the canvas sides back, then they all disappeared to the canteen with the exception of security.

Mervyn turned to Ted. 'I will go and get something to eat and drink, then return to relieve you.'

'Mervyn, Les has left me something for tea and it's my favourite, so take your time.'

Two armed guards stood at the bottom of the gangplank. Ted got his meal and enjoyed sitting in the galley eating it. He picked up his dirty dishes and washed them, then went back, sat down, and closed his eyes. In total surprise, in his mind he could see Colin Garland's face smiling at him and his voice saying, *'I can now leave, all is well!'* and he was gone. Ted opened his eyes and smiled to himself.

Just on dusk they started unloading the sixty crates. A number was placed on each one, there was a set of scales on the wharf, and each crate was weighed and recorded.

At 4.30 am Mervyn and Ted were standing there all alone. There wasn't any security, nobody seemed to be worried any more.

'Sleep Ted?'

'Yes Mervyn.'

Ted went to his hammock, Mervyn went to his cabin.

At 7 am Ted woke to the sound of voices in the forecastle. A man said, 'I'm taking that hammock. Look how it's made with the headpiece and all the trimmings.'

Ted lifted his head up. The three men looked totally surprised. Ted shouted to them, 'This is my hammock! It doesn't belong to you, or to the Navy. Now, what do you want?'

'We have been told to report to Captain Ted Coe. We have been told to remove all hammocks, mattresses, blankets and any other items that are not required.'

'I am Captain Coe. Thank you for letting me know you all have light fingers. Keep them off my hammock.' He swung his legs out of the hammock and put his trousers on. 'Are you three men in the Navy?'

'No sir, we come under the dockyard. When the vessel is in dry dock, we clean and paint it, and anything else they ask us to do. We have been assigned to you. Is there anything you would like us to do?'

'Take my hammock, roll it up and carefully put it on the Bridge with the rest of my belongings. Anything that is in the drawers, stays in the drawers. All the charts and any logbooks stay there. You can remove the mattresses, but that's all. There are mattresses in the stern cabins, but I will check first. Don't move anything from the galley. There is wood for the stove and briquettes. Leave them there. Are you cleaning the hull?'

'Yes sir, when the equipment arrives.'

'I have been Bosun on this vessel for a very long time. I know everything that's aboard: Marlin spikes, spears, rope stores in the stern. You play it straight with me, I play it straight with you.' He put his shirt and shoes on. 'I'm going to have a good, hot shower. Don't wake the Captain up in the single cabin.'

Ted had his shower, shaved and cleaned up, and walked back to the vessel. He passed Mervyn with a towel over his shoulder and carrying his wash pack. 'I hope you enjoy your shower as much as I enjoyed mine.'

Mervyn nodded.

Ted went onto the Bridge and sat down on Lesley's bunk. Her nice soft blanket was still there. He said to himself, *they're mine*. He opened the top drawer. There was Walter Wright's telescope. Bill's was also still there. 'Walter's telescope stays on board with me,' and with a croaky voice, he said 'and Bill's goes to Mervyn.'

Ted and Mervyn had their breakfast in the galley. Mervyn's two secretaries sat down in front of them. 'Sir, there is a car arriving for you at 9.30 am. It is your personal car, and the driver is your personal driver. You have been summoned to Buckingham Palace along with Captain Ted Coe.'

Mervyn looked at his watch. He stared at his two secretaries, wondering what was in store for them. They all returned to the *Daisy May*.

A Naval Officer came on board and went into the galley and saluted them. They returned the salute. 'Captain Coe, sir, I have been assigned to you as Bosun. I have also been informed, sir, that you are going to London, but will return. What are your instructions for me?'

'Come up onto the Bridge.' Mervyn followed them. He handed the Bosun a pencil and paper. 'These will be my quarters. In these drawers are all the documents for this vessel relating to everything you need to know about her. Study them. I believe there are three men aboard to clean her up. Watch them! This vessel doesn't have any ballast, and it relies on its cargo. If you move her from here to a dry dock, no sharp turns and only in calm water, but something tells me I'll be back before then, so I don't need to tell you how to start the motor. Just study these documents.'

Ted opened the top drawer and handed Bill's telescope to Mervyn. 'The other one is mine, and it belongs to this vessel.' He thought for a moment, picked it up and slid it into his personal pack. 'These are my personal belongings, along with the blankets, leave them in here. That's all I can ask you to do at the moment. We'll talk when I get back.'

The four of them walked down to the waiting car on the wharf. It was a beautiful Bentley. A man stepped out of the driver's seat and saluted Mervyn, who laughed and said, 'Don't ever salute me again. How is the wound in your side. Is it all healed up?'

'They re-opened the wound and did something, I don't know what, then they stitched it back again. All is well. Mervyn, we had better get moving, we don't have much time.'

When they left the dockyards, a police car followed them. Mervyn said to his driver, 'Do you always wear a side arm?'

'You don't miss anything. You haven't changed one bit, but that is why we're both still alive.'

Mervyn turned to his secretaries. 'We were in the special forces together. I wouldn't say it was fun, but it certainly wasn't boring.'

They finally arrived at the gates of Buckingham Palace, drove through into a courtyard, got out of the car and walked into a foyer. A very polite gentleman ushered them into a waiting room.

Mrs Henderson came through another door and shook hands with them. 'Mervyn, if you would come with me first, along with your secretaries.' She smiled at Ted, 'Totty, if you would like to have coffee and sandwiches, they will bring them out for you.'

Ted frowned at her.

Mervyn and his secretaries were ushered into another office and directed to the chairs at a table. Mervyn's eyes scanned the room. There were dark timber panels, pictures of important Naval Officers, Nelson, Army Officers, Churchill, various politicians and well-dressed ladies. There was also an impressive painting of the King and Queen.

Green leather folders were put down in front of them. Three men sat down on the opposite side of the table and introduced themselves. They were lawyers.

'Gentlemen, if you would read through your documents.' As they were reading them, coffee and sandwiches were brought in and Mrs Henderson came and sat down alongside Mervyn. 'Do you have any questions?'

Mervyn mentioned, 'Mrs Henderson, these are like the papers I signed for special forces. Never did I ever think I would turn up on an old sailing clipper. So now I am an Adviser for new technology for weapons and naval vessels and military equipment. I will be assigned to discussions and conferences on warfare around the world, and how to prevent it happening, and the sanctions we can put on those who create war.'

Mervyn went on and Mrs Henderson just kept saying, 'Yes Mervyn.' They finished going through all the documents.

Mrs Henderson looked at him very seriously. 'Have you read these documents before?'

'No, but I have had a briefing with a colleague, Captain Jacko, who said to look over the horizon.'

Mrs Henderson said, 'Yes, he is a crystal ball.' She handed him a pen and Mervyn signed the papers, each one, very carefully. He pushed the papers back over to Mrs Henderson and handed her the pen to co-sign. She did so.

Mervyn looked at the three lawyers, and in a very commanding manner, said to them, 'Where is my copy?'

'We will get them to you later.'

Mervyn stood up, looked down at the lawyers and said, 'You will get them now, and if there is anything different, I will politically tear the three of you to pieces. Do I make myself clear? Now, where is my copy?'

Mrs Henderson put her arms on the arms of the chair, put her fingers together and smiled, thinking to herself, *he is certainly the right person to replace me*. Mervyn's copies just seemed to turn up out of nowhere. He signed them, and so did Mrs Henderson.

Mervyn handed his copy to his secretary, looked at him and raised his eyebrows. 'No sir, I don't have any questions.'

Later on Mervyn and Ted were taken into another room, much more impressive than the last, with beautiful furniture, paintings, and curtains on the big windows. The high ceilings were beautifully decorated. To their total surprise, the King walked into the room and smiled at both of them. He shook their hands.

He stood in front of Mervyn, 'Mr Mervyn Nelis, you are an incredible man, the service you gave before and during the war, the outstanding achievements you and your colleagues performed to the utmost of valour, did a great part in re-pricing the Treasury. You did not hesitate to become a decoy so that this could be done. Mr Nelis, it is I who should kneel before you.' He put his hand out, and a sword was placed in it. The King knighted Mervyn. 'You are now a Knight of the Highest Order in the British Commonwealth.' He handed the sword to Mervyn. 'This is yours, for the office you are about to undertake.'

Mervyn took the sword and stared at it. The King put his hand on Mervyn's shoulder and said, 'Thank you, sir Nelis.' He put his hand out again and the Victoria Cross was handed to him, which he placed around Mervyn's neck. The King stuttered a bit. 'I look forward to meeting you in our discussions in the future.'

Then the King stepped in front of Ted. 'Captain Ted Coe, you have been one of the most important keys to success for others and for the role you have served to your Captain. You've always been there, at the mainmast, tempest, storms, no matter what the circumstances you have served as second in command of a dreadnought during the war. What you have achieved has helped preserve England's future in the financial world. We are still the banking centre for the world. We can hold our heads up high. Thank you, Captain Coe.' He put his hand out again and the St. George cross was put in his hand. The King placed it around Ted's neck. 'This is for the services you have given to the Realm, but I also give you this document from me. You are charged with the responsibility of being the Captain of *Daisy May*, I repeat *Daisy May*.'

He put his hand out and a leather folder was placed in it. 'In this folder are my instructions for you. You have total command.' He shook Ted's hand and held it. 'I look forward to my family and myself sailing with you. Winston Churchill has told me of his memories of being aboard a bark sailing Clipper. Now, if you would excuse me.' He smiled, 'Totty, I have to go.' He patted Ted's shoulder, nodded to Mervyn, and left.

They were all taken back to the other room where drinks and food were served. Mrs Henderson walked up to Mervyn. 'I'm now officially retired. You will be taken to a hotel in London with your two secretaries. Tomorrow morning, you will officially take over my office. There are two ladies there. Please look after them for me. Ted, when you're ready, there is a car waiting for you. If you want to go anywhere else, you are in command. There is one of those,' she pointed to Ted's medal, 'for Les.'

She turned to Mervyn, saying, 'Watch your back! Goodbye gentlemen,' and she left.

Mervyn's secretary walked up to him. 'Sir, you will be taken to your office first thing tomorrow. You have a meeting with the Ministry in the afternoon. Your flight to Australia is booked for the following day. At your convenience, you will have a meeting with the Maribyrnong Government Research Laboratories, Melbourne. When you leave Melbourne, I should say when we leave Melbourne, we will fly to America to inspect military hardware.'

Mervyn smiled at him. 'Does that mean our holiday is over?'

'Yes sir.'

CHAPTER 59

I sat up a little stiff. I had fallen into a deep sleep. A voice on the inter-com said, 'This is the Captain, we are now preparing to land. Fasten your seat-belts. We only expect to be thirty minutes on the tarmac, just to refuel. This is a naval runway, and it is extremely busy, so this is our time slot. For those of you who are disembarking, there is transport waiting for you.'

'Where are we, Bill?' Lesley asked.

'I don't really know. There is a lot of activity around this aircraft.'

Two Naval Officers disembarked, and another two boarded the air-craft. Jacko was slouched in his seat, his hair was untidy, his beard was looking scruffy, but his medal lay on top of his beard. His kilt had split up over his knees. He was wide awake.

The First Officer boarding in his smart naval uniform stopped abruptly. He stared at Jacko and his medal, then glanced at Lesley, saw her rank, then glanced at me, and saw my rank. I winked at him. Then he looked at Jacko, who sat straight up, looking surprised, and with a very British accent said to the Naval Officer, 'I say, old chap, you do look most terribly ill. I would suggest that you see a doctor, could be a bad back, old chap.'

The officer had a surprised look on his face, put his head back in a very arrogant manner and went to his seat. The other officer followed him.

The steward walked down the aisle to check on the new passengers. As he passed Jacko, he said, 'sir, more ice-cream aboard!' Jacko put his thumb in the air.

The aircraft took off again. Jacko looked more comfortable this time, but he was still holding Lesley's hand. I picked up a magazine and glanced through it, just looking at the pictures. I realised that being at sea, I had lost touch with society and women's clothes. Some of those clothes and dresses Mum would have been disgusted, but I smiled. I liked them.

I looked over at Jacko and Lesley. The steward brought Jacko his ice-cream, a cup of tea, one mug of coffee and sandwiches. I was so tired I fell off back to sleep, dreaming that I was standing on the helm of *Daisy May*. Cat was sitting on the bench, and we were watching the sunrise. The best time to be on the Bridge, looking at the beauty of the sunrise and all her colours. I opened my eyes. Sunlight was streaming through the little window straight into my face. My body ached. I turned my head. *Where is Jacko?*

Lesley was asleep in her seat, but no Jacko. Had he gone to the toilet? I needed to go to the toilet. I got up and squeezed past Lesley, not waking her, but when I got to the toilets, they were empty. I glanced around the cabin but couldn't see him. *Where is he?* I was just about to walk down the aisle to look for him when the steward came up behind me saying, 'Are you looking for your friend?'

'Yes, I am.'

'Well, he's in the cockpit with the pilots.'

I looked surprised.

'We couldn't argue with him sir, he outranks all of us. This is a Naval Aircraft.'

I thought for a moment. The only person who outranks him is Lesley. I went to the toilet, then back to my seat.

Lesley was awake. She asked me, 'where is Jacko?'

'In the cockpit with the pilots.'

Lesley replied, 'Oh my God, he'll be flying the aircraft next.'

I laughed. 'So long as he doesn't try to land it.'

The steward walked back to us and said, 'the Captain is enjoying his conversation with your colleague, and they're sharing ice-cream.'

We landed in Darwin to re-fuel and pick up some more passengers. Jacko started a conversation with one of them. Apparently, this officer was flying to Melbourne for a meeting at a research laboratory with a high ranking British diplomat. Big, big smoke. The three of us looked at each other thinking Mervyn Nelis, but we didn't say a word.

We eventually landed at Laverton Military airport just outside of Melbourne. There was a car waiting for us. The driver put his hand out and shook our hands. 'I'm Chris O'Hara. I'm working for Jarrett Collins.'

'My name is Bill, this is Lesley, and this is Jacko.'

'I'm very pleased to meet a fellow brother.' Chris smiled. 'I'm to take you to the British Admiralty in Flinders Street, then onto Ted and Peggy Jones's private home.'

As we were driving towards the city, I asked him, 'So you work for Jarrett?'

'Yes and no. I own a hire car company and a couple of garages, business-wise it is convenient for both of us.'

We pulled up outside Admiralty House in Flinders Street and went up the steps to the foyer. A secretary saluted us, we returned the salute, and were ushered into an office. The man we supposed was a secretary asked if he could get us some tea and refreshments. Jacko naturally said yes. We were ushered to some chairs at a table. A man walked in. Jacko and I started to stand, but Lesley said, 'No.' She outranked his man.

He bowed his head to her. 'Good morning madam, good morning gentlemen.' We nodded. 'I will start with the business first. You have been returned to your home port, that is Naval Law. I am a Naval Solicitor, so please forgive me if I'm over tactful.'

Lesley spoke. 'Talk to us straight, no protocol, just straight. Bill and I have to return to England once a year to attend His Majesty's Court, we are flown there in a British government aircraft. We will be residing in the Channel Country. We are ready to sign those papers for that financial agreement with his Majesty the King. Here are the papers.' She produced the papers.

'Thank you madam, that makes my job more simple. There are a number of business people and politicians putting on a dinner party for you. To further simplify things for themselves, they want you to be involved in their enterprises. You can now mix in society where they can offer you a directorship in their companies or other positions to do their manipulating in your name, to hide items and many other things to further their course, and offer you money favours, luxury estates, cars, etc.'

Jacko spoke out. 'Yes, we have been to sea and we may be illiterate to the ways of the city, but we will not sell our souls to anybody. All we want to do is go home. We have done our part, these medals,' he patted his, 'prove that.'

The solicitor stared at him. An indigenous man dressed in Scottish regalia, rank of a Captain, wearing a Victoria Cross.'

'Yes,' I said, 'he is a Captain. He holds the highest honour as a Scotsman. He has a Victoria Cross, but he has a higher rank than all of those. He is the keeper of our people. We will not be attending such a function. I believe we have some paperwork to sign.'

I could see Jacko out of the corner of my eye picking up a sandwich with two fingers and just ever so gently stuff it into his mouth, and so could the solicitor. 'Well sir, you have made my job very simple. It would not have been in the interest of the Crown because of the circumstances of your missions. I don't know exactly what they were, but I'm told they are top secret, as far as the paperwork is concerned. The King has signed them, the British Prime Minister has signed them, so has the Australian Prime Minister, and in the interests of the indigenous people of Australia all I need now is for you to sign them to prove that you've received them.'

'Could you ask our driver, Mr Chris O'Hara, to be the witness,' I said. The solicitor spoke to his secretary and Chris walked in the door, looking very confused.

'Chris, we just want you to witness the signing of some papers.' He looked around the room, looked at the solicitor, looked at us, and shrugged his shoulders.

'Yes.'

CHAPTER 60

Soon we were back in the car heading for Brighton. I could see the anticipation in Lesley and Jacko, they were to be reunited with Peggy.

We turned into a cul-de-sac lined with beautiful poplar trees, which overhung the road. We turned into a driveway. The house was a two-storey, typically English-styled house with a pitched roof and little lead-light windows. It had a large front door with two panels on either side. The garden was beautifully trimmed with a typical English flowerbed.

The front door opened. Peggy came running out, her hand over her mouth, trying not to cry. Lesley got out of the car and just stood there for a moment, staring at her sister, Peggy. It was as if all the trauma of the past years had finally caught up with her. She slowly sank to her knees, weeping. Peggy sat down beside her, put her arms around her, and wept as well. She remembered reading about the turmoil Lesley had lived through, though she was now free.

Jacko leaned up against me. I put my arm around him. Both of us could not stop the tears. A man slowly walked out of the front door. He was of medium height, with grey hair and had a dog by his side. It was a Cavalier King Charles Spaniel. It ran up to Peggy and licked her face, knowing that she was upset. Peggy put her arm around the dog to comfort him. Lesley did the same. Something had happened. The dog had eased their pain just by being there.

Jacko and I walked up to Lesley. Peggy's husband, Ted, walked up behind his wife. We helped the two women stand up. Chris O'Hara unloaded our bags from the boot of his car. He handed me his card. 'If you want me, just call.' He nodded to Ted Jones, who nodded back. He drove away.

Their dog Charlie just kept running around in circles. He was so excited. We all went into the house. You would have thought we were back in England, with the ceiling beams, panelled walls, paintings on the walls, and beautiful furniture. The two ladies sat on the couch, holding each other, not saying a word, just enjoying being together.

Ted said, 'So you are Jacko.' Jacko put his hand out. Ted shook Jacko's hand. 'And you are Captain Bill.' He shook my hand. Ted said, 'We will leave the women alone for a while. By the way, Bill, Jackie sends her regards. Yes Bill, we are old colleagues. Jacko, bacon, eggs, onions, tomatoes, sliced potatoes and fried bread. We will always be English, never change. If you sit down, I will make you coffee first.'

As Ted made the coffee, he started to talk. 'I reached quite a high rank in the police force in England, but I wouldn't play the political game for the politicians. I am a policeman for the public of England, but they wanted to play the political game with me and I was transferred to the Australian police force, the same rank. I met Peggy in the courtroom.' He chuckled to himself. 'Something came over me. She was the one I had been looking for. Don't ask me how, or when, but I found myself married to Peggy. She has a very high sense of ethics. She can cut through the bull dust very quickly and find the wrong and right of the situation and put it to others so they can't argue with the truth. She is extremely good in the court room, totally in control and way ahead of the other legal beavers in the court room. Do you both take milk and sugar?'

'Yes, I do,' Jacko said, 'but Bill likes his coffee black, strong and no sugar.'

I raised my eyebrows. Ted started to cook breakfast, but kept on talking. 'When we received the correspondence from England to say that Lesley had died, Mr Fredericks, Lesley's solicitor, suggested we should return to England, if possible.' Ted grinned to himself as he was turning the sizzling maple bacon over in the pan. 'That's when the game began. I must admit now that I thoroughly enjoyed it. Meeting all my old colleagues, it certainly was my cup of tea. They helped Peggy and I to sort out the tangled web of deception, political plunder. I got to see my mother and my brother and the rest of the family, but when Peggy read through Lesley's journals and the trauma she had gone through during the war, and how Jacko and you, Bill, had pulled her together. She spoke about her bodyguard, Mervyn Nelis. I certainly would like to meet with him.'

I said to Ted, 'I think you may do some day. They are so much a part of each other. They have both seen too much together and lived the same traumas deep in their minds.'

Jacko's eyes were watching the frying pan and the food sizzling away in the dripping fat. Ted put food on three plates, then put three slices of bread in the dripping fat and fried them. He took them out and put them on the prepared plates. 'How about we have these on the patio?'

We picked up our plates and coffee, went through the back door of the house, and sat down at a table. Jacko's voice boomed out, 'I can see the sea.'

'Yes Jacko,' Ted said, 'walk down through the garden and you're on the beach.'

Jacko did one of his little dances and said, 'good place to live.'

'Yes, Peggy and I are very happy here.'

We finished our meal and then talked about the *Daisy May*, the Channel Country and the people there.

'It's been a long time since you have been there. Things might have changed a lot,' Ted said.

Jacko replied, 'My people are my people. They wouldn't have changed. They will always live in the desert. Like me, we are part of it, like the wild flowers, like the birds that fly high, looking down on everything.'

Jacko was looking at a swinging chair hanging from chains on the verandah with soft cushions on it. He got up and walked over to it. He didn't sit on it, he just curled up on it. With a full tummy and jet lag, the movement of the seat, a gentle breeze in the open air, and the sound of the little waves on the beach, he was soon sound asleep. In his mind, Jacko was back in the desert.

Ted and I drank more coffee and talked. I was totally relaxed. Eventually, the two women appeared. Peggy asked Ted, 'Could you get our car out please? We have an appointment, don't we?'

'We need to buy clothes,' Lesley said. 'Peggy has suggested her favorite men's shop, John McCoys.'

Lesley looked at Jacko asleep in the swinging chair, their dog Charlie had jumped up on the chair with him and was also asleep. 'Just leave them there.' she said.

Ted and I had more coffee while waiting for the women to get ready. I didn't feel comfortable in my naval uniform, I felt out of place, and was looking forward to my new clothes.

We drove to the shops. Ted and I sat in the warm sun watching the beautiful young ladies go by on their way to the beach. We were quite content.

Two voices behind us said, 'Don't just sit there. We want new clothes.' We didn't argue, just got back into the car and went to John McCoys Men's shop. John was very obliging. His staff were very friendly, and we found everything we wanted. Peggy bought Ted a new suit, and

I must admit, he looked good. Lesley would pick out a shirt and put it up against me, shake her head, and put it back. Then she'd pick out another one, put it up against me and grin. She glanced at Peg, they both approved. I didn't even get the chance to say yes or no. A wise man once said *yes, dear*. We shook hands with John, said our goodbyes, and headed back to Peggy and Ted's home.

When we got there, Jacko and Charlie weren't there.

Ted said, 'I know where they are.' We walked down the path to the beach. There was Jacko and Charlie sitting in the water, enjoying it. Ted didn't want to disturb them, so we came back to the house. Lesley seemed to be very happy, laughing and giggling at anything. I enjoyed watching her be happy and content.

After tea, all we wanted to do was to go to bed and sleep. In our bedroom was a large four poster double bed, with a lace canopy. There were big windows overlooking the beach, with beautiful curtains hanging down on either side. There was a large dressing table opposite the end of the bed with a big mirror, nearly touching the ceiling. There was beautiful ornate timberwork on either side of the mirror and two large wardrobes at each end of the room at a slight angle and facing the bed. Both wardrobes had mirrors on the doors. There were two pictures of Roman statues on the walls, depicting beautiful women.

I took my wash things out of my bag and went into the adjoining bathroom. I took my uniform off and draped it over the chair, and stood there looking at it. *Will I ever wear it again? Do I really want to wear it again? No, I do not!* I stood in the shower with the hot water flowing over my body, thinking this is pure luxury. I enjoyed lathering up my body with the soap. Am I cleaning my body or trying to clean the past away? But I was enjoying the hot water. I eventually stepped out of the shower, not really wanting to leave that hot water, but I cleaned my teeth, trimmed my beard and combed my hair. I went back into the bedroom and climbed into bed. It was so comfortable. Lesley came into the room, looked at me with a cheeky grin, she shook her finger at me. 'Don't you go to sleep!'

She went into the bathroom. I could hear the shower and hear her singing. I've never heard her sing before, and I was enjoying it. My eyes were heavy. I just wanted to close them, but Lesley walked out of the bathroom and stood at the end of the bed. She was completely naked. I was totally surprised. I could see her reflection in the dressing table mirror and the wardrobe mirror. She was absolutely beautiful. She made all my senses become alive and tingling. She put her hands up above her head and just ever so slowly swirled around, like a Greek goddess. I was totally mesmerised. I have never seen anything so beautiful. She just slowly turned around, saying, 'I'm free, I am now free, just you and I, and the world belongs to us. We no longer have to answer to anybody. We are free.' She kept swirling around slowly. I was stunned by the total beauty of her body. She is mine, and I am hers. I didn't want her to stop. She smiled at me. 'Tonight, I am yours.' She went to her side of the bed, pulled back the blankets and put both her hands down on the bed, with one knee on the bed so that I could see the absolute beauty of her breasts. Then she laid down alongside me, put one leg over me and snuggled into my shoulder. I waited for a moment, still trying to take it all in, then I heard heavy breathing and realised she was asleep. Damn jet lag. What do I do about my problem now?

We both slept soundly. I awoke to the sun coming through the window illuminating all the colours in the room. Lesley hadn't moved all night. A voice said to me 'you're not getting up yet,' and she snuggled into me, pressing her body up against mine. My problem was back! About an hour later, we dressed in our new clothes and went downstairs. We found Ted reading his newspaper on the verandah. He looked at us and smiled.

'Now I can start breakfast. Jacko is on the beach with Charlie. That dog has never taken to anybody like he's taken to Jacko.'

Peggy came downstairs in her dressing gown and her big floppy slippers. 'Where is my slave?'

Ted's voice came from the kitchen. 'I'm coming with your breakfast mistress.'

Peggy replied, 'It's hard getting good service nowadays,' and shouted out, 'where's my coffee?'

Ted shouted back, 'I was once a free man. What happened Bill?'

Jacko's voice broke in, 'You want *cheeky, cheeky* you have to perform for it, don't they, Charlie?'

Peggy, with her flip-flops, flipped flopped over to Jacko and put her arms around him. 'Charlie is mine. You can't have him, but you can have Ted, after he's cooked my breakfast.'

We all sat around the table on the verandah, talking, drinking coffee and laughing. 'Your man, Chris O'Hara, is an interesting character,' I said.

'Yes, he is one of those really rare men. They call him Ricochet. Real bullets and other political bullets just ricochet off of him.'

'In my position in the police force, I need such a man. He can go places I can't. He can receive information I need to protect others. He has a hire car, he can pick up somebody very discreetly from the airport or any other place. He has a network of friends which are very valuable to me, all in their own businesses, or should I say in business with him.'

'Never under estimate him. His principles are very high. Cross him and you've got trouble.'

'Bill, would you like to take a walk along the beach?'

'Yes, we'd enjoy that.'

Charlie stood up in his basket. He knew exactly what Ted had said and was wagging his fluffy tail. His body moved to the movements of his tail.

Jacko went first, along with Charlie, and we followed, walking in the water up to our ankles. It was very relaxing, feeling the squelching sound under your feet. We noticed Jacko was looking at the women on the beach and in the water. Lesley leaned over to me, and in a soft voice said, 'Would you believe Jacko is a virgin? Being at sea so long in *Daisy May*.'

'Come to think of it Lesley, you're probably right. Girls in swimming costumes like that one over there would stir any man up.'

Lesley giggled, 'Keep looking, Bill, and stay up until tonight.'

Jacko's head went up and turned around to give Lesley a serious look. Lesley's mouth moved, but no words came out.

'Shut up Jacko, I was looking at the boats with their red sails.'

'Yes, Bill, they're becoming very popular. They are Couta boats. I have been thinking of buying one. Out there in the bay, you are alone. Nobody can annoy you. Peggy and I are in the professions where being alone is very important.'

We returned to the house. Ted said in a very loud voice, 'Put the kettle on, wench!'

Peggy slowly lifted a hand up, twirled it around, slightly bowed, 'Yes sir, O great master. Do you want me to put water in it as well?'

Jacko said, 'Good surprise today, good day tomorrow, lots of good friends.' Then he and Charlie went back out to the swinging chair and made themselves comfortable. Ted had a frown on his face.

'That's Jacko, only half the information,' I said.

Just then, the doorbell rang. Peggy said to Ted, 'Chop chop boy, answer the door.'

'Isn't she lovely when she's bossy,' Ted said, and went to answer the door. We heard voices and Ted saying to them, 'come in, come in.'

Jarrett Collins walked in, followed by Chris O'Hara, Mervyn Nelis and another. We all stood up, laughing and cheering. Ted shouted out, 'more water in the kettle dear.'

We all went and sat out on the verandah, but first Mervyn went up to Jacko and rubbed his hands through his hair.

'Keeping out of trouble, Jacko?' He put his hands on Jacko's shoulders and squeezed them.

Jacko laughed. 'I've got no troubles. You're the one who has all the troubles.'

'Yes, Jacko, you warned me.'

I looked at Number 11. 'From now on, I'm just Bill. This is Lesley, and you are Frank, not number 11. Ted, this is Mervyn's secretary. This lady is Peggy, she is Lesley's sister, and this gentleman, Ted, is her trusted servant, or should I say her husband, and that dog over there is Charlie.' I don't know what made me say it, but I did. 'Chris, they tell me that you are a very knowledgeable person. Do you know anything about diamonds?'

'Yes I do. I use them as collateral.'

I looked at Lesley. She got up and went to our bedroom to fetch the diamonds. Ted looked at me with a policeman's frown. Lesley came back, put down the tin box and opened it. She took out the folded piece of paper containing the diamonds and gave them to Chris.

He took his black-rimmed glasses out of his pocket and a small magnifying glass. He put on his glasses and examined the diamonds. Then he examined them with his magnifying glass. 'Whoever bought these knew what they were doing. They're from Africa. Whoever cut them was the best, and I know he has passed away. I would suggest to you, do not put them into jewellery, use them as collateral. Make them generate money for you.' He looked over at Jarrett. 'Jarrett's company is entering a new world in shipping containerization, invest in them. Peggy knows the system. That's right, isn't it Peggy?'

'Yes, it is.'

'I need good investors,' Jarrett said.

Chris put the diamonds back into the piece of paper, folded it up and handed it back to Lesley. She took them back and looked at me. I nodded. She handed them to Peggy. 'I will take care of them, Lesley.' Jarrett sighed and grinned. We all laughed.

'How about we all go out for tea?' Ted said. 'A unanimous decision, yes. I know a place where we can take Charlie as well.'

We had a damn good meal and hardy conversation. We returned to their home. Jacko and Charlie disappeared and went straight on to the verandah, and soon they were asleep.

We had coffee, and all turned in for the night. As we were going up the stairs, Lesley said to me, 'You have your shower first. I've got to finish what I started last night!'

'Yes dear,' I grinned.

I woke just on daylight, quite content, dressed and went downstairs. Mervyn and Frank were sitting at the table going through paperwork.

Frank said, 'This is your first speech in America. I have outlined some small suggestions on stealth technology and the future satellite navigation. This section here, hiding military equipment from enemy ships at sea.'

I made coffee and Jacko's voice broke in. 'You funny white folk take a long time to learn. You used to ride into battle all dressed up like peacocks, as if to say, *look at me, I'm here, aren't I pretty?* My people learn from the animals in the bush. When you see us with white on our bodies, we have learnt that's how we can hide in the desert. We stand perfectly still. You don't see us. We use sticks with leaves and we disappear. The lizard, he changes colour to suit his environment. Birds hide in bushes with the same colours on their wings, an Emu sits down in the grass or dirt, you can't see him, his colours blend in with his surroundings. Kangaroo can smell you. Crush leaves in your hand, rub them all over your body. He can only smell the leaves and he is happy. We learn all these tricks many dreamtimes ago. Go and sit in the garden and observe. Be there, but not be there.'

'Could I read that back to you so I haven't missed anything?' Frank said.

Mervyn grinned. 'Still teaching us, aren't you, Jacko? If I used your speech, perhaps change one or two small words, I think it would go down very well and be Australian. If I started by saying, a very dear

Aborigine once told me, and I repeated what you said, I would probably get more attention than if I made it technical.'

I said, 'Anybody for coffee? No? We don't have Kentucky fried chicken yet.'

I took Lesley a cup of tea and put it on the side table. She looked at me with a frown. 'Bill, you have been holding back on me. That performance last night has to continue.'

I just said, with a grin, 'Yes dear. We are going for a walk on the beach before breakfast. Would you like to come?'

'I'll get some shorts on and a T-shirt and be down.' As I was going out the door, I stopped and looked back. 'Just a T-shirt.' I turned quickly and went down the stairs. We had a nice long walk on the beach, laughing at Charlie chasing seagulls. They were far too quick for him. We returned for breakfast. Jacko was well in front of us and as we walked up the path we could smell the coffee, bacon and eggs. Bread and dripping were sizzling away in the pan. A typical cockney breakfast. After we had finished eating, Mervyn talked about his new career.

'Mrs Henderson set me up nicely. I'm going to enjoy it. Putting everything I have learned the hard way together for the future. Lesley, do you think I could have Jacko?'

'No Mervyn, Peggy found her puppy dog Charlie. Jacko is my puppy dog, you can't have him.'

Peggy clapped her hands. 'We have a big afternoon in store for you all. Could you go up and change into some fancy duds. Lesley, could you brush your puppy dog's hair and Ted will brush Charlie's.' She clapped her hands together and said, 'Chop, chop, now.'

We all bowed. Peggy fussed around her house, making sure there wasn't anything on the big table. She put a big tablecloth over it. When we came down, she ushered us out of the back door onto the verandah.

'You wouldn't believe she was very shy and timid as a little girl, would you?' Lesley said.

I grinned, wondering what was happening next. To our surprise, caterers turned up with flowers, food, little bits and pieces, and were very busy.

Lesley and I sat there, waiting. She said to me, 'The £5 notes in the safety deposit box, should I give them to Peggy as well to invest?'

'Yes, I think that's the best way and we will make Collin Garland's wife a partner in the shares, but she would get a bigger portion of the share.'

Lesley said, 'I agree, and that tidies that up, no loose ends.' She grinned at me. 'Jacko knows exactly what is going on. He is too quiet.' Then we saw the grin on this face, the doorbell rang and in walked Chris O'Hara.

'Lucky I had brought the bus, I found a few stragglers.' Margaret walked in with Trevor, they were both carrying babies.

Lesley jumped up out of her chair, with her hands on her mouth, but still screaming out, 'Margaret, Margaret!'

She slowly walked over to them, turned and looked at Jacko and said, 'You're in trouble!' She put her arms out to cuddle the four of them. I walked up behind Lesley, wanting to see the babies and trying to keep the tears out of my eyes. Lesley was crying as well. Margaret reached out and put the little girl in Lesley's arms. Trevor stepped forward and put the little boy in my arms.

'Bill, I would like you to meet your grandson, Bill.'

I felt a shiver go up my spine. My emotions were singing out, 'enjoy.' Then Trevor said to Lesley, 'I would like you to meet your granddaughter, Lesley.'

I knew Lesley needed to sit down with the baby, and Jacko had the chair ready. He said, 'I don't have to meet them, I met them a long time ago.'

Margaret nearly knocked him off his feet, cuddling and shaking him. 'You are Pop Pop from now on.'

Jacko put his head back. He had a very serious look on his face. 'I was Pop Pop a long time ago when you first got your cabin together.'

I went over to the lounge and sat down on the couch, looking down at the little face smiling at me. My whole body went to water. I couldn't take my eyes off his beautiful little face. Lesley got up from her chair with the baby and came and sat down beside me. She put her head on my shoulder.

I looked around and saw there were three men behind me, Snowy, Tommy and Dominic, and his wife. We all sat there for at least an hour. Jacko walked over to me. 'I think it's my turn now, Bill.'

I put the little boy into his waiting outstretched arms. I got up, and he sat down next to Lesley, looking at the little girl with tears in his eyes. The little boy was looking at Jacko. If he could have talked we knew he would have been saying this one's different. As he watched the tears roll down Jacko's white beard, Jacko gave a little sniff.

I shook hands with Snowy. 'Still doing paperwork, Snowy?'

'Yes Bill. Jarrett's got me working hard.'

I shook hands with Dominic. 'What are you doing now, Dominic?'

'I'm a crane operator for Jarrett.'

'Tommy, have you got your cows and settled down to married life?'

'Yes, Bill, no paperwork, no politics. Breakfast is on the table and so is my tea. What more could a man want?'

We all chatted for a while. I walked over to Mr and Mrs Collins to talk to them for a few moments, then I met Trevor's father and Trevor walked over to us.

'When I heard my son was on a Barque sailing clipper I was worried, but then I heard he had married and I found out he was a Captain in His Majesty's Navy. Now I have a daughter-in-law and two grandchildren, and my son is in the upper crust of a shipping company. When they drafted me into the Navy I had no say in it. I left my wife and children to fend for themselves and I was so worried. Now I'm so proud of my son and I would like to thank you for taking care of him and giving him a future.'

'Your son has earned everything he has. He got it the hard way and I'm extremely proud of him as well.' Trevor's father took his handkerchief out of his top pocket and wiped his eyes.

'What are you going to do now, Bill?'

'Well, there are no more places in Jarrett's company for an old sea Captain, so Jacko, Lesley and I are going back to the Channel Country. We have a small property there, about 16,000 acres, to keep us busy.'

The afternoon and evening were very good, but keeping our emotions to ourselves was very hard. We had travelled a long way with these people, we had done so much, but it was all secret, only we know. So much history is not recorded. Did medals or titles put it right? I suppose that's up to the individual.

Saying goodbye at the door was the hardest part, and Jacko didn't want to give the baby back. We sat there drinking coffee, watching the caterers cleaning up. I couldn't stop yawning, I was so tired. I was mentally drained.

CHAPTER 61

I woke up with a start in the morning, asking myself, *what's the course? What is the barometer doing? What sails do we have aloft?* Then reality set in. I sat up in bed and felt a little lost. I could hear birds singing. I could hear the traffic outside on the road. What has happened to my life? It is going to take me a little time to put it all together. I had a shower and went downstairs, wondering where Lesley was. She was sitting on the verandah with Peggy, going through the documents for our investments. Ted was cooking breakfast. I couldn't see Jacko or Charlie. I guessed they were down at the beach. Ted handed me a coffee. I nodded a thank you to him and went out onto the verandah and sat down with the women. Peggy slid some paperwork over to me. 'Sign these, Bill.' I thought, *should I read them first?* No, I just signed where the crosses were. Jacko's nostrils were like radar. He had picked up on the smell of bacon and was soon standing there alongside us with Charlie. Ted came out with our breakfast. He looked at Charlie. 'You have put on weight, Charlie, since we have had visitors.'

Peggy said, 'Look in the mirror Ted, both of you are on diets tomorrow. Don't you look at me like that Charlie, I know it's not your fault, it's

Ted's. He won't stop feeding you bits and pieces whenever you ask, and don't you look so innocent Jacko, you're just as bad.'

We talked about our future for a while. When the doorbell rang, Jacko said, 'We are on the way home, back to my people. He has come to fetch us.'

Ted got up and went to the front door. He was frowning at Jacko. He opened the door and said, 'Come in, Chris, breakfast is still on.' Another man was standing behind him. Ted put out his hand and shook his. 'Come in Peter.'

Ted closed the door behind them. 'Bill, Lesley, this is Peter. He works for Special Branch.' We both shook hands with Peter.

Peggy, in her best lawyer's voice, said, 'Christopher, sign these papers with this pen. Not yours. The ink in your pen will fade away in half an hour.'

Peter said to Chris, 'That's why they all call you shifty.'

Peter sighed. 'And I believe you're Jacko. Somebody in the UK press has informed the press here that you are here and have given all the particulars. Forgive what I'm going to say, but we have to hide you. You are still top secret.'

'We perfectly understand,' Lesley said.

Peter nodded. 'We have a plane waiting for you at Laverton Military Air force Base.' He rubbed his hands together. 'So while you are packing, we'll have breakfast, won't we Ted?'

Jacko stepped forward. 'I'm already packed, so I can have breakfast too.'

Ted put his hands in the air. 'Jacko, you've just had breakfast.'

Jacko replied, 'That was an hour and a half ago!'

Ted walked into the kitchen, shaking his head.

I brought down our bags and put them in the back of the car, and went up to get Jacko. Lesley was still standing in our bedroom. 'Good memories, Bill.'

'Yes Lesley. I won't forget it, or the mirrors!'

We both went downstairs. I put Jacko's luggage in the car and went back inside. Lesley and Peggy were sitting on the couch quietly talking to each other. After the others had finished their breakfast, I shook Ted's hand. 'Thank you for everything, Ted. We'll see you in the near future.'

'Yes, I've got holidays coming and I want to see this Channel country.'

Jacko shook Ted's hand. 'You come in good clothes, not those fancy duds. I will cook you a good breakfast. You bring Peggy home.'

Lesley and Peggy said their goodbyes inside where it was private. When Lesley came out to the car she had her handkerchief to her mouth, holding back her tears.

Before we could blink, we were on our way, through St. Kilda, along the Beach Road, into the city, and out through Footscray Road to Laverton.

A DC Six aircraft was waiting for us, and before we could say anything, we were in the air on our way to Brisbane. Once at Brisbane, there was another aircraft waiting to take us home.

The second aircraft was a lot smaller. It had propeller motors on each wing. Jacko sat next to the pilot. We sat behind Jacko and the pilot. Our luggage was on the two seats behind us. Jacko started a conversation with the pilot, asking him questions about the flight. This time he wasn't nervous and enjoyed it. The pilot said to Jacko, 'We have two stops before we get to the Johnson property. I have to deliver mail and parcels.'

Jacko asked him, 'Where do you land at the Johnson property?'

'There is an airstrip at the back of the property.' He chuckled to himself. 'I can nearly drop you at the back door of the house. I will be staying there overnight to pick up passengers. They're going to Brisbane Hospital for x-rays, and I pick up the mail at two other properties.'

'So the Johnson property has an airstrip,' Jacko said. 'That's very interesting.' He glanced around towards us. 'That makes it easier for

Peggy and Ted. Lesley, I didn't like the first landing, it was very rough.' A few minutes later we were back in the air. The second landing was the same. Both were cattle stations, and I had noticed two elderly Aborigines. They nodded to Jacko. He nodded back, but it was the way he nodded back. He had spoken to them, not with words, but with his mind. He turned and glanced at Lesley, and looked back at the two elderly Aborigines. He didn't say another word, he just sat there quietly.

The sun was low in the sky when we landed. I was surprised to see so many Aborigines waiting. As we got out of the plane, they made a circle around the plane and stamped their feet on the ground chanting. Three elderly Aborigines stepped forward, holding their bark shields with smoking gum leaves on them. They slowly walked backwards and Jacko followed them. We had passed the plane and a circle of people had surrounded us, and they tightened the circle around us.

Jacko stopped, turned and put his hand out to Lesley. She walked up alongside him. Jacko took his shirt off. Two of the women stepped forward and put markings on his body in white, across his forehead and on his cheeks. They did the same to Lesley's face. Another elderly Aboriginal man, very thin with long white hair and a white beard, leaned on a long spear for support, chanted out some words. All the Aborigines clapped once, and they all sat down cross-legged. The three elderly Aborigines sat down as well. The single old Aborigine chanted some more words and stamped his feet on the ground. A voice behind me said, 'He has to thank the witchy for bringing the Peacemaker home and bringing their daughter back to them.' A younger man stood up with a spear and handed it to Jacko, a young woman stood up and handed Lesley a nulla nulla, and they both helped the old man to sit.

Jacko put his head up high and looked around at his people, then he looked at the setting sun and the desert which surrounded them. He spoke to the people in his own tongue. I knew some of the words, but not all of them.

A voice behind me said, 'I have traveled beyond the setting sun. I have traveled over the horizon. I have learnt many things, I have been to many places. I have learnt a lot about the white man and his funny ways, which I will share with you, for your knowledge of the future coming from over the horizon. We cannot fight it, but we will slowly bend it to suit the witchy. We will sit quietly and listen, as we listen to the wind when it is cool and fresh, or when it is hot and dry. Our knowledge will grow as it has done in the time before the time. The white man is a fool. He rapes and destroys. He does not share. He believes anything belongs to him. He still has to learn you must live. You must bow your head to it. We will become teachers living our way with what he calls nature. The witchy sent me over the horizon to fill my eyes with what we need to know. Talk to me and I will give you what the witchy wants you to know.'

Jacko turned and looked at Lesley and smiled, then he turned back to his people. 'The witchy showed her the way the white man twists and bends the truth to suit himself for his own greed and power. He opened her eyes wide and showed her pain, but also showed her joy and peace.' He took Lesley's hand. 'Listen to her wisdom and her knowledge, you who create the witchy's children.' He slowly bowed to his people and Lesley, and he sat down cross-legged. They all sat cross-legged, chanting and tapping their nulla nullas together.

I turned around to the voice behind me. It was a man just a bit shorter than me, with olive skin and dressed in European clothes. He put his hand out to mine. 'I'm Lenny Mitchell, your station manager.' I shook his hand, studying him. 'You have lost your wife and brother until tomorrow.' He grinned and looked around at all the people. 'I've got coffee waiting, and food.' He nodded to the pilot, and we followed him into the house, but before I went in I glanced over to the old cookhouse. In my mind's eye I could see our mum grinning at me, once a cook's boy, now the owner. Jacko's words were in my mind, but what did I own?

This land belongs to everybody. I am only the custodian for a very short time, as Jacko would say:

Can you own the sky? Can you own the air we breathe? Can you own the sea? Can you own all the birds that fly? The fish in the sea? We are here for not even the blink of an eye. How old is the desert? In the past history it was said that the indigenous people owned where they are now.

I went through the door and was quite surprised. The house I remembered is not this house. It has been freshly painted, and the kitchen is new and modern. I remembered it being dark, but now it is full of light with electric lighting and I would imagine hot and cold running water.

An indigenous lady stepped forward. She was wearing modern clothes and her hair was long and beautifully brushed, with curls at the bottom.

'Bill, this is my mother Joanne. My dad calls her Sunshine, so I call her Sunshine as well. She is the daughter of the desert. She was born here on this property and she is now the schoolteacher.'

We shook hands. 'My husband isn't here at the moment. He is looking for ancient rocks. Since he retired, he calls himself a rock hound. Would you like a coffee? I've cooked a roast for tonight.'

We sat at the table and talked. 'Are you married, Lenny?' I asked.

'No, not yet. I was told to wait until the Peacemaker arrived then ask his permission. He is now home.'

'Do you have a lady in mind?'

'Yes, I do,' Lenny said.

'Talk to Lesley. She will arrange it for you. She was also born here.'

'Yes, I know. They have told me the history, and so were you, Bill. They told me you were the Cook's boy.'

'Yes, that's true. If I may call you Sunshine as well, would that be alright?' I said.

'Everybody calls me Sunshine, Bill. You want to know about me?'

'Yes, I do.'

'After old man Johnson had died and his daughters had left for England, their mother died of a broken heart. She is buried next to her husband at the Billabong behind the big stump. The government didn't know what to do with this property. They had it surveyed and marked the boundaries with piles of rocks, and numbers painted on them. My people just laughed. My husband was one of those surveyors. We fell in love, married and he took me back to Brisbane, where I studied and became a teacher. That is where my son Lenny was born. My husband knew I wasn't really happy. He knew deep down I wanted to come home. He read an article that they were looking for teachers in the outback, one was at the Johnson property, and that they were also looking for a manager. We both applied and got the jobs. They built a school and a house for us. We sent Lenny back to Brisbane to further his education, then my husband retired and Lenny took over the job as manager. We were always paid by the government. Now we are told that you will pay Lenny, and the government will pay me and any expenses for the school.'

'I still have to go over the paperwork, but on paper Lesley, her sister Peggy, and Jacko and I own this property. Legally, it is very complicated. Lesley is a member of the Crown, she's in that circle, she has been knighted for her services to the British Crown and its people. If we were in England, these would be her estates under the Crown. Don't ask me any more than that, as it just becomes too complicated, far above me!'

The evening went by quickly. We had dinner, and I went to bed. I woke up in the morning to the sound of an aircraft taking off. I rolled over, looking for Lesley, but she hadn't returned to the house. I got dressed and went towards the kitchen. I could hear the chanting and clapping going on outside the window. The Aborigines were sitting around in a circle, with Jacko and Lesley sitting in the centre, their hands on their laps and their eyes shut. They appeared to be in a trance.

Lenny's voice came from behind me and said, 'They are with their ancestors from the time before the time to gain wisdom and knowledge. They are facing the rising sun. When the rays of the sun warms their bodies, they will return to us. Do not worry.

CHAPTER 62

Back in Brighton, Ted Jones said to his wife Peggy, 'I'm going to bed Peggy. I need an early night.'

'Ted, I will finish this paperwork and be up.'

Ted woke in the early morning. Peggy wasn't there and her side of the bed hadn't been slept in. He got up, put his dressing gown on, and went downstairs. Peggy's untidy paperwork was still on the table.

Ted thought that's not Peggy's way, she's normally extremely efficient and tidy with her paperwork. He looked around the house but couldn't find her. He went out on to the verandah, she wasn't there either. To his total surprise, he saw her sitting cross-legged on the grass, facing the direction of the rising sun. Her back was straight, her hands were in her lap, and her eyes closed. A wave of panic went through Ted. He started to go down the steps from the verandah but stopped himself. Or did something/somebody stop him? He thought if there was something wrong, she wouldn't be sitting straight up like that, so he sat down on the steps and patiently waited. The sun was just starting to rise over Port Phillip Bay. He watched the beauty of it as the rays gently touched the calm waters and spread out, touching everything. As the sun rose, he watched the leaves on the trees change colour. The light touching Peggy was becoming brighter and engulfing her. Then Peggy opened her eyes and stood up. She turned and smiled at Ted, who seemed frozen in time, not fully understanding what he had just seen.

Peggy kissed him on the end of his nose. 'I'll explain it to you later, but I'm hungry. Breakfast, my darling?'

CHAPTER 63

Meanwhile, back in the Channel Country, Bill also stood watching through the window. The light was growing stronger, and the sun was starting to rise, the faint rays spreading out on the horizon, touching the mountains and illuminating them in many colours—red, yellow, green, purple, and orange. The sun's rays started to spread over the desert, touching the many dotted trees and bushes, then the rays spread over the Billabong and all the colours in the water. The cattle seemed to be watching the sun as well. Jacko and Lesley were now illuminated in the sun. There was a silver glow all around them. The chanting stopped, and all was quiet. Jacko put his hand out and took Lesley's. They both stood up and everybody in the big circle stood up and slowly started to walk away. Jacko and Lesley walked over to the house and came in through the back door. I stood there, staring at them, totally confused. No, that's not the word. I know Jacko's world, but I'm not really a part of it. He is the Channel Country, the Diamantina River and the surrounding desert.

Lesley said, 'Breakfast Bill?'

'If that is your command, I will cook breakfast.'

But Jacko said, 'No, Lesley's a better cook than you, but coffee would be good.'

I watched Lesley's eyes flitting around the house and the kitchen. 'It is a little different, Bill.'

'Yes, Lesley. They have done a good job in painting this house.'

We had breakfast and the rest of the day for me was paperwork with the station manager, Lenny.

Days slid by quickly, then the months turned into years. We had watched Jacko with his people. He had changed. He was now the teacher, sitting in circles talking of the past and the future, and how they must adapt, but still live within the laws of the desert. As the white man will be your teacher, you will also be his teacher to protect the desert.

We noticed he had found himself a female companion. They were getting closer and closer, and finally the time had come to be as one. They were married according to their customs. Lesley and I sat on the verandah talking together and felt very satisfied. Everything is in its place, everything is in order.

We watched the sun slowly setting comfortably on the horizon, the rays glistening on everything. I said to Lesley, 'I will go for a walk around to check that all is well.' I could see Jacko and his new bride sitting on the old stump by the Billabong. A sense of peace came over me. My brother is doing well. I walked back to the verandah. The light was quickly fading.

A voice said, 'Who are you?'

I said, 'Bill Farquhar, what do you want?'

'Boss cocky sent me over to the big boss. You are the cook's boy, aren't you?'

'Yes.'

'Come inside. I've got big plans for you.'

And we walked back through the big door hand in hand.

Is this really the end of my story?

Is it true, or is it just my imagination?

Thank you for reading this. You have made my life complete.

THE END OR IS IT?